TABLE OF CONTENTS

CHAPTER 1	TANYA
CHAPTER 2	RODRIGUEZ
CHAPTER 3	FIRST WORLD JUSTICE
CHAPTER 4	ÁLVAREZ
CHAPTER 5	THE PLAN
CHAPTER 6	*DESTINY*
CHAPTER 7	SAN PEDRO SULA
CHAPTER 8	THE HAMPTONS
CHAPTER 9	BANDIDOS
CHAPTER 10	SOUTHBOUND
CHAPTER 11	MORALS
CHAPTER 12	CAPE MAY TO NORFOLK
CHAPTER 13	MOTHER CHAVEZ
CHAPTER 14	NORFOLK TO COINJOCK
CHAPTER 15	COUSINS
CHAPTER 16	COINJOCK TO BEAUFORT
CHAPTER 17	PUERTO LEMPIRA
CHAPTER 18	BEAUFORT TO CHARLESTON
CHAPTER 19	HONDURAN COSTA POLICA
CHAPTER 20	CHARLESTON TO JEKYLL ISLAND
CHAPTER 21	TAXES
CHAPTER 22	JEKYLL ISLAND TO CAPE CANAVERAL
CHAPTER 23	OPEN WATER COURT
CHAPTER 24	CANAVERAL TO FORT LAUDERDALE
CHAPTER 25	FEED THE LEMMINGS
CHAPTER 26	*DESTINY* HONDURAS
CHAPTER 27	STEALING *DESTINY*
CHAPTER 28	THE EXCHANGE
CHAPTER 29	*DESTINY* USA
CHAPTER 30	THE FEELING
CHAPTER 31	FOG
CHAPTER 32	HURRICANE TANYA
CHAPTER 33	OCEANIC WHITE TIP
CHAPTER 34	BLACKOUT
CHAPTER 35	REVENGE
CHAPTER 36	BY THE WAY
CHAPTER 37	NO MERCY
CHAPTER 38	ADRIFT
CHAPTER 39	UNITED STATES COAST GUARD

CHAPTER 40   LOCAL SAVIORS
CHAPTER 41   PROVIDENCE
CHAPTER 42   NEW RIVER
CHAPTER 43   THIRD WORLD JUSTICE
CHAPTER 44   BAHAMAS
CHAPTER 45   OBSESSED
CHAPTER 46   TRUE LOVE
CHAPTER 47   *DESTINY* CLEAR
CHAPTER 48   DEFINITION OF WEALTH

NAUTICAL GLOSSARY

A NOTE FROM THE AUTHOR

CRIME AND PUNISHMENT

REFERENCES

PHOTO/IMAGE CREDITS

ABOUT THE AUTHOR

EXCERPT FROM *IMMINENT HAZZARD*

LOCO

A Story of Love, Loss, and Moral Decay

By

Jeff Ford

PUBLISHED BY FORDIFIED PRODUCTIONS

This book is dedicated to those who choose morality over money.

Published in the United States by
Fordified Productions
411 Walnut Street, Suite 7463
Green Cove Springs, Florida 32043

Library of Congress Control Number: 2013948935

www.locoford.com

Photo/image credits appear following References.

Cover design by Todor Vasilev

Edited by John Fiske

ISBN 978-0-9898591-0-3

Printed in the United States of America

10 9 8 7 6 5 4 3 2 1

First American Paperback Edition

This book was printed on high quality, acid-free paper and meets all ANSI standards for archival quality.

CHAPTER 1   TANYA

CARIBBEAN SEA, OCTOBER 22, 2010.

Captain Billy Forbes switched channels on the VHF radio to see if he could get any weather forecasts, but the eighty-five foot yacht was now more than 100 miles off shore in the middle of the Caribbean Sea. Nothing but static belched from the small speaker.

A wave of apprehension swept over him as he turned on the satellite television. It took more than five minutes to locate and track the geostationary satellite due to the rough seas and swaying of the yacht. As the mechanized satellite dish roamed the skies in search of the correct satellite, Billy began to feel nervous. He had been forced to kill four people and there were drugs onboard, but they did not seem to be the reason for his unease. He couldn't quite put his finger on *the feeling,* but he knew from experience, that what it signaled could be deadly.

The TV finally flickered to life and he quickly turned to the Weather Channel where a commercial was just ending. Billy's pulse quickened. Frantically swaying palm trees blasted by rain came into view, and the words, "Hurricane Tanya," filled the screen.

Weather. The one thing he always checked at least three or four times while underway, he hadn't checked in five days. Five days! He had been so preoccupied with the drug deal and Honduran officials that he had failed to perform one of the most basic rules of seamanship: respect the weather.

The massive hurricane on the TV screen was headed right for him! Billy grabbed a small notepad he kept in the side pocket of his shorts and frantically scribbled down the latitude, longitude, direction and speed of the hurricane, but he didn't need to plot the coordinates on the chart to know that he was in serious trouble.

"Marco!" Billy yelled to his first mate, and only other person on the yacht. "We've got some heavy weather ahead of us! Make sure the engine room is secure and that nothing will go flying. Tie down anything that is not tied down! Check the bilges, too. See if they are dry and make sure the bilge pumps are working!"

"Okay, amigo."

Marco headed out the aft door of the salon towards the engine room, while Billy looked back at the television screen. A bald meteorologist explained, "The storm has been gaining strength since it passed the Lesser Antilles early yesterday and is moving west at almost twenty miles per hour. Fortunately, it will only impact the sea for the next twenty-four to forty-eight hours."

"Yeah, fortunately," Billy muttered. He hurriedly walked over to the wheelhouse and plotted the hurricane's location on the chart, using the computer navigation system to quickly compare the yacht's position relative to the storm. As he gazed at the screen, he heard a drop of water hit the nautical chart below him. He looked up to see if the wheelhouse windows were leaking, but realized it was his own sweat that dripped onto the chart. Billy grabbed the bottom of his shirt sleeve and wiped his forehead and face. He could feel his head throbbing with every heartbeat. The pressure was getting to him. Thoughts were ricocheting around his head like a bullet in a bank vault. *The boss doesn't know I'm down here and could have me arrested for stealing his yacht. I've got millions of dollars of cocaine onboard. I've just killed four people. We don't have enough fuel to get where we need to go, and now we're headed straight for a hurricane. If, and that's a big "if" I live through this, I'll be lucky not to spend the rest of my life in jail, much less hold onto my job. What the hell was I thinking?*

Billy walked over to the galley sink and splashed some cold water onto his face. He felt the three day's growth of beard.

At six feet tall, Billy was about the same height as Marco, but built differently. His chest and arms were naturally thick and kept toned by daily pushups and manual labor on the yacht. He had dark hair and his father's rugged, good looks.

He grabbed a couple of paper towels, wiped his face off, and took a few deep breaths. He couldn't afford to lose it now. There was too much to do. *Keep it together. Keep it together. Focus on the storm. Then,* if you live*, you can deal with the guilt of being a murderer.*

Marco came in through the aft deck door. "Engine room is set and the bilges look good, just a little water in the, em, rudder room bilge. I tested the bilge pumps and they all work."

Marco had native Central American skin color that made him look like he was perpetually tanned. He had jet black hair and an angular jaw. At fifty-one, he was fifteen years older than Billy, but living on the ocean all his life had kept him fit.

"Okay, thanks Marco. Check the fly bridge and tender. Take all the cushions off and stow them. Take down anything that can blow away. Make sure the tender is fastened securely to the deck, but tie it so we can cut it loose quickly if we have to abandon ship." Marco started to move, but Billy noticed his hesitation when the words, "abandon ship" registered. Marco shot a glance over, and Billy looked directly into his eyes.

"It's a hurricane, Marco, category five. We can't get out of its way. We're just going to have to fight it."

Marco's perpetual tan faded to a look of pale shock, and he stared at Billy with an expression that did not require any words. Both men knew they would not survive.

In another type of yacht maybe they'd live, but this was a show piece of wealth, not a blue water vessel. If one of the fancy glass windows blew out, there would be no way to stop water rushing in. Once that happened, the electrical system would flood and short out, in turn stalling the engines. Without power, the yacht would swing broad side to the waves and get ripped to shreds or roll over in the high surf. Once completely flooded, the yacht would sink like a boulder to the bottom of the ocean.

CHAPTER 2   RODRIGUEZ

THIRTY EIGHT YEARS EARLIER,
THE MOSQUITO COAST OF HONDURAS, OCTOBER 18, 1972.

Little Marco Villanueva walked excitedly towards his first paying job. Though he made mere pennies per day, for a twelve year old boy, it was a great job in Honduras. A soft spoken, conscientious boy, Marco had a strong work ethic that he had learned from his father, who had suggested the job. He could still go to school during the day and make a little money at night washing dishes and cleaning up at the local bar in the small seaside town of Ahuas, Honduras.

The bar itself was far from a fancy establishment. The tables had been converted from fifty year old wooden beer kegs that would have been chic in a New York City nightclub. But at *Enrique's,* they were just the materials at hand. The raw, unpainted wood was gouged and battered. The owner, Enrique, confirmed his late fifties age with receding salt and pepper hair, and a pot belly that was usually covered with a soiled apron. He had painted the concrete floor several times in an effort to spruce up the bar. However, over the years the paint had chipped and peeled in many places, revealing a dirty patchwork of muted colors.

The ceiling appeared as if it could collapse under its own weight at anytime. Originally white, the ceiling tiles had turned dark from years of smoke and grime. At the corner of one of the now defunct air ducts, a drop of mystery fluid, with the color and viscosity of used motor oil, defied gravity waiting to drop onto the head of an unsuspecting patron, or simply blend into the discolored floor.

Some nights the bar would get very busy, and Marco would be rushing about nonstop for hours. The customers were mostly fishermen, who came in when they got paid, which could be any night of the week. On this particular Tuesday night, the majority of the fishing fleet had brought in an impressive catch of yellow fin tuna. The sell price at the pier was unusually high, so after two weeks at sea, the fisherman left their boats with lots of money in their pockets.

It was standing room only at the bar that night. Along with thick, heavy smoke, loud Spanish music filled the air, occasionally drowned out by outbursts of drunken laughter. Marco had to turn sideways and sift through the crowd as he performed his chores. The fishermen had been drinking since about three in the afternoon, so only a few were left at eleven, Marco's usual time to go home.

Enrique had had a lucrative night and paid Marco for the past week just before he gave him one last chore to do. "Una persona se enfermó en el baño. Puede usted por favor límpielo antes de irse a casa? Someone got sick in the bathroom. Can you please clean it up before you go home?"

The crowd was mostly gone when Marco carried the bucket and mop over to the bathroom. His small, brown hand pushed the old wooden door open. Marco smelled the foul stench before he actually saw the splattered vomit. The drunken buffoon had managed to get about one third of the total volume into the toilet, and had neglected to flush even that down. *What a smelly mess!* Marco thought. He tried to put his mind somewhere else, anywhere where he wouldn't have to see and smell the splattered puke in front of him. He had been thinking about buying a bicycle. Not a new bike, of course, but a used one from a man in town. That would be great. His very own bike! Little Marco was daydreaming about riding his new bike into town when some commotion in the bar snapped him back to the foul stench of regurgitated food.

Marco walked over to the bathroom door and peeked through the crack with one eye. A man he had never seen was standing in the doorway. Marco was scared, but he didn't know why. Maybe it was the expression on Enrique's face. The stranger was not a fisherman. His clothes were fancier than a fisherman's, but not gringo-fancy.

The sharply dressed intruder swaggered toward the bar and began speaking loudly displaying an inflated ego to the three men remaining in the bar: two seated on bar stools and Enrique, behind the bar. The man began to almost preach, spreading his arms wide and motioning around the room. "Bueno, bueno, bueno. Allí estás, mi viejo amigo, Chato! Ah yes, yes, yes, there you are, my old friend, Chato! Yes, much joy in the village!" When he spoke, the stranger revealed a big, fake smile, exposing his gold front tooth. "I see you have enough money for drinks. Yes, yes! Drinks all around, Enrique, on my good old friend, Chato, here!"

The man sitting at the far end of the bar got up and staggered out in a hurry, leaving only Chato, Enrique, and the gold-toothed stranger.

Marco's eyes darted to the nervous expression on Enrique's face. Enrique pulled a bottle off of the top shelf behind the bar and poured the stranger a tall shot. He placed another cerveza in front of Chato, who had come to the bar straight from the fishing boat. His tattered clothes and two week beard was in stark contrast to the neatly dressed stranger.

Chato began to squirm in his bar stool, and turned to talk to the man. "Iba a verte mañana, te lo juro! I was going to see you tomorrow, I swear! I came in for a drink after the hard trip. Two weeks at sea, you know what it's like."

The stranger put the small glass to his lips, snapped his head back and drank the shot in one quick gulp. Chato did not touch his beer. He stared down at the bar, avoiding eye contact.

"That is one way to look at it my friend, but you must realize that Mr. Álvarez sees it another way. You owe him much money. You have a good catch on your fishing trip and make good money, yes? But do you come to him and pay? No, instead, you come here and get drunk. You spend money that isn't yours. Mr. Álvarez sees that as stealing from him. You don't want to steal from *Mister* Álvarez, do you?"

Chato looked up with a pleading look on his face and said, "No, no, of course not, but I..."

The stranger cut him off with a dismissive wave of the hand. "What did I tell you the last time, eh? You don't listen to me? You don't think I'm serious, what I say to you? Think I'm a liar? Eh? No one calls Juan Rodriguez a liar!"

In an instant, the man pulled out a gun and shot Chato in the head from less than two feet away. Blood sprayed from the back of his head in a ten foot diameter pattern as Chato's body slumped over and his head hit the bar, his body limp. Dead.

Marco had gasped at the sight of the gun, but the shot followed so quickly that the loud blast drowned out his inhalation of surprise.

Unfazed by the cold blooded murder he had just committed, Rodriguez looked up and asked Enrique, "How much did this piece of shit drink?"

"Um, he, ah, had ten beers and bought two rounds of whiskey shots," Enrique mumbled as he lifted his apron with shaking hands to wipe sprayed blood off his face.

Rodriguez went through the dead man's pockets and took all the money he found. He flipped several bills on the bar top. "This will cover the tab and," nodding to the lifeless body, "there is a little extra for the mess he made." Then Rodriguez picked up the beer next to Chato's lifeless head, took a long swig from the bottle, and walked out of the bar.

Little Marco couldn't move. Trembling, he was in total shock staring at Chato's dead body. *So much blood!* Marco stood frozen in fear and could not avert his gaze. He watched the blood flow down from the bar top where it swirled with cigarette butts and slowly formed into a large puddle on the dirty floor.

Marco stood motionless for what seemed like an eternity. He wasn't sure if he was breathing and became even more frightened. Unconsciously he let the mop slip from his hands; it hit the floor with a dull whack. Enrique looked up in a flash, ran around the bar and ripped opened the bathroom door.

"Marco!" Enrique cried. "Oh, Christ, I forgot you were here! Did you see what happened here? Did you? No! No, you didn't see! You must go home right now and tell no one! Tell no one of this, not even your parents! Do you understand me? You can never tell anyone what happened here tonight! Look at me and swear that you will tell no one what happened here!"

"I... I... I promise." Tears streamed down Marco's face.

"Good, now go home! Go straight home!"

Marco ran home as fast as his small legs could carry him, and he never spoke to anyone about what he saw that night. However, he never forgot the shot, the blood and the careless attitude of the killer. Like the sizzling from a red-hot cattle brand, the raspy voice and evil, gold-toothed smile of Juan Rodriguez burned forever into little Marco's brain.

CHAPTER 3   FIRST WORLD JUSTICE

THREE WEEKS BEFORE HURRICANE TANYA,
LONG ISLAND, NEW YORK, OCTOBER 1, 2010.

Billy Forbes sat on the aft deck of the yacht, *Destiny*, and gazed west, across Three Mile Harbor, toward the East Hampton sunset. The eighty-five foot, seven-point-five million dollar yacht was both his home and his full time job as captain. *Destiny* spent the summers in East Hampton and the winters in Florida, and Billy was getting ready for the southbound trip. The owner of the yacht, Billy's boss, worked in New York City and lived in a sprawling mansion on Long Island, about an hour east of the city.

The sunset displayed a magical array of colors and should have been cause for elation. However, the recent activity of the government had stirred deep anger within Billy. He kept thinking, *for the last ten years I've been a hardworking, law abiding citizen, and now, what do I have to show for it?* Like millions of people, he had lost most of his savings due to the global economic collapse.

Discussing the matter earlier in the week over lunch with two other captains, Billy expressed his frustration. "Look, if I'm a captain and I run the yacht into rocks and sink the boat, I don't get a new boat and a raise, I get fired and arrested. Just look at the captain of that Italian cruise liner,

Costa Concordia. He screwed up, got too close to the rocks, and got punished for it. It was a seriously neglectful act, and people died. But look at the fucking economy! Have any of the executives responsible for this financial crisis been brought to justice for their crimes? No! Not one person from AIG or the big Wall Street banks has been indicted or even questioned by authorities!"

His friend, Tom, who ran a seventy foot Swan sailboat, interrupted, "How the hell do you know that?"

"Did you ever see the movie *Inside Job* or that thing on *60 Minutes*? Steve Kroft asked the assistant attorney general at the Justice Department why no one had been charged. Know what the Justice Department said? 'This is a department that's working hard, and we're going to keep working hard.' What absolute, complete, and total bullshit! Fucking Congress exonerated Goldman Sachs for Christ sakes!"

"Christ Billy, calm down."

"Calm down? Calm down! I've lost most of my net worth! I'll have to work another twenty years to get my savings back! Look, should the public have to pay for the damage done by the BP oil spill in the Gulf of Mexico? Or, what about when the oil tanker, *Exxon Valdez,* ran aground in Alaska spilling millions of gallons of oil in one of the most beautiful places in the world? How absurd would it have been to ask the taxpayer to finance the hazardous waste cleanup, and then give the Captain a *fucking* bonus? The whole Wall Street slash investment bank debacle was far worse than any oil spill, but those responsible for the global economic meltdown were rewarded for their greed and ineptitude."

The fact that the CEOs, the *captains* of Goldman Sachs, JP Morgan, Citigroup, AIG and others had been paid huge bonuses with taxpayer bailout money after leading the world into economic chaos infuriated Billy.

Billy's dream of retiring early, buying a catamaran, and sailing the Caribbean was shot to hell. *Well, two can play at that game,* he thought. *If the ringleaders are held unaccountable for blatant negligence, then there is no justice. If there is no justice, what is the point of abiding the law?*

Billy had decided to roll the dice in the game of life, but if he was going to roll them, the stakes had to be enormous. It had to be all or nothing. He would use the yacht he was working on to smuggle a fifty-five gallon drum full of cocaine from Honduras to Florida. He took a sip from the icy cold Corona in his hand, smiled at the wondrous colors of the sunset and thought, *this time next year I'll be on my own yacht with millions of dollars in a foreign bank–if I don't get caught, or killed.*

CHAPTER 4   ÁLVAREZ

THIRTY EIGHT YEARS EARLIER,
THE MOSQUITO COAST OF HONDURAS, OCTOBER 19, 1972.

Rodriguez walked into Álvarez's office and could clearly see that Álvarez was in a foul mood.

"Cuando han sido ustedes? Where have you been?" Álvarez yelled.

Rodriguez knew to be very careful with his words. He had once witnessed Álvarez use a baseball bat to club a dedicated employee in the head just for being late, even though the man's daughter had needed to go to the hospital for emergency stitches. "No excuse, sir," he replied.

"Yes, that's right there is no excuse!" yelled Álvarez. "Where the hell is my money?" Rodriguez threw a wad of bills on the table in front of him.

"I took what he had, but that is all we'll get from him. The others will pay up quickly now that he's dead." News that the fisherman had been killed seemed to quell Álvarez much the way fresh rabbit placates the ravings of a rabid jackal.

Luiz Pedro Álvarez was the living embodiment of Lord Acton's famous phrase: "Absolute power corrupts absolutely." Álvarez had worked his way up the Honduran drug trade his entire life. Over the years he had become so arrogant, narcissistic, and conceited that he truly lost grasp of reality and believed he was omnipotent. During the day, he strutted about authoritatively in army fatigues like Iraq dictator Saddam Hussein, then, later that night, be seen downtown dressed in a shiny silk suit and designer sunglasses, just like Libyan strong man Muammar Gaddafi. Álvarez had major players placed in what passed for government in Honduras on his payroll. Immune to anything resembling law and order, he could do as he pleased, but he was no fool. Several men had tried to take him down over the years, but extreme paranoia and a small, devoted team had kept him alive.

During the planning stages of the last attempted coup, a subordinate named Filipe Gomez approached Rodriguez with the intent of turning him against Álvarez. Rodriguez played along, but informed Álvarez of the plot to over throw his empire. Wasting no time, Álvarez called a meeting of twenty-five of his top men. When Álvarez gave the signal, guns were drawn and the three defectors were held down in their chairs. They sat there helpless, pinned down by brute force on either side of them.

Álvarez turned to Filipe Gomez. "You think you can kill me? I've known of your plans from the start," he lied. "I know what you think, what makes you happy and what makes you sad, what you love and what you hate. I even know what you dream. This way, I know your nightmares. In fact, I know you so well, that I feel that it is almost a shame to kill you. So, before I kill you, I'm giving you a going away present." Álvarez snapped his fingers like an obnoxious patron at a restaurant, whereupon a large security man quickly walked over and placed a gift wrapped box on the table in front of Gomez. The security men on either side of Gomez removed his gun and released his arms so he could open the gift.

"Open it!" Álvarez ordered. Gomez tried to be stoic, but as he reached for the box, his trembling hands could be seen by all at the table. He pulled on the ribbon at the top, and the sides of the box fell away. There, in front of him, lay his youngest child's severed head with his wife's ring finger protruding from his son's mouth. Light from above made the wedding ring diamond sparkle with macabre perversion against blue lifeless lips. Gomez screamed as he leaped on the table towards Álvarez. Security had been anticipating this type of response and instantly shot all three defectors in the head. The execution had been so precisely timed, that the three simultaneous gun shots echoed as only one report.

It would have been a simple matter to kill Gomez's wife, but Álvarez allowed her to live, less one finger. She was a constant, living reminder of who was in control and a warning to those who contested Álvarez. Gomez's two daughters were also allowed to live. But these acts of mercy did not erase Álvarez's brutality. Word travelled quickly of the repercussions against those who had challenged him. This way Álvarez kept the peasants terrorized through mortal fear. It worked.

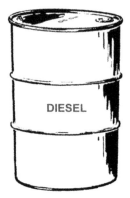

CHAPTER 5   THE PLAN

EAST HAMPTON, NEW YORK.

Billy loved being docked in Three Mile Harbor during the summer. Almost every night, a dazzling array of beautiful colors was displayed on God's canvas. The sun had gently ducked down below the trees. Just the right amount of clouds reflected the setting sun's light in a wondrous spectrum of vibrant colors. The lower clouds were soft yellow-orange, while the top of the clouds beamed bright magenta. The reds were set off by rich greens from the pine trees below. In between the clouds, beautifully interspersed shafts of white and blue light burst brightly as if sent from heaven.

    Billy was constantly astounded by the awesome power and beauty of nature. With a long sip from his icy cold Corona, he leaned back in the deck chair and gazed at the sunset. *Ah, yes, summer in the Hamptons.*

As Mother Nature's light show slowly began to fade, Billy closed his eyes. His dream was becoming more vivid and focused. *More of a business plan, really. In theory, it's quite simple. So is splitting the atom,* he thought with a chuckle.

Prior to getting a 500 ton U.S. Coast Guard Captain's license ten years ago, Billy had worked as an environmental engineer for a large engineering firm in Boston. He had designed and built remediation systems for hazardous waste sites, and had seen the ramifications of excessive corporate greed firsthand; large corporations who had dumped toxic chemicals into the ground instead of paying to have it properly disposed of. While working in Woburn, Massachusetts, he had discovered a large underground soil area contaminated with trichloroethylene (TCE). The TCE had migrated to a municipal water supply well and affected hundreds of people. Many small children developed cancer, and several died as a result of drinking water contaminated with TCE . Corporate lawyers played their slimy game and no one admitted anything.

When the government began to bail out the corporations responsible for the economic collapse, Billy had looked up the definition of Chief Executive Officer: "The highest ranking executive officer within a company who has the responsibility for overall management of its day to day affairs."[2]

Sitting on the aft deck Billy felt his blood beginning to boil just thinking about it. *The CEOs must have known! They must have known they were getting into financial trouble long before the situation reached crisis level. If you're paid 165 million dollars a year to be the captain of the company, you have to look at the financial depth gauge and fiscal charts once in a while. CEOs can't have it both ways, being paid ridiculous amounts of money because they say they are unbelievably good at what they do, and then declaring, "Well, it wasn't my fault," when they run the company hard aground.*

Bullshit! It was YOUR responsibility! You didn't see the storm clouds on the horizon? Didn't notice the depth getting shallower? Refused to accept reports that you were taking on water in the form of overextended leverage?

How nice it must be to have no accountability! Billy shifted in his chair, no longer aware of the beautiful sunset before him. *Not only did they run their own country's financial solvency into the ground, but many other countries as well. In the process, they ruined the lives of millions, perhaps billions, of people all over the world. And when it came time to explain? 'Gee, well, like the other guy was doing it, so, like, I started doing it, and, well everyone was doing it.'*

Oh, why didn't you say so? Here, have 700 billion dollars of taxpayer money, and another twelve trillion in guaranteed funds.[3] We won't give it to public schools, or try to make health care more affordable. No, no investment bankers and insurance companies really need it more than anyone else. What madness.

He remembered a line from a great Bob Dylan tune: "Steal a little and they throw you in jail. Steal a lot and they make you king." *Wonder what Bob has to say about the neighborhood bullies on Wall Street?*

Billy took another swig of beer, and shook his head, thinking, *you had to give Treasury Secretary Paulson credit, though. He snowballed Congress and got all that money almost instantly with the smallest bill in the history of the United States.*

Billy found himself getting really worked up, so he had to deliberately move his mental energy in another direction. Using his engineering background, he began calculating the quantity of product he planned to bring back to the states. *A gallon of water weighs 8.3 pounds. Cocaine, with its fine* *powder form, probably weighs slightly less, say 8 pounds per gallon. Therefore, at 8 pounds per gallon, a 55-gallon drum would contain 440 pounds of cocaine. Since there are 2.2 pounds per kilogram, 440 pounds divided by 2.2 equals 200 kilograms. There are 1,000 grams per kilogram, so one drum would contain 200,000 grams. Cocaine ranges anywhere from $50-100 per gram, so one drum of cocaine is worth somewhere between 10 and 20 million dollars.*

Billy knew that he wouldn't get street value when he sold such a large quantity, but dealers could cut his stuff in half and still have an excellent product. The high quality coke currently being produced in Central America would enable continuous cutting as it made its way down the selling ladder to the end user. By the time it hit the street, the coke would probably have been cut eight to ten times, resulting in 1-2 parts coke, and 8-10 parts laxative.

If one drum was cut one-to-ten, then the street value would increase to anywhere between 100 to 200 million dollars. You didn't need very sharp math skills to realize that there was a hell of a lot of money in the drug business.

Billy felt a sense of guilt rising up through his soul, but he quickly suppressed it. *The war on drugs has been going on for more than forty years with a cost of over one trillion dollars,*[4] he thought. *My taxes pay bonuses to super rich white collar criminals, and finance a war that can't be won. Didn't the government learn anything from prohibition? I'm just going to get in and get out, take my money, and run. So people want to party a little longer on a Saturday night, big deal.*

CHAPTER 6   *DESTINY*

Motor yacht *Destiny* was constructed in Italy and then shipped to the United States where all the electronics and other owner-specified options were installed. The designer of the yacht used contemporary, flowing lines for the external topsides, hull, and windows, but maintained elegant, classic beauty on all interior furnishings. Entering the yacht, the first impression was the feel of luxurious carpet on bare feet. Shoes were removed prior to entering, and kept in a wicker basket near the aft door. Thick, incredibly soft wool felt magical underfoot. It was far too cost-prohibitive to manufacture carpet like that in America, so it was impossible to find domestically. Unfortunately for Billy, the carpet was white, and required a watchful eye, particularly when serving red wine.

Interior walls constructed of elaborate wood veneer and coated with a lustrous, super-high gloss finish created a brilliant, shiny new experience whenever viewed. Master woodworking craftsmanship could be seen throughout the yacht. The grain patterns of wood veneer aligned meticulously to create spectacular visual displays on the walls and doors that were art pieces in themselves. The focal point on the main salon ceiling consisted of a grain pattern as beautiful as the back of a custom made guitar. Pear tree wood, with a vivid, golden wheat color, achieved a truly magnificent bubbly champagne grain display on the salon ceiling. Soft lighting accented the elliptical art piece in a subtle, yet elegant manner. The pear tree ceiling art created much discussion with visitors, particularly in the evening when the soft, cool blue night lights were illuminated.

Walking from stern toward the bow, guests would make their way through the salon, followed by the galley, then the main helm station. Stairs next to the helm brought guests below the main deck, to four luxurious state rooms. In stark contrast, a ladder provided access to the cramped crew quarters located in the bow. Italian yachts are well known for preposterously small living areas for crew, and as such, the crew quarters quickly became a storage room. Fortunately for Billy, the boss knew that it was unrealistic for anyone to actually live in the so called crew quarters. Instead, he offered Billy any room, save the master suite, when the boss and his family were not onboard. Billy quickly took the VIP room, second only to the master suite for size and comfort.

The yacht boasted luxury everywhere possible. Fourteen carat gold-plated faucets glistened in the bathrooms. The galley countertops consisted of one inch thick, finely polished, blue pearl granite that dazzled the most discerning eye. And the super-high gloss finished woodwork proclaimed elegance throughout the interior. Even the trash compactor was silver plated.

Both of the massive diesel engines were larger than that of an eighteen wheeler. So large, in fact, that construction of the yacht took place *around* the engines. Once completed, if one of the engines had to be removed from the yacht, an access hole the size of two living room couches would have to be cut through the hull. It was a good idea to get the engine installation correct the first time.

CHAPTER 7   SAN PEDRO SULA

HONDURAS OCTOBER 2, 2010.

Officer Miguel Chavez responded to the radio call in his native Spanish. "Roger esta expedición es Chavez. Roger dispatch, this is Chavez." He looked the part of a Honduran police officer in an olive drab military jacket and pants and black military boots. Aviator sunglasses hid his eyes just below a matching cloth hat. However, looking the part of an officer had just lost its credibility, again. Eight people had just been gunned down by men wearing stolen police uniforms in broad daylight in downtown San Pedro Sula. Chavez had been called to the scene.

Chavez was not proud of the recent United Nations Report listing Honduras as the homicide capital of the world for the second year in a row. The published rate was just shy of one homicide per 1,000 people,[5] and he was doing his best not to become part of that statistic. He knew many people who had been killed. In fact, he could not think of a single person who didn't know someone, a friend or relative, that hadn't been brutally murdered. If the same homicide rate was applied to New York City's population of eight million, it would equate to twenty-two killings every day.

The police radio squawked to life, and Chavez was redirected to yet another crime. Apparently, the eight people gunned down earlier were quite dead, the killers had fled, and his services were no longer needed. Instead, he was ordered to an area not far from the airport where there had recently been a rash of robberies, muggings and murders.

The dispatcher alerted him over the static of the police radio that, "Un autobús lleno de turistas justo al lado del plano... A bus full of tourists just off the plane is being held at gunpoint. The bus was on its way to a resort hotel when it was forced off the road by armed gunmen. One of the passengers was able to make a cell phone call before the bandits confiscated all cell phones. I just took the call!"

Chavez replied, "¿Cuál es su posición? What is their location?"

Dispatch quickly relayed the location of the hijacked bus, and Chavez hit the accelerator. He was less than four minutes away!

CHAPTER 8   THE HAMPTONS

Seventy-five miles east of New York City, Long Island splits into the north fork and south fork at the town of Riverhead. The Hamptons began about twelve miles south of Riverhead. Running from west to east were the towns of West Hampton, Hampton Bays, South Hampton, Bridge Hampton, and East Hampton. Each town had its own personality and appeal. Certain neighboring towns like Sag Harbor and Amagansett had been swept under the veil of The Hamptons and might never again be able to claim their independence.

On the south fork located all the way out at the farthest easterly point lay Montauk; a beautiful village desperately trying to hold onto its fishing roots. Often referred to as, "a small drinking village with a fishing problem," it was surrounded by water and boasted one of the best fishing fleets on the east coast. The Montauk locals were down-to-earth folk, and wanted nothing to do with pompous attitudes that were an unavoidable byproduct of the extreme wealth of the Hamptons. In fact, if Montauk were ever actually referred to as being part of the Hamptons, there would be a village uprising and revolt that would no doubt include a mad, drunken march of fishermen yielding flaming torches at midnight as though they were in search of Quasimodo.

Billy woke up to the sound of rain drumming on the deck of the yacht. He dressed quickly and walked out on the aft deck of *Destiny* where he instantly felt chilled by the cold, wet fall air. Wind blowing in cold from the northeast at twenty to twenty-five knots, combined with driving rain, made this Saturday of Columbus Day weekend just plain nasty. *Man, it's coming down! No mountain biking today. Better hit the gym,* Billy thought. He made a cup of coffee in the galley using the little two cup coffee maker that he used when the owner and guests were not onboard, and then he tried to get the satellite TV tuned in. *With rain this hard, I won't get anything.* Sure enough, the satellite couldn't cut through the rain, so no Weather Channel and probably no TV all weekend. He listened to the marine weather forecast on the VHF radio while the coffee brewed, and as he expected, the weekend was going to be a wash out accompanied by strong winds.

Billy drove down Three Mile Harbor Road into the Village of East Hampton and parked behind the trendy New York style grocery store, Citerella. Billy opened the door and walked down the steps into the basement of the building, below Citerella, and entered the gym. Sitting behind the front desk, Bridget was a blond haired cutie with sparkling blue eyes and luscious, full lips.

In addition to the front desk, Bridget worked as a personal trainer. Billy had first noticed her in the gym at the beginning of the summer training another woman while he sweated profusely on the Versa Climber machine. Later that evening, Billy ate dinner at a local Mexican restaurant when Bridget walked in. She sat down at the vacant bar stool next to him, placed a motorcycle helmet on the bar top and announced, "I did it Michelle!" The bartender, Michelle, turned around, looked at the helmet, shook her head, and smiled, "I'm not surprised!"

Billy was intrigued. Without eavesdropping, he was privy to their conversation by proximity. He learned that Bridget had just purchased a used on/off road motorcycle. After several minutes, Billy got up the nerve to talk to her and asked what kind of bike it was. "Want to see it?" She flashed him a dazzling smile. They made their introductions on the walk out to the parking lot.

"So Billy, what do you do?"

"I'm a captain of a motor yacht."

"Like a fishing boat, or...?"

"No, it's a luxury motor yacht."

"Cool. So, what kind of license do you have, a six pack?"

Billy's curiosity was piqued. He had never met a woman who knew anything about the types of licenses issued by the U.S. Coast Guard. Hell, most of his male friends didn't know anything about Coast Guard licenses. What was more interesting was that the term 'Six Pack' was slang for a license that allowed an operator of an uninspected passenger vessel to take no more than six passengers onboard. She obviously knew something about boating. During the conversation that ensued, Billy learned that she had worked part time as crew for one of the fishing fleets out of Montauk.

Now Billy was really interested. This cute girl in great shape rode a motorcycle *and* knew how to fish! They really hit it off that night and talked for hours until last call, when they hastily made plans to go mountain biking the next day.

The following morning, Billy loaded her mountain bike onto his car rack and they drove out to Cedar Point Park. Billy had ridden the park trails more than a dozen times the previous year and knew the area well. Nevertheless, he was a little nervous that he was about to go riding with a personal trainer in top physical shape who might very well be an excellent mountain bike rider. They started off slow, but after a large downhill section, Billy kept up the pace and could hear her right behind him. They zipped over a knoll at high speed and surprised four grazing deer that exploded off in all directions. One of the deer tried to run away in the same direction as the bike path, much like someone trying to outrun a train by running on the tracks. Billy and Bridget were soaring along the path with a deer running alongside them for what seemed like five minutes. The deer finally bolted off to the right and bounded into the dense woods.

Later, they stopped to rest at Billy's favorite spot where the massive Hampton sand dunes gave way to a majestic view of Gardiner's Bay. The bluff rose more than 100 feet above the water, creating a magnificent, panoramic view of the bay. "Wow! This is beautiful," Bridget said. "I've never been here before, and I've spent every summer in the Hamptons since I was little!"

Billy removed a carefully wrapped peach from his backpack, cut it in half and handed her the side without the seed. The sweet, soft fruit was beyond delicious, and they savored every bite. Licking the juice from her thumb, Bridget smiled and said, "I thought that deer was going to run with us forever!"

Billy had been rehearsing this moment in his mind all morning, but now that it was upon him, he wasn't sure if he had the nerve to follow through. They were standing and looking out at the water when Billy put his finger to his lip, tapped it, and said, "You've got a little peach right there."

She brushed her lips, stuck her chin out and said, "Did I get it?"

"Not quite, here," Billy took a step closer and raised his hand as if he were going to brush away the peach, then at the last second he leaned in and kissed her. At first, Billy felt her body become rigid, but then he felt her relax. He wrapped his arms around her, and she returned his kiss. After a warm embrace they parted. "Got it," he said.

"That was delicious. The kiss wasn't bad either." Laughing, she jumped on her bike. Billy followed in pursuit on his mountain bike, grinning from ear to ear.

They continued dating frequently throughout the summer, and their relationship grew to the point where they were spending all of their free time together. Billy met Bridget's parents two months later, in July, when they enjoyed the Bastille Day fireworks over Three Mile Harbor.

Billy was continuously impressed, not only with Bridget's admirable goals, but with her significant achievements as well. She was a serious athlete and had run several marathons. However, even though Bridget was in great shape, she wasn't obsessed with diet and exercise; rather, it was a way of life that she embraced naturally. Billy loved the contagious effect of Bridget's healthy lifestyle. He consciously noticed that he had more energy, and felt better about himself when he was with her.

Their relationship flowed so easily that it seemed like they had known each other for several years, but it had only been several months. They first met in mid-May and now it was early October.

When Billy walked down into the gym, he immediately saw Bridget being hit on by a man dressed in spandex shorts that were so tight they looked like they were painted on. The man hitting on Bridget had acquired the nickname, Dexter, which had evolved from Spandex. Apparently, he wore skin-tight spandex shorts all the time, not just in the gym. Dexter sat on the reception desk with one cheek and was motioning around with his hands, completely absorbed in telling his story.

Bridget saw Billy walking down the stairs and her expression lit up with an ear to ear smile. "Good morning

Captain! How may I be of service?" She gave Billy a stealth wink.

Being interrupted caused Dexter to momentarily close his well-oiled mouth. He looked confused as if he couldn't understand that the world did not revolve around him. Clueless to the fact that he was completely in Bridget's space both professionally and personally, he stood up, ignored Billy and said, "Hey, I've got to get back to lifting, but I'll finish my story later." Bridget did not reply.

Billy waited until Dexter was out of earshot before he said softly, "Hey Bridget."

She gave him a serious look and said, "You answered my prayers, babe."

"Really?"

"No, I'm serious. I was just literally praying for someone to come in to get Dexter's ass off my desk!" They both laughed, and then she asked, "You're still taking me out for sushi tonight, right?"

"Absolutely! When do you get off?"

Bridget did a little shuffle, moving her shoulders one way and her head the other, gave Billy a sultry look and said in a throaty voice, "With you babe, every time."

Billy smiled and said softly, "I *know* when you get off, but when do you leave work?"

"Caroline is coming in for me at six, then I'm going for a run, so why don't you pick me up at, say, eight?"

"Sounds perfect."

"Oh, Marco's here. He's on the floor somewhere."

"Thanks. See you in a bit," Billy said, and walked into the locker room to change.

Billy spotted his friend and part time first mate, Marco Villanueva, on the nautilus machine and walked over. Billy and Marco had been working together for several years and had become good friends. "Hey Marco, how are you looking for the southbound trip?"

Marco smiled, and responded with a Spanish accent, "Emm, oh, I'm ready anytime, but... Em, the weather?"

"I checked the weather this morning, and this low pressure will last through the weekend, but we should be good to go later in the week. Let's provision the yacht on Wednesday and leave at first light on Thursday."

"Okay, I will plan on that."

Billy's boss had a close friend who also had a luxury motor yacht where Marco worked. Even though the owners of Billy and Marco's yachts commuted to work in helicopters, they wanted to save money where they could, so Billy and Marco would team up to move the yachts between New York in the summertime and Florida for the winter. Together, they would deliver one yacht, fly back, and move the second yacht. This way, the owners didn't have to hire any additional crew, and had just one full time employee on each yacht. Billy was the captain, but Marco didn't have a Captain's license, so he was first mate.

After a good, long workout, Billy was relaxing in the sauna thinking about the upcoming voyage and leaving the Hamptons. *Yeah, it's that time of the year again. Time to head south. It seems like I'm ready to get out of here a little earlier each year.*

Billy picked Bridget up at eight, and they drove out to Amagansett for sushi and sake at a restaurant called Mt. Fuji. The owner of the restaurant knew Billy and sat them at a table at the far end of the dining room.

Bridget had eagerly accepted Billy's invitation to be crew for the southbound trip aboard *Destiny*, and Billy was elated to hear the excitement in her voice when she talked about taking the trip. "I've never done the intracoastal waterway before. I did one trip south to deliver one of the fishing fleet's boats to Florida, but we stayed in the Atlantic and ran twenty-four-seven. We only pulled in for fuel once, down in the Carolinas."

The server placed a bottle of hot sake and two small cups on the table. Billy poured the hot clear liquid into the cups, handed one to Bridget, and said, "I think you'll enjoy this trip more because we stop to refuel every night, and you can get off the boat."

Bridget raised the small cup to her lips and took a sip. She smiled and said, "Great, I'll bring my running sneakers."

Several fillets of sashimi and many sakes later they decided to do a little skinny dipping, and Billy knew exactly where to go. The boss owned a multimillion dollar mansion in the Hamptons, complete with the requisite pool. Billy kept an eye on the mansion when it was vacant for any length of time, but generally he slept on the yacht. He knew the Boss was away for the weekend at his chalet in Beaver Creek for some early season powder skiing.

The moon glowed softly upon them as they stood naked in the shallow end of the pool. Billy held her in his arms and passionately kissed her as the gentle moonlight reflected off the surface of the water. She had beautiful, full lips that Billy could never get enough of. He took her lower lip in between his and held it there for several seconds before he slowly kissed his way down her neck. Taking a deep breath he went underwater and pleased her with his tongue. He came up and kissed her full lips again and slowly released a mouthful of water that erotically flowed down both of their mouths and fell from their chins onto her breasts, then into the pool. Billy pulled her away from the side of the pool and she wrapped her legs around his waist. He slid inside her and held her in that position, relishing every detail. He nibbled on her neck while she gyrated, and they both moaned with pleasure.

Their passion continued for several hours and moved from the pool, to the kitchen, and then the living room before they finally collapsed, exhausted in bed.

The next day, they grinned and blushed over coffee while they discussed the previous night. "I can barely walk," she confided.

"Look at this," Billy pulled his shirt off and turned around, exposing zebra like scratches across his back.

"So *that's* how I broke a nail!" she said. They both laughed.

The following night, Billy met Marco at a long-established, if not elegant, bar on Main Street in Montauk. He didn't want to run into anyone that he, or his boss, knew in East Hampton. The vertical lights of the neon sign both highlighted and dated the bar which had been there for more than forty years. Upon entering, Billy was relieved to see that the rustic old place was quiet, just the way he planned it. The summer crowds had gone and the entire region seemed to emit a collective sigh of relief now that each town once again belonged to the indigenous folk.

Several large shark jaws were mounted over the bar. Lights hung from anchor shaped fixtures that could almost pass for authentic. They illuminated dozens of photos, both old and new, of proud men, embracing a massive halibut, arm around a mako shark, dwarfed by a giant blue fin tuna. There was even a photo of a youngster struggling to hold up a massive striped bass. One man was holding both arms out in front of him clutching the claws of the largest lobster Billy had ever seen. The claws were above the man's head and the tail was below his waist. Hemingway would have approved.

Marco arrived and joined Billy at a table in the back corner of the bar. "Hey Marco, what can I get you?"

"Emm, oh a draft cerveza is a nice thing."

The waitress returned and set two frosty mugs of mahogany colored pale ale on the table. Billy waited until she left. "Marco, I need to talk to you about something, but if you don't want to do it, just say so, and I won't mention it again…"

CHAPTER 9   BANDIDOS

SAN PEDRO SULA, HONDURAS.

Chavez spotted the hijacked bus off the road near the airport in less than three minutes. His police unit consisted of four men who bounced wildly in the old, battered Jeep as they sped along toward the seized bus. Fortunately, the Jeep's large engine had been maintained, and the men were flying across the spotty asphalt. He yelled over the noise, "Obtener a hombres listos! Estos chicos están armadas! Get ready men! These men are armed and will not hesitate to kill us!" The unmistakable *click* of metal on metal was the only response from the men as they loaded and cocked their weapons.

Chavez quickly evaluated the scene as they approached: two vehicles, one on either side of the bus; passengers still onboard; at least four bandits, maybe more. He swerved sharply off the road just in time to take cover provided by a small embankment as rapid flashes emitted from the bus windows and dust exploded all around the Jeep. One shot hit the Jeep sending sparks and shrapnel into the air. They bounced along at high speed keeping just below the embankment, until they skidded to a stop, only twenty yards from the bus, creating a large dust plume. Using the dust for cover, all four men jumped from the Jeep, hit the dirt, and shuffled along the ground on their forearms to the top of the embankment.

Chavez noticed one of the gunmen running away behind the bus, heading toward the mountains where it would be impossible to capture him. Using hand signals, he motioned to Juarez, his best shooter, to take him out. Juarez trained his rifle scope on center mass and took him out with one shot. The gunmen on the bus responded with a barrage of AK-47 gunfire, causing Chavez and his men to duck down.

Chavez yelled, "¿Cuántos armado? How many shooters?"

"He visto al menos dos, tres muchos en el bus. I saw at least two, maybe three on the bus," replied Juarez.

Chavez pointed to Juarez. "¡Vos! You! Crawl to a location where you have the best shot and signal us when you're ready. We'll provide cover, and you take out as many as you can, but try to get at least two!" Juarez nodded and began to arm-crawl away, keeping his hips pinned to the ground.

The gunmen on the bus continued to fire wildly toward Chavez then paused, possibly to reload. Juarez seized the opportunity to slide his rifle below a thorny bush that gave him superior camouflage, while maintaining line of sight to his target. He did not fire until he knew exactly where two of the gunmen were located on the bus, and then gave the signal. Instantly, Chavez and his men began unloading their weapons as fast as they could. Juarez took the first bandit out with a direct head shot. Hysterical screams from the captive bus passengers pierced the air.

The second gunman came into view through the crosshairs and instantly ducked down. "¡Maldita sea! Damn!" A few seconds later the same gunman shoved a hostage against the bus window. Through his high powered gun scope, Juarez could see terror in the hostage's eyes. The gunman was being clever and barely revealing any of his own head as he tried to see where the police were located. However, the gunman assumed that the shot that just killed his partner had come from the barrage of gunfire, not twenty yards away where Juarez was taking careful aim. "Sólo un poco más. Just a little more..."

The .234 Winchester round exited the rifle barrel at more than 4,000 feet per second and blew through the bandit's head less than one-tenth of a second later. Loud screams erupted from the bus as the men moved in.

Chavez ran up the steps and announced, "Policía! No te muevas! Do not move!"

With his gun drawn, Chavez inspected the passengers and ordered the first five rows to exit the bus. As the passengers rose from their seats and began to exit, a woman looked into Chavez's eyes with more than fear, and he instantly knew something was terribly wrong. In a flash, another gunman leapt up from behind the last seat and fired two shots from less than ten feet away. The loud explosions in the confined space of the bus were deafening. Chavez saw the gunman's motion in his peripheral vision and was swinging his gun into position when the first bullet struck his left shoulder. Fortunately, Chavez was right handed. He quickly positioned his pistol on target and rapidly fired four rounds. The gunman jerked and convulsed as each bullet blasted into his flesh, sending the second shot wildly off target through the roof of the bus.

Recovering from his bullet wound in the hospital several weeks later, Chavez learned that the man he had shot and killed on the bus was the police chief's nephew.

After fully recuperating, Chavez returned to work for what he thought was active duty. However, when Chavez was called into the chief's office for what Chavez thought was a citation, or a possible promotion, he was shocked when the chief said, "You used unnecessary force, and endangered the lives of civilians on the bus. Effective immediately, you are suspended indefinitely without pay." Chavez became infuriated and stormed out of the police station.

One month later, Chavez threatened to contest his dismissal and go public with the whole event, whereupon he learned that the official police report stated that the person running away from the bus was not one of the gunmen, but a passenger. Chavez's fellow officer and expert sniper, Juarez, had inspected the body and found not one, but two weapons. The other passengers on the bus confirmed that there were four assailants. Witnesses on the bus identified the man who ran away as one of the bandits!

Forces beyond Chavez's control had made a drastic impact on his life and he felt angry and cheated. In a vain effort to ease his pain he proceeded to drown his frustration over drinks with an older officer at the local bar. The older cop, who had been drinking for hours, leaned over and slurred, "Si se insertar cualquier más lejos, voy a matar. If you push this any farther, they'll kill you."

Overwhelmed with the feeling of loss, Chavez had become a broken man at the hands of corruption.

CHAPTER 10   SOUTHBOUND

EAST HAMPTON, NEW YORK.

It was still dark when Billy woke up on the yacht Thursday morning at 5:25 a.m. He opened his eyes two minutes before his cell phone alarm was scheduled to go off. He rolled over, kissed Bridget's shoulder and gave her a warm rub. Grabbing the remote from the bedside table, he fluffed up his pillow and silently switched on the Weather Channel to get the local on the eight's report. *Let's have a nice first day,* he thought. The forecast indicated cool temperatures, but there didn't seem to be much in the way of precipitation on the Doppler radar.

He made his way to the small bathroom and splashed some water over his face while he listened to the marine weather forecast on a portable VHF radio. He kept the volume low and the door closed so as not to disturb Bridget. A monotone, computerized voice relayed that the winds were forecast to be from the southeast at ten knots with waves one to two feet. *Sounds like it should be a good day weather wise,* he thought as he finished dragging a razor over his face.

After his usual morning routine in the bathroom, Billy quietly did fifty push-ups and sit-ups. It got the blood flowing and cleared his mind for the day ahead. When he finished his last sit-up, he looked over and saw Bridget lying across the king size bed seductively smiling at him. "As a personal trainer, I'm well versed in a multitude of aerobics." Billy hurriedly leapt up onto the bed and passionately kissed her. Her aerobics were much more pleasurable than push-ups and sit-ups.

After Billy dressed, he walked upstairs to the wheelhouse to double check the course he had plotted out on the navigation system. Marco popped up the steps a few minutes later. "Good morning Amigo," he said with a cheerful smile.

"Yes, yes, good morning Marco. It looks like we have a nice first day ahead of us. Southeast winds around ten knots with no storms visible yet."

"Excellent. Should I start the gen-or-aye-tors?" Marco asked.

"Sunrise isn't for another forty five minutes, so have some breakfast. I made some coffee. Fire up the gennys in about fifteen minutes, and then we'll head out."

"Okay, Amigo."

The main engines rolled over sluggishly due to the cold weather and belched a plume of white smoke to confirm their dislike of the cool fall air. Billy gave one final look around the dock and gave Marco the okay to begin untying the lines. Bridget joined Billy on the fly bridge and asked, "What can I do to help?"

"Oh, thanks, babe, but we're all set. This slip is pretty straight forward."

Marco yelled, "All clear," indicating that all the lines were untied, Marco was onboard, and they were ready to maneuver away from the dock. With confident, gentle ease, Billy backed the yacht out of the slip and headed north out of Three Mile Harbor.

In the pre-dawn light, they were greeted by a family of swans, two very large adults and six offspring. The young ones had not yet turned white and were a mottled dusty gray color. The bright white feathered bodies of the enormous adults measured over three feet long, and could easily be seen in the faint, early morning light. The swans were not impressed by the yacht and kept to their business of swimming toward the shallows in search of their morning meal. When *Destiny* came alongside the two adult swans, they showed their disinterest by dipping their large orange beaks down deep into the water causing their rear ends to rise up high in the air. Bridget had been watching them and burst out laughing.

Marco chuckled. "They are... How do you say? Mooning us."

As they rounded a section of channel that took them very close to wetlands and saw grass, Billy recognized the cackle of a giant blue heron. He searched the grassy area for the bird, but in the pre-dawn light it was difficult to spot the master of camouflage. In fact, Billy didn't spot the mammoth bird until it silently took flight. He admired its soft blue grey color and gentle grace as it glided over the bow.

By mid-October in the Hamptons, things had quieted down substantially from the crazy days of summer. As such, the harbor channel was deserted, save for one lone fisherman in a small, fifteen foot boat casting for striped bass on the incoming tide. Billy recognized the boat and the two men exchanged waves without a word. *Destiny* quietly passed the East Hampton Yacht Club and the town dock, before turning to port and heading out of the harbor.

Billy checked the coolant temperature of the massive diesel engines, and slowly accelerated by pushing the throttle forward. It was amazing that a yacht *Destiny's* size could actually get up on a plane on the water. He could feel the engines strain against the eighty-ton load they were pushing as the yacht got closer and closer. At eighteen knots, the bow dropped down and the yacht was now on a plane. Maximum speed was twenty-four knots, but to go easy on the engines and maximize fuel efficiency, Billy cruised at twenty knots.

The majestic orange glow of sun rise began to take hold of their surroundings. The soft morning light bounced off the brightly colored lobster pots. The wind had not had a chance to build, so the sea was flat calm. As they made their way north toward Plum Island, they saw the Cross Sound Ferry passing through Plum Gut to the west. The sun was up high enough to illuminate everything now, but it hadn't warmed up the air temperature yet. Billy was wearing his trusty old wool cap and a pair of gloves to keep his hands warm while holding the stainless steel steering wheel. He put his arm around Bridget and pulled her close, and she rested her head on his shoulder.

In good weather, Billy liked to run the yacht from the fly bridge. The visibility was far better and it was a much more pleasant, outdoor experience. In foul weather, the fly bridge station was a wet and sloppy affair, so he ran the yacht from the main wheelhouse. However, today with perfectly clear conditions, the visibility was limited only by the curvature of the earth.

As they rounded Plum Gut, they saw a horde of fisherman working the riptide. Billy counted no less than sixteen small boats as they bounced through the rip. The sun was at their backs now, and Billy switched on the auto pilot for a waypoint that was off Port Jefferson, about forty miles away. Except for dodging lobster pots and debris in the water, they had a straight shot for two hours.

As if on cue, Marco poked his head up through the doorway that led to the fly bridge and asked, "Do you want to take a break, Amigo?"

"Thanks, Marco, but I'm good for a while. Once we get south of Ambrose Channel, I'll take a break."

"Em, I will do an engine room check now." He disappeared down the steps.

Bridget took a sip from her coffee mug and leaned into Billy. "This is nice," she said. They sat in silence taking in the beauty of being on the ocean early in the morning. Cruising along at twenty knots, the yacht made a continuous *shhhhhh* sound, as it sliced through the water. The cool, crisp fall air contained minimal moisture, making the visibility crystal clear. They could easily see Connecticut across Long Island Sound.

He rubbed Bridget's shoulder and pulled her tight against him. The thought of telling her about Honduras crept into his mind, but she would be utterly opposed, so he quietly took in the scenery.

Marco appeared from nowhere snapping Billy from his gaze across the water and reported, "Em, everything looks good, no problems."

"Thanks Marco."

They passed the entrance to Huntington Harbor and continued hugging the coast, heading toward Sands Point. Two hours after sunrise they rounded Great Neck and saw the historic Stepping Stones Light up ahead. Six minutes later, they were cruising on the East River, heading under the Throgs Neck Bridge. Traffic looked to be moving fairly well at that early hour. The Bronx-Whitestone Bridge was another story. Major delays appeared in store for those heading into Queens. Billy remembered all the hours he spent in a car during his commuting days at the engineering firm where he worked ten years earlier. He pointed up at the bridge full of stationary vehicles and said to Bridget, "I don't miss that!"

With unlimited visibility, jets were busy landing and taking off from LaGuardia Airport, next to the East River. Jet engines roared loudly as they flew low overhead. The yacht bounced gently over the invisible boundary line transferring them from Queens to the Bronx as they rounded infamous Riker's Island. "Look Marco, a prison with water views!"

"Em, I like this view better."

Entering New York County by boat via Long Island Sound literally meant they had to cruise through the gates of hell. *Welcome to New York...* Hell Gate was located on the East River, which connected three major bodies of water: New York Upper Bay, Long Island Sound, and the Hudson River via the Harlem River. The tidal flow could reach speeds of up to five knots depending on the lunar cycle and prevailing weather. The East River formed a switchback right at Hell Gate and could create treacherous situations for mariners.

Marco studied the navigation chart, looked up with concern and said, "Execution Rocks! Hell Gate! Oh, nice place!"

Billy chuckled and replied, "Yeah, amigo, this area can get a little tricky."

As they passed under the Hell Gate Railroad Bridge, he turned up the VHF radio and listened for any oncoming traffic. Billy heard a security call from a tug boat pushing a barge coming out of New York City. The tug and barge had the current flowing with them, making maneuvering more difficult. Billy called the tug boat captain on the radio and asked if he would like a slow pass. The tug operator responded: "Thanks Captain. That would be appreciated." Billy slowed the yacht which reduced the size of the wake from three feet to about half a foot. He gave a wide berth to allow the tug captain plenty of room to make the turn under the Robert F. Kennedy Bridge.

The sun had risen high enough to warm the air. Billy removed his hat and gloves as he rounded the lower portion of Hell Gate and the Gracie Mansion came into view up ahead.

While the yacht continued south on the East River, vessel traffic became more and more congested. At the East 35th Street heliport, there was a flurry of activity as a helicopter took off amongst the numerous water taxis. Bridget and Billy felt the rotor wash of the helicopter as it flew low over their heads. Just another day in New York City.

As *Destiny* passed the Staten Island Ferry Terminal on the starboard side, with Governor's Island in the foreground, Billy remembered coming through this part of the trip in October, 2001. His thoughts cascaded back in time and he vividly recalled their southbound trip after nine-eleven.

The U.S. Coast Guard had closed the East River to all vessel traffic for an entire month after the cowardly attack. It wasn't until late October, 2001 that Billy was finally granted passage down the East River. When they approached Ground Zero, not only could they smell the destruction, but they could *feel* it. Billy experienced an overwhelming sensation of profound melancholy that day. Goosebumps rose on his arms, and he physically shivered with thoughts of the victims. The feeling was tangible, as if thousands of souls were crying out from the grave in disappointment. It was disappointment, rather than anger, for once again the evolution of the human species had been set back by religious lunacy.

Congratulations guys, Billy thought, nine years after the attacks. *You've succeeded in perpetuating worldwide hatred, revenge, war, and murder for the foreseeable future. This is your belief? No God would ever condone such actions.* He exhaled a heavy sigh as he gazed at the void space where the mighty World Trade Towers once stood. As long as belief exceeded reason, there would never be true evolution.

All onboard waved to Lady Liberty in the distance as *Destiny* rounded Governor's Island off the port side. In no time the mighty Verrazano Bridge connecting Staten Island to Brooklyn became clearly visible dead ahead. Billy took a long look back at the New York City skyline and thought, *See you in six months. I hope.*

Billy, Bridget and Marco gazed up as they swiftly cruised under the massive center span of the Verrazano Bridge. They exited Ambrose Channel by making a dog leg turn and headed east, out to sea. Once they had cleared New York vessel traffic and gotten into deeper water, Billy set a way point on the auto pilot near the main channel marker for Atlantic City, New Jersey, about 100 nautical miles to the south. He stood up and motioned for Marco to take the helm. "Are you good for a while, Marco? We're going to take a break and get a snack." Billy winked at Marco so that Bridget couldn't see him.

"Oh, em, I'm fine. Enjoy your snack," Marco said with a smile.

Billy and Bridget walked down into the VIP room and as soon as she shut the door, he pulled her close, wrapped his arms around her, and they fell onto the bed kissing. They were past the point of hesitation and caution in their relationship. Billy was aware that he had let go of any apprehension caused by the potential of getting hurt and was thrilled to be opening up and sharing. They both wanted it, needed it. He was really falling for her. He knew the only way to really get to know someone wholly was to truly reveal his emotions, but in doing so, he was exposing himself to deep pain if the relationship didn't work out. But, he didn't care. It was worth the risk. He felt euphoric with her. The sex was fantastic, but it was much more than that. Billy was in love.

Although they had made love just six hours earlier, their passion was so intense it felt as if it had been six months.

Billy held the back of her head in the palm of his hand and kissed her neck as he felt himself getting close. He quickly rolled over while holding her in his arms and then she began to gyrate on top of him with such intensity that Billy yielded to primordial urge and lifted his hips off the bed to get as deep inside her as possible. They both collapsed on the bed with hearts pounding.

"I think I like this whole yachting thing," she said smiling. Billy leaned over and kissed her, then shut his eyes, enjoying the afterglow.

During most trips, Billy never really slept while underway. However, the warm flow of endorphins combined with the gentle rocking of the yacht and the hum of the engines was a lullaby. This leg of the trip was fairly straight forward, with no rocks or obstacles, and plenty of water depth. All Marco had to do was dodge lobster traps and the occasional boat along the way. Billy felt himself drifting off to sleep and it felt so good, he let himself go.

He caught a micro nap and opened his eyes to the familiar Doppler radar on TV. Nice and clear all the way down to Norfolk, Virginia. *Yes!* Bridget was sitting up in bed reading a paperback with the TV sound muted. From the time stamp on the Weather Channel, Billy saw that he had slept for thirty minutes. Since they were cruising at twenty nautical miles per hour, only ten miles had gone by and there was no need to check up on Marco. The rumble in his stomach reminded him of when he last ate, so they got dressed and walked up to the galley.

Billy opened the fridge, which overflowed with all kinds of meat, cheese, fruit and veggies. Bridget looked over his shoulder smiling and said, "Wow! I guess we're not going to starve on this trip!"

He wanted to tap into the deli meat and cheese, and make a huge sandwich complete with lettuce, tomatoes, pickles and banana peppers. His mouth started to water as he detailed the sandwich in his mind, but then had another thought. "The place we're eating at tonight is really good with ample portions. As much as I want to make a big sandwich, I'm going to save my appetite." Reluctantly, he grabbed the bag of raw broccoli that Bridget had washed and cut up prior to departure.

"Raw broccoli, babe? Really?"

Having dulled the hunger pangs with half a dozen broccoli florets, Billy made his way back through the salon for an engine room check while Bridget made a salad in the galley. The salon was separated from the aft deck by two massive sliding glass doors set in six-inch wide stainless steel frames. The highly polished doors were mounted on precision bearing rollers, allowing the 250 pound doors to slide open and closed with ease. The salon doors were equipped with a key lock for security, but also contained locks that secured the doors in the fully open or closed position. The heavy doors rolled freely in any other position. While underway, Billy had to make sure that the doors were secured, or they could slide into each other and smash the $10,000 glass panels.

He ensured that the doors were securely shut behind him and walked out on the aft deck. The deck consisted of two-inch wide strips of teak wood, separated by black caulking. The golden brown teak strips ran in perfect parallel fashion from bow to stern. The location of the engine room below the aft deck ensured a very quiet ride while underway. In fact, it was easy to carry on a conversation in the salon at normal speaking volume while cruising at twenty knots.

Billy's eyes did a cursory review of the aft deck table and chairs to ensure that they were secure, and he stuck his head over both the port and starboard sides, looking from bow to stern for any abnormality. Everything looked good, so he walked around to the port side and rotated the two-foot long latch handle counterclockwise to open the water tight door to the engine room. Billy heaved on the bulky, white door and moved it four inches towards him and then slid it toward the bow on a semi-circular track. Pushing the locking pin in place, he secured the door in the fully open position. He reached inside, grabbed ear muffs, and placed them over his ears with both hands.

Entrance to the engine room was a little tricky, and in heavy seas very dangerous. The floor of the engine room was a full seven feet below the main deck. When he stepped through the engine room door, he stepped onto the top rung of a ladder that extended vertically straight down to the engine room floor. So Billy quickly turned around, backed into the open engine room door, and bounded down the ladder in the tight three foot by three foot square vertical shaft. At the bottom of the ladder, Billy turned towards the bow, where the main electrical panel was located.

The electrical system on large yachts like *Destiny* could only be rivaled by the electronics on aircraft of similar size. Completely self-contained with two, 25 kilowatt generators, the yacht supplied both AC power at 220 and 110 volts, and DC power at 24 and 12 volts. The DC system consisted of four separate battery banks: starting batteries for the main engines and generators, bow thruster, and service (or "house") batteries. With the power equivalent of twenty-five car batteries, the house battery bank needed to be enormous, and expensive. The large amount of energy stored in the house batteries allowed Billy to shut off the generators while anchored for up to two days, enabling a quiet, peaceful experience, far from the smell and noise of combustion.

Billy inspected the analog and digital gauges of the electrical panel and confirmed that the generators were producing sufficient power and that all the batteries were fully charged. He grabbed a spotlight that he kept in the engine room and began his methodic sweep of all critical systems looking for anything irregular. Visual cues were not always the leading indicator that alerted him something was wrong. Many times he had smelt or even *felt* the problem before identifying it visually. After a close inspection of the fuel distribution system, engines and generators, Billy pulled up one of the floor boards of the engine room to inspect the bilge. He pointed the spot light on the seal where the propeller shaft penetrated through the hull. Both shaft seals were dry. *No water. Good,* he thought. Then he returned the spot light to its charger, climbed up the ladder, turned around and secured the water tight engine room door with a clockwise twist of the latch handle.

Back inside, he walked past the galley to the main wheel house and grabbed the cruising log that he had generated in Excel prior to the trip. He filled out the log and noted their position on the paper chart with a large, removable, sticky red arrow. He glanced forward through the windshield, and made out Trump's Atlantic City about five miles away to the south. He looked over at Bridget, who was just finishing her salad, and winked as he said, "We still have two hours until we reach Cape May." He grabbed her hand and led her away from the galley toward the VIP bedroom.

Later, Billy resumed control of the fly bridge helm station about a half hour before arriving at the entrance channel to Cape May. The sun was still sufficiently high enough so that Billy didn't have to look right into the setting sun as they made the westerly turn into Cape May Harbor. He pulled the throttles back and eased the yacht off of a plane far before they reached the no wake zone.

On flat grass, two hundred yards off the port side, a small group of new recruits marched in tight formation at the U.S. Coast Guard station.

Billy radioed the marina where he had a slip reserved, and the dock master said that there would be two dock hands to guide him to the slip, and assist with the lines if needed.

"Can we fuel from the slip?"

"No problem Captain."

"Great, we'll see you in less than five minutes. *Destiny* out." Billy instructed Marco to rig for a port side tie up. That way they could leave more easily in the morning; there would be no dock hands at the early hour. Billy swung the yacht around 180 degrees and eased it up to the dock with the finesse of a seasoned Captain. The young dock hands were eager to please and ran to catch the lines Marco and Bridget threw. Once the lines were secure, Billy yelled down to the dock hands, "We'll need about 700 gallons of diesel."

"Yes Sir! I'll get the hose to you right away!"

Billy covered up the fly bridge while Marco made the preparations to take on fuel.

Earlier, Marco asked if Billy wanted to eat dinner alone with Bridget, but Billy had insisted, "No, no, Marco. Please join us. It's fine, really. I may want to do a romantic night later in the trip, maybe Jekyll Island, but I'll let you know when it feels right."

The three of them enjoyed a delicious dinner of fresh Mahi-Mahi, dusted with just the right amount of Cajun seasoning without being overpowering, which flaked apart in moist, succulent chunks. Accompanied by a cold draft beer for the men and white wine for Bridget, there was little conversation as they savored every bite of their meal.

Feeling completely satiated, they enjoyed their half mile walk back to the yacht. It felt good to stretch their legs and walk a little after a large meal and being at sea all day. The cool fall air hinted of the months to come, but was not yet bone chilling. The crisp coolness felt refreshing on Billy's wind burned face; he could see his breath when he exhaled.

They walked down the ramp to the floating dock where
Destiny lay tied up. She looked at peace, elegantly
illuminated, with the soft, ice blue colored LEDs highlighting
her sleek European lines in the dark.

"Em, what time for the morning do you think?"
Marco inquired as they approached the aluminum steps that
led to the aft deck entrance.

"Let's have props turning at six thirty, Amigo."

"Okay, em, see you in the morning."

All three of them walked through the salon and down
the steps to the state rooms. Billy and Bridget bid goodnight
and retired to the VIP suite. Marco walked down the hallway
and shut the door to the port guest cabin. Each room came
equipped with satellite TV, and Billy could faintly hear CNN
emanating from Marco's room. Billy already had the TV
tuned to the Weather Channel, and he caught the local on the
eights before he set his alarm to five twenty seven a.m.

Billy was lying on his stomach when Bridget returned
from the bathroom and started rubbing his back. "Oh, that
feels unbelievable!" She worked his back for a blissful ten
minutes then instructed him to roll over. She started rubbing
his shoulders then moved down his chest and worked her way
down to his quadriceps. Using both hands she massaged up
and down his large legs and soon Billy was hard. She took
him in her mouth with long, slow deep sucking and they
began their fourth love session of the day.

CHAPTER 11   MORALS

SAN PEDRO SULA, HONDURAS.

Chavez had no illusions about the systemic corruption in Honduras. Everyone knew corruption was rampant throughout the country in every way imaginable.

A year ago, when he bought his used Jeep Cherokee, he considered going to the motor vehicle department to register it, but the thought of waiting in line for a day or two seemed ridiculous. Instead, he paid a middle man to get the Jeep registered. The middle man literally went to the back door of the registry, bribed a government worker and walked out with the new registration. Corruption had become so evident, it might as well been advertised in the newspaper. It was just an established part of daily life and had been going on for years. Having grown up with corruption all around him, Chavez had become accustomed to turning a blind eye. Actually, he wasn't really turning a blind eye; it was just the way of life in Honduras. Most of the daily corruption he experienced appeared fairly benign.

However, the recent events with his job had his full attention, and his anger had focused his mind to truly comprehend the magnitude and extent of corruption in his country. In the days following his termination from the police force, Chavez had done some private investigation of his own and discovered that the chief of police had been getting a cut from the robberies near the airport. The regularly scheduled dispatch operator had called in sick the day of the bus shooting, so a substitute dispatch operator had taken the call. Chavez should never have been sent to the high jacked bus. The plan had been for the police chief's nephew to let the police chief know the time of the robbery. The chief would then alert the dispatcher, who would delay getting officers to the scene, allowing the bandits a thirty-minute window without police. The documentation could be easily falsified later.

As it happened, the day of the bus robbery, the unexpected shootings by men disguised as police officers in San Pedro Sula required the chief's full attention, therefore he didn't know his special dispatcher had called in sick. It would have been a simple matter to call his nephew and postpone the robbery.

By performing his job above and beyond the call of duty, by risking his life and taking a bullet in the process, Chavez had lost his livelihood and made a very powerful enemy. His career was over, and he had nothing to show for it. Stripped of his benefits, with his retirement plan confiscated, he had no chance of ever working in the city he called home.

Falsifying the police report to accuse him of killing an innocent passenger was the last straw. For Chavez, the line between good and evil had vanished. The police were criminals but what could he do to fight the system? Corruption was everywhere.

CHAPTER 12   CAPE MAY TO NORFOLK

Billy awoke to his cell phone alarm and systematically switched on the TV to catch the weather on the eights. Bridget moaned and rolled over in bed. The forecast looked good, with the winds increasing in the afternoon and the possibility of thunderstorms late in the afternoon and evening. Prior to splashing water on his face for a shave, he switched on the hand held VHF radio for the marine weather forecast. As Billy expected, the winds would be on the stern, from the north for the majority of the day as they headed down the Delmarva coast. The winds would then swing around as the front moved in from the west.

He crawled back into bed and rubbed Bridget's back. "Stay in bed, babe. It will be an hour before we'll have props turning and another hour before we get out of the harbor. Come up when you hear the engines rev up to cruise."

Billy enjoyed being up before sunrise, still an hour away. He used *Destiny's* soft night lights to see his way around the galley and pour his coffee. He sat down at the main helm station to double check the route he planned out on the chart. Although he'd cruised the exact route more than twenty-five times, he still reviewed every waypoint and plot line to ensure there were no obstructions or hazards. It was always best to do this with fresh eyes, first thing in the morning.

Marco came up the stairs and greeted Billy. "Good morning. Let's drink coffee!" Marco didn't drink coffee every day, but on the deliveries, he would indulge in what he viewed as a treat. "Em, I will start the gen-or-aye-tors, now?"

"We're in good shape. Relax and have your coffee, Amigo," Billy replied.

The first light of dawn would not occur for another twenty minutes; however the ambient light had increased enough for Billy to maneuver *Destiny* away from the dock. They rounded the fleet of old steel hull fishing boats to port, which were rafted up to one another to reduce docking expenses. Rust wept down the sides of their steel hulls in a silent moan. In the distance, Billy and Marco could hear the robust call and response from a group of young cadets performing morning calisthenics as they passed the Coast Guard Station off to starboard:

> *We're always ready for the call,*
> *We place our trust in Thee.*
> *Through surf and storm and howling gale,*
> *High shall our purpose be*
>
> *From Barrow's shores to Paraguay,*
> *Great Lakes or Ocean's wave,*
> *The Coast Guard fights through storms and winds*
> *To punish or to save.*

There were very few boats out at the early hour and Billy proceeded east out of Cape May inlet and made the turn south before the sun crept over the horizon. Had the weather been uncooperative, Billy had the option of heading inland via the Chesapeake and Delaware Canal which would have brought them into Chesapeake Bay. It would have added an extra day to the trip, but in a strong east wind, the bay offered solid protection.

With the wind from the north, *Destiny* picked up almost two knots, cruising just shy of twenty two knots on a course of due south. Billy had to alter course when he crossed the entrance to the Delaware River to avoid a huge cargo container ship with "Maersk" stenciled in twenty foot tall, white letters on the side of her black hull. And if he couldn't read that, there were several hundred containers stacked on deck with "Maersk" painted on the side of each steel container. "What do you suppose the name of that shipping company is, Marco?"

"Em," Marco said with a smile. The speed of the massive cargo ship was deceiving. The 50,000 ton ship was moving through the water faster than *Destiny*, yet due to its size, it appeared to be moving slower. Billy was well aware of the speed of the ship and had already altered course to pass behind her. He looked at the radar and estimated the ship was cruising at twenty-six knots. With that type of speed, the wake generated by displacing more than 50,000 tons of water was over eight feet high. Billy throttled back and brought *Destiny* off of a plane to ride out the ship's large wake.

Bridget came up to the fly bridge clutching an insulated mug. "Now I know why you put the coffee pot in the sink! Those waves would have sent it flying!"

"Oh, sorry about that. I should have yelled down, but I thought you were still in bed. Any casualties?"

"No, when I felt you slow down, I figured it was waves and held on."

Marco took the helm and Billy and Bridget ducked down into the VIP for what Billy hoped was becoming their mid-morning routine. Bridget was thinking the same thing. They made passionate love twice, once when they first retreated to the VIP, and again after Billy awoke from a nap, which was most definitely induced by their first go round. They made a snack and ventured back up to the fly bridge to enjoy the view.

Morning softly turned to noon, which turned into a pleasant afternoon as *Destiny* made its way uneventfully down the Delmarva coast. They took turns with the binoculars combing the quiet sandy beaches, but did not spot any of the elusive wild horses.

It began to rain just as Billy altered course more to the east as they passed the Chincoteague Inlet, and he could feel the weather building. He was glad when they finally made the turn into Norfolk channel at three in the afternoon. *Destiny* smoothly glided over where the mighty Chesapeake Bay Bridge dips down into the water, and transforms into a tunnel for one mile of its twenty mile length.

The wind had begun to swing, or "clock" around, and was now on the bow, occasionally blowing sea spray up to the fly bridge.

"Looks like we timed that pretty good, amigo," Billy said. They cruised into Hampton Roads and gazed at the enormous aircraft carriers off to port. Billy finally pulled the throttles back as they approached the no wake area. The eighty ton yacht came off of a plane with exceptional grace, similar to a swan coming in for a landing on a flat pond. They pulled into the marina just as the rain tapered off.

With the largest naval base in the U.S., downtown Norfolk ran around the clock. The local establishments constantly competed for off duty navy personnel's attention, and paycheck, with drink and dinner specials. This particular Friday night, some sort of waterside festival kicked off, so Billy and Bridget relaxed on the fly bridge and enjoyed live music emanating from a tent set up next to the Marina.

Marco appeared freshly showered and shaved with a big grin and said, "Em, oh what a nice thing! We have music! All I need is a cold cerveza!"

"Make that two," Billy replied, and then being the perpetual host, quickly shot back, "Marco, we have been at sea far too long! Where are my manners? Make that tres cervezas, por favor!" Bridget giggled and politely thanked Marco as he handed her a beer.

Sitting on the fly bridge, they could clearly hear the band playing in the tent nearby and the musicians sounded fairly talented, so Bridget suggested that they head over to check out the band, and then maybe get a bite to eat off the yacht.

They switched from beer to fruity rum drinks in red plastic cups for the walk over to the band stand. When they arrived, all three of them could feel the energy in the crowd as the band began to play a Joe Cocker version of *Feelin' Alright*, complete with funky keyboard. *Ba-ba-doot-dat. Bah-ba, da-da, ba-ba, doot-dat.* Bridget knew the song and immediately started to gyrate to the infectious rhythm. While spinning Bridget around, Billy noticed Marco smiling broadly as he danced with an attractive Latin woman.

They danced for a full hour before the band took a break, and everyone decided that more drinks and food were absolutely required. The four of them walked over to a nearby restaurant where they sat down and enjoyed hot wings and pitchers of draft beer. It wasn't long before they were all back at the bandstand dancing.

They all felt good and loose when the band began the song, *Turn Your Lights down Low,* by Bob Marley. Bridget moved in close, wrapped her arms around Billy and said, "Oh, I love this song," and they started to sway as one. Billy felt the warmth of her body through her thin cotton top as he slowly rubbed his hands around the small of her back. She reached up and draped her arms around Billy's shoulders and the two gently swayed back and forth to the sensual rhythm. The drinks had their desired effects, and the sudden realization that he held a beautiful woman in his arms, combined with a healthy buzz on, made Billy feel euphoric. He could feel her ample breasts pressed against his chest and he pulled her in tight to let her know that he wanted to do more than dance. She moved her head so that his right ear was positioned against her right ear, and then she nodded her head ever so slightly to rub both ears together, locking her ear behind his. Billy felt blood flowing into an area that would very soon become quite obvious, so he pulled his head back slightly and blew gently into her ear. He felt Bridget shiver as goose bumps rose on her arms. "Oh," she muttered, "You're bad." He smiled as he pulled his head further back and pressed his lips against hers. Billy slid one hand up and held the back of her head while they kissed, his fingers interlaced with her soft hair. As the song ended, he gently pulled her head back in the palm of his hand and suggested they head back to the yacht. "One more dance!" she exclaimed as the band changed the mood and jumped into an upbeat *Late in the evening* by Paul Simon.

The whole crowd exploded in dance, complete with several primal screams. Billy and Bridget spun and grooved to the enticing rhythm. As the song neared its climactic ending, Billy grabbed her wrist and spun her away, only to reel her back in. With a huge embrace, he picked her up off of the ground, just as the song ended with *Dat-dat-dat!*

They walked hand in hand back to the yacht and laughed about how fun it was to dance to such great music. "I haven't had that much fun dancing in years!" Bridget said, as they climbed up the steps leading to the aft deck.

"Yeah, I think I've had my cardio for the week," Billy replied.

"Not yet," she said softly as she shuffled up close to Billy.

Billy and Bridget bid goodnight to Marco, walked into the VIP bedroom, and proceeded to enjoy the most pleasurable aerobics of their entire life.

Billy awoke at six a.m. He rolled over silently and gazed at Bridget sleeping peacefully, her blonde hair gently scattered about her face. Oh how he loved her. He wanted to tell her about the risk he was taking by going to Honduras, but knew that Bridget was too pure to be associated with anything like a drug deal. She would surely be against it and might leave him. Billy felt guilt rising up through his soul as he stared at her.

Not wanting to wake her, he gently slid out of bed and quietly made his way up to the galley. Billy hit the brew button on the coffee maker when he spotted Marco coming into the galley. He held up a finger to his lips and motioned to the aft deck. The men slipped outside as the coffee pot started to hiss and gurgle.

Once on the aft deck where they could speak without waking Bridget, Billy asked, "Did you have fun last night, Amigo?"

"Em, oh yes! Fun, fun night! My dancing is, em, not as 'With the Stars,' but em, oh what fun!"

They gazed about Norfolk Harbor while chatting when Billy noticed movement out of the corner of his eye; Bridget was awake in the main salon. The two men walked back inside the yacht and greeted her with smiles. "The smell of coffee woke me up," she announced as she stretched her arms out.

"Should be just about ready. Would you like some?"

"Sure, that sounds great."

The wind and rain from the small front they experienced yesterday had long gone. The morning air was cool and clear. Marco went to work removing the covers on the aft deck chairs and table, while Billy poured the coffee and fetched the half and half from the fridge. The three of them enjoyed coffee, smiled and laughed, while recounting what a great time they had the previous night.

CHAPTER 13   MOTHER CHAVEZ

SAN PEDRO SULA, HONDURAS.

Chavez confided in his mother over dinner at her house and described the events that had changed his life. He would love to have spoken to his father, but Chavez's father was long dead, killed by a stray bullet in a mid-day gunfight over drugs and money. It was one of the reasons Chavez became a police officer. His mother looked at him with wise, dark eyes surrounded by deep wrinkles that were a combination of age and worry. "Tenía miedo de este día podría venir... I was afraid this day might come my son. You're a great man, Miguel, and your father would be proud of you. I have lived a long life, not a small feat in this country as you know, and it saddens me to say that we will not see justice in our lifetime. The corruption here is like a cancer that keeps spreading. Who knows how it will end? You need to do what is necessary to survive; that is what it has become, survival. Your father's older brother has a son, your cousin Rafael, who works for the coastal police. Maybe he can help you find a job."

"Sí, mamá. Recuerdo le. Yes momma, I remember him. I haven't seen him in years, but do you think he can help?"

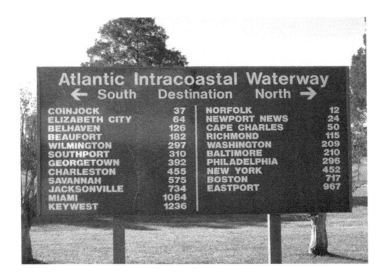

CHAPTER 14 NORFOLK TO COINJOCK

Even though they were more than three hours behind their usual departure time, it didn't really matter to Billy, because they were heading for Coinjock, North Carolina that evening, located only 60 miles south. It was one reason why Billy had decided to get off the yacht and have some fun while in Norfolk. The next southbound section of the trip was located in the Intracoastal Waterway or ICW. The ICW was renowned for being more technical than open water cruising because the captain must follow the channel markers very carefully. In many sections of the ICW water color did not change with depth. Instead, the color remained a constant turbid, dark tea color. The uniform water color could be very deceiving and provide a false sense of security because it was impossible to determine the deep-water channel simply by water color. One could be cruising along, bend down to pick up a cell phone, sway five feet out of the channel and go from a depth of eight feet to eight inches of water. Those were the worst and often the most expensive phone calls to answer.

Another substantial component of ICW navigation was bridges. There were more than 140 bridges in between mile marker 0.0 in Norfolk, Virginia and mile marker 1,085 in Miami, Florida. The bridges ranged in size and type. Some were fixed bridges; others opened and closed on a certain schedule. Depending on tide, wind, bridge height, and vessel vertical clearance requirements, the bridge might or might not have to open for a particular vessel. Part of the Captain's duties included determining if an opening was required. Billy knew from experience that the first bridge in Norfolk required an opening for *Destiny*'s vertical clearance, and the bridge had scheduled openings on the hour. He planned to catch the next opening at nine o'clock.

With Swiss watch precision, Billy maneuvered away from the dock and headed south toward the first bridge, where six boats lined up, waiting for it to open. The vertical clearance of the bridge was only ten feet, so two of the stationary boats were fairly small. He pulled the throttles back to neutral and let *Destiny* coast so as not to come too close to the waiting boats, but he never came to a complete stop and cruised easily under the bridge upon its opening. He did not try to move ahead in the line of boats, because in all the years he had traversed the ICW, he knew that trying to get to the head of the line was like rushing to a red light. The next bridge was two miles away and opened in thirty minutes, so if he kept the speed at four knots, he would get there in plenty of time. He pulled one engine into neutral and ran with only one engine in gear. Billy smiled when one of the sport fish boats sped off on a plane following right behind two smaller boats, and knew that the sport fish would be waiting at the next bridge for the scheduled opening.

The surrounding area became more industrial as they left the City of Norfolk, and continued south on the waterway. A few hundred yards off to port, a massive sand and gravel plant used several large conveyor belts to carry different sized raw stone toward loud grinding machines. A large dust plume hovered around the whole area which reminded Billy of Pigpen from the old Charlie Brown cartoon. They rounded a bend in the waterway and came upon the approach for the next bridge where, sure enough, the sport fish boat was waiting for the bridge opening, like a dog next to his bowl at feeding time.

As they continued on past the bridge, the sights and sounds became more pleasant as they emerged from the city area and moved into the more rural sections of the waterway.

The rain showers that had passed through the day before had left yet another beautiful day in their wake. The sun, beaming in all its glory, fully illuminated the infinite shades of green that burst forth; from the almost day-glow bright green saw grass on the edge of the water, to the solid, dark greens of the robust pine trees far above. Billy leaned back in his chair and thoroughly enjoyed the aroma as he took a large sip of hot coffee from his stainless steel travel mug. He had bought the mug the previous year at Coinjock Marina, their next destination. The mug had a cylindrical shaped top which flared out at the bottom, giving the mug a very low center of gravity, rendering it nearly impossible to tip over, even in the heaviest of seas. The stainless steel insulation also kept the coffee piping hot, just one of the little things that Billy enjoyed on delivery trips. A quick look at the navigation system and Billy knew they had another hour of travel before the next bridge. He asked Marco to take the helm for a second and ran down to use the head. On the way up, he plugged his iPod into the yacht's sound system and turned on the fly bridge speakers.

Billy thanked Marco and resumed control of the helm. He sat down and soaked up the sensation of being on the yacht on a nice, easy and peaceful day, cruising down the Intracoastal Waterway and getting paid handsomely for it. Maneuvering the large yacht had become second nature to him, and at low speed, he let his mind drift off to last night with Bridget. One level of his mind always remained aware of his surroundings, yet on another level, he thought about how good it felt to hold someone in his arms and drift off to sleep last night. She had fallen asleep before he did and the feeling of human touch was so appealing that he just lay there, running his fingers through her soft hair and rubbing the smooth skin of her back. *I hope she enjoys this lifestyle as much as I do,* he thought.

Several hours, and five bridges later, *Destiny* approached the Great Bridge Lock, which connected Albemarle Sound to the Chesapeake Canal via the North Landing River and the Elizabeth River. Great Bridge Lock allowed two water bodies at different elevations to be connected, and it was unique because it handled tidally influenced water from the Elizabeth River and fresh water from the North Landing River. The lock was shaped like a huge swimming pool with water tight doors on both ends. One end opened up, boats entered, and the doors shut behind them. Once the doors were secured, water was pumped in or out of the lock to equalize the water elevation, then the opposite doors were opened and vessels continued on.

Hundreds of vessels made the seasonal pilgrimage north and south in the spring and fall. Commercial vessel traffic, seasonal travelers, and local vessels on a beautiful long weekend usually added up to a long waiting line. But on this beautiful fall Saturday, there were only a few boats waiting for the next lock opening.

Once they were tied up securely, they had a fifteen minute wait for the water height in the lock to equalize. Billy and Marco took the opportunity to use the head and quench their thirst with cold, bottled water.

"Should I make up some sandwiches?" Bridget asked.

"That sounds great, but we're headed for yet another great restaurant tonight, so how about something light?" She prepared some veggie roll-ups with balsamic dressing, which Billy thought were delicious. When he finished, he looked down at his chest, ecstatic that he was able to keep balsamic vinegar off of his white shirt and khaki shorts. Bridget noticed him doing wardrobe inventory and laughed. He smiled and said in a throaty pirate voice, "Aye, lost many a good shurt dat whey."

The ICW ran back and forth in serpentine fashion for the next ten miles, which created an abundance of natural beauty. Billy felt like a master of his domain rounding the bends in the waterway cruising along at twenty knots on a seven and a half million dollar yacht. In most places, the waterway was an actual river or naturally occurring water body like a sound or bay. In other spots, it had been man-made by dredging to connect different water bodies, thereby creating a continuous water highway from New Jersey all the way to Key West, Florida.

Exactly thirty miles south of Norfolk, the confines of the river banks gradually widened as the North Landing River met Currituck Sound. Ten miles later, the waterway magically opened up to a vast, lake-like area. The water color in the sound resembled strong tea, with virtually no underwater visibility. The depth of the waterway was maintained by the Coast Guard, but like any government operation, it was far from perfect, and the waterway could have shoaling areas, particularly where a tributary river flowed into it. Just like construction on the highway, dredging and repair operations constantly occurred on some section of the Intracoastal Waterway.

The sleepy expanse of Currituck Sound contrasted radically from the hustle and bustle of New York City. Over the years of cruising thousands of miles up and down the east coast, Billy had developed a deep appreciation of how the aesthetics of the waterway changed from state to state. The surroundings also influenced his emotional being. It was difficult to be completely relaxed in the craziness of New York Harbor; however like a vacation in the mountains, he soaked up the still beauty around him as they cruised along the flat, brown water with only the sound of the wake audible. With the exception of slowing down to meet an oncoming tug and barge, they were able to cruise at twenty knots.

After they made their way past Bell Island into Coinjock Bay, he brought the yacht down off a plane as they approached Long Point. It wasn't a no wake zone per se, but Billy remembered a tricky shoal off Long Point. He watched the depth gauge as they slowly passed over the shallow spot with a mere four inches to spare. With a mock Bahamian accent, Billy turned to Marco and said, "Skinny watah-mon." Marco smiled and started down from the fly bridge to get the lines and fenders ready.

About a half a mile from their destination, Billy grabbed the VHF radio and hailed, "Coinjock Marina, Coinjock Marina, this is motor vessel *Destiny* on channel one-six, over."

"This is Coinjock Marina to motor vessel *Destiny*. Switch to channel six-eight please." Billy acknowledged and switched the VHF radio up to working channel sixty eight and listened.

"How ya doing there, Billy?"

"Doing great, Louis, how about you?"

"Just fine, just fine. We've got you right outside the restaurant stern to stern with a hundred footer who's gonna be here a while. So you'll want to spin her around and rig for starboard side."

"Roger that. We'll see you shortly."

Billy spun the yacht 180 degrees and slid into the dock space with ease. The experienced dock hands at the marina were polite and calm and the whole docking procedure went smoothly. Billy leaned over and looked down from the fly bridge to ensure the lines were secure before shutting the engines off for the day. As the engines wound down and ceased, the yacht seemed to exhale an, "Ah" as if it were human. Billy covered up the instrument panel and headed down to the main deck. "Marco, it was flat calm all day, and we didn't take one wave topside, so there's no need for a wash down. Let's refuel now so I have time to get a workout in."

Billy found Bridget lying on a towel on the fly bridge sun pad and asked, "Want to get a workout in before dinner?"

She turned her head sideways, lifted her sunglasses, and squinted as she grinned up at him. "What did you have in mind?"

"I was thinking about a roller blade, but you can run if you want."

She sat up. "Yes! That's exactly what I need."

They stretched out on the aft deck for a full ten minutes before they disembarked. Billy sauntered over to a nearby picnic table where he put on roller blades.

"Your pace is faster than mine, so go on ahead and we'll catch up back here," Bridget said.

"Sounds good." Billy started to walk toward the road, paused and said with a deadpan expression, "Oh yeah, watch out for snakes, particularly water moccasins."

Bridget's eyes popped wide open. "WHAT?"

Slipping his earphones into his ears, he hit play, and began his forty-five minute roller blade on Waterlily Road, the back country road toward Piney Island.

Skating along the beautiful low country of North Carolina was therapeutic. The road was basically flat and Billy could see for miles in both directions

Billy kept the music volume loud enough to mask his heavy breathing, but was well aware that he was getting a good workout.

On the way back he was hoping to catch up with Bridget, but she was nowhere in sight. *Hmm,* he thought with a sly grin, *maybe I shouldn't have mentioned the water moccasins...*

Back at the marina, Billy untied his roller blades, took off his socks and walked barefoot down the pier to the yacht. Although he was hot and sweaty, the post exercise endorphins gave him some additional energy, so he climbed down into the engine room to check all the fluid levels. With such a short, easy day, he knew he wouldn't have to add any oil unless something was way out of whack.

He finished the engine room check, and headed for the shower. Billy opened the door to the VIP room and saw Bridget lying on the bed. She looked up at him with her trademark grin. She was wearing a matching set of light blue silk lace bra and panties that must have been from Victoria's Secret because it was over the top sexy and Billy was instantly excited. "Stay right there. Don't move an inch. I'm going to take the quickest shower of my life!"

She stood up and strutted like a runway model over to him. Pulling his body close to her, she whispered, "Don't bother. You're just going to get sweaty again anyway." She pushed his chest causing him to fall back onto the bed. Ripping off his shorts, she jumped on top of him.

The VIP shower was a little cramped, but they enjoyed washing and massaging each other. On her knees, Bridget used the removable shower head to treat Billy to the most pleasurable hygiene of his life.

They emerged from their room feeling rapturous. They walked upstairs and met Marco on the aft deck, where everyone enjoyed a cold, light beer while chatting with other boaters who happened by. "Okay Amigo, it's 6:30. Let's head over to the dock house and say hi to Louis. Then, we'll grab a bite."

"Em, maybe one cerveza for the walk." Billy smiled as Marco handed him and Bridget another beer.

Both Billy and Marco had purposely not eaten all day in anticipation of the meal they would have at the marina restaurant. Renowned for its prime rib, the Coinjock Restaurant offered a thirty-two ounce cut of beef, measuring over two inches thick. Louis would often go through 500 pounds of beef in a week. The local meat distributor loved him! So did the residents of the adjacent towns. A busy weekend often resulted in a substantial wait for a table.

Louis, the owner of the marina, had two dogs: *Riva*, a beautiful black lab with uncanny water skills, and *Rudder*, a friendly dachshund. As the crew of *Destiny* walked down the pier and approached the dock house, Billy noticed motion inside the ship's store at the bottom of the full length glass window in front of them. Rudder was looking out the window, his tail wagging faster than a humming bird's wings. Rudder was fully extended on his hind legs and couldn't get any higher vertically. His nose print smudge line was perfectly horizontal across the entire bottom of the window. Billy and Bridget smiled at the dog, which quickly dropped down on all fours and waddled over to greet them at the door.

Greeting each other with big smiles, Billy and Louis shook hands. Billy introduced Bridget, and no introduction was needed for Marco, as the men had met many times before. They sat down at stools near the main counter of the ship's store and chatted about the events of the last six months since they had seen each other. Billy learned that Louis' wife was pregnant with their second child.

"That's great, Louis. Congratulations!"

Louis leaned down and reached into a rectangular cooler. "Thank you. I believe it's cause for celebration." He handed each of them a cold beer. Rudder sensed the camaraderie between Billy and Louis and waddled over for a pat from whoever would oblige. Billy leaned down and scratched Rudder under the collar which sent his tail wagging into overdrive. "Anybody catching any fish?" Billy asked. Louis had some good friends who were serious commercial fishermen.

"A friend of mine just came in two hours ago with some fresh Wahoo." Rudder's tail was beating rapidly against the side counter creating a drum roll beat, and Louis grinned and said, "The Wahoo's so fresh, the fish is still flappin'!" All four of them laughed and continued talking and nursing their beers until the VHF radio crackled to life with a call from another approaching vessel. "I'll see y'all over at the restaurant," Louis said as he headed out to direct the next tie up.

Both Billy and Bridget ordered the Wahoo fish for dinner. Marco decided to see if he could conquer the thirty-two ounce prime rib special.

After they finished their salads, the main course was served. The Wahoo was cooked to perfection, surrounded by rice pilaf and steamed broccoli. Billy imagined the size of the fish based on the cut in front of him. Instead of the typical fillet cut, the Wahoo had been cut into steaks, with the vertebrae still in place. The steak, a perfect oval shaped cross section of the fish, measured a full eight inches across the longest side.

"That must have been a hell of a fish," Billy said.

Bridget smiled, obviously enjoying the moment and said, "Do you guys know how lucky you are?"

"Yeah, right," Billy replied. "Wahoo this time of year?"

Bridget shook her head, "No, no. Not the fish! I mean the life you have? You get to be outside in the fresh air all day; experience cool aquatic creatures; no commuting traffic, and yeah, you *do* eat pretty well!"

They all smiled and raised their glasses in a toast, then continued finishing up their meals.

Later that night, Billy tossed and turned in bed while Bridget slept peacefully by his side. The trip to Honduras was haunting him. He wanted to tell Bridget, but deep down he knew that she would not approve. It was tearing him apart; finally, he had found someone very special that he wanted to be with forever, but if he told her his plans, he might lose her. What was more important? Although he hadn't broken the law *yet*, guilt eerily crept through his soul, and he could feel it affecting him.

CHAPTER 15   COUSINS

On the drive from San Pedro Sula to Puerto Lempira, Miguel Chavez had much time to think. He knew he could not single handedly change the ways of Honduras. Those with money and power had firmly set their teeth into virtually all of the income streams in the country. If he tried to fight those with power, he would certainly wind up dead. *Christ, I was almost killed by the police chief's nephew! Maybe the coastal police will be different.* Chavez sighed to himself doubtfully.

    Thoroughly depressed, he drove mindlessly through the city of San Pedro Sula. The dirty, loud and overpopulated city did little to enhance his mood. Nor did the stop and go traffic. The rain drizzled down upon his windshield, and his movement in the Jeep mimicked that of the intermittent wiper. Rain accumulated, and the wiper passed. Traffic cleared, and he pulled his foot off the brake. Two hours later, he passed the smaller city of Choloma where the surroundings were more rural and pleasant. The rain eased, as did the traffic, and lush green forest extended on both sides of the road.

    The natural beauty of his surroundings began to lift his spirits. He always enjoyed the tranquility of the more rural parts of the country. As he gazed off into the mountains, he thought, *Honduras has so much potential. There are so many beautiful places. Why is it such a mess?*

Miguel arrived at the small coastal town of Puerto Lempira in the early afternoon. He drove slowly along the dirt roads making his way through the sleepy town toward the harbor. He had not seen his cousin, Rafael Chavez, in a very long time. As he stopped the Jeep to let several goats cross in front of him, he tried to recall exactly how long it had been since they had drank too much cheap beer and chased women in the city when they were younger. Miguel had lost touch with his cousin after Rafael had moved to the coast more than ten years ago.

Miguel pulled up to a small lean-to tortilla shack, where Rafael suggested they meet, and parked. Miguel got out and looked around. He did not recognize his cousin until Rafael yelled out, "Miguel! ¿Cómo estás? Exactamente el mismo aspecto! You look exactly the same!"

"Hey Rafael, it's been a long, long time. You look well." In fact, Rafael did not look so well. The years had not been kind to him. His belly was hanging over his pants, obscuring his belt buckle, and his face resembled rawhide, seasoned by too much whiskey and cigarettes.

Rafael gave a half smile and said, "Bueno, veo que su mentira no ha mejorado, pero muchas gracias de todos modos. I see your lying has not improved, but thank you anyway."

The two men embraced, slapping each other on the back, smiling, and then made their way over to the food shack to order lunch. The "restaurant" consisted of little more than a corrugated aluminum roof barely propped up over a make shift coal stove, with a few battered chairs pulled up to the service counter. "No juzgar un libro por su portada, amigo. Don't judge a book by its cover, my friend," his cousin mused.

They walked over to a small table made from milk crates and plywood and sat under the shade of a palm tree. The fish pastelitos were surprisingly good, and the beer was ice cold. Rafael smiled in between bites and said, "Creo que puede... I think I may have a job for you."

"Really? Doing what?"

"Well, one of the guys that works with me on the police boat got bent scuba diving for lobsters last weekend and is in bad shape. Good for you, bad for him. You ever see that, the bends? What a painful, nasty thing. Anyway, this just happened, so my boss is waiting for the Doctor's diagnosis before putting out an official notice for the job. I stopped in to see him at the hospital, and it doesn't look good. If he lives, he won't be able to work."

All of the government jobs in Honduras were bought and sold. Hard work and honesty meant nothing. In fact, as Miguel had just learned, they could get you killed. "How much will it cost me?" Chavez asked.

His cousin leaned back in his chair, adjusted his belt about his large stomach and wiped his mouth with the back of his shirt sleeve. "One month salary, but you can pay it over the first six months. You must understand; the money is not for me. It goes straight to my boss, Juan Rodriguez. If I didn't know you, the price would be two month's salary, but you are blood, so I take no money."

Rafael explained that Chavez would be spending half his time in the office and half on the water doing patrols. "Hay unas cuantas cosas de procedimientos. There are a few procedural things," Rafael said, then paused to wash the last of his pastelito down with beer. "You must pass a drug test, but this is no big deal. I know the manager at the testing lab. It costs $200."

Miguel noticed the ease at which his cousin spoke of obtaining falsified drug test results and wondered how many times Rafael had bribed the lab manager for his own clean test results.

Before he left San Pedro Sula, Miguel had become so infuriated with the blatant corruption in the police force that he considered going out in a blaze of glory by telling his story to the largest newspaper in the city. He contacted a lawyer who had known Miguel's father when he was alive. The lawyer listened very carefully to his story and told him in no uncertain terms that he should not publish the story if he wanted to live. The police chief had the newspaper editor on the payroll. Not only would the story never be published, but Chavez would be killed or worse. He would just disappear or be framed and go to prison where they could kill him slowly.

After everything he had just been through and with rampant corruption everywhere, Miguel Chavez saw no way out but to join his bandit cousin with a badge.

CHAPTER 16   COINJOCK TO BEAUFORT

The morning after their dinner at Coinjock's, Billy and Marco were ready to depart the dock at six a.m., two hours before the marina officially opened. The dock master, Louis, prided himself on using every linear foot of dock space, and the previous night was no exception.

The bow of the yacht behind Billy was hanging over the stern of *Destiny.* He could reach up and touch the anchor of the neighboring yacht while standing on *Destiny's* swim platform. Likewise, the bow of *Destiny* was hanging over the stern of the yacht in front of them.

Marco was looking at the tight squeeze when he turned to Billy and said, "Em, as sardines!"

Billy smiled and said, "Yeah, Louis is the only guy I know who can squeeze an eighty-five foot yacht into eighty feet of dock space!"

"Bridget, you grab the lines from Marco when he unties them from the dock."

The two other yacht owners watched in earnest as Billy fired up the engines from the fly bridge. Billy leaned over and called down to Marco, "Aft spring, bow, and then stern. Get the forward spring line last, from onboard."

"Okay, Amigo."

Billy spun the wheel so that the tidal current passing over the rudders would ease the yacht away from the dock, while the forward spring line kept the yacht from moving with the current and hitting the yacht behind them. The other captains watched intently as Billy crab-walked the eighty-five foot yacht out of the sardine can without even using the bow thruster. "Okay Marco, remove the forward spring." Marco whipped the line off the dock cleat from onboard and yelled, "All clear."

The early morning air felt heavy with the scent of low country. Billy interspersed his sips of coffee with gentle dog leg turns as they cruised along at twenty knots. For fifteen miles they sped along enjoying the solitude as the North River gradually expanded to meet Albemarle Sound, where the official Intracoastal Waterway veered off toward the west and connected with the Alligator River. That route turned into a twenty-two mile man made cut called the Alligator River-Pungo River Canal. The other more easterly route included cruising through the Albemarle, Croatan, and Pamlico Sounds, located just inside Carolina's legendary Outer Banks. The Alligator River route was more protected in foul weather, but the long, manmade cut could be slow going with a lot of vessel traffic, particularly sail boats. If the weather was cooperative, Billy liked running inside the Outer Banks through more open water.

Billy and Bridget sat on the fly bridge enjoying the scenery as they cruised across the open water of Albemarle Sound. He felt on top of the world with Bridget by his side. Could he tell her about the plan to go to Honduras? Billy imagined her response. "*So, you're angry that you lost a bunch of money to white collar thieves. Now you're going to break the law and risk everything, risk us, to try and make that money back?*" Bridget would be seriously concerned, her beautiful face frowning. "*You've just joined the morals of the CEOs you're upset with! Can't you see that?*"

"What's on your mind, babe?" Bridget said, snapping Billy from his thoughtful gaze.

"I'm just really enjoying having you here by my side."

Later that afternoon, they arrived at the Beaufort Docks at three thirty in the afternoon and took on fuel. Looking out across the river from the marina they watched the majestic wild horses grazing on Carrot Island.

CHAPTER 17   PUERTO LEMPIRA

HONDURAS.

The morning after their lunch meeting, Miguel Chavez met Rafael Chavez at the coastal police headquarters in Puerto Lempira. The small, intimate seaside village that made up the surrounding area strongly appealed to Miguel. It brought him back to his childhood where he grew up near the ocean in Puerto Cortes.

The men shook hands and walked up the lopsided steps into the main office. The building was in desperate need of painting. The combination of lack of maintenance and salty air had wreaked havoc on the badly peeling exterior. Miguel took a seat in the waiting area and looked around, taking in the surroundings of his new potential workplace. He noticed a woman behind a tall counter, and he smiled at her when their eyes met. She looked back at him with no expression. Miguel wasn't sure if she thought he might be a criminal or a new recruit. There was little difference.

Rafael disappeared and returned twenty minutes later with a man slightly taller than him who revealed a gold front tooth as he smiled. He shook Miguel's hand and said, "¿Por lo tanto, ustedes son el primo, eh? So, you are the cousin, eh?"

"Sí."

The men continued speaking in Spanish. "My name is Juan Rodriguez, I'm the chief of the coastal police. Chavez, I mean, *Rafael,* here has told me a little about you, but first things first. Why don't you come back to my office and we can talk further?" Miguel saw Rafael give him a wink and slight nod.

Miguel followed Rodriguez down a hallway that led to a corner office with a view of the dock and surrounding harbor. He looked around Rodriguez's office with interest and noticed several fishing pictures. Once the door was shut the two men could speak in private. Rodriguez sat down, looked across his desk and said, "So you want to be a coastal policeman?"

"Yes, I do. I worked on the police force in San Pedro Sula for eight years."

Rodriguez surveyed Miguel up and down and asked, "Can you drive a boat, and do you get sea sick?"

"I grew up on the water, in Puerto Cortes, so I have experience driving boats and I've never been sea sick. In fact, I worked on the fishing boats for weeks at a time when I was a young boy."

Rodriguez nodded with approval, revealed the gold tooth again, and said, "Excellent!"

Chavez wanted to warm up the conversation and pointed to a wall photo, "That is a huge Goliath Grouper!"

"Ah, yes. Nine hundred fifty pounds that one." Rodriguez said with smug satisfaction. "It was like reeling in the bottom! It took over four hours."

The two men volleyed back and forth in a pleasant discussion about fishing and growing up in Honduras until Rodriguez steered the conversation back by looking into Chavez's eyes, "So, what else did your cousin mention about this job?"

Chavez had never had to buy a job in his life, and was not used to negotiating criminal activity with another police officer, so he mustered his best poker face and replied sternly, "He said that it would cost one month's salary."

"He did, did he? Well, as you know times are tough and there are many men who would like this job. In order to put your name on top of the list it will cost two months' salary, but you can pay it over eight months. Not bad, really. You work for four weeks and get paid for three for the first eight months." Rodriquez leaned back in his chair and folded his hands behind his head. He exposed his gold tooth yet again with another smile and said, "But if you work hard and keep your mouth shut, you can make that plus much more in no time."

CHAPTER 18 BEAUFORT, NC TO CHARLESTON, SC

Billy reviewed the weather and decided to run outside the Intracoastal Waterway and make the long, 220 nautical mile cruise from Beaufort, North Carolina to Charleston, South Carolina on the Atlantic Ocean. It would be a long day at sea, far from the sight of land, but the marine forecast called for one to two foot seas and variable winds. *Better take it while we can*, he thought.

Bridget slept quietly in bed when Marco yelled, "All clear," and *Destiny* departed Beaufort docks. The first light of dawn would not occur for another hour as they rounded Radio Island off to starboard. Billy had to maneuver around a shallow spot on the south side of the island where the river flowed into the main channel, but other than that, the channel provided a straight shot out to the Atlantic. He set the autopilot for a waypoint off Frying Pan Shoals 100 miles away. Marco came up to the fly bridge and Billy asked if he'd mind taking the helm for an hour or so.

Billy quietly crept back into bed and found Bridget lying on her side fast asleep. He curled up next to her and she made a little grunt like sound as he wrapped his arm around her waist and pulled her close. He could feel her chest expand with each slow breath while he gently kissed the back of her shoulder. He had never cruised the east coast with someone he cared about so much, and he loved every minute shared with her. Whenever she smiled at him, he would grin from ear to ear. "What?" She would ask.

"Nothing, just smiling. You make me smile." Billy closed his eyes and blissfully fell back asleep.

The flat calm sea, combined with being so comfortably wrapped up in Bridget, enabled Billy to sleep for over an hour. He woke to see Bridget standing at the foot of the bed freshly showered and wrapped in a towel. She smiled at him as she let the towel fall to the floor, revealing the wondrous curves of her ample breasts and slender waist and said, "So, you're up?"

Billy gave her a wide eyed smile. "Oh, I'm up. I'm *definitely* up."

Four hours later, Billy threaded the needle of deep water that cut through Frying Pan Shoal. He set a course for the entrance channel to Charleston located 110 miles away. The ocean had remained flat calm all morning. They had spotted a pod of dolphin surfing the wake of the yacht and a giant manta ray lazing on the surface.

"I can see why you like this," Bridget said. "Most people live an entire lifetime and never see the beauty that we've experienced in just the past few days."

"Yeah, you're right," Billy said and changed the subject. "So will you have time to stay with me in Fort Lauderdale for a day or two, or do you have to get back?"

"Well, I have to take my finals in two weeks, and I took a lot of time off work, so I should get back." Bridget was getting a master's degree in nutrition and fitness while working at the gym.

"Well, how about this: you fly back up to New York, I think we have to do a trip to the Bahamas anyway, but after your exams, come back down and we can enjoy some warm weather."

She smiled and looked deep into his eyes. "I'd love that."

Billy and Bridget managed to fit in two more love sessions between shifts running the yacht and engine room checks. They pulled into Charleston a little after five in the afternoon. All three of them were a little salty from eleven hours at cruise and it felt great to shut the engines down.

Charleston, South Carolina is a wonderful city populated with some of the friendliest people in the world. Billy wished they could stay a week as they walked downtown through Marion Square. After a short walk through downtown, they ended up at a sushi restaurant, where they shared several different sushi rolls over a bottle of pear infused sake. After a seventeen hour day, eleven of which were at cruise, all three of them were in a state of tired euphoria. Feeling elegantly satisfied, but not overly full, they walked outside and caught the shuttle back to the marina, where they all headed straight for bed.

Billy lay in bed exhausted, but once again, thinking about the trip to Honduras kept him awake. He gazed at Bridget fast asleep and ran his fingers through her soft hair. Did he really need to go? He thought, *What if I get caught?* He remembered the Turkish prison scene from the movie *Midnight Express,* and shuddered at the thought of a Honduran prison. He rolled over and pulled Bridget in close to him.

Billy had props turning at six a.m. sharp the next morning. He wanted to arrive at Jekyll Island, Georgia, with time to show Bridget around. It was one of his favorite places on the entire east coast, and he hoped that she would feel the same way.

CHAPTER 19   HONDURAS COSTA POLICÍA

Miguel answered the cell phone call from his cousin, "Hola Rafael, ¿cómo estás?"

"Enhorabuena, amigo tenes el trabajo! Congratulations, amigo you got the job!"

"Oh, good, when do I start?"

"You start tomorrow morning. Meet me at the office at eight."

"Okay, gracias Rafael. Hasta manana."

Excited to have a job again, he quickly walked downstairs from the second floor hotel room and found a dilapidated bar nearby. He ordered a cerveza and asked the bartender if she knew of any apartments for rent or even a room to share in a house. She got the wrong idea and thought he was trying to pick her up, so she brushed him off. He finished his beer and went to another bar down the street. After visiting a few bars he obtained several names and found that dropping his cousin's name helped. He had half a dozen leads when he returned to his hotel room later that night.

When he arrived at the police headquarters the following morning, Chavez was fitted for a uniform. Well, not really *fitted*, he just happened to *fit* into the former officer's clothes. The name tag was sewn into his shirt, so he'd have to be *Goito Martenz* until his new name tags arrived. "Parezca un Goiter. You look like a Goito," his cousin teased. They finished up the required paperwork and jumped onboard the coastal police boat tied to the dock adjacent to headquarters.

After the cousins returned from their patrol, Rodriguez called the men into his office for a briefing. Miguel and Rafael walked in and sat down next to another officer named Filipe Valdez.

Rodriguez stood behind his desk looking down at the men and began his brief. "Hay un cargamento de cocaína salgan de puerto... There is a shipment of cocaine leaving port tonight, and we are going to intercept. We got a tip that the exchange will be between two small boats about twenty miles offshore. We need to make sure we obtain the coca and the money. They will have guns, so be sharp. No more drinking for the rest of the day."

CHAPTER 20 CHARLESTON TO JEKYLL ISLAND

Destiny departed the Charleston docks before first light. Billy wanted to be tied up in Georgia at his favorite stop, Jekyll Island, with plenty of daylight. They pulled into the sleepy island marina eight hours later. Billy took on fuel while Marco began washing down, and they finished their work by three in the afternoon.

Billy settled the bill at the marina office and was ecstatic when the dock master told him that the marina had just bought new courtesy bikes for its guests. Billy inspected the bikes on his way back to the yacht. They were beach bicycles, the kind with only one speed and wide tires.

Back onboard, Billy found Bridget in the galley munching on vegetables and proposed a ride around the island. It just so happened to be low tide, which meant they could ride on the beach at the water's edge. They grabbed some bottled water and walked up the pier to pick out two bikes.

They pedaled south on a side road for a little over two miles passing tall marshland filled with willowy reeds soaring over eight feet high. Billy took an off road path that brought them to the south end of the island where they hopped off their bikes. They walked their bikes over a large sand dune and down toward the water, past the soft sand to the low tide area where the sand was hard packed like a clay tennis court. Billy and Bridget soaked in the panoramic view of the ocean with Saint Andrew's Sound to the south and the mighty Atlantic to the northeast.

The hard packed sand made it feel as if they were riding on asphalt, so they pedaled with ease as they began their eight mile ride to the north. The beach was deserted, so Billy and Bridget had the magnificent view to themselves. Riding along the secluded beach created a feeling of tranquility. There were no loud motorcycles, car horns or sirens, just the soft crushing sound of sand beneath the tires, combined with the subtle splash of the waves upon the beach. Soon, they came across an enormous flock of small birds that ran toward the ocean as the waves receded, plucking up minute specks of food, only to scurry away from an incoming wave as if it were a ball of fire. Bridget smiled at the retreating birds. "I think those are sanderlings."

With their workday complete, Billy and Bridget were in no particular hurry, and took their time riding along the beach. A half hour later they came upon a soft sand area and disembarked from their bicycles. "Let's take a break up by the willows." They left their bikes down by the water and walked up toward the sand dune, where the beach met the saw grass. The 180-degree panoramic view of the Atlantic Ocean was nothing short of astonishing.

They sat on the soft sand and silently soaked in the abundance of natural beauty all around them. The ocean gently bounced light off small waves on the outgoing tide, and Billy noticed a shrimp boat far off in the distance. Bridget took a long sip from her water bottle and turned her head scanning the area from left to right and said, "Look, there's not a soul on the beach! We have it all to ourselves." They lay back in the sand and listened to the gentle sound of the ocean washing ashore. It felt magical.

"This just feels *sooo* good," Billy said. He was just about to kiss her, when she leaned over and kissed him. She climbed on top of him, and they held each other in a passionate kiss. Billy rubbed his hands up and down her back as their tongues danced erotically in each other's mouths. Bridget began to grind her hips into Billy, and he instantly became rock hard. In an explosion of clothes and sand, they were naked. Bridget remained on top, and Billy caressed her breasts as her hips moved in slow, deep circles on top of him. He closed his eyes and became overwhelmed with sensation: the sound of the ocean on the beach, the feeling of being deep inside her, and the soft, warm sand on his back and body.

He opened his eyes and the image of her perfectly curved, ample breasts and sensual lips pushed his pleasure to the limit. He lifted her off the sand by raising his hips and tightening his butt. Bridget's full lips gently parted as she moaned with pleasure, and Billy lost all control. She fell flush on top of him and he wrapped his arms tightly around her. Billy gave way to the surge of endorphins that coursed through his body, and they both erupted in an avalanche of bliss.

She stayed on top of him for two full minutes before rolling off, and they both lay on their backs, hearts beating fast, and breathing heavily. "Wow," she gasped, "That was amazing!"

"I'll never forget that for the rest of my life. I love you, Bridget."

"I love you, too, Billy."

Together, they walked down the beach naked and jumped in the warm water to wash off the sand before dressing and climbing back on their bikes.

Billy and Bridget shared everything now and knew what made each other tick. She was pure; her morality beyond reproach and Billy loved that about her. Over the last few months he had tried to show her how painful the economic crash had been to all but the super rich. They had even watched the documentary movie, *Inside Job* together, which clearly illustrated how the greed of a handful of men had brought the world to its knees. She agreed with him at the unfairness of the whole market crash, but it did not affect and consume her the way it did Billy. As the trip to Honduras edged into his mind, guilt rose up through Billy's soul. No matter how he tried to rationalize it, by not telling Bridget about Honduras, he was not being honest with her.

A few miles later they came upon an area of driftwood jetting up from the sand. Entire trees lay partially buried. The dead, gray twisted tree branches stood in stark contrast to the lively tan colored sand. It felt as if the trees were reaching toward the heavens in one last attempt at survival. For a distance of more than 100 yards the graveyard of driftwood created an oddly compelling Ansel Adams-like art display. Both of them had been taking in the scene for several minutes when Bridget broke the silence. "I've never seen anything like this. There is a divine beauty here, yet at the same time it's chilling."

"Yeah, I know what you mean. There is a palatable feeling here, like a haunting sensation. The first time I came across this I was by myself, and I found it very difficult to describe the feeling it evokes. You really have to see it. I was told that a hurricane blew down all these trees up river, and they were washed down by the excess runoff from the flash flood. They would have been washed out to sea, but the wind and tide blew them back up on the beach and then covered them with sand."

They continued riding up the beach toward the tip of the island just as the sun was beginning to set. The sandy beach morphed into a state park at the very northern tip of the island, where Billy located the asphalt bike path that lead back to the marina. They meandered along the serpentine bike path as it wove in and out of massive oak trees. "These trees are well over 100 years old," he said.

"How can you tell?"

"I remember weird formulas and stuff like that. For oak trees, a good estimate of their age is their circumference in inches, measured about five feet off the ground." Billy quickly rattled off the math behind a three foot diameter tree. Most of the trees were much larger and Billy continued to calculate the ages of the trees as they rode by. "Wow! Look at that one! It must be six feet wide!" Billy quickly deduced that the tree was well over 200 years old. Bridget smiled. She liked a man with a brain.

The mighty oak tree branches filled with hanging moss hung silently in the twilight and created a sense of mystical timelessness and soft grace. The fading light reflected off the Jekyll Island Club's massive façade, highlighting its historic architecture, and emitting an air of nobility. Billy explained how the elite families of the last century–the Rockefellers, Vanderbilts, and Goodyears–had visited the island and been members of the Club in its heyday.

After a shower, Bridget joined Billy for a glass of wine on the aft deck as the final glimpse of light faded into darkness. Marco had decided to eat his dinner onboard *Destiny* that evening, so the two of them walked back up past the dock house and straddled their bikes, thankful for the large, comfortable seats, and rode back through the mighty oaks to the restaurant two miles away. They walked their bikes down the long pier that led to the waterside restaurant and left them unlocked–just one of the many things that Billy loved about the island.

The restaurant had recently been redecorated, yet it held onto island history through the use of exposed mahogany beams and dark wood trim. The walls contained old black and white photos of families enjoying island activities over the past hundred years. Bridget pointed out a photo from the early 1920's of an antique car driving along the same beach where they had just ridden. The driver was smiling happily and dressed in classic early century attire, complete with leather goggles. The hostess seated them next to a floor to ceiling window with a magnificent view of the waterfront. Their waitress personified a true Georgia peach, a gracious blonde with a joyful attitude. Recalling the shrimp boat he had seen earlier, Billy inquired about the local catch. As it so happened, the special of the evening included fresh caught local shrimp. Both Billy and Bridget feasted upon large, succulent shrimp, sautéed in an olive oil and garlic sauce over whole grain pasta tossed with mixed vegetables. Bridget read that some of the white wines on the menu were from locally grown grapes, so they tried a bottle from a nearby Georgia vineyard. The crisp wine complemented the shrimp perfectly, without being overly sweet.

Billy looked across the table at Bridget and watched as she casually brushed the hair back from her face and curled it around her ear. She was looking down at her meal and didn't notice him staring. Was there such a thing as perfection? He savored the vision of her far more than the meal before him.

She picked up her wine glass and motioned for a toast, "To yet another spectacular day with a spectacular guy."

Billy kinked his glass, smiled and took a sip while he gazed at her. He let the wine linger in his mouth as her words lingered in his mind, and he fell in love yet again.

Wonderfully satiated, they climbed aboard their bicycles and rode back toward the yacht along the path winding through the massive oaks. Volumes of hanging moss draped silently from oak branches like a minister's robe. The soft light of the moon illuminating the moss was beautifully haunting. To their complete surprise, they rounded a corner and beheld a vision that was most remarkable. Before them, in a massive thicket of tall grass, light from several thousand fireflies flickered on and off. The low watt illumination of each firefly randomly pulsed here and there throughout the thicket like an enormous Christmas tree. Bridget looked astonished and said, "I understand why this is your favorite stop on the trip."

"Babe, in all the times we've stopped here over the years, I've never seen anything like this. One or two fireflies, maybe, but this is truly amazing."

They watched in awe as Mother Nature displayed a magnificent light show on a stage of vegetation, using one of the lowliest creatures as the star performer.

It seemed as if something was trying to show Billy that even the simplest things in life could be extremely beautiful, and should never be taken for granted.

The next morning, they asked Marco if he had ever seen anything like the firefly exhibition growing up in Honduras. He replied he had never seen what they described *anywhere*.

CHAPTER 21 TAXES

PUERTO LEMPIRA, HONDURAS.

Juan Rodriguez walked into the office of Francisco Lopez, the most powerful man he knew in Honduras. The lavish office was quite large, with an oriental rug running across the entire floor. The walls consisted of dark mahogany, trimmed with teak, and elegantly accented by solid brass light fixtures imported from Europe. Rodriguez sat down and waited to be noticed. Lopez, who sat behind a large, leather top desk, was his superior, but not in any official police capacity. No record of employment or job description of any kind existed between the two men, yet they both knew their roles in an organization with no written policies. Rules of conduct were never posted on the wall for their type of business.

Lopez looked up, cocked his head sideways, and spread his arms out wide as he asked Rodriguez, " ¿Qué es con ese chico? What is with that boy? This is the third time he has tried to smuggle without paying me. He was caught the last two times. What does he think will happen?"

Rodriguez paused in thought and said, "His father owns a large rum distillery in the hills and makes a lot of money. The son wants to make money fast, but doesn't like to work. The father sells the liquid, and the son sells the powder. Who knows?"

Lopez scowled and said, "Well, teach him a lesson this time. He needs to be told how to do business properly. His father pays taxes on the liquor he produces. My fees are the same for cocaine."

Later that evening, Miguel Chavez joined his cousin, Juan Rodriguez, and Filipe Valdez on the coastal police boat. Rodriguez had obtained the exact time and coordinates of the boats involved in the drug deal, but the three other policemen did not know that. Chavez looked on intently as Rodriguez tracked the two drug boats by radar from three miles away. The police boat had no running lights on, and the overcast sky provided little moonlight. The four stroke engine of the police boat purred silently as they waited nearby. The plan was to let the two drug boats meet each other and then approach in the police boat at top speed. Chavez hoped the other drug boats were not equipped with radar.

The police timed their arrival just as the two drug boats were tossing lines to each other. Rodriguez gave the order, "Now!" Valdez held two powerful spotlights, one in each hand and blinded the men at the same instant Rafael fired a warning shot close enough to splash water into one of the boats. "Se trata de la Policía Costera! This is the Coastal Police! Put your hands up or you will be shot!"

Each drug boat contained two men. Miguel saw fear in the eyes of the men on one boat, but anger and madness in the eyes of the other men. Things happened very quickly. One of the men on the second boat bent down in a flash, picked up an assault rifle and began shooting at Valdez. The spot light in his right hand exploded into a thousand pieces while the flash from the exploding xenon bulb temporarily blinded the men. Rafael already had his gun drawn and put two bullets into the man with the assault rifle in less than one second. Wild staccato gunfire erupted into the sky as the man fell back dead into the boat. "Disparar otro! Shoot the other one!" Rodriguez ordered. The second man looked up and pleaded for his life, causing Rafael to hesitate for a second. Rodriguez quickly swung his pistol toward the pleading man and rapidly fired two bullets into his chest. Then he turned his gun on the men in the other boat who were clearly shaken by the brutal killings they had just witnessed. "¿Qué haremos contigo? What shall we do with you?"

Valdez kept the remaining spotlight on the two terrified men in the drug boat. "Which one of you is the son of the distiller? Both men looked at each other, then back at Rodriguez. "Speak!"

"I, I am..."

Rodriguez pointed his gun toward the other man.

"No! No! Please! Don't shoot me!"

Rodriguez paid no heed to the man's pleas and shot him in the forehead. Following the loud blast of the gunshot, a deafening silence descended upon the policemen.

"Chavez!"

"Sí?" Both cousins replied simultaneously.

"Christ, I will never get this right! Miguel! Handcuff that man!" Miguel jumped over to the boat and cuffed the trembling hands of the last living member of the drug deal.

CHAPTER 22
JEKYLL ISLAND TO CAPE CANAVERAL

Billy checked the marine weather, and the forecast called for
wind on the bow at twenty knots if they ran outside on the
open Atlantic, so he decided to run on the Intracoastal
Waterway for the day. They departed the marina at Jekyll
Island at seven and headed south into Saint Andrew's Sound.

The waterway kissed the Atlantic Ocean just south of
Jekyll Island, at mile marker 690, and Billy could clearly see
that the ocean was rough offshore. Delighted to be running on
the waterway, Bridget studied the paper charts while
monitoring their position as they cruised south. Billy loved
having her by his side on the fly bridge while they sped along
at twenty knots on the multimillion dollar yacht.

They escaped the unprotected area of the sound and
followed the waterway into the protection of the Cumberland

River, where the water became flat calm. The river banks were interspersed with massive pine trees and low country vegetation. Cat o'nine tails lined the banks in some areas, followed by tall saw grass. The vegetation's brilliant green contrasted along the river banks with the turbid, tea color of the abutting water. Billy spotted a pod of dolphins approaching from the bow. "We're going too fast for them to surf the bow wake, but watch the stern wake, they're going to surf the waves!" The dolphin rode the three foot waves with the precision of professional surfers. One even performed a back flip to confirm his enjoyment. As Bridget snapped photos, they continued to play in *Destiny's* wake for several minutes before disappearing.

No large monument welcomed them to Florida as they crossed the Georgia/Florida border on the waterway. However, Billy and Bridget were both smiling as they watched the little boat-shaped icon cross the state line on the navigation screen. They celebrated with a kiss. *Destiny* approached Amelia Island, slowing down as they passed the Fernandina Beach docks and then returning to cruising speed.

Billy reduced speed once again when *Destiny* passed through the city of St. Augustine, as the entire area was a no wake zone. Bridget made roast beef and turkey sandwiches for the men, complete with lettuce, tomatoes, cheese, and spicy banana peppers. Billy's mouth began to water before he even took a bite. The men took turns at the helm in order to thoroughly enjoy their lunch.

"You know," Billy said in between bites of his sandwich, "St. Augustine is the oldest city in the U.S."

Bridget thought he was kidding. "C'mon Billy, Florida, really?"

"I'm serious! Let's bet a half hour backrub on it."

She frowned. "There's no way Florida has the oldest city in the U.S. It's got to be Boston or some place in New England."

"Okay, let's make it an hour!"

Bridget thought he was bluffing and shook on it.

Billy winked at her and said, "Cool thing is, even if I lose, I win."

Several hours later, they pulled into the Cape Canaveral Lock. As they were waiting for the water elevation to equalize, they saw four manatees ten feet off the bow. "How in the world do they know to go through the lock?" Bridget asked.

"The first couple of times I saw them in here, I thought they were trapped by accident, but I asked the lock tender, and he told me that they swim through the lock all the time and probably learn when they're young to just wait until the water starts moving again."

"Amazing," she said.

They pulled into a marina that Billy had used before, which was located directly across the channel from the launching area of Kennedy Space Center. While they were refueling, a dockhand told Billy that a rocket was scheduled to launch later that evening. It was not a manned space craft launch, but a satellite rocket. Billy was thrilled that he could share the event with Bridget. A night time rocket launch from Cape Canaveral would surely be an extraordinary visual display, and a spectacular way to spend their last night of the east coast cruise.

While surfing her iPhone, Bridget reluctantly acknowledged that Billy was right about the age of St. Augustine, and also found out that the rocket was scheduled for a 10:05 p.m. lift off. "Perfect," Billy said, "I've never seen a liftoff at night. Let's grill out on the fly bridge with a bottle of wine and watch!" Bridget prepared a salad while Billy thawed some frozen fillet mignon.

They enjoyed a glass of wine together on the fly bridge as the sun began to set to the west. Bridget reclined back on the long white sun pad and rested her head in Billy's lap. Looking up at him, she smiled and said, "These seats are exceptionally comfortable."

"Must be the head rest," Billy replied grinning. They reminisced about how quickly the trip went by, yet when they departed New York, it had seemed like Florida was light years away.

Billy sautéed some mushrooms in the galley with a splash of Worcestershire and white wine, and then cooked the fillet mignon on the fly bridge grill. Bridget played one of her iPod playlists through the stereo, which pumped music up to the fly bridge. Billy even broke out his old chef's hat which he wore while grilling the steaks with one hand and holding his glass of wine in the other. A feeling of elation and camaraderie was palpable to all three of them as they sat around the fly bridge dining table eating salad and fillet mignon, covered with sautéed mushrooms.

"You boys know how to eat," Bridget said with a smile, adding, "I'm a little sad that tomorrow is our last day of the trip."

"Well, you'll just have to come back down when you finish your master's."

The wind had died down, and the night air was warm and void of sound with the exception of an occasional creak and groan from the dock. Billy opened a second bottle of Pinot Noir for the three of them as they finished up dinner. Only a quarter moon was visible as the liftoff time of 10:05 p.m. neared. Bridget found the official NASA website on her iPhone, which had a countdown to launch timer in the upper right hand corner. They turned off all the lights on the yacht to allow their eyes to adjust to the darkness.

The Kennedy Space Center consisted of a massive complex, more than 200 square miles in size. They gazed about, not sure exactly where to look for the rocket. "Don't worry, we'll see it," Billy assured Bridget and Marco.

All three of them began the countdown as they approached liftoff, "Ten, nine, eight... LIFTOFF!"

It took several seconds for the sound to travel from the launch site to the yacht, but when it arrived, they had to shout to each other to be heard. A massive roar, like an airport full of competing jets, enveloped them and they could feel the vibration of the mighty rocket's exploding fuel.

"Sounds like a go!" Billy yelled, and pointed, "There it is!" A massive white ball of light appeared, blinding the three of them as it slowly began to rise above land. The rocket continued its thunderous roar as it proceeded to climb vertically toward the heavens. Once the rocket was several thousand feet in the air, the angle of trajectory changed, and the white ball of fire extending from the bottom began to elongate into an oval shape as the rocket accelerated. The perimeter of the white fire ball of exploding gas was fringed with orange and red, followed by a long trail of white fire. The rocket continued to gain altitude with elegant grace as the decibel level of combustion slowly faded.

Bridget smiled and said, "Dancing under the stars, viewing amazing aquatic creatures, hundred year old oak trees silently screaming out of the sand, a magical display of fireflies, and now, a rocket liftoff from Cape Canaveral! What an absolutely amazing voyage!" Billy hugged her close and kissed her.

They finished their wine while recounting stories of the trip; all three of them were in high spirits. Billy said, "This time tomorrow we'll be in Fort Lauderdale, and I'm not sure we'll be able to top tonight."

"Em, yes amigo. Thank you for another great trip!" Marco bid goodnight and departed down the steps, leaving Bridget and Billy alone on the fly bridge.

Billy had his arm around her and was running his fingers through her soft hair as they lay back and gazed up at the stars. "This feels really nice, I'm so glad you enjoyed the trip. You really made it special for me, and I loved having you along. I've done the trip up and down the east coast many times, but this was by far the best one. Thank you."

He could feel guilt rising from within as the voyage to Honduras crept into his mind. It took several minutes to force the thought out of his head.

She nuzzled her head into his chest. "I really did enjoy it and loved sharing such special times with you. I know this is work for you, but it doesn't feel like it. Do you have this much fun when the owners are onboard?"

"It's a different program. We don't do long runs at sea. They generally fly their jet and meet the yacht in the Bahamas or wherever. We might do a short trip somewhere, but never eight hours of cruising. You know, sometimes I hire a chef/stew when the family is onboard. Would you like to try working with me on the yacht sometime? We would have so much fun!"

"Sure! I might need to brush up on some recipes, but I'd love to try it!"

Billy was overjoyed. Bridget had what it took to live and work on a yacht. If she could work a few trips as a chef/stew with the boss and his family, and she liked the boating lifestyle, when he came back from Honduras, he could buy the catamaran he'd always dreamed about, and sail away with her. It was perfect!

All he had to do was borrow his boss's multimillion dollar yacht, and smuggle 400 pounds of cocaine into the United States.

CHAPTER 23   OPEN WATER COURT

TWENTY MILES OFFSHORE PUERTO LEMPIRA, HONDURAS.

On the voyage back to police headquarters, Miguel Chavez stood at the helm of the police boat and steered them on a course for the station dock. The only living prisoner from the drug deal sat on the bare deck of the boat, without a cushion, so that his ass slammed down hard with every wave.

Valdez was tasked with running the drug boat containing the three dead bodies back to shore, and Rafael drove the second confiscated drug boat.

Miguel Chavez could hear Rodriguez talking to the prisoner. "Usted debe haber escuchado a mi asociado. You should have listened to the message from my superior. Now you are going to jail. Or, we could just shoot you and throw you overboard. Yes, that would be easier."

The prisoner was finally coming out of shock and the reality of his situation was upon him. He looked up at Rodriguez and said, "Lopez is insane! He wanted more money than I could pay!"

Rodriguez shook his head and replied, "You came up with the money for the drugs, so you could have paid Lopez. And if you had, you wouldn't be here right now."

Rodriguez leaned over and told Miguel to stop the boat. The other two boats were following close behind, and pulled up alongside. Valdez reached over, grabbed the midship cleat, and asked, "What's up?"

Rodriguez replied in Spanish. "I'm not paying for a funeral for these pieces of shit. How deep are we?" It took Miguel a moment to comprehend what was happening. His cousin grabbed two of the dead men and threw them overboard one at a time. Rafael was going to throw the third body over when Rodriguez raised his hand and stopped him. "No, we need one. Everyone listen up. This is what happened. We saw these two boats meeting in the dark and boarded them. He," Rodriguez pointed to the dead man, "opened fire and I shot him. We'll keep two thirds of both the money and the coke. I'll give you your share of money tomorrow after I meet with Lopez. Obviously, he gets the rest."

Rodriguez used the one remaining spot light to search the duffle bag full of cash. He didn't bother to count it. Instead, he divided up the mound of cash by volume, like taking a slice of pie, a big slice. He did the same with the cocaine and stowed the confiscated goods down below.

Rodriguez addressed everyone again, "There will be news reporters at the dock. Let me do the talking." He looked at Miguel, pointed at the prisoner and said, "Gag him. I don't want him trying to yell to the reporters. If he does, knock him out."

Their duties complete. Miguel brought the police boat back up to speed. Rodriguez leaned over to Miguel, revealed his gold tooth in a moonlight smile and said, "I like our new boats."

Miguel Chavez was now officially a Honduran coastal police officer.

CHAPTER 24
CAPE CANAVERAL TO FORT LAUDERDALE

The weather fully cooperated for their last day of cruising down the Florida coast from Cape Canaveral to Fort Lauderdale. They departed before first light because Billy didn't want to navigate directly into the sun coming out of the east facing canal. Bridget was in a cheerful mood and smiling from ear to ear sitting next to Billy on the fly bridge in the semi darkness of pre-dawn.

Billy turned to her and said, "We got such a good start this morning that maybe we'll slow down and fish for a while on the way south."

"All I've made on this trip are salads and sandwiches," Bridget said. "So, if we catch some wahoo or mahi, I'll cook tonight."

"You don't want to go out on the town tonight?" Billy asked.

"I'm cool with whatever you want to do, but since it's our last night together, I wouldn't mind just hanging out with you."

Billy's heart melted; he had finally found someone truly special. He felt the same way and secretly wanted to just chill out and relax with her on their last night together. On other deliveries with Marco, the two of them always went out and celebrated after a long voyage on the water, but this time with Bridget, Billy felt different.

The sun burst up from the ocean horizon soon after *Destiny* made the turn south from Cape Canaveral. Bridget came back up to the fly bridge, handed Billy his favorite mug of coffee just the way he liked it, and sat down next to him. "Thanks, Babe. The Gulf Stream is many miles off shore from here, so we'll wait a few hours and get into some deeper water to the east before we fish."

She took a sip of coffee and smiled. "Okay, just let me know when, and I'll go down and rig up the rods." Billy had never dated a woman who actually liked to fish, and fell in love all over again.

About three hours later, Billy slowed down to a speed of six knots in 400 feet of water. Bridget and Marco attached rod holders to the port, starboard and center handrail sections around the aft deck. Bridget rigged up three boat rods with trolling lures and set them in the rod holders. Then she tethered the massive Penn reels to the handrail with a small nylon line and carabiner clip. She had a portable VHF radio clipped to her waist, so she could easily radio Billy on the fly bridge if they hooked up with a fish.

They trolled for about twenty minutes when Billy noticed some action on the water near the lures. He radioed to Bridget, "Get ready, we've got a follow." Bridget studied the water behind the lures, but it was harder to see into the water from the aft deck. Billy's elevated view high up on fly bridge provided a better vantage point.

Less than a minute later, Bridget yelled, "FISH ON!" She didn't bother with the radio, and Billy heard her loud and clear. He slowed down, took the engines out of gear and ran down to the aft deck. On his way out of the salon door he heard more commotion, but couldn't make out what was said.

Bridget wore a leather rod holder around her waist and worked the fish like a professional. With an ear to ear smile, she looked over at Billy and said, "Double header!"

Marco wrestled a fish on the port side while Bridget struggled against her fish on the starboard side. Billy started to speak when suddenly the tip of the center rod bent down with the weight of a large fish, and then yelled, "No way! A triple header!"

He quickly removed the center rod from its holder. "Keep the lines clear! Don't let em' get tangled!" Yelled Billy, as he walked down to the swim platform to get closer to the water and keep his line away from the others. His fish jumped high out of the water shaking his head violently as it tail walked along the surface. "Mahi!"

All three of them grinned like children on Christmas morning as they struggled against their fish. Billy reeled his catch near the stern, but when the mahi-mahi sensed the yacht, it took off like a thunder bolt sending the reel into a whining buzz. After a few more minutes, he was able to reel his fish up to the swim platform, but as he reached down to grab its tail, the fish took off again splashing his face full of water. "Buggah!" He cried in a mock cockney accent, while shaking the saltwater from his face. He worked the fish back in and successfully grabbed its tail and hauled it onboard. Billy could tell it was a female mahi-mahi by its gently sloping forehead. It measured over three feet long and weighed more than twenty pounds. He placed the fish in a large white cooler where it began a wild percussion solo.

"Em, I have one here!" Marco said. Billy followed Marco's line into the water and saw that he had hooked a yellow fin tuna.

"Hold on Marco, let me get the gaff." Billy ran up the steps, grabbed the gaff out of the locker and returned to the swim platform. "Okay, I'm ready." Marco brought the fish up toward the stern of the yacht, but the tuna would not yield so easily and made another run. Marco's reel emitted a *zzzzzzzz, zzzzz-zzzzzzz,* as the line spun off the reel. After several more minutes of struggling against the powerful fish, Marco finally worked the tuna up near the stern, and Billy grabbed the fishing line where it connected to the heavy duty wire leader. He pulled the fish closer to the swim platform and saw that it was a nice size fish. In one swift motion, Billy lowered the gaff and swiftly pulled it into the fish. Grabbing the gaff with both hands he hauled the tuna up onto the deck. "Nice fish Marco!"

Bridget was sneaking a glimpse of the action when she could, but was still vigorously fighting her fish. Marco held the cooler open as Billy placed the tuna inside. Both fish fluttered wildly in one last vain attempt at escape.

"Okay, Babe, you're up!"

Bridget walked down the steps to the swim platform and maneuvered her fish closer. She had fought the fish longer than the others and tired it out, so it did not make a run as it approached the yacht. Billy gaffed her fish and pulled it aboard. The blunt, angular head confirmed it was a male mahi-mahi, and Billy could feel that it weighed more than his fish. "Nice work! Wow, a triple header and all fish onboard!" Billy placed the last fish in the cooler, and they exchanged high fives. "What did that great white shark say in *Finding Nemo*?" In an Australian accent, Billy said, "We're havin' fish to-noit!"

Back on the fly bridge, Billy felt on top of the world. The weather provided calm seas and a spectacular view of the Atlantic. They were cruising along on an exquisite yacht. He had his arm around the woman he loved. He was healthy and happy, and he felt that he had finally met someone with whom he could share the rest of his life. Every time the thought of her leaving started to edge into his mind, he forced it out; he didn't want to waste any mental energy in the negative. He had his arm around her now and was living in the moment.

He kissed the top of her head and said, "Babe, not only are you gorgeous, but you're one hell of a good luck charm!"

They pulled into the dock space that Billy rented for the season in downtown Fort Lauderdale a little after three in the afternoon. By now, Bridget was well accustomed to the tasks associated with docking and was wrestling with the aluminum steps when Billy came down from securing the fly bridge. They connected the two shore power cables and Billy climbed down into the engine room to shut off the generators. The yacht fell silent as the second diesel generator sputtered to a stop.

"Let's take a walk and get a nice wine to go with the fish you're cooking tonight," Billy said.

They disembarked from the yacht and took a few steps on land, when Bridget staggered and said, "Whoa." Eight days of living on the water made terra firma feel strangely foreign. "I don't have my land legs back yet," she said laughing.

Marco left to visit his son in Miami for the night, leaving Billy and Bridget the yacht to themselves.

Billy showered, feeling fantastic having completed another east coast trip. He heard Bridget playing Van Morrison on the yacht's Bose stereo system as he walked up to the galley, and suffered a pang of sadness when he thought of her flying back to New York tomorrow. She was cooking away and he watched for several moments before she noticed him standing there smiling.

"What?" She smiled back.

"I'm just happy to see you so at ease in the galley. You look right at home."

"You know, this galley is really pretty functional. I think it actually has more counter space than the kitchen in my apartment."

"Anything I can do to help?" Billy asked.

"I'd love a cold beer." Billy smiled to himself and fell in love yet again. He grabbed two frosty beers from the fridge. Bridget prepared a plate of sashimi tuna with the fish they caught, complete with wasabi, soy, and ponzu sauces. They snacked on it standing around the galley as she prepared a Cajun rub for blackened mahi-mahi. The wonderful aroma from the galley made Billy's mouth water.

Bridget served the blackened mahi-mahi with lightly sautéed vegetables, and they sat at the aft deck table looking out over the water. For such a special occasion, Billy decided to use the yacht's custom made crystal wine glasses, which contained a laser engraving of the word *Destiny* on the side. He popped a bottle of wine, poured it into the crystal wine glasses, and lifted his glass in a toast, "To the end of a wonderful journey and the beginning of a new one." They touched their glasses creating the timeless sound of celebration. They ate in silence for a few moments as Billy's words lingered, then he added, "This is an absolutely perfect meal. Every bite is overflowing with flavor."

"Thanks. Well you know, it's always better when someone else makes it."

Billy paused from eating, savored the moment, and said, "What a nice way to end our trip. I'm so content that it's hard to think of you leaving."

"I know, and I'll miss you terribly, but after I finish my exams, I'm free. I can come down and maybe we can do a trip like you mentioned."

"Absolutely! We have a trip to the Bahamas coming up, and it's perfect for us. We'll take the yacht over to Nassau a few days early and then meet the boss and his family over there. They won't want to make the trip across the Gulf Stream this time of year, because it's much too dicey with weather. Don't worry too much about the role of chef. They eat out almost every night, so all you really need to do is make breakfast and they fend for themselves at lunch. If you do have to cook dinner onboard, I'll give you a hand, but if you served something like this, they would love it!"

They continued to make future plans. Billy was thrilled with the idea of cruising the Bahamas together with Bridget.

They finished doing the dishes together in the galley and as she dried her hands, she turned around from the sink and wrapped her arms around Billy. He pulled her tight against his body and embraced her with both arms around her back. They kissed passionately, tongues exploring each other's mouths for what seemed like an hour when Billy finally confessed, "You feel so good that I don't want this moment to end, but let's take this downstairs."

"I thought you'd never ask."

As they lay in bed, Billy was once again vacillating with telling her about his plan to go to Honduras. It was on the tip of his tongue many times, but he knew she would not approve and guilt ate at his soul. Why was he really going? Money? Didn't he have all of the things in life that were really important? Why couldn't he just continue on the way things were? Maybe the boss would hire her full time? He didn't want to overload her with *everything* he was thinking, but if she liked working the trips with his boss's family onboard, then she'd love cruising alone with him on a catamaran next year. After much deliberation, he decided not to tell her about the drug deal. Maybe he would explain the windfall of money later on when he returned to the states, but for now he just couldn't tell her. With the money he made from Honduras, he could stop working on the yacht and buy his own catamaran. Then, he would start a charter business on paper which would enable them to travel wherever they wanted under the pretense of working. Billy hadn't worked out all the details of the business plan yet, but the charter business was nothing compared to what he needed to accomplish over the next several days.

The next morning, Billy woke up automatically at six and rolled over to see Bridget wide awake staring at him. They embraced silently, made passionate love once again, and fell back asleep. Bridget's flight was late in the afternoon, so they slept in. Later, as Bridget packed her things, there was a palpable sadness in the air. "I'm really going to miss you and can't wait for you to come back down," he said.

She walked over and hugged him, putting her cheek flat against his chest, and then she looked up deep into his eyes. "When I get my schedule finalized with work and school, we'll make plans for me to come back down. I really hope I can make the trip to the Bahamas with you."

Billy rode with her in the taxi to the airport. They had a drink at the airport bar near security and waited until she absolutely had to leave. He wanted to be with her every minute he could until she had to board the plane.

"I love you Billy."

"I love you too, Bridget. Have a safe trip and I can't wait to see you again."

Billy watched her pass through security. They gave each other one last wave goodbye before she walked toward her gate. He turned and walked away overwhelmed with mixed emotions of both missing her and anticipating her return. It was an odd combination of a heavy heart, combined with exciting possibilities of things to come.

Now that she was gone, he had to focus on getting down to Honduras. If he got caught by the authorities, he would never see Bridget again. Billy shuddered and forced the thought from his mind. He walked up to the Jamaica Air ticket counter and paid cash for a round trip ticket to Montego Bay.

CHAPTER 25   FEED THE LEMMINGS

Miguel Chavez drove the police boat with Rodriguez standing by his side. His boat was the first to pull up to the station dock. Numerous bright flashes briefly blinded him as photographers took photos for the morning papers. Seconds later, the entire dock was illuminated by flood lights for television cameras. A tall, dark haired, attractive woman in a low cut suit coat pushed through the photographers to get near the boat as Chavez secured the lines to the dock. Rodriguez turned his back to the crowd and reminded Chavez. "Me deja hacer el hablar. Let me do the talking."

Rodriguez turned toward the cameras and put his hands up in an attempt to quiet the crowd, but the reporters were all yelling questions at the same time. "Por favor, por favor! I will give a two minute press conference now, and a full statement will be issued in the morning. We have a dead body and a prisoner who needs to be secured."

When the reporters heard about the dead body, their activity on the dock became piranha-like, each one shuffling for the best photo-the best bite of bloody meat. Rodriguez gave a quick debriefing of the night's events, quite similar to what he had told his men earlier. Several reporters tried to corner Miguel as he got off the boat but he did not speak. Instead, he just shook his head and pointed to Rodriguez.

CHAPTER 26   *DESTINY* HONDURAS

FORT LAUDERDALE, FLORIDA.

Billy returned from the airport the next day and found Marco back onboard. "How is your son? Did you have a good time in Miami?"

Marco's son, Ernesto, sometimes helped out on the yacht buffing and waxing. "Ernie," as his American friends now called him, had come to the United States to visit his father. While living outside of Miami in little Honduras, he had become reacquainted with his childhood sweetheart, Zara and had never returned to where he was born.

Ernie had just barely escaped the madness of Honduras. In his teens, he had been tempted by the promise of quick cash in the Honduran drug trade, and managed to stay alive for two years while his father worked in the States.

"Em, oh, yes. Everything was nice. He is good."

"Did he talk to the necessary people in Honduras?"

"Yes, but em, we will have to meet them when we're down there, so as, em, how you say? No bowling pin set up."

"Okay, I understand. We could get down there in a little over three days at twelve knots. We'll have to slow down to conserve fuel and extend our range. It'll be tight, but we can make it."

There was much to do to prepare for another 1,000 mile trip. They needed two drums for extra diesel fuel, navigation charts for areas they would travel, provisions, and Billy needed to make sure there was no way the boss would want to use the yacht while they were gone. They divided up the required tasks and planned on meeting the next night to finalize everything and go over the plan one last time. If they worked quickly, they could leave for Honduras in two days.

Billy spoke to his boss on the phone, but as always, the owner wouldn't confirm anything; they might use the yacht and they might not. It was as if his boss always wanted to keep him on his toes. Billy learned long ago not to press too hard. He knew that the owner never used the yacht right after the southbound delivery to Florida, so Billy decided they would just have to risk it.

The reality and magnitude of the crime Billy planned to commit robbed him of any meaningful sleep over the next two nights. He tossed and turned as all the repercussions of his actions bounced around his brain. The voyage to Honduras would result in all or nothing. He tried to think of it as buying an initial public offering of stock, but he knew that there was a hell of a lot more at risk than just losing all of his life savings. Billy had cashed in his IRA, sold all his stocks and liquidated everything from his bank accounts to come up with a little over $182,000 in cash. Marco also withdrew all of his savings and was able to produce $25,000. Together, they had come up with a little over $200,000, the amount necessary to purchase one drum of cocaine. They needed at least another $10,000 for fuel. For the first time in Billy's life, he withdrew a cash advance on two credit cards.

He decided to leave at two o'clock the following morning and run straight through until they reached Honduras.

Marco's son was able to contact an old acquaintance in the Honduran cartel who was still alive. The contact had assured that the product could be delivered this week, but the exchange would be tricky. Billy seriously worried about handing over $200,000 in cash to Honduran drug dealers. He didn't even have a gun onboard.

It was mid-October when they departed Fort Lauderdale. The temperature was still quite warm, low eighties, in the early morning. Billy had broken a solid sweat helping Marco with the shore power cables, aluminum stairs, and securing two drums of extra diesel fuel to the aft deck. They made a stealth departure from the dock a little after two thirty in the morning. Billy made a last minute decision to cruise at full speed for 200 miles down to Key West, refuel, and then depart for Honduras. Even though the yacht might be recognized in Key West, it would give them a good reserve supply of fuel for the long trip. Because of the paper trail, and possible delays with Customs, Billy did not want to stop at any other foreign port, so the extra drums of diesel fuel were mandatory for the 800-mile trip from Key West to Honduras.

They pulled into Key West at ten and were back underway, fully fueled within an hour. Billy paid cash for the diesel, hoping to minimize any evidence of the yacht being anywhere it wasn't supposed to be.

The next twenty-four hours were actually pleasant. The weather was cooperating with five to ten knot winds and relatively calm seas, so Billy and Marco took turns at the helm in three hour shifts. They tried to catch a little sleep whenever they could, but it was really a wink here and a wink there.

Destiny cut through the warm, Caribbean waters slowly. Billy deliberately cruised at a low speed to maximize fuel efficiency. The next morning, they passed Cuba in the distance. Billy did not want to get too close to the island for many reasons. Once they rounded the west side of Cuba, they turned south on a course of 163 degrees for a final ocean run of roughly 450 miles. They were too far offshore to see Cancun or the whole Yucatan Peninsula, but that was fine with Billy. He didn't want to be seen in any resort locations. You never knew who might be on vacation and recognize the yacht. Billy had been monitoring their speed and fuel tank levels constantly, and was pleased with their fuel burn rate. There would be no problem making it to Puerto Lempira in Honduras. In fact, it looked like they would have more than 100 gallons to spare.

Destiny eased into Puerto Lempira a little after eleven p.m., and they tied up at the Lempira Marina dock. The dimly lit area was eerily quiet with no employees at the late hour, so they quickly secured the docking lines, locked all the doors and tried to get a few hours sleep.

Far too anxious to sleep, Billy paced the aft deck long before sunrise. However, there was not much he could do at the early hour. The sedate marina did not open until eight or nine, so he sat down with a cup of coffee and planned out how he wanted the exchange to go down. During the long trip down from Key West, Billy had pressed Marco for any information about the Honduran drug cartel. Based on the notorious stories that Marco conveyed to him, Billy knew they could not leave the yacht and perform the exchange onshore. If they did, they would be kidnapped, or simply killed. Two hundred thousand American dollars was a motive far too tempting to ruthless killers with zero morals.

As much as Billy didn't want to have *Destiny* involved with the actual exchange, there was no alternative. They would have to exchange the money and the drum right there on the dock.

The marina office finally opened at nine and Billy walked up to make arrangements for their stay. The office was located at the top of the ramp that led to the floating docks, and consisted of a small, eight-by-eight box with a corrugated sheet metal roof. Billy noticed an old rusted *Esso* sign hanging on the wall of the small building. He walked into the office and nodded to the dock master, who was a slender man with hair combed straight back and a couple of day's growth on his beard. When the man smiled, Billy noticed several missing teeth. It could have been Billy's apprehension and general anxiety, but he was fairly certain that the dock master had been anticipating their arrival. They spoke in English, and the dock master seemed just a little too friendly. Billy decided to improvise. "Hello, I'm Phil, the captain of that yacht." He pointed down toward the only, and thereby most obvious, yacht tied to the dilapidated dock.

"Good morning Mr. Phil! How can I help you?"

"Well, I had some mechanical problems yesterday and need dock space for a few days for repairs. I was scheduled to come in yesterday afternoon in the daylight, but we lost an engine, so we didn't get in until two this morning." Billy saw the wheels turning in the man's head and was glad he lied. "Do you sell diesel here?"

The dock master continued in broken English. "We had to yes, but, eh, the pump broken down and boss no pay for fix. But, there is truck I call, and he get hose to boat. No problem. I do it many times. I get you good price. How much you need?"

CHAPTER 27   STEALING *DESTINY*

Rodriguez picked up the newspaper with his coffee the morning after returning to the police dock with two prisoners, one dead, one alive. The reporters had featured the bloody body of the dead drug dealer in gruesome detail. Rodriguez was pleased to see his name in print portraying him as: "Risking his life in the line of duty to protect the Honduran people." That line in particular created a smile that revealed his gold tooth once again.

      Rodriguez had dressed in civilian clothes. He did not want to tempt a nosy reporter photographing him in his police uniform entering Lopez's residence. Such a reporter would most certainly be hunted down and killed, but the photo could be released to other countries via the Internet and create several days of troubling press that no one wanted to deal with.

      Rodriguez arrived at the entrance to Lopez's massive estate a little after ten and proceeded through the first of three security check points. The 200-acre estate was located on, or more precisely, encompassed a small mountain rising a little more than 2,000 feet above sea level.

      Francisco Lopez had worked as a protégée to his beloved mentor, Luiz Pedro Álvarez, until Álvarez was arrested at the Guatemalan border by U.S. DEA officials in

1988. The event was highly controversial in Honduras because the country had no extradition policy. The event was a clear violation of the Honduran Constitution. The then Minister of Natural Resources, who detested Álvarez, said in a phrase that became famous: "I understand that with the surrender of Álvarez to the United States, the Constitution was violated, but, if it is for the benefit of Honduras, the Constitution must be violated as many times as necessary."

Lopez had learned two valuable lessons first hand from the sneaky Americans; *might makes right, and do not underestimate your enemy.*

Lopez immediately filled Álvarez's place as supreme lord of the entire region's drug production and distribution operations, and quickly crushed any attempts to infringe on his territory with excessive force. One such example of force was the elimination of a competing drug lord's entire operation.

Rodriguez reflected on that bloody week-long war as he drove two miles up the serpentine road through checkpoints two and three. Eleven years ago, Lopez had launched a surprise attack on the rival drug lord with military precision. Lopez lured the paranoid rival drug lord away from the protection of his villa under the false pretense of creating a partnership and expanding their business together. Lopez knew his competition would be suspicious, and had factored that into his plan.

Rodriguez quickly proceeded through the final checkpoint and drove up to the massive villa. As he pulled the car to a stop, he shook his head as he remembered the exact words Lopez had said over the phone to his competitor eleven years earlier, "One of my highest ranking men will accompany you to the meeting to ensure my word of forming a partnership." Sitting in the corner of the room, Rodriguez thought that he, himself, would have to be the human collateral to enable the meeting of the two drug czars. But Lopez hung up the phone with his rival and described his intent to overthrow his competitor.

Lopez's plan included killing the rival drug czar, all upper echelon personnel, and their loyal men, but allowed those willing to defect to live. The attack had to be carried out quickly in order for the surprise to have its desired effect. Lopez went on to describe the assassination, "We will hit them on route to the meeting. I have picked a location that is approachable by only two routes, and we will set up an ambush on both approach roads. At the same time we will attack and capture his villa. We'll need 100 men for the villa and fifty for each road ambush. We'll kill him and all men in his convoy and simultaneously capture his villa."

The so called 'high ranking' person Lopez had offered as collateral to his competitor turned out to be a very shrewd move on Lopez's part. Rodriguez sat in awe as he learned that there was an informer posing as a young mule trying to work his way up the organization. The mule worked for a very small fraction of the Honduran government loyal to the U.S. in its vain attempt to thwart the drug trade. Lopez told Rodriguez to brief the young mule on his new role. "Promotion" was the word he used, for the mule would be the high ranking man to escort the rival czar to the meeting. Naturally, Rodriguez waited until the last minute to tell the unsuspecting mule of his assignment, who had no choice but to accept the role of escort on such an auspicious occasion as the meeting of two drug czars.

The day of the meeting, when the dust finally settled on the bloody roadway, all twenty-five men in the czar's motorcade, including the informant, were killed. However, the attack and attempted takeover of the villa did not go as smoothly as Lopez had preached to Rodriguez.

Lopez hired over fifty new recruits for the villa raid, and as such, their loyalty was to staying alive, not fighting to the death. The several mile hike through dense, tropical vegetation to the villa proved to be much more difficult than originally thought. After hours of bushwhacking through thick rainforest, several unsuspecting new recruits stepped on land mines set up around the perimeter. The explosions alerted villa security and frightened off most of the remaining men.

It wasn't until the two ambush brigades arrived and stormed the villa from the road that they were able to seize the villa after much bloodshed. For six days after that, sporadic attacks occurred on Lopez's men, but all those who resisted were eventually silenced. The coca farmers and refiners really didn't care who they worked for as long as they got paid, so conversion to Lopez was rapid and unanimous.

After the attack, Lopez had been impressed with the villa's opulence and natural defenses and quickly moved in. It had been his home ever since.

Rodriguez walked up the same steps he had traveled eleven years ago, but this time he was a welcome guest, not storming the villa of a competing drug czar. One of the armed guards at the front entrance met him on the steps, and after a brief exchange, walked over to the car to retrieve the cocaine and money purloined the previous evening.

Usually, Rodriguez waited to meet his boss, even if Lopez was completely free and available. The waiting used to bother Rodriguez, but that frustration had faded away long ago. He understood that it was a matter of respect, and Rodriguez had no intention of ever challenging his boss. If the boss wanted him to wait, he would wait.

Therefore, Rodriguez was a little surprised when, not only didn't he have to wait, but was greeted by the boss himself. "Hola viejo amigo. ¿Cómo fue tu viaje anoche? Tenemos mucho que discutir. Venir, vienen en. How was your trip last night? We have much to discuss. Come in, come in."

They walked into Lopez's large office and Rodriguez waited for his boss to sit down behind the large, mahogany leather-top desk. Rodriguez sat in a comfortable arm chair on the other side and reported, "I had to keep some of the cash and product for the news reporters to see and to include in the official police log, but I brought the rest of it here to you. I had one of the guards get it from the car. We should compensate my men on the boat. They are loyal."

Just then there was a knock at the door. "Come!" Lopez ordered. A guard with an AK-47 assault rifle slung over his shoulder walked in carrying two bags and placed them on the leather top desk. Lopez waited until the guard left the room before saying, "Of course your men will be paid. We need them, especially now. Do you like your new boats?"

Rodriguez revealed his gold tooth with a wide smile and replied, "Oh yes. We may sell one of them to fund some improvements to the dock and office, but I will definitely keep the other one."

Rodriguez watched intently as Lopez leaned back in his chair and said, "Speaking of boats, a luxury yacht came in last night and is docked not far from you. They want to buy 200 kilos. It is a nice yacht, and I want it. They have trouble with their engine and have reserved a slip for several days. They can't leave until the engine is repaired. We'll sell them the product, but I want you to confiscate the yacht." Lopez leaned forward, rotated the computer screen on his desk toward Rodriguez and said, "Here is a photo that was taken this morning. It's nice, don't you think?"

Rodriguez shifted in his chair. He would never openly oppose his boss, but there was a big difference between high jacking a twenty-five foot center console boat and confiscating a large yacht. He raised an eyebrow. "They will be tied to the dock for several days?"

"This information is from the captain himself," Lopez said with confidence.

Rodriguez thought for a moment and replied. "Such a yacht is worth much money, and the owner will want it back. We'll need to prepare some evidence so that if it reaches the high court, we can prove it was used in an illegal drug deal. I'll need to take some incriminating photos."

Lopez nodded in approval. "I estimate the yacht is worth seven or eight million, so I will have to get some official court documents eventually, but I'm not worried about that, a mere formality. You confiscate the yacht and give it to me. I'll reward you and your men handsomely. I don't care about the men on the yacht. Kill them, if you need to. In fact, it's probably better if they are dead. That way, they can't talk, and we'll create a story for the press if needed, but I'd rather keep it as quiet as possible."

CHAPTER 28   THE EXCHANGE

Billy had given Marco money to buy a cell phone SIM card that allowed four hours of cell phone time in Honduras. They used Marco's phone because he still had relatives in Honduras, so if they ever had to explain the calls, it would make much more sense for Marco to have a Honduran SIM card than Billy.

The two men ate lunch on the yacht, but Billy was not hungry. He forced some food down anyway. They were scheduled to call the contact number at 1:00 p.m., and the hour was rapidly approaching.

"Okay Marco, let's go through it one more time. You've got to make them do the exchange here, on the dock. No matter what they say, we can't leave with them, or they might kill us."

Marco didn't need the lecture from Billy; he knew firsthand the vicious wrath of the drug cartel. "Em, yes. I know, but what if they say the deal is off if we don't go? Do I just say, em, 'deal is off'?"

"Yes. We can't risk getting kidnapped, or worse. Right now, I'm only out a few grand in diesel fuel, but if we're held up somewhere, all of our savings are gone and probably, our lives as well."

"Okay, amigo, I understand and will do as you say."

Marco's son had provided the code word, *lionfish*, which had to be used in the initial part of the conversation to prove who they were. Marco looked at his watch and dialed the number provided by his son.

He spoke in Spanish, "Hello, I was told that you take people scuba diving, but I wanted to know if *lionfish* have taken over the reefs."

"We were expecting your call. Right on time, good. Do you have the money?"

"How many kilos do you have?"

"We have more than you need. Do you have the money?"

"Yes."

"Excellent. You want 200 kilos, the price is $250,000."

"No! The price was $200,000."

Marco realized that the man on the other end of the phone was fishing for more money. The price had been confirmed at $1,000 per kilo, and the man was just trying to get a little extra for himself.

"I will need to speak to my superiors, but we can do business if you have the money. Is it cash-U.S.?"

"Yes."

Billy was listening nervously, picking up only a word here and there, desperately wishing he understood Spanish better so he could hear the exact conversation.

Marco continued, "We need you to bring it to us at the dock, and it must be in a fifty-five gallon drum that says 'DIESEL' on it."

The man on the other end of the call laughed loud enough for Billy to hear. "I will talk to my superiors and call you back in two hours." The man hung up without waiting for Marco's reply.

Just then there was a loud knock on the hull that jolted both men. They looked at each other quickly. Billy ran out to the aft deck and looked down over the side of the yacht. The dock master stood on the dock smiling with a fuel hose grasped in both hands and said, "I have fuel truck for you. He must make trips because small truck no hold so much, but I get you good price." Billy relaxed a little and allowed himself to smile.

"Thank you. We'll fill the drums first." He grabbed the fuel hose from the dock master and ran it over toward the drums on the aft deck.

They drained the fuel truck of its contents in forty-five minutes and the driver left to refill. During the third trip of the fuel truck Marco's phone rang.

Marco answered after the first ring speaking in Spanish, "Hello?"

"We will meet you at the dock at eleven tonight. If you are one dollar short of 200,000, I will shoot both of you." Again, the man hung up without waiting for a response.

Marco relayed the conversation to Billy three times. Billy wanted to be sure that the man had said, "Both of you." Marco was absolutely sure and Billy believed him, but he wondered how the dealers knew that there were only two of them onboard. *It had to be the dock master,* Billy thought.

They finished refueling, and Billy walked up to the dock house to pay for the fuel. Once again, the dock master was a little too eager to please. "Yes, Captain, I get you best price at dock. Extra super good deal just for you. The truck pumped 2,115 gallons. Here is the ticket."

Billy already knew how much fuel had been pumped onto the yacht, and looked at the old fashioned carbon print ticket from the fuel truck pump. It was a simple matter to forge the ticket, and Billy knew for a fact they had received only 1,895 gallons. The extra 220 gallons was probably the dock master's cut.

Billy decided not to bring attention to the discrepancy. Instead, he toyed with the dock master a little and said, "Fine, my friend. Muchas gracias. I assume you take credit card."

The dock master's face became deadly serious. "Oh, I'm afraid phone lines no work. We no take credit card for much time. Cash only my friend."

Billy feigned surprise. "I see. Well, I'll have to go back to the yacht to get that kind of cash. However, I need another favor."

The dock master nodded eagerly, "Yes, yes, whatever you need."

"Since we're going to be here for what looks like a week now, I'm going to do an oil change, but I need a specific type of oil." Billy picked up a pen and wrote down the oil specifications.

"Can you call around and find me a 55 gallon drum of this?" He handed the dock master a piece of paper with *Mobil Delvac SAE 40 synthetic oil* written on it. "It must be synthetic. I can't use multi grade; get exactly what's on that paper. Get me a price and delivery time and I'll be back up to pay for the fuel. See if you can get the drum of oil here in two or three days."

The dock master nodded obediently. "I will make phone calls now. I will use my own cell phone just for you." As Billy turned to leave the office he noticed a small digital camera behind the counter. He would have thought nothing of it, but in an office with no land line, it looked out of place in the dilapidated surroundings. He walked out of the office and back down the ramp toward the yacht.

The dock master picked up his cell phone and dialed Lopez.

Back onboard, Billy went down into his state room and began counting out $200,000 with shaking hands. He paused at $100,000. He could start the engines, leave now, and be back in the United States in less than three days. *I've come this far*, he thought. He finished counting the money, recounted it, confirmed the amount was correct, and placed the neatly bundled cash in a canvas bag. Then, he placed a beach towel on top to hide the currency. At a quick glance, Billy thought it looked like a beach bag. *Yeah, a Nantucket beach bag.*

Billy took $10,000 of the remaining cash and placed it in his back pack. He walked up to the dock house and spoke to his old friend. "Any luck with the synthetic oil?"

"Ah, was most difficult to find, but eh, yes I find it. Very expensive."

Not surprised that the dock master would take every opportunity to mark up whatever he sold, Billy asked, "How much?"

"I get drum for you in two days, but it is special order from 100 miles away, so it cost much, $3,000."

Billy could not hide his look of surprise. "Three thousand!" Billy knew the price was three times what he paid in the U.S. for the same drum of oil. Synthetic oil was expensive, but not fifty dollars per gallon!

Billy had had enough of the con man and got serious in his tone. "Look, we must do an oil change, but that price is way too high. The diesel fuel ticket is also too high. The truck came four times and it only holds 500 gallons, so there is no way it could have pumped over 2,000 gallons! So, here is what I'm willing to do; I'll pay for 2,000 gallons of diesel, and I'll pay you $1,500 for the drum of oil. Seven fifty now, and seven fifty when it arrives here. Otherwise, cancel it and I'll go someplace else."

Billy watched as the dock master recoiled like a serpent from the accusations. The exaggerated response was intended to gain sympathy, but Billy saw through the act. With a pleading look, the dock master said, "I'm only telling you what information I have. How can I change the diesel ticket?"

Billy responded angrily, "Look, I might be American, but I'm not stupid! Do you want my money or not?"

The dock master put up his hands in defense. "Okay, okay my friend. We have no problem here, just let me work with price. I think we can be fine."

Billy counted out the money and paid the dock master, then walked back to *Destiny*.

Down in the engine room, Billy worked well into nightfall to get the yacht ready to head back to Florida. He had absolutely no intention of performing an oil change in Honduras. He was counting on the dock master being an informer for the cartel, and didn't want anyone to know his real plans.

Time passed exceptionally slowly that evening. Eleven o'clock came and went. At midnight Billy thought the sellers would not show. Just a few minutes later, headlights turned into the parking lot. It was a small pickup truck with a yellow fifty-five gallon drum in back. Two men got out, and a third stayed inside the cab. Billy couldn't see if they had weapons, but was sure they did. Marco walked up the ramp and spoke to the men in Spanish, while Billy stayed on the yacht. He could hear the men speaking, but could not make out the conversation from the distance. Marco returned two minutes later and informed Billy, "They have the drum on the truck. I saw it. They won't move it until they get the money."

"Okay, Marco. We have to make sure the drum is full and that it's what they say it is before we give them the cash. Tell them that I'm coming up to test the contents, and *then* they can have the money."

Marco walked back up the ramp and spoke to the men.

Earlier in the day, Billy had been thinking about how to get a drum that weighed 200 kilograms, or 440 pounds, onto the aft deck of *Destiny*. It was not easy to move a full fifty-five gallon drum out of a pickup truck. He figured that they would roll the drum down the ramp, all the way to the side of the yacht and then use the davit, the small crane used to launch the tender, to haul it aboard. He had rigged up a sling for the drum to make it easier and lowered the davit cable to the side of the dock. All they had to do was roll the drum down the ramp and haul it aboard.

Marco returned to the yacht and told Billy, "The men will allow us to inspect the, em, product, but the drum must stay on the truck until they get money." Billy stood motionless, deep in thought. *I wonder if they plan on just shooting us and taking off with both the drum and the money.*

They left the yacht and walked up the ramp. Billy got his first look at the men he was dealing with. The two visible Honduran men were fairly young, less than thirty, but looked like they had seen their fair share of violence. One man had a scar that ran down from his hair line to just above his left eye. Billy was sure it was from a knife fight, and felt incredibly ill equipped for any kind of combat. He was certain that the man sitting in the truck was armed and was glad he had not brought the money with him. *It would be so easy for them to kill us,* he thought.

Marco said, "Necesitamos ver el interior del tambor. We need to see inside the drum."

The man with the scar jumped up into the bed of the truck and proceeded to remove the cover of the drum with a large socket wrench. Billy brought a long piece of one-inch-diameter aluminum tube and a hammer. When the man removed the cover he motioned to Billy. Billy jumped up and looked down at the drum full of cocaine. Even though there wasn't much light in the parking lot, the product was bright white. He dipped a moistened finger into the drum and put it to his tongue which went instantly numb. Billy nodded in approval and then hammered the hollow piece of aluminum tube all the way to the bottom of the drum. He pulled the tube out while keeping his thumb over one end and removed a core sample of the entire drum. He tested the bottom of the tube with another moistened finger, but this time he spread it over his top gums. The fine white powder numbed his front teeth. Billy watched closely as he let the sample of powder fall from the tube to make sure that it was all uniform. He sampled one last point from the middle of the drum and used his bottom gums. Within a minute, he could not feel his entire mouth.

Billy nodded to Marco, who said, "Muy bien. Tenemos un acuerdo. Conseguirá el dinero, pero tenemos que conseguir el tambor de la camioneta. We have a deal. He will get the money, but we have to get the drum off the truck."

The leader of the men said, "Lol! Tenemos que ver el dinero antes de que el tambor deja el camion. No! We must see the money before the drum leaves the truck."

Billy walked back to the yacht and removed the beach bag from his room. *This is it*, he thought. He resolved to try and appear calm, but he was trembling with fear as he walked through the salon toward the aft door. He paused and took several deep breaths, He could feel sweat running down his back. Billy's heart was pumping so loud, he could not hear his feet as he walked back to the pickup truck holding his life savings in his right hand. The leader of the group grabbed the bag from Billy, walked up to the truck cab and opened the door. Putting the bag on the seat, the man removed the towel and examined the contents of the bag. He leafed through one of the folds of money and appeared to be satisfied. He nodded to the other man in the bed of the pickup truck who pulled two pieces of wood off the truck bed and laid them up against the folded down bed door. The other man secured the cover back on the drum. The two men slowly tipped the drum on its side and rolled it down off the bed. The man with the scar threw the two pieces of wood into the bed of the truck and shut the bed door. Both men got in the cab and drove away.

Billy shuddered with a huge sense of relief. He and Marco rolled the drum down the floating dock and wrestled it into the sling. Billy ran up to the fly bridge and used the electric davit to hoist the drum onboard while Marco guided it into place.

One hundred yards away, a gold-toothed smile briefly reflected in the moonlight as Rodriguez slid an infrared, night vision camera into a case.

Billy wanted to start the engines and leave right away, but they had to transfer the product. They shut off all the lights on the yacht in an effort to make it look like just another yacht at the dock. Only problem was, there were no other yachts on the dock, just a work barge and some old, rust-laden fishing boats, so the yacht stuck out like a diamond in a turd.

Rodriguez remained in the shadows watching the yacht for another half hour after he saw them stow the drum onboard. He had his men on call in case the yacht tried to leave right away, but based on what the dock master had told him, he didn't think they would leave tonight. He failed to notice the absence of shore power cables in the darkness. Rodriguez was reassured by the reported engine trouble. *It could be a lie,* he thought, *but why bother special ordering synthetic motor oil?* He believed that Billy would remove the cocaine from the drum and stow it onboard somewhere, probably over the next day or two, do the oil change, and then leave. A fifty-five gallon drum in plain view on the aft deck was far too obvious a location for any official to inspect. Rodriguez decided to give Marco and Billy a false sense of security and return just before daylight, at five thirty, with several well armed men and surround the yacht. He radioed his men and told them to rendezvous at the dock station at five a.m.

The next morning, Rodriguez finished his second cup of coffee just as his men arrived at the dock station at five a.m. He quickly briefed them, unlocked the gun cabinet, and removed three AK-47 assault rifles. He ordered Miguel and his cousin, Rafael, to run the police boat over to the marina where the yacht was docked five miles away. They would simultaneously descend on the yacht from land and sea in the pre-dawn light as quietly as possible. No need to alert the two men on the yacht. If there was any resistance, the criminals would simply be shot. "Estos hombres están armados y peligrosos. These men are armed and dangerous." After what all the men had witnessed just three nights earlier, there would be no hesitation in shooting the criminals this time. Rodriguez was counting on that.

Rodriguez kept in cell phone contact with Rafael so they could coordinate their approach to the yacht. They didn't use the police radio in the event the yacht or a news reporter had a scanner. Rodriguez stopped by the side of the road a half mile from the entrance to the marina and waited for Rafael to bring the police boat into position. Ten minutes later, Rafael called him from the channel entrance. Rodriguez hit the accelerator. Both the police boat and Jeep quietly sped into the marina without their lights flashing.

Rodriguez flew through the entrance to the marina and looked down in disbelief at the empty, yellow fifty-five gallon drum on the dock. The yacht was gone.

CHAPTER 29   *DESTINY* U.S.A.

Billy couldn't wait to get the hell out of Honduras. They had disconnected the shore power cables earlier in the day and run on battery power so that they could leave as quickly as possible. In the pitch black night, both men removed the aluminum stairs, started the engines and departed the dock without running lights. In an effort to leave the dock as quietly as possible, Billy purposely did not start the generators. He could have kissed the Italian yacht designer who ensured the engine room's soundproofing! The eighty-five foot yacht silently slipped away from the dock at two a.m. in total darkness.

The sun broke the ocean horizon at 5:30. The extremely bright reflection off the water illuminated the ocean for miles in all directions. Billy grabbed his polarized sunglasses and checked the radar, which showed no boats in a ten-mile radius. "Don't go counting your chickens, Billy," he said out loud.

Billy wanted to put some distance between them and Honduras as fast as possible, so he ran at twenty knots for the first two hours, and then slowed to around twelve knots. Based on the southbound fuel burn rate, he figured they'd have enough fuel to make it safely to Key West.

"Good morning, amigo," Marco said as he walked up to the fly bridge.

"Yes, it is a good morning," Billy replied. "Good weather and no targets on the radar. Marco, can you pump the auxiliary fuel from the drums into the main tank? We've burned enough fuel this morning to add 110 gallons."

"Em, sure thing, Amigo." Marco turned and started downstairs to the aft deck.

Marco used a small, portable pump and transferred the fuel in less than twenty minutes. He walked back up to the fly bridge. "Em, fuel is in the main tank now. Should I toss the drums over?"

"No. Let's hold on to those," Billy said. "Why don't you take it for a while? I'm going to try to get a little sleep."

Billy left Marco on the fly bridge and walked down toward the VIP to lie down. Sleep was impossible, so he checked the engines, ate some food and studied their position and heading. At 8:30 a.m. Billy returned to the fly bridge.

"Why don't you take a break, Marco? I'll take it for a few hours."

"Em, as you say, amigo."

Billy looked down and inspected the radar. He increased the gain and tried several different ranges to look for any possible targets. On the twenty-mile range, his heart skipped a beat when he saw a little green dot on the screen. Was it a boat, or had he increased the gain too much and it was just false positive noise on the radar? The target pulsed intermittently just outside the ten mile range ring; visible one second, then gone the next, and then visible. He checked the charts again to see if it could be a buoy of some sort, but the target was right in line with his course, directly behind the yacht, so he would have passed it an hour ago, but there had been nothing back there. *Right? Right.* He thought.

Billy continued to monitor the radar with the attention of an air traffic controller, adjusting the gain, fixated on the intermittent target.

Marco returned to the fly bridge and asked, "So, em, what you see?"

"It's a target on the radar and it's gaining on us," Billy replied. "It's a small boat. Anything with some size would not be so hard to spot on the radar. It's probably a fishing boat that happens to be on the same course as us." To be sure, Billy adjusted his course twenty degrees to starboard moving the compass heading from three-forty-five to zero-five degrees. "Now let's see what happens." Billy used the radar's variable range marker and electronic bearing line to monitor the target's position relative to theirs. Marco stood by anxiously, eyes glued to the radar screen, without saying a word.

Whatever was coming up behind them had to be going faster than they were. If not, Billy and Marco would never have seen it appear on the radar. Parallel courses on the open ocean happen occasionally, but it is unusual to be on a collision course with another boat in the middle of nowhere with 440 pounds of cocaine onboard.

One minute seemed like one hour. Five minutes felt like a month. Just after five long minutes, the target began to move off to the left of the screen. "Whew! Oh man, maybe now you can get some sleep! I'll yell if anything comes up." Billy said.

"Ok, emm, no problem," Marco replied. "I'll see you in a while."

Billy looked down at the radar in disbelief. The target had changed course and was now on a collision course, approaching from behind, a little over ten miles away.

Billy's smile faded and his heart began to race. Marco noticed his expression and didn't' move from the fly bridge. Billy felt beads of sweat forming on his forehead. *Keep it together*, he thought. *You don't even know what kind of boat this is. We're more than 90 miles off shore for Christ sake. It's probably just coincidence.*

But Billy could not argue with *the feeling* in his gut; that uncomfortable, nagging feeling that something was going to go very wrong. "Marco, rig up the fishing rods."

"Fishing Amigo, *now?*"

"Yes, Marco. That has to be a small boat back there and, if they have radar, there is no way they can calculate our speed with any accuracy on such a small radar screen."

Since the other vessel altered course it meant only one of two things: either the other boat was indeed a fishing boat, and it just coincidently turned twenty degrees in the same direction as *Destiny*, or it was the authorities of Costa Rica or Honduras who were pursuing them.

Billy took a fix on his position using the GPS and looked at the chart to determine exactly where he was. If it was the authorities back there, they would not be stupid enough to believe that an American yacht was fishing in 2,000 feet of water with no shelves or reefs or some sort of underwater topographic relief that would offer a fishing habitat. Billy took the longitude and latitude from the GPS and made an "X" on the chart with a pencil, noting the time just below it. Billy scanned the chart quickly to see if there was some direction they could head in that would give more credence to whole fishing charade. Much to Billy's surprise and satisfaction, he saw an upwelling about five miles up ahead, just north of his present course. The chart indicated that the sea floor rose from 1,900 feet to 400 feet.

"That's certainly a wall worth fishing." Billy said as he pointed out the spot on the chart to Marco.

"Ah, yes amigo." With that, Marco quickly escaped down the stairs from the fly bridge to get the fishing gear ready.

Marco attached rod holders to the handrail, rigged up the rods, and got the lines out quickly before someone could spot them with binoculars. Billy pressed the yacht's intercom button, "Marco, we need to have lines in the water now!"

"Right away!" Marco replied.

Billy watched as the target on the radar came closer and closer. The mysterious green dot was less than ten miles away and approaching fast. He wondered who and what these people were. *Pirates?* He thought. *No, we are in the Mid-Atlantic, and there hasn't been a pirated boat in these waters for years. It definitely has to be police of some sort. Coast Guard or military boat from either Costa Rica, Honduras, or Guatemala. Cuba is too far away and in the wrong direction.* "Shit. Stay cool, Billy," he said under his breath. Then he yelled, "Marco what's the status on the lines?"

"They are in the water, amigo."

Billy throttled the engines back to 800 rpm, which gave the yacht a speed of about seven knots through the water. Just about right for the fast, pelagic Caribbean fish, such as Wahoo. He switched on the auto pilot and scurried down to the aft deck to see what the other boat would see in about fifteen minutes. "Take the main helm station," Billy said to Marco. Marco started to walk away. "Marco, if we get boarded, you have to stay calm. If you panic or they smell panic, it's all over. Do you understand?" Marco's eyes revealed that he was nervous, but he just nodded and walked inside toward the main helm station.

The mysterious target on the radar was now visible on the horizon a little over three miles away; however, the type of boat could not be determined from that distance. Billy looked down at the binoculars, but paused. He didn't want to be seen looking through his binoculars at someone looking through binoculars back at him. Not a crime in and of itself, but it would be viewed as suspicious activity by any law enforcement agency.

There's no doubt about it now, Billy thought. *They are coming right toward us.* "Marco, grab the binoculars and see if you can tell what kind of boat it is without being seen." Marco grabbed the binoculars and crouched down inside the salon, resting his elbows on the couch. With his head just above the window he was able to get a fix on the approaching boat.

"Em, okay, they are coming this way. Yes, they have uniforms, of what kind I cannot tell." Billy was thinking, *we are in international waters. Who could be way out here, and what the hell do they want?*

As the small boat approached, Billy could make out four men onboard, and there was no mistake they were heading straight for *Destiny.* Billy did his best to complete the fishing ruse, which looked quite good, actually. Two boat rods were angled out off the port and starboard sides of the yacht, and one more rod was positioned in the center of the stern. As the mysterious boat approached, Billy stood up and waved franticly, as any avid fisherman would, to signal the small boat to get away from the trolling fishing gear trailing behind the yacht. The boat altered course slightly to come up alongside *Destiny.*

"Marco, go up to the fly bridge helm and slow us down to three knots. Let's see what these clowns want." Billy knew he had to maintain character and not give the slightest hint of guilt of any kind. "Keep cool Marco. We've done nothing wrong."

The small boat approached *Destiny,* running parallel to her starboard side, keeping the same speed of three knots. Billy could barely make out the scratched and faded law enforcement logo on the side of the twenty-eight foot boat. It read: *Guarde de Aqua Costa Honduras.* The Honduran

Coastal Police. Billy did his best to look surprised and puzzled as to the presence of the Honduran authorities way out here.

"Good morning. Habla Englaise?" Billy said.

"Yes, yes, Captain. I speak English." The man who was obviously in charge took two steps forward, hands on his belt, elbows out to his side in an effort to make his body mass larger than it was. *Similar to an animal moments before a fight,* Billy thought. *They inflate themselves in an effort to intimidate the other.* Being a fairly large man, Billy didn't need to artificially inflate himself. He could be intimidating when he needed to be, but rarely choose to do so. *Why fan the fire,* he thought. *Just let this guy do his routine, and we can get out of here.*

"What can I do for you Mr...?" Billy said.

"Constable Juan Rodriguez, of the Honduran Coastal Police," he said in heavily accented Spanish, "And there is plenty you can do for me, Captain." Senior Rodriguez took two more steps forward and pointed at two cleats on *Destiny.* "Captain, could we tie our boat to those two cleats and come aboard and have a word with you? You can keep this speed. We don't want to interrupt your fishing," Rodriguez said with an eerie, fake smile that revealed a gold front tooth.

"With all due respect, Constable," Billy said, "We are in international waters and I'm quite surprised to see you this far from land. I'll need to see your official identification papers, and you must explain why you would like to come aboard."

"Yes, of course, Captain," said Rodriguez with a wry smile. "That is a wise thing you say. But I can assure you, if we were pirates, you would be dead by now." This, Billy understood. Pirates were rare, but not unheard of in these waters. A twenty-first century pirate's objective was simple: board the boat, kill the inhabitants, and take the boat to a safe haven for selling on the third world black market. Or, like a hermit crab, keep the boat as the new pirate ship.

Rodriguez swaggered over to the center console of the small patrol boat and reached down into a water tight compartment located near the steering controls. He removed a large manila envelope and handed it to Billy. "Here you will find the information you need."

Billy took the envelope. "It will just take a minute."

"Take your time, amigo," Rodriguez said, again with the gold-toothed smile. Billy heard a couple of low grunting chuckles from the crewmen on the police boat as he walked across the aft deck and slid open the door to *Destiny.*

He closed the salon door behind him and walked over to the main navigation table to review the documents. Marco pressed the intercom button on the fly bridge control station and quietly spoke into the microphone, "Captain?"

Billy leaned forward into the helm station and pressed the talk button on the intercom, "It's okay Marco, it's just me," Billy whispered. "I'm reviewing their paperwork to see if they are legit. Keep your eye on them. If one of them makes a move to come on board, hit the throttle. We may have to let them onboard. Just keep us on course and speed, and I'll let you know what to do when the time comes."

"Okay, amigo. Standing by."

Billy slid the contents of the manila envelope onto the table and began to inspect the documents one by one. The first page consisted of a very official looking, multi-colored letter with the Honduran Government seal as the letterhead, and Honduran Coastal Police stamp at the bottom. It was written in Spanish, so Billy couldn't fully understand every word, but got the general meaning. It stated that the Honduran Government had given whatever authority was necessary to the Honduran Coastal Police and that vessels within their jurisdiction shall comply with those requests made by the Coastal Police. The second page looked quite similar in appearance, but differed in content. It stated that if the Coastal Police had reason to suspect that a vessel had left Honduran waters without paying export tax on items aboard the vessel it could pursue the vessel into international waters to redeem the export taxes, plus fines and penalties. Or, they could contact the government of the ship's hailing port for retribution and/or persecution of said vessel.

This started to make sense to Billy, and he breathed a sigh of relief. Maybe the Honduran authorities thought he left port without paying proper duty tax, and he'd have to bribe them now. He had no problem with that.

The next page caused Billy's mouth to drop and his stomach to flip over. It was an infrared, night photo of Marco and Billy loading the yellow fifty-five gallon drum onto the yacht.

"So, you see, Señor Forbes, unless that was diesel you were loading onto your yacht, we have a problem." Billy immediately shot a glance toward the stern, where Rodriguez had quietly jumped onboard and silently slipped through the salon door. Rodriguez confidently walked through the salon towards Billy, sat down across the table and said, "You see William Forbes, we have you. We have you loading the drum onto this yacht, and I'm here to take you back to Honduras."

Panic raced through Billy. What were the options? There were too many men to try to fight, and surely one would survive and live to tell other authorities of the events. No, fighting was too risky. Billy wanted to avoid violence if he could.

"Why would diesel be a problem?" Billy asked, buying time. It dawned on Billy that no mention of the drum's contents had been made yet. *Did Rodriguez know what was in the drum?* Billy thought, *Is he bluffing? All the way out here in the middle of the ocean? Is he fishing just like we are?*

Billy examined Rodriguez carefully as the Honduran official spoke, "Diesel would be no problem. Cocaine, on the other hand, that would be a problem." Billy studied his nemesis from point blank range. Puffy, bloodshot eyes stared back at him surrounded by wrinkled, yellowish skin. Rodriguez looked just like a criminal. Instantly Billy realized, *he knows. Damn it, he knows! The drug cartel owns the coastal police!*

Marco had warned him that there was an imperceptible line between authorities and criminals in Honduras. Billy gave Rodriguez a wide smile and said, "My friend, we would both have big problems if that was cocaine! But as you can see, we have no yellow drum onboard. Only the two empty drums on the aft deck." He did his best to sound sincere, but deep down he was just trying to buy some time and come up with a plan.

Rodriguez stared back into Billy's eyes with a deadly serious, cold glare and said loudly, "Then we have a problem."

"You can't think that we're drug smugglers!" Billy stretched his arms out wide, "That's ridiculous!"

Billy tried his best to act innocent, but his mind was racing wildly on what to do and say. *Could I bribe Rodriguez and his men? Or will they take me back to Honduras so I can spend the rest of my life in a God-forsaken prison?*

"That drum was filled with cocaine!" Rodriguez was getting more frustrated and his voice was getting louder and vindictive.

"Nonsense!" Billy yelled, his voice matching the volume and authority of Rodriguez. "That drum was full of diesel fuel! How the hell are we supposed to get back to America? We need extra diesel for the long voyage home!"

Outside on the Coastal Police boat, Chavez and Valdez could hear the argument growing between Billy and

Rodriguez and quickly jumped aboard *Destiny*. With their AK-47 rifles in hand, the two armed men briskly entered the salon.

"Mr. Forbes and I are just having a little conversation about the contents of the fifty-five gallon drum," Rodriguez said to his men. "The captain here says that it was full of diesel fuel." The two men at the door smiled at each other and then looked back at Billy with stern faces. Just then, Rodriguez started rapidly shouting orders in Spanish that Billy could not understand. Before he could even get a word out to object, the two men rushed forward and raised their weapons at Billy's head. "You will call your mate down here at once!" Rodriguez yelled.

"And if I refuse?" Billy asked.

"You are in a position to refuse nothing!" Rodriguez snarled. "I have total authority here and you will do as I say. Even if you disagree with my authority, you are outmanned, and more importantly, out gunned. Therefore, you will call your mate down here at once and stop this vessel."

Billy hesitated for a moment as he stared into the barrels of two AK-47 assault rifles, raising the tension in the room another notch. Sweat dripped down his face as he desperately tried to think of a plan. He knew these men would not hesitate to kill him. Rodriguez gave a short nod to Valdez, who was holding a gun at Billy's head. Valdez swung the butt of the rifle around so fast Billy did not have time to duck. The butt of the rifle struck him on the side of the head with a crack that sounded like dropping a dozen eggs on a granite floor.

When Billy came to, his hands were tied behind his back, and he was sitting back to back next to Marco. Marco felt Billy's head rise and whispered, "Are you okay, amigo?"

"Yes, but my head is pounding."

"I had no choice; they had a gun to my face."

"I know, I know, it's not your fault, Marco." Billy looked around and tried to figure out what the intruders were up to. There was a murmur of voices down in the guest cabins that Billy could not quite hear.

"Marco, where is everyone? How long have I been out?"

"Em, about ten minutes, I think. They searched the drums on deck, then there was much, em, commotion. Right now two men are checking the cabins below, and I think the leader is in the engine room with one other man. I haven't seen the two men in the engine room, but I could hear them. I don't think there is anyone left on their boat."

"Marco, let's see if we can get over to the intercom and hear what's going on in the engine room, but we must be quiet; we can't let the men downstairs hear us."

Back to back, both men pressed hard against each other and slowly rose up from sitting position to an awkward stance. They walked crab-like over toward the wheelhouse where the intercom was located. Since the intercom was a push-to-talk system, Rodriguez couldn't hear them, but Marco and Billy could listen through the microphone in the engine room. They bent down together and Billy pressed the listen button with his tongue while Marco held his ear as close to speaker as he could. Immediately, they both heard Rodriguez speaking through the intercom.

Billy saw Marco's eyes widen and his face turn ashen white as soon as he heard the voice through the small speaker. "What is it, Marco?" Billy asked.

"I know of this man speaking," Marco whispered. "He is a madman. I've seen him kill with my own eyes when I was a boy. He is the Devil himself, and works for another madman named Lopez. He must have seen the yacht in the harbor and now he wants it. This man, Lopez, he just takes what he wants and kills anyone in the way. He has many guns and has bought the police. They will kill us. For this I am sure. Our time has come."

Billy had never seen Marco look so scared, and the effect was contagious. Billy quickly felt himself starting to panic, but knew he couldn't afford to lose control, so he closed his eyes and concentrated, fighting both terror and his throbbing head. "Marco, we must find out what they want. What is he saying?"

Marco closed his eyes and listened intently. "Rodriquez must be on the phone with someone, because the conversation is, em, one-sided," he said softly. Then he continued to slowly whisper the English translation: "I don't know. I've looked all over the yacht. Yes, I know that, but I haven't found it yet. No, there was diesel in the drums, but they're empty too. He might have seen us coming and thrown it overboard. I tried, but he won't talk. Not yet, they're both still alive. If you want the yacht, then we have to show some signs of a fight, because a lot of locals saw the yacht at the marina, and if we come back in with this nice new yacht and two dead men, there will be too many questions from local people. We'll lose the faith of men at the dock, and I don't have to tell you how much we need them."

Billy's mind was racing and his thoughts were flying through his head at the speed of light. There was no way out. Nothing was clear. *Think, think, think! You can get out of this.*

They heard one of the men down below coming up the stairs, so Marco and Billy quickly made their way back to their old spot. Billy pretended to wake up in front of one of the men, looked up and said, "Why are you doing this? What do you want?"

"Shut up or I will knock your teeth out this time!" Valdez said, as he walked past them and went out the salon door towards the aft deck.

"Marco, do you really think they will kill us?"

"I have no doubts. That is how Lopez works. At first, I bet he just wanted to steal the cocaine back, but once he saw the yacht he wanted it, too. Lopez will give some cocaine to the police, and they will make up a story of how they busted a big coke deal. The police chief will be made a hero, but all who know his name will know the truth. If we go back to Honduras, we will not live. Lopez can't have the yacht if we're alive to talk. This much I know."

Just then, Rodriguez strutted through the aft deck door and yelled, "Valdez, get them in the engine room, now!" Rodriguez turned, bent down and spoke directly into Billy's face as they were being hauled upright, "I have spoken to my superiors, and they are convinced that the drugs are on the yacht, so we are taking you back to Honduras where we will tear the yacht apart."

Billy screamed, "But we are in international waters, you have no right to do this!"

Rodriguez laughed so hard that spittle hit Billy's face and said, "Heh, you stupid fuck-king American! Look around you! No right!? Ha! Who will save you now? Fuck-king *American* Coast Guard? They won't come down here, *noooo*, too dangerous. But you? No! You come down here and buy drugs. What you think will happen, eh? We get back to Honduras, you go to jail, and we take yacht. How you like that? Stupid fuck-king John Boy! But we have nice jails in Honduras, nicer than U.S. *Trust me.*"

Billy and Marco were untied, and with guns pointed at the base of their skulls, they walked outside to the aft deck and started to climb down the ladder to the engine room. Once in the engine room, they were ordered to sit down. Then, they were tied up back to back at the wrists with their arms threaded around a stainless steel vertical pole. Valdez looked down at the two bound men, spat on Billy, kicked him in the ribs, and said, "Piece of sheet."

Billy coughed as the boot went into his ribs and bent over, pretending it hurt more than it did. The men left Billy and Marco and climbed up the ladder to join the others. The engine room door made a loud thud as it came flush with the watertight frame. Billy and Marco heard the swivel latch seal them to their fate.

Outside, the wind was slowly beginning to build.

The two men remained silent in the engine room and a huge wave of emotion swept over Billy as he sat tied up next to Marco. He tried to use the scant mental energy still remaining in a positive way and think of a means of escape, but his mind kept telling him what a fuck-up he was and how bad things really were.

Marco broke the silence and said, "They will surely kill us. I saw Rodriguez shoot an unarmed man in the head when I was only twelve years old."

"Why didn't they do it yet?" Billy asked.

"Amigo, many people saw us in Puerto Lempira. If Rodriguez comes back with just a yacht and two dead bodies, the local fishermen will not stand for it and revolt. He's trying to figure out what to do. If he can find the cocaine, then he doesn't have to kill us, but we go to jail. If he can't find it, then he kills us, makes it look like a fight, and maybe plants something on the yacht. Either way it doesn't look good for us, my friend."

Completely dejected, Billy said, "I'm sorry I got you into this, Marco."

"Well, I am a grown man and could have said no."

Billy tried so desperately to think of a way out, his head felt as if it would explode. He already had a severely throbbing headache from the guard's rifle butt to his head, but now, every beat of his heart felt like a jack hammer to his brain. Then he remembered his multi tool knife attached to his belt.

"Marco, can you reach my Leatherman? It's tucked in under my shirt on my belt near my right hip. They didn't see it on me when they tied us up."

Marco squirmed in place. "I'm not sure I can reach it. Am I close?" Marco moved both of their tied hands together as he slid his hand around Billy's belt.

"You're close!"

"Yes, yes, I can feel it, but I can't quite reach the top. Ahh! So close!"

"You only need another inch, Marco, you can get it. What if we try to move together?" With every ounce of remaining energy, both men strained against the rope as it cut into their skin.

"Yes, yes, I feel the Velcro! I can get it!"

"Be careful, don't drop it."

Sweat dripped from Marco's forehead as he blindly placed his index and middle fingers on the knife, and began to lift it up. Billy could feel the knife being slowly wedged out from his waist and tried to squirm in unison with Marco to help him remove it. Just as the knife slid out of the top of the sheath, it fell, but Marco quickly pinned it to Billy's body with his index finger.

Marco gasped, "Don't move!"

Billy sat motionless as Marco carefully maneuvered the knife down Billy's side the way a blind man reads Braille. At last Marco felt the cool metal of the folded knife in his palm.

"Got it!" he said.

"Can you open it?" Billy asked. Both men were sweating in the hot engine room and Marco's palms were slippery. Trying to open a Leatherman with one hand resembled opening a flip phone with one hand. You need a chin, or a tooth to grip one side and flip out the blade.

Marco squirmed and said angrily, "Damn! I'm almost there, amigo!"

"Marco, take a deep breath and concentrate." Billy could feel the loops of rope tighten against his chest as Marco filled his lungs. There was a brief pause, and then the rope tension began to ease slightly as Marco exhaled a long, deep breath. Ever so slowly, Marco pushed the folded knife against Billy's body and hooked his thumbnail into the grip slit for the blade. When the blade was half way up, Marco repositioned his hand so that the knife was in his palm.

"I've got it, amigo!" Marco moved the blade back and forth over the rope. He couldn't cut at a perpendicular angle; rather he was cutting almost lengthwise along the rope. Billy felt the tension of his right hand ease as the braids began to sever.

Just then the engine room door opened up above them. Billy froze as he heard the heavy boots of the men coming down the ladder.

"Well, well, nice and warm I see!" Rodriguez said mockingly as he, and two of his men, stood over them looking down in apparent disgust. "I just wanted to let you know that we found the cocaine, and you are going to jail. You are under arrest, and we are confiscating the yacht and bringing you back to Honduras for prosecution."

Billy knew this was a lie. What was Rodriguez trying to do?

"Or maybe we shoot you, eh? What do you say to that, my friend? Yes, I think this is good idea. We shoot you, so you don't rot in our jail, eh? Then we say, 'You fight us,' see? And all is good for me with the peoples of my town, yes? Yes, I like."

Billy looked directly at Rodriguez and yelled, "You didn't find the coke, because there is none on the yacht!"

"American FOOL! You think I won't find it? It's just a matter of time. But I think I will enjoy watching you die. Yes, that will be nice. I don't want to shoot you down here. No, no, we might damage these fine engines with a bullet that goes through your soft American head. No! We will shoot you where only the sea can have the bullets, yes?"

Billy knew that he had to do something now, or he was going to die. He pretended to be stoic. "You better shoot us up on deck, or you might start a fire down here." When Billy said the word, "fire," he pinched Marco with his left hand and hoped Marco understood. If not, they would both be dead in a less than a minute.

Rodriguez gave the order, "Get them up on deck, now!" As Chavez reached down to untie them, Billy lunged toward Rodriguez and knocked him down. At the same instant, Marco stood up and jetted his elbow into Rafael Chavez's jaw. He had been aiming for his neck, but Chavez ducked his head at the last instant.

Billy saw Valdez reach for his holster with his right arm, but Marco still had the knife in his hand and made a quick, hard sweep over Valdez's forearm with the sharp blade.

"Ahhhhhhh!" Filled the engine room, as the gun dropped from Valdez's hand, scattered on the metal floor, and fell into the bilge. Valdez staggered in shock while holding up his right wrist with his left hand, staring at blood pouring from his arm.

Marco dove towards the small door that exited out of the engine room into the rudder room. Billy caught the movement out of the corner of his eye as he was shimmying up the ladder to the main deck.

There were only two ways out of the engine room and Marco and Billy were at the doors of each exit. Rodriguez, being older and fatter than the other men, was slower to react, but had just enough time to get one shot off. The bullet missed Billy's head by a fraction of an inch just as he slammed the engine room door shut.

Billy could hear someone climbing up the ladder. He held the door latch tightly with one hand, and pulled the handle of the fire extinguishing system with his other hand. Immediately, he heard the loud hiss of carbon dioxide as the 200-pound cylinder began discharging the deadly gas. The men in the engine room screamed briefly as the reality of their situation literally hit them in the face.

Billy heard pounding from the other side of the door and could feel the latch handle trying to move in his hands, but he held it with all his might. It was a morbid sensation; he would never forget it. Then he heard the "click" of the firing pin from a pistol. The CO_2 fire extinguishing system was designed to eliminate oxygen and stop a fire. Since there was no oxygen in the engine room, the gun could not fire, and the men were dying of asphyxiation. Marco *had* understood. Billy's mind was racing. *Where's the last man? Is Marco okay? Did anyone get out of the engine room?* The banging on the other side of the door became slower. The lack of oxygen was taking its toll.

Just then Billy heard an outboard motor turn over trying to start.

"Shit!" he yelled. It was the last of Rodriguez's men. Miguel Chavez had jumped into the police boat and was starting the engine. Billy could still feel Rodriguez on the other side of the engine room door, desperately trying to open it. Billy had to hold onto the latch to keep the door shut, or the engine room would be flooded with oxygen and the men would revive. Then, he heard the outboard motor start.

"Shit!" Billy's mind was racing wildly. *If that man gets away, we'll be killed for sure.* Billy screamed, "Marco, get that guy!" Marco ran around the aft deck towards the sound of the motor and just as he stuck his head out to see where the police boat was, Miguel Chavez fired his pistol. The bullet missed Marco's head by less than an inch, spraying splinters of fiberglass into his face and eyes. The impact of the gunshot sent Marco flying down to the deck. Chavez hit the throttle and the police boat took off at full speed.

When Billy heard Marco hit the deck after the shot, he let go of the door and ran around to the other side of the yacht. "Holy shit, Marco! Are you okay?"

"Yes, it just missed my head. I have fiberglass in my eye, but I'm okay."

"Come on!" Billy shouted as he helped Marco up and they made their way into the main salon.

It seemed as if Billy was in another world, as if he was looking down on the whole scene from another dimension. Time was simultaneously racing by and standing still. With every second, the police boat was getting farther away, but Billy couldn't start the engines because the fire system had sucked all the oxygen out of the engine room. *How much time has gone by? Are all three men really dead? Where is the police boat? Shit, shit, shit!!*

Suddenly, the VHF radio crackled to life: "Mayday, mayday, mayday! Se trata de Miguel Chavez con la Policía Costera de Honduras. Estamos bajo ataque! Cualquier buques en la zona responda! This is Miguel Chavez with the Honduran Costal Police. We are under attack! Any vessel in the area respond!" Every passing second was critical. If someone heard that transmission, Billy and Marco would be caught and executed.

They had to get the police boat immediately.

"Shit! Marco, turn the engine room blower fans on and take all the weapons from Rodriguez and his men."

"Yes!" Marco said, and dashed out the salon door toward the engine room.

Marco tried to open the engine room door, but the handle motion was very sluggish. Something on the other side impeded motion of the latch. Stepping back, he kicked the latch handle with one swift kick. A distinct *snap* emitted from the behind the engine room door, followed by two muted thuds, like dropping a bag of wet laundry down the stairs. When he opened the engine room door and stuck his head inside, air rushed by his head as carbon dioxide from the fire extinguishing system reacted with the atmospheric oxygen all around him.

Marco looked down at the bottom of the ladder steps. Rodriguez was lying haphazardly on the floor of the engine room with one arm unnaturally twisted behind his back, obviously broken. Rodriguez must have been stuck on the other side of the door with his arm wedged onto the latch handle when Marco kicked it open.

Taking a deep breath, Marco climbed down the ladder, past Rodriguez, and quickly looked around the engine room. Two men lay on the floor unconscious with eyes bulging from their sockets and discolored blue faces.

He leaned over and flipped on the circuit breakers for the blower fans. Immediately, the large fan blades started pumping fresh air into the engine room. Marco tried to take a breath, but the carbon dioxide level was still too high. He moved his head into the air stream created by the blower fans and took a deep breath. Moving very quickly, he opened up the electrical tool box and removed three large, plastic wire ties. Then he rolled all three men onto their stomachs and used the wire ties as hand cuffs behind their backs. He removed the remaining side arms and scurried up the engine room ladder. Marco burst through the salon doors and yelled, "Go!"

Billy had already turned the ignition switches on and was waiting for Marco's cue to press the start buttons. Both engines roared to life and Billy yelled, "Come on!" as he slammed the throttles down to full speed. The eighty-ton yacht didn't jump up on a plane nearly as fast as the police boat, but it could out run the smaller boat over time in rough seas. The wind was stronger now, creating waves in excess of four feet. It had taken Marco and Billy three agonizing minutes to get the yacht moving. At twenty knots, three minutes gave the police boat a full one mile lead. *Destiny* planed off, and Billy could see the police boat bobbing up and down intermittently through the large waves in the distance.

The VHF radio squawked again, "Mayday, mayday, mayday! Se trata de Miguel Chavez con la policía hondureña Costal. Estamos bajo ataque! Los buques en la zona responden!"

Destiny bashed full throttle into the waves at twenty-four knots as she slowly gained on the smaller boat.

"Marco when we get close enough to shoot, take him out."

Marco picked up the AK-47 assault rifle from the salon floor and headed to the fly bridge. Chavez looked back, saw them gaining, and began to fire his pistol. The shots were wild. In the smaller boat Chavez was bouncing all around in four-foot seas at twenty knots. It was like trying to shoot a tin can while riding a bull. *Destiny* provided a far steadier ride. Billy could definitely feel the waves, but the large yacht's motion was predictable and smooth. Marco steadied himself on the fly bridge and tried to get into sync with the waves and rocking of the yacht. He could see Chavez now. The smaller boat bounced wildly in the waves with spray flying all around it. Marco took aim and fired. The shot hit the boat to the left of Chavez, sending splinters of wood into the air. Chavez turned and unloaded the remaining rounds from his pistol.

Marco heard one round hit the yacht somewhere in the bow. They were closing in on the smaller boat now. Marco carefully synchronized the motion of the two boats as best he could. Aiming for body mass, he fired again. Marco saw a piece of the outboard engine soar into the air. Miraculously, Marco hit the electronic distribution box on the outboard, and the engine stalled out immediately. The police boat stopped so quickly that *Destiny* was going to run right over it.

"Shiiiiiiiit!" Billy screamed as he turned the wheel hard over.

Destiny rolled hard to port, missing the police boat by inches. A massive wall of water fifteen feet high, weighing eighty tons, engulfed the small boat, swamping it instantly. When the second wave from *Destiny's* wake hit the police boat, it rolled over and bobbed upside down in the water. There was no sign of Chavez.

Billy turned the yacht around and approached the overturned police boat with caution. He throttled back to neutral, and ran up to the fly bridge to see what the hell was going on. "What happened?" Billy asked.

"I hit the engine, and it stopped."

"Is he alive?"

"I think he's out of ammo, but I never hit him," Marco said.

Both men surveyed the area around the small boat. "I don't see him," Billy replied.

All around them, the wind was growing stronger and the sea was building. Even the large yacht was feeling the waves now. Billy and Marco were getting whipped side to side on the fly bridge as they rocked broad side to the wind. They watched the small boat rock in the waves for almost five minutes with no signs of life.

Billy knew what they had to do. "Marco, get the weight belts from the scuba locker. There are two in there, and I have a belt with my gear in the bow. Meet me in the engine room.

"Yes, amigo."

Trying to get Rodriguez and the other two men out of the engine room was not easy. It was just too difficult to lift the lifeless bodies up the ladder. Instead, they had to shimmy the bodies through the rudder room, where Marco had hid when the CO_2 fire system went off.

Billy pulled as Marco pushed, and slowly they dragged the three lifeless bodies through the rudder room, and onto the aft deck swim platform. The waves were now five to six feet, and water was splashing all around their feet as they fastened weight belts around the dead men's waists. Billy grabbed the hands and Marco took the feet, and one by one, they heaved two of the men over the stern of the yacht.

Just as they were about to heave the last body over, a large wave hit the stern knocking Billy and Marco off their feet onto Rodriguez's lifeless body. For what seemed like eternity, the three men were entangled in four feet of water rolling around on the swim platform. Billy gasped a breath of air, opened his eyes, and saw a gold tooth and Rodriguez's lifeless blue face inches from his own. He grabbed the hand rail with one hand and reached out for Marco with the other. Their hands met just as water receded off the swim platform and sucked Rodriguez into the abyss. It seemed as if Rodriguez was reaching out from the grave and trying to pull them down with him. Billy helped Marco up onto his feet, and the two men made their way off the swim platform, up the steps onto the aft deck. Billy bent over and put his hands on his knees and his ass against the side of the yacht to keep from falling over. He could feel himself breathing hard. His head was throbbing, but he knew that they had to keep moving.

Billy gave Marco several instructions for getting the yacht ready to bounce around in the rough seas. Marco ran bungee cords through all of the cabinet and drawer handles in the galley, and tied the refrigerator doors shut to prevent their contents from becoming one big galley floor jambalaya.

Billy fired up the engines and got his bearings. They had drifted several hundred yards while taking care of the bodies, but he located the overturned police boat in the distance. He inspected the chart and saw that the depth was a little more than 3,000 feet in the area around them. Even if someone found the smaller boat, it would look like an accident. It would be logical to think that the small boat had engine trouble, stalled out, and became broadside to the waves. It would not take very long in rough seas for the small police boat to become swamped full of sea water, and the men drowned. It happened every year. It seemed a more likely scenario than a shootout over drugs where all of the Honduran officials were killed. In fact, if no one were alive to tell the story, the closest someone might come to the truth would be foul play. And that was very large field of play in Honduras.

As they approached the overturned police boat, Marco asked if they should shoot some holes in the hull to let the air out so it would sink more quickly. There was no sign of the last man near the overturned boat. The ocean was rough, maybe he had become separated, and it seemed that if he were alive, he would not be able to survive long in the large, crashing waves.

Billy's thoughts bounced around like the boat itself in the high seas. *No one could find this boat in 3,000 feet of water. Well, maybe the noted oceanographer, Bob Ballard, could, but would the fiberglass hull even register on side scan sonar? The engine would. Shit, well it sure as hell was less likely to be seen way down there at the bottom of the sea versus up here on the surface.* "Good idea, Marco. Go ahead and put some holes in the hull, and then throw all the weapons overboard." Marco returned with one of the guns from Rodriguez's men and fired three shots into the bottom of the overturned boat. Then he tossed all of the confiscated guns into the ocean. Most likely, the boat would have sunk in time, but now, with three gaping holes through its hull, it would sink right away.

Billy plotted a course and pushed the engines up to 1100 rpm. They would not be able to cruise back to the U.S. any faster for two main reasons. First, the Caribbean Sea was now very rough with waves exceeding eight feet, and *Destiny* couldn't do twenty knots for any length of time in seas much over four feet, never mind eight. Secondly, they had to conserve fuel. The range of the yacht was about 400 nautical miles at their cruising speed of twenty knots. They needed to more than double that in order to refuel in Key West. They would have to find fuel somewhere closer, but where?

Billy began to replay the events that had just occurred over and over in his mind, and thought, *if anyone heard that mayday call, the local authorities will be on full alert. Any fool can see the two bullet holes in* Destiny. *We need to avoid Cozumel and the whole Yucatan Peninsula. We'll have to refuel in the Cayman Islands. Hopefully, they didn't hear the mayday.*

Billy did a quick check on the chart and changed the heading from three-forty-five to zero-five degrees, straight to the Cayman Islands. With the new heading, the yacht was ramming right into the oncoming seas. The bow would rise up over and then the yacht would slide down the wave with so much momentum that the bow would nose dive into the next wave sending a huge spray, thirty feet high over the fly bridge. Once Billy got the yacht stabilized and heading on the right course, he adjusted the speed so that the yacht was making headway into the wind with the least amount of pounding from the waves.

The two men did not speak as they bashed into the waves for several hours, until Billy turned and said, "Marco, take the helm for a few minutes while I check the weather."

"Okay amigo, as you say."

As Billy rushed down stairs from the fly bridge, he realized that he hadn't checked the weather since the day before they left Key West, five days ago. In an instant, Billy got *the feeling*, a sensation he couldn't describe to others, but he knew it well. Even though he had felt the profound trepidation only twice in his life, there was no mistaking the bone-chilling sensation of *the feeling* that something disastrous was about to occur.

CHAPTER 30   THE FEELING

The last time Billy had *the feeling* had been eight years ago when *Destiny* was hauled out at the yacht yard. With the yacht out of the water, there had been no air conditioning inside the yacht, and in the Florida heat, it felt like a greenhouse inside the salon.

     The engine room provided only sparse relief from the heat due to the massive blower fans, and Billy had spent the whole day down there sweating away. As he finished up the job, he realized that it was almost six o'clock. The yard was closed when he climbed up out of the engine room, so he had to walk around the locked fence to get to his car. He had made arrangements to stay aboard a friend's yacht while his yacht was 'on the hard.' During the fifteen-minute drive to his friend's yacht, Billy got *the feeling* that he needed to call his parents. Not just a, "Hi Mom and Dad. Haven't talked to you in a while," type call, he needed to call them *right now.*

     Billy picked up his cell and called the land line to his parent's house in Palm Beach, Florida. When his father answered on the second ring, Billy knew something was wrong. "Where are you?" His father asked with no introduction.

     "What's wrong Dad?"

     "Mom's just had an episode!"

Billy told his father to hang up and dial 911; he would be there as soon as he could. Just seconds earlier, Billy's father had found his mother in the bathroom and was carrying her to bed when Billy called. There was no coincidence in the timing of Billy's phone call; his father just happened to be in arm's reach of the phone while holding his mother. The emotional panic and fright that his father felt were somehow conveyed to Billy from seventy-five miles away, creating *the feeling*. Billy drove straight from the yard in Fort Lauderdale to the hospital in Palm Beach. His mother had had a stroke.

As Billy hurried toward the helm station, he felt a surge of guilt as he thought about his parents. They would be beyond disappointed with him. He knew what they would have said to him if they were alive. He sighed and switched channels on the VHF radio to see if he could get any weather forecasts, but the yacht was now more than 100 miles off shore, in the middle of the Caribbean Sea, so nothing but static belched from the small speaker.

He walked back to the salon and a wave of apprehension swept over him as he turned on the satellite television. It only took one look at the high surf, swaying palm trees and rain spattered television camera lens for Billy to understand where *the feeling* was coming from.

Hurricane Tanya.

Never in his life had Billy experienced such a sensation of impending doom. *The feeling* had graduated to panic, and he was trying very hard just to keep it together. There was simply no way out. They couldn't radio for help. Who would help? They were way out in the middle of the Caribbean Sea, hundreds of miles from land, and way out of range of the U.S. Coast Guard. Even if the Coast Guard did help, it would mean air lifting them and leaving the yacht adrift.

His boss would want to know what the hell he was doing 400 miles south of Cuba, miles from the Yucatan Peninsula, and there would certainly be an investigation. If the yacht sank, he was liable for seven-point-five million dollars. If it didn't sink, the officials were bound to find the cocaine, and he would be arrested. There would also be serious damage to the yacht and the ensuing litigation. That was the best case scenario. Otherwise, he would be arrested and charged with murder.

After Marco had done everything he could to secure the boat, Billy asked him to take the helm for a minute. Billy had to hold the handrail tight as he staggered down the stairs. He bounced off one wall and stumbled into his room as the yacht rolled hard to one side, and collapsed onto the side of his bed.

Billy's mind had produced so many emotions in the last twenty-four hours that he felt absolutely numb. He couldn't finish a thought to its end. Time seemed to be flying by and standing still at the same moment. Every time he thought of something that needed to be done, his mind raced off in another direction. All he wanted to do was curl up under his covers and pass out, but there was no way he could sleep. He felt control slipping away, and began to panic.

Then, as if the extreme pressure in his head caused a synapse in his brain to explode, he had a vivid flash back to an experience he had nearly twenty years earlier.

CHAPTER 31   FOG

One summer when he was home from college, Billy and a
friend, who was just out of Navy boot camp, decided to go
scuba diving. It was mid-July, and the north Atlantic had
warmed up from downright freezing to just damn cold. "A
balmy fifty-eight degrees, Mike," Billy said, as he took the
thermometer out of the water.

"Great," Mike responded unenthusiastically.

It was fifty-eight degrees at the surface, where the sun
had warmed the water, but it would be about five degrees
colder at a depth of sixty feet where they were headed. Billy
had a ten pot lobster trap license with a diving stamp, so he
could catch lobsters while scuba diving in Massachusetts
waters. Although the water was cold, both men were looking
forward to diving at a new spot, catching some "bugs," and
boiling them up in the back yard over a few cold beers–all the
ingredients of a perfect summer day.

The morning Billy and Mike were scheduled to dive, a
small front moved in. Billy wanted to wait and see what the
weather did. If it was just a squall, they could wait it out and
push their dive time back a couple of hours and be safe. If it
was something stronger, then the last thing Billy wanted was to
get out to the dive site and have the weather hit the fan, or

worse, come up from the dive in the middle of a raging lightning storm.

As it turned out, it was just a small summer squall that dropped a fair amount of rain, but passed the area quickly. After waiting out the squall, Billy jumped aboard the family boat and picked Mike up at the commercial dock right next to the Driftwood Restaurant in Old Town, Marblehead, Massachusetts.

They loaded their dive gear onto the twenty-three foot Mako center console motor boat and headed out of Marblehead Harbor towards Halfway Rock.

Billy figured they would dive the Gooseberry Islands. There were two Gooseberry Islands, north and south, and he hadn't dove either one yet. He wasn't sure which one they would dive, but they'd check out the conditions when they got out there and pick the better of the two islands. On the way out of the harbor, the air was full of moisture from the recent rain, but the sun was trying to break through and it seemed like it was going to be a pretty nice day after all.

Mike was a strong, well built man and had done a little diving in his brief stint with the Navy. Billy assumed that since Mike had done some Navy diving, he had decent underwater skills and would make a good dive partner.

The ocean was flat calm, and they had a nice, easy run out to the Gooseberry Islands. Billy decided to drop the anchor at the north Gooseberry Island and dive the drop-off on the southeast side. In the past, he had had some decent luck with his lobster traps there and hoped they would find a few nice "keepers" for their afternoon feast. Due to the lack of any breeze, the tide was the only thing affecting movement of the boat while at anchor. The tide had turned about an hour ago and was starting to ebb, so the boat swung slowly with the tidal current towards the south.

The anchor seemed to be holding, and Billy became quite hot in the direct sun through his thick neoprene wetsuit.

"How you doing? 'Bout all set?" Billy asked.

"Yeah, just my BC vest and I'm good to go." Billy gave Mike a hand with his buoyancy compensator vest, and soon, they were sitting on opposite sides of the stern of the boat looking at each other ready to go over backwards into the water.

"How much air do you have?" Billy asked.

"Little over 3,000 psi."

"Yeah, me too. Okay, we'll follow the anchor line down and check the hold and then I thought we'd check out the drop off to the southeast."

"Sounds good to me."

"If we get separated," Billy said, "look around for me for three to five minutes before surfacing."

"Okay, Bill."

They placed their masks on and checked the air flow through their regulators one last time. With a nod to each other, they leaned back, falling into the water about mid revolution backwards. The water felt good, cold, but refreshing.

The visibility was extremely poor. Billy and Mike almost hit each other, getting together under the boat. They swam up to the bow, found the anchor line and began their descent. *Damn, this is bad visibility,* Billy thought. *It must be only three or four feet!* As they followed the half inch thick nylon anchor line down towards the bottom, an eerie feeling began to creep into Billy. As the boat rocked gently in the water, the anchor line tightened and recoiled like a long, white serpent in the murky water.

Billy kept checking his depth gauge with one hand and kept the other hand on the anchor line as he continued to descend. He couldn't see anything but a cloudy haze of water.

All of a sudden, out of nowhere, the ocean floor appeared. Dark brown seaweed swayed gently from a rock right in front of him. The bottom, what he could see of it, consisted of small, fist sized gravel with some larger one-to two-foot boulders intermixed along the bottom. He swam along the bottom, gratefully following the anchor line until he came upon the six feet of chain attached to the anchor. Billy stopped and turned around, but couldn't see Mike. He sat on the ocean floor, bent his knee, and pulled his foot back and forth to determine the visibility. He could not see his fin when his leg was outstretched all the way. He could only make out a hazy glob until his fin was three feet away. *This is going to be tough*, he thought. Mike came into focus and they looked at the anchor together. It was set fast with little chance of coming loose, so Billy gave Mike the okay sign, and they started to swim off toward the southeast.

Billy understood why the visibility was so poor. Over the years on the water, he had observed the phenomenon several times from above. In the second or third week of July, the water warmed up to the point where the underwater flora released their equivalent of pollen. The temperature of the water had to coincide with the correct moon phase and then all of the seaweed and kelp released a tiny, yellowish puree en masse, drastically reducing underwater visibility. It took a couple of weeks before the visibility would get back to eight to ten feet.

Billy and Mike were swimming side by side, but without constantly looking at each other, they kept getting separated. They would wait a few minutes, and if they didn't find the other, they would go to the surface.

After the third trip to the surface, Mike said, "The viz really sucks!"

"Yeah," Billy replied, "I know. I can't look for lobsters and you at the same time. We're only in fifty or sixty feet of water, so if we lose each other again, let's just stay down and we'll see each other back on the boat with 500 pounds of air, okay?"

Mike nodded, and they descended back down to the bottom.

It wasn't thirty seconds before Billy was on his own. He kept swimming southeast following his compass which was the third in a string of gauges attached to his tank, including air pressure and depth.

Billy swam through the applesauce visibility almost the way a person walks during a blackout. He was staring intently into the immediate distance when a massive, ten-foot high rock instantly appeared directly in front of him. As the shock of surprise began to subside, an eerie feeling crept through his body as he watched the dark brown seaweed attached to the rock slowly sway back and forth with the ocean current. He took several minutes to gather his wits and calm down, and then continued swimming.

Mike was not doing so well. The beers from the night before were making him feel sick and he was a little freaked out not knowing where he was in such limited visibility. He swam around under the boat and didn't let the anchor line out of his sight. Maybe he had exaggerated his diving experience to Billy, who was nowhere to be seen.

Billy followed the contour of the bottom staying about fifty-to sixty-feet deep. He was able to catch two lobsters and some mussels, which improved his mood, and was actually singing to himself as he swam along. *I'd like to be, under the sea...*

With 1,000 pounds of air left in his tank, he decided to go up to the surface and take a look around. It might be a long swim back to the boat, and he wanted to get his bearings. Billy rose slowly to the surface, ascending at about half the speed of his exhaled bubbles, and wondered how Mike was doing.

When Billy surfaced, he looked around, but could not see a thing. There was dense fog in all directions. He turned his head again and again, but could see nothing but thick fog, 360 degrees of zero visibility. Pure, eerie stillness enveloped the air, however, a thousand thoughts flashed through his head. *Where's the boat? Where am I? Did Mike make it back to the boat? Oh shit. Don't get hit by a boat. You won't hear them coming.*

"Oh shit, oh shit! Mike!" *What was that?* "Miiiiiiiiiiike!" Billy yelled at the top of his lungs. "Miiiiiiike!!" He thought he might have heard something, but the sound was barely on the threshold of hearing. Just at that moment, a seagull flew by and Billy wondered if the sound he heard was a squawking gull. *Follow the bird,* he thought. *What's if he's more lost than me? Shit! Do I go back down and try to head back the way I came?*

Billy had moved his mask up to his forehead to see more clearly. Now, he reached for it to replace it. But it was gone. The reality hit him hard. When he was listening for Mike, he had moved his hood behind his right ear. In the process, he must have knocked the dive mask off which meant it had sunk to the bottom. Startled by the fog and ensuing adrenaline overload, he hadn't even felt it slip off his head through the thick neoprene hood.

No choice now, he thought, *I've got to stay up on the surface.* Billy's mind was still racing. *I wouldn't hear a sail boat coming. There's no wind, so they'd have to be under motor power, but still, I wouldn't hear them, and I can't dive down if I have do. Where the fuck am I that Mike can't hear me? Is he okay? Oh shit. What if he's lost? Wait, I came up with 1,000 pounds of air, and we said 500, so maybe he's still down? Oh, shit.* "Miiiiiiiike!!" Intense, deafening silence was Mother Nature's only reply.

Billy pulled his hood down around his neck so he could hear without a layer of water filled neoprene over his ears. *Keep it together and don't freak out. You're not going to die. You could last a couple of days out here if you had to. You've got food.*

He knew from growing up on the water that Boston fog in the summer usually didn't stick around for more than a day or two at the most. It wasn't like Maine fog that could last more than a week. He kept trying to keep his mind clear and not panic, for he knew that once panic started, it slid very quickly into an emotional avalanche, and then he would be in very serious trouble.

As thoughts cascaded through Billy's mind, a lobster pot bobbed into view. Billy grabbed it by the wooden dowel and tied the line to his ankle. Then he inflated his BC vest as much as he could. He waited there getting control of himself, and tried to figure out what to do. He cursed himself for not having a dive watch because trying to gauge time was nearly impossible. A real second in time oscillated between the stillness of the fog and the drum roll of his heartbeat. He started to count out loud," One-one thousand, two-one thousand..." just to occupy his mind and slow his thoughts down so he could think. *OKAY, I'm tied to a lobster trap and I have mussels and lobsters in my catch bag that I can eat if I have to. I'm warm enough and could definitely last through a July night if I had to stay out here.*

Billy wasn't sure how long he'd been tied to the lobster trap. He looked at the fog and how it slowly drifted across the water. He also noticed how hard the line from the lobster trap was tugging at his ankle. The tide was moving pretty swiftly, and he wasn't sure how far out the tide had already dragged him before he surfaced. He thought he heard the faint crash of the ocean washing up onto the island in the distance, but which way? Is the density of the fog uniform, or did the fog make it seem like the sound was coming from that direction?

After what seemed like hours, Billy decided he had to do something. He untied the lobster pot and started swimming toward the sound of ocean washing ashore. He swam for a long, long time and as more and more time passed, his mind began playing tricks on him. *Did I swim past the island, and now I'm swimming away? I can still hear it, but the sound is more that way, over there now.* He should have landed on the island a while ago and he hadn't seen any lobster traps since he started swimming. There would likely be traps near the island. If he missed the island on an outgoing tide, he could wind up in hundreds of feet of water, miles from anything in shark infested waters.

Maybe I should have just stayed tied to that lobster trap and waited it out, he thought. Then he heard a much louder splash on the rocks. Billy swam hard towards the sound and ever so slowly a rocky beach began to materialize out of the fog. "Oh, thank God. Thank you God!" He cried. Due to his dive fins, he was walking backwards getting out of the water, trying to keep his balance as he awkwardly emerged from the ocean onto the rocky beach. He slowly continued walking backwards up the beach to the rock outcrop of the island. As he turned around to lean on a ledge, he looked down and a dead seagull was staring at him through a decayed eye socket. "Ahhhh!" Billy gasped, as he recoiled and stagger-stepped backwards around the corner of a rock crevice. Billy almost lost his balance when he was shaken again, this time by two seagulls caught together by a fishing lure and line. Both gulls tried frantically to get away, but being bound together with line, they created a flurry of flapping wings and feathers, adding more madness to the moment. "What the fuck? This is right out of Alfred Hitchcock!" Billy said out loud to the gulls, who awkwardly hopped away squawking.

He collapsed on the rocky beach and leaned back against solid rock breathing hard. He was numb, yet his mind was spinning wildly as his gaze slowly focused in on the dead gull. There was no eye in the skull, but the bird stared at him nonetheless. Both seagull episodes took less than ten seconds, but as the dead seagull stared into Billy's soul, it was as if time had stopped. His entire surroundings seemed to become strangely silent. Several minutes later and still breathing hard, Billy realized he was gazing at the dead gull. He shook his head and stood up. *Okay, now I'm alright. I can live here for weeks if I have to.* But now his concern shifted to Mike; where was he? How much time had gone by? Billy took off his fins and started to climb up to the top of the island.

Billy had swum to a long, rocky spit about twenty yards long. Then, the island sloped up to solid rock. At the top was a small, oval spot of grass about twenty-feet wide. Billy climbed up and stood on the grass and looked all around the island. The fog had lifted just enough to see about thirty or forty yards from the shore. Billy searched about frantically, but there was no sign of Mike or the boat. *Is Mike in the boat looking for me? Or is he lost in the fog?* Billy knew that if he could just get back to the boat he could make it back to Marblehead Harbor with the compass on board. Mike didn't know how to navigate, much less in the fog, so he might even have run aground. *Oh man, this isn't good.*

Billy sat down and tried to collect himself the best he could. *Okay, I should be able to see where I anchored the boat, but it's gone. That means either the anchor slipped loose and it drifted away, or Mike's in the boat looking for me.* Both of those scenarios were terrible. *It doesn't leave me much choice. I'm not going anywhere. I've just got to stay here until the fog lifts and flag another boat down, and then I*

*can try to get back to town. Oh, Christ, what if he's gone?
What will I tell his parents? Oh man!*

After what seemed like two weeks, but was more like
an hour of agonizing over how to describe Mike's death to his
parents and the newspapers, the visibility slowly started to
improve. The fog hung low over the water, but from the high
spot on the island where Billy stood, he could see the spindle
of Baker's Island Lighthouse in the distance.

"What? No way!" Billy yelled out loud. Once Baker's
Island Lighthouse was in perspective, Billy realized that he
was on the wrong island! He was on the *South* Gooseberry
Island not the *North!* He swam half a mile in the fog to the
other island. *No wonder the boat wasn't there!* Both islands
looked remarkably similar. They both had a rocky outcrop
that was awash at high tide and a gentle slope up to the vertical
rocks that led to an identical grass patch on the top of the
island. Soon a slight breeze helped to lift the remaining fog
and the North Gooseberry Island came into view, complete
with the boat anchored right where he left it.

When Billy spotted Mike onboard, he felt a tidal wave
of relief. Billy tried yelling over the water to Mike, but was out
of range. He flipped his wet suit hood inside out from black to
bright red and began waving it and his yellow catch bag like a
maniac. Mike took notice, pulled the anchor and made his
way slowly over to the southern island. Billy left his seagulls
behind and swam out to meet the boat.

Reaching out a hand to help Billy up into the boat,
Mike said, "I was trying to figure out what I was going to say to
the police."

"How long have I been gone?"

"I surfaced a little over two hours ago. I wasn't doing
too well."

"Could you hear me yelling?" Billy asked.

"A couple times I thought I heard something, but it was very faint and I was so freaked out, I didn't know if it was real or not."

As they made their way back to the harbor, Billy reprimanded himself for not seeing the situation coming. *A hot, July day with morning showers, the sun comes out and warms up the air to the dew point, why didn't I think of that?*

Billy never forgot that day and the lessons he learned. The one time he decided to leave his dive partner and swim off on his own was the one time fog came in. Coincidence or what? Billy chalked it up to Mother Nature giving him a lesson. If she wanted him dead, that would be no problem. It was more a matter of respect. All she did was give him a little backhand, and a soft one at that, and she had managed to scare the living shit out of him. He shuddered at the thought of the true wrath of Mother Nature.

CHAPTER 32   HURRICANE TANYA

Billy snapped out of his daze as if he had been hit in the face with a bucket of ice water. This was no fog bank. No soft backhand. He was on a collision course with a grand mal seizure of Planet Earth. His shirt was soaking wet with sweat, his head was pounding, and a hole was burning in his gut.

Get it together. Get it together, Billy thought. *Focus, focus. Make a plan. Plan your work and work your plan. Start with the basics, what you know, and go from there.*

Billy got up from his bed, and shuffled down the hallway. A large wave violently rocked the yacht, smashing him into the wall. He climbed to the top of the stairs where Marco stood at the helm with his hands tightly gripping the steering wheel. Billy staggered over to the nautical charts and double checked *Destiny's* location and heading toward Grand Cayman Island.

"Marco, get your ditch bag and mine, and stow them in the salon. Make sure you have everything you might need, amigo." Marco came up with one bag at a time, due to their size, weight, and the shifting footing caused by the rough seas. Billy grabbed a hand held VHF radio and a portable GPS and put them in his ditch bag along with extra batteries. Light faded from the setting sun on the horizon behind them, and they had only a half hour of daylight left.

The hurricane grew stronger with every passing minute. Billy could feel it with each wave. The yacht barely made any headway against the powerful wind. They were in an ominous situation that only got worse with the passage of time. Like all seasoned mariners, Billy knew that in the North Atlantic, hurricanes generally moved from east to west. Their best chance of survival was to try to and head south and let the storm pass them to the north. If they were caught in the northern section of the hurricane, the spiral rotation would suck them deeper into the center of the storm where the wind and seas would be higher. If they could just get south of the hurricane, then the winds would blow them away from the eye, and they might just have a chance of living. They couldn't get caught on the dangerous side of the hurricane, or the yacht would be torn to pieces.

The satellite TV displayed nothing but a black screen. The yacht rocked so fiercely from side to side that the satellite dish mounted on *Destiny* could not tune into the satellite in space. Billy had the VHF radio on, but all of the weather channels emitted only static.

With only two reports of the storm's position, Billy had no choice. After plotting the latitude and longitude of the two positions on the chart, he drew a line connecting them and was forced to use the line as the projected path of the hurricane. "Shit," Billy said. He extrapolated the projected path of the hurricane 200 miles, and it ran smack into their current position in the middle of the Caribbean Sea.

Billy knew they had to alter course. There was no way they could head directly to the Cayman Islands now; it would be suicide. He had to try to skirt the eye of the storm as much as possible to the south. Furthermore, he would have to slow down, because they didn't have enough fuel to make it to the Cayman Islands at their current speed.

Billy's mind filled with doubt. *If we slow down to save fuel, we might actually get pushed backwards by the storm and have to travel even farther. There's no way we'll make it with the fuel we have. No choice, it's what we have to do.*

"Marco, make sure those fifty-five gallon drums are secure on the aft deck. If they come loose, they'll roll around and smash everything in their path. Use the extra half-inch line, wrap each one, tie them to the cleats, and then secure them together. They can't get loose!"

"Okay, amigo!" Marco turned from the helm station and bounced through the salon like a pinball as the yacht rocked from side to side with each massive wave. Billy took over the helm and double checked the coordinates on the chart before he altered course by thirty degrees. Then he brought the throttles back to 1,000 rpm.

The new course gave sparse relief from the raging ocean, as the sea now bashed more on the port side of the yacht, instead of head-on. Billy was concerned about the windows on the port side. He could hear the twenty-foot waves slamming into the side of the salon. *If we lose one of those windows,* he thought. The pitch black night offered virtually no visibility. As the yacht rose up over the giant swells, the windows only revealed rain and angry black sky, and when *Destiny* came down the swell, the windshield was awash with angry sea and foam. The rain poured down like an

African monsoon, and the sun had set a half hour ago, but that would not have mattered much. It had become ominously pitch black from the formation of the massive hurricane storm clouds.

The yacht rolled over from side to side farther than Billy had ever encountered before. It was probably good he couldn't see what the hell was going on outside because he would be even more scared. On one roll that seemed to last forever, Billy looked over at the starboard window and saw it flush with sea water. He grasped the wheel hard with both hands. Marco stood next to him at the chart table, both hands glued to the stainless steel handrail. Billy was checking their heading on the computer when, *Bam!* It felt like they had run aground. Billy quickly looked at the navigation screen to see if there was anything around them that they could have hit. He didn't think so, and had checked the paper chart earlier, but the yacht rocked with such force, he was sure they hit something.

"Christ, that felt like we hit something!" Billy yelled to Marco over the driving rain and howling winds. Just then the same sound came crashing through the yacht again. *Bam!*

"Jesus!" Billy cried, as Marco fell into him, jolted loose by the giant wave. They were deep in the storm system now, with no way out.

Bam, Bam, Bam! With each massive wave, the whole yacht shook as if it had been struck by a giant sledge hammer. Billy tried his best to keep standing up, but he was being tossed around so much, his legs could barely support him.

He tried to keep one eye on the engine gauges and the other eye on the navigation system, but his vision was becoming blurry. The auto pilot could not stay on course with the massive waves pushing the direction of the yacht plus or minus forty-five degrees. Billy's arms were getting tired of spinning the wheel trying in vain to stay on course, and loud beeping from the auto pilot's off course alarm only added to the mayhem.

"Marco, make sure the..."

Bam! Crash! The unmistakable sound of broken glass filled the room. Billy immediately looked at all the windows. No water coming in. "What the hell was that?"

"I will check it," Marco replied. "Sounded like the VIP room."

Marco used both arms to ping pong down the stairs and was able to make it down to the lower level of the yacht without falling. Then, he crawled on his hands and knees toward the VIP room. When he opened the door, he immediately saw what had happened. The full size wall mirror behind the bed had shattered into a million pieces. Marco looked around the room. Water was coming in from one of the portholes. He crawled over, careful not to cut himself on the chards of mirror, and cranked down on the latch to the porthole. He shut the door to the VIP and crawled back up the steps to the wheelhouse. "The wall mirror blew out."

"Anything else?" Billy asked.

"There was some water coming in from the porthole, but I tightened it. Not much water."

"I know you already dogged down the hatches, amigo, but do another check. Things are bound to loosen up."

"Okay." Marco awkwardly crawled back down the stairs on all fours.

Fierce wind whistled through the radar arch sounding like a screaming lunatic as huge waves crashed upon them from all sides. It was all Billy could do to try and keep the yacht going somewhat straight, but *Destiny* was pitching and swaying all over the place. The enormous amount of stress was catching up to him. His muscles ached. His mind ached.

Marco reappeared from below and staggered to his post. "One hatch was loose, but all are tight now." He reported.

Destiny rolled far over to starboard and hung there. Billy began to think she might not right herself, when slowly she started rolling back over to port. Just as the yacht leveled out and started to roll to port, the bow of the yacht became submerged in a massive wave. The engines groaned as the yacht physically shuddered when they bow-plowed smack dab into an enormous wave. Billy felt the momentum of the yacht stop and reached out to keep from falling forward. He knew the waves were becoming steeper and more dangerous, and *the feeling* started to edge into his emotionally shattered mind. He thought, *shit, did the hurricane change paths and now we're approaching the north side?*

Just then an alarm went off on the main circuit panel, its red light blinding in the darkness. Billy quickly switched on the overhead night light at the helm station so he could see which alarm had sounded. His heart beat wildly when he determined the source. It was the engine room bilge high water alarm.

"Marco, take the helm!" Billy said. "Try and keep us on a thirty-five degree course. It's tough, but use the compass. We're bouncing all over the place."

Billy staggered back toward the salon door which led to the aft deck. *Destiny* rocked so violently that he had to have both hands or his ass on something, or he would fall over. As he walked by the TV in the salon, he saw that it had broken loose from its mount and was hanging by the power cord. *No time for that, first things first.* He got to the aft deck door, where he took off his shirt and kicked off his boat shoes. He would get soaking wet the second he went outside, and he wanted to be able to feel what he stepped on underfoot in case the engine room lights had gone out. He paused several seconds to think through how he was going to get down into the engine room. The access door was on the port side of the yacht. Once the door was opened, he had to climb down the ladder to get to the engine room floor. The second entrance off of the stern could not be used. Five feet of water violently crashed about the swim platform and would certainly sweep him away. If he fell overboard, he would die. It was as simple as that, over equals dead. It would be impossible for Marco to find him in the darkness of the raging seas.

The yacht rolled over and hung there much too long. *There must be a lot of water in the bilge,* Billy thought. *Christ, we might not come back up from one of these rolls.*

The yacht had rolled hard to port and Billy was waiting for *Destiny* to begin its sway back to starboard. When she rolled hard to starboard, the engine room door on the port side would be high out of the water and give him the best chance of getting in. The yacht began to roll to starboard, and he seized the opportunity. Billy slid the salon door open and immediately felt a blast of rain and tasted the wind driven saltwater. As the yacht continued to roll starboard, Billy bolted around towards the port side, but just as he rounded the aft port corner he was blown backwards by the incredible force of the wind. He grabbed the stainless steel handrail and pulled himself forward, but not fast enough. The yacht rolled over hard to port and hundreds of gallons of water crashed onto Billy, knocking him off his feet, sending him flying backwards toward the steps leading to the swim platform. Desperately reaching for anything to hold onto, his arm swung and hit the aft deck table stanchion. He wrapped his other arm around the stanchion and bear hugged it as hard as he could while the sea tried violently to drag him overboard. The water slowly flowed off the deck as the yacht once again started to roll over to starboard.

Last time he had waited too long to make his move, so he jumped up and pulled himself forward using the handrail. He managed to get to the engine room door and rotated the water tight door hatch. Pulling against the wind he heaved the door open and stepped inside. Just then the yacht rolled back to port and a massive wall of water crashed into the port side. With the force of one hundred fire hoses, saltwater blew the door shut and flung Billy backwards. He lost his balance and started to fall down the ladder, but one leg got caught in the rungs stopping his fall. He reached up and secured the water tight door. *Thank God the lights still work,* he thought. Backing down the ladder he came to the engine room floor and turned around, bracing himself with every step. He got down on his hands and knees and removed one of the bilge plates that make up the floor. He peered into the bilge and saw three feet of water. He tasted it, but already knew it was saltwater. Fresh water would have meant a controlled, manageable leak with a fixed amount of water onboard. Saltwater meant another story altogether. Marco had checked the bilge pumps, so where was it coming from? He looked up at the indicator panel. No bilge pumps were on! *What the...?* Crawling over to the 24-volt DC circuit breaker panel, he saw two bilge pump breakers had tripped. He reset them; they worked for a second, and then tripped off again. "Shit!"

He pulled the engine room floor plate off above the first bilge pump and used a hand held spot light to see what was going on. *A damn oil spill pad!* Billy reached down into the water up to his arm pit, and pulled at an old, oil absorbent spill pad that had been left behind by a careless mechanic.

Pulling gently, so as not to rip the spill pad right at the intake, Billy wedged it back and forth until it came free. He tried the circuit breaker again. This time, the green light came on and the breaker didn't trip.

Thank Christ, he thought. *Okay at thirty gallons per minute, that should help out. Now if I can just get the other one to...*

"Ahhhhhh!" The yacht rolled hard over in a flash, and Billy, still on his knees, went flying through the air in the engine room. He tried to break his fall by reaching for something, but he couldn't get his hands up quick enough. His right arm hit the starboard engine turbo charger creating a *tsssssssss* sound. The turbo charger fan got incredibly hot at almost 1,300 degrees Fahrenheit and instantly gave third degree burns when touched.

He looked down at his bicep and could clearly see the imprint of the turbo charger in red lines, oozing a clear fluid. Ignoring the pain, he crawled on his hands and knees and cleared away the flooring above the second bilge pump. While looking down through the water at the bilge pump, he could not see an obvious blockage, but feeling around the pump intake, he touched the remnants of a nylon wire tie. Billy removed the culprit and hit the circuit breaker. Now he had two pumps running at thirty gallons per minute each. After three minutes, he could see where the water was coming in.

Billy pointed the spot light at the location where the propeller shaft penetrated through the hull of the yacht. The stuffing box was gushing saltwater into the bilge.

"Damn!" Billy tried to gauge the volume of water rushing in. It definitely wasn't thirty gallons per minute; it was more like five to ten gallons per minute. That was good news, and Billy thought, *okay, it's a controlled leak for now, but we've got to keep an eye on this. We flood the engines, and we're dead.*

Billy looked around at all the usual areas that he inspected during a regular engine room check. Belts and fuel lines looked good and the water in the bilge was noticeably starting to drop. He crawled back over to the base of the ladder and started his climb up. Getting out of the engine room door would be tricky. If he opened the door into a wall of ocean, he would be smashed down the ladder steps. Hundreds of gallons of sea water would flood the engine room.

He climbed up to the top of the ladder and waited. His right bicep was oozing puss and blood, and aching badly. He could hear the fierce power of the ocean pounding on the other side of the door. Just then the yacht rolled hard to port and Billy seized the chance. He counted to three, spun the door hatch and leapt through to the port side. The yacht began rolling back over to starboard, so he had a just a moment before the waves crashed into him. Ninety-five mile per hour wind blasted saltwater in every direction. He held on with every ounce of remaining strength while his bicep burned like mad. Holding the steel handrail with both hands he took several deliberate steps and dove toward the salon doorway. He grabbed the door handle and slid inside the yacht, relieved to be out of the howling wind and driving rain, and most thankful to be alive.

"Amigo," Billy said panting, "the pumps were clogged, but I fixed them and they're working now. The leak is coming from the port shaft stuffing box and it looks like about five to ten gallons per minute, but both pumps are working, so we should be pumping about sixty gallons per minute overboard. We'll need to keep an eye on it. Be damn careful if you go out there. I was almost blown over. There's a lot of water in the bilge, that's why we rolled over so far for so long. The water was rolling with the yacht and changing our center of gravity. I knew I felt something off."

Billy took over at the helm and asked Marco for the hydrogen peroxide from the first aid kit. Marco quickly fetched it, unscrewed the top, and handed the bottle to Billy, who poured it all over his right bicep, letting the excess fall to the floor. Immediately his bicep began to foam vigorously.

"What happened, amigo? Are you alright?"

"It's rough as hell down there, Marco. I got slammed into the turbo on one of those waves and took the full fall on my right arm."

Just then the yacht slammed into another wave head on, and an explosion burst from the salon behind them. Sparks filled the air along with the foul smell of electrical fire. Billy yelled over the blaring smoke alarm. "Marco! What the hell was that?" Marco staggered into the salon and through the smoke he saw that the forty-eight-inch TV had been blasted out of its mount and smashed into the marble coffee table. The screen had exploded and glass was everywhere.

"It's the TV!" Marco shouted.

"Is there a fire?"

"No, I don't see flames."

"Kill the circuit breaker quick, that's 240 volt!" Marco rushed to the main circuit panel and had some difficulty locating the breaker, because he never had to shut it off before. Billy turned around, noticed, and yelled, "Third one from the right on the 240-volt line!" Marco quickly found it and shut it off.

The smoke alarm was still ringing loudly when they were hit by another series of colossal waves. *Bam, Bam, Bam!* Billy tried to keep them on course, but it was pitch black and everything was chaos. They were rolling and pitching in all directions. "Damn it!" Billy yelled. He spun the wheel hard to starboard hoping to get some kind of relief. *Bam!* Then again, *Bam!* There was just no escape. It felt as if the sea had gone mad.

We must be getting into the center of the storm, he thought. *We can't take much more of this. Destiny* groaned and squeaked like a wild boar caught in a steel trap. Billy had never heard her moan like this before, but she was being twisted like a wash cloth. He saw Marco's terrified expression and tried to offer some inspiration. "Okay, just a few hours more, and we'll be on the other side! Come on girl you can..."

Just then, a sixty-foot wave blasted straight into the yacht. The impact felt like driving a car into a stone wall at eighty miles per hour. Billy and Marco were thrown off their feet. Marco flew through the air and landed on the salon floor, cutting himself in several places on the broken glass from the TV. Billy's arms reached out as he soared through the air, but his chest took the impact of the fall as he hit the chart table hard, knocking the wind out of him. Violently rolling around on the floor, he desperately gasped for breath as the second massive wave smashed into the yacht. Billy couldn't tell if the second impact was more powerful than the first. It felt like trying to compare the wrath of two hippos.

In an instant, Billy was soaked again. Saltwater and broken glass sprayed into his face with the force of a fire hydrant. Gasping, he rolled over out of the water and swallowed a precious breath of air. "The port window blew!" He screamed.

Both men struggled to their feet as water continued to blast through the blown out window. "Marco! Get something in there. Stop the water! I'm going to try to get the port to lee!"

Marco grabbed two large cushions from the salon couch and ran towards the broken window. Gallons of water poured in as he tried to wedge the cushions in the open space, but it was simply too large. The window frame was four feet long by two feet high. It was all he could do hold one cushion over a portion of the blown out window as the sea continued to flood the wheelhouse.

Billy staggered over to the helm and began turning the yacht around, trying to put the heaviest seas over on the starboard side. He had to navigate the way a blind man reads, totally by feel. He could hear water hitting the yacht from all directions, but that was rain and wind driven sea spray. The largest waves had been coming from the port, so he had to turn *Destiny* around if he wanted to put the starboard side into the waves. *Turn around.* That meant traveling with the storm and added hours of chaos. *How much longer can we hold out? What about fuel?*

Billy turned the wheel hard to starboard, but as if sensing their plight, the sea struck back with another monstrous wave. The water crashed through open window and blew the cushion out of Marco's hands. Several hundred gallons of saltwater poured into the port window and down over the chart table. Seconds later, all the lights went out.

They could smell the mix of salty air and acrid smoke. They could hear the wind and water against the yacht. They could feel the wetness and cold, and they tasted salt, but they could see nothing at all. Total blackness. Their eyes had previously adjusted to the minimal light given off by the instruments, but without their limited light, it was pitch black. There were no stars and no moon because the sky was a Godless, evil black.

The yacht came down off of another large wave, and it felt like coming down off of the first pitch of a roller coaster. Billy knew they hadn't fully turned the yacht around yet and were in serious trouble of yawing. Thank God the engines were still running.

Billy hit the throttles with his right hand. "Ahhhh!" He yelled, as he tried to accelerate the eighty tons below his feet. But the sea would not let them escape. With unimaginable power, the enormous wave spun the 85-foot, 160,000 pound yacht like a child's toy. The centrifugal force caused by the yawing of the yacht sent Billy flying. In total darkness, the only thing he could do was instinctively put both hands out to break his fall. He flew blindly through the air with his hands out in front of him, but they missed the ground and his head hit the corner of the chart table, knocking him out cold.

Fireflies. Fireflies? Yes, those are fireflies. What are fireflies doing here? I must have fallen asleep in a field. Now it's dark, and the fireflies are out tonight. Six, no, four of them hovering around, moving back and forth, up and down. Wait, now there are only two. Maybe they are mating, because the two are so close together. Yes, definitely mating, there is only one now. Horny little fireflies.

Billy blinked slowly as Marco flashed a pen light around his head and said, "Amigo, amigo, can you hear me? You've got a cut on your head, amigo." Marco's voice gradually brought Billy back to the present.

Billy ran his hand over a large, protruding lump on his upper right forehead and felt a warm sticky fluid, blood. He groaned and tried to sit up. Everything slowly started to come back to him: the broken window, turning the yacht around, and the storm. *The storm! What had happened to the storm?* Billy's senses began to come back around and he realized the yacht was barely rolling, and there was no rain or wind. He could feel the yacht rise and fall with the passing of a swell, but other than that, they were quite still. An eerie silence enveloped them. "How long was I out Marco?"

"I don't know exactly, time is hard to judge, but em, five or ten minutes." Marco found the spot light and pointed the beam towards the ceiling and turned it on. The light diffused through the salon and wheelhouse, and they could see again.

"Marco, we must be in the eye of the storm and we don't have much time. Go down to the rudder room and get the two pieces of scrap plywood that we have. Get the cordless drill, drill bits and screws and attach the plywood to the outside of the window frame. You've got to drill pilot holes in the fiberglass. Use at least eight screws per piece of wood, make it secure! There is a headlamp in the tool box. I'll need that spot light. I'm going to see if I can get the navigation system working again."

Without wasting time to respond, Marco ran to the salon door and disappeared into the darkness. Billy grabbed the spot light and quickly looked around to survey the damage. The floor was flooded. Saltwater had drenched the chart table and flowed down into the electronics area below. He opened the access door and flashed the spot light in. Water was dripping off of the computer. It had been doused with saltwater. "Shot." He looked around to see what else had been affected by the saltwater and could see that some of the DC components were still dry, but most of the 120-volt AC circuits were fried. On the main control panel, a red alarm light glowed brightly for the generator, but Billy couldn't worry about that now. He hoped the service batteries would last for a while.

Billy ran down the steps to his room and grabbed his laptop computer. Scurrying back up the steps, he snatched the portable GPS from his ditch bag and began to work furiously. He duct taped the GPS unit below the windshield so that it had the best view of the sky. Then, he wedged the laptop in between the radar and the now useless navigation screen. It was a snug fit, and he had to really force it in, but it seemed like his lap top just might stay put in rough seas. *It will have to do*, he thought. He noticed that the radar had gone into standby mode, but still had power. *Of course, it's DC!* Billy hit the transmit button and the radar came to life.

Billy spotted light from Marco's headlamp out of the corner of his eye as Marco began working fast on patching the blown out window.

"Wholly shit!" Billy said as he stared down at the instrument panel. The radar screen looked like the 18th hole. Bright, fluorescent green surrounded an almost perfect black hole in the center. He could clearly see they were in the eye of the hurricane. He scaled the radar range down from three miles to one mile. The wall of the hurricane was approaching them fast. At twenty miles per hour, the storm moved a mile every three minutes. They had to act fast.

"Marco! We don't have much time! Two or three minutes max! Get that window covered!"

Marco yelled back, "One side is almost on!"

Billy rushed to hook up the cable from the GPS to his laptop. He knew he had to get the GPS tracking before they hit the wall of wind that was fast approaching them. Otherwise, the little handheld GPS would never hone in on the satellites with the yacht rolling in all directions. Everything seemed to take forever. He turned on both the laptop computer and the GPS and ran outside to help Marco, while the computer booted up.

"I'll hold the plywood. You drill and screw." Marco had the drill bit in his mouth along with several long Phillips head screws. He got two screws into the last piece of wood, when Billy heard the Windows theme on his computer as it finished booting up. The little jingle seemed to be mocking them; it sounded so out of place in their current predicament. "It's all yours, Marco. I've got to get the navigation system running!"

"Okay, I got it." Marco replied.

Billy ran back inside to the helm station and double clicked on the navigation software. The GPS was still searching for satellites. *Damn.* He zoomed out on the radar and saw just how large the hurricane was. If he only had more time he could figure out which way the hurricane was moving by watching the direction the eye moved. He analyzed the wall of the storm as it jumped towards them with each revolution of the radar vane and calculated a quick and dirty estimate of the hurricane's path. He looked over at his computer and saw a green light meaning that he had GPS tracking. "Yes!"

Got to buy some time, he thought. Billy spun the wheel again and hit the throttles. The yacht slowly turned around and now they were moving with the storm. *Yeah, yeah! That's it!*

Marco stepped in the back door. "The two pieces are screwed in, and I overlapped them for strength, but I have to plug the little holes around the overlap."

"Good, good. "I'm going to run with the storm for a few minutes until we figure out its speed and direction. Once you get the window water tight, go down and check the engine room. Check the leak on both stuffing boxes, and make sure the bilge pumps are working!"

"Okay, amigo."

Billy got the yacht up on a plane, and they were speeding along at twenty-four knots in the pitch darkness. He headed in the direction he thought the hurricane was moving. Ever so slowly, he could see on the radar screen that they were heading back into the center of the eye, that perfect circle of black, surrounded by bright, fluorescent green. He could tell from the radar scale that the eye was about seven miles wide. Now he just needed to determine the direction of the hurricane. He adjusted the radar scale several times, slowed the yacht down to eighteen knots, and studied the radar screen closely. After several moments, Billy determined that *Destiny's* speed matched that of the hurricane, but he needed to adjust their course fifteen degrees to stay right in the center of the eye.

Okay, the storm is moving at about eighteen knots in a direction of 250 degrees. Ah, the direction of the storm did change! It swung south by thirty degrees! That's why we got our asses handed to us!

Billy tried to think of the best scenario for survival. *I could stay in the eye of the storm until we run out of fuel or reach land and then run the yacht hard up on shore and run like hell. We might live, but the yacht would be trashed. Or, we could run with the storm at a slower speed than the storm itself and let it pass over us. We'd definitely run out of fuel if we did that, and then we'd be dead in the water. Shit, if we're broadside to waves the size we just went through, we wouldn't make it. Another window or two will blow out, we'll fill up with water and sink, or get flipped over. Our only chance is to brave the second half of the storm head on and try to get through it as quickly as possible.*

Marco came in through the salon doors and quickly shuffled up next to Billy. "Em, the through hull is still leaking. Seems what you say, five to ten gallons per minute. Other one is fine, and bilge has some water, but, em, pumps keeping up."

"How much water?"

"Em, about three or four inches," Marco replied.

"The hurricane's course dropped unexpectedly to the south while we were fighting it. That's how we ended up in the eye. We're going to try to blast our way out of the other side. Can you make that wooden window as watertight as possible?" When Marco had screwed in the two pieces of plywood over the blown out window, the rectangular cut wood didn't make a perfect seal over the oval shaped window frame, leaving two void spaces.

"What should I use?" Marco asked.

"Take a chamois cloth and cut it in two. Tie a knot at one end and run the other end through the hole from the outside. We'll still get a little water in, but the force of the ocean will keep pressure on the plug-knots."

"Okay amigo," Marco said and hurried out towards the aft deck.

All the while, Billy looked at the gauges to check the condition of the engines and the status of all the alarms. He also kept one eye on the navigation system, trying to learn as much as he could about his nemesis before their next round of battle.

Marco got the first plug in with no problem, but the second, lower plug needed to be grabbed from the inside. Billy engaged the auto pilot and quickly ran over and pulled the sleeve of the plug up from the bottom of the patched window. The void spaces were small and shaped like a wedge of cheese. The plugs would work well and Billy didn't think that much water would come through with the plugs firmly fastened in place. Marco ran back inside the wheelhouse and fastened the plugs securely in place with several Phillips head screws. "Em, that was a good idea, amigo. It looks pretty tight."

"Let's hope they hold!"

Back at the helm station, Billy observed that in the thirty seconds it took to help Marco, *Destiny* had remained in the center of the eye.

"Okay! Here we go! We're just going straight into it. It's moving at eighteen knots. If we can just make two knots headway, then for every hour we stay alive, twenty miles of the storm will pass us. If the hurricane is 150 miles wide, then this side is 75, so that's between three and four hours. Marco, if we can stay afloat the first two hours, we just might live!" Billy's voice sounded confident, even to himself.

"Anything you have to do, do it now, amigo," Billy said.

"I have to pee," Marco replied.

"While you're down there, check all the rooms and double check the hatches." Marco nodded and dashed down the steps towards the nearest head.

Billy looked at the fuel gauge. They had burned a lot of fuel fighting the storm, and he hadn't had time to get a good fix on his position relative to the Cayman Islands. *Doesn't matter if we can make it to Grand Cayman or not,* he thought. *First things first; survive the hurricane.*

Marco came up and reported that one of the shower doors had jumped off of its tracks and shattered all over the bathroom floor, and that one of the hatches had come loose and let in enough water to soak one of the mattresses in the port cabin.

Billy slowed down and quickly turned the yacht around so that the behemoth was now approaching them head on. It was eerie and unnerving to know that hell itself was coming right at him, but he couldn't see it. Only the fluorescent green of the radar gave any inclination of where the storm was. With each rotation of the radar vane, the east wall of the deadly hurricane approached.

Billy brought the speed down to ten knots. He didn't think that he could maintain that speed once they were in the thick of it, but it gave them enough momentum to break through the fast approaching wall of the storm. They couldn't go into it at twenty knots; *Destiny* would be smashed to bits. Billy looked deep within him and thought, *if that window will just hold out for two more hours, we might make it.*

Billy didn't need to say anything to Marco. Both men knew their predicament and low odds of survival, but they had to try and stay alert and fight it out. The green line of the east wall of the hurricane marched towards them on the radar screen like thousands of men charging into battle. *How insignificant we really are,* Billy thought. *We're a flea's egg on an elephant. Mother Nature could kill us as easily as we step on an ant.* They were seconds away from hitting the wall of the storm, "Brace yourself, amigo."

The winds increased faster than a jet taking off the runway. Within fifteen seconds, Billy and Marco were holding on as tight as they could just to stand up. The yacht rolled side to side and pitched feverishly in the wild seas. They heard something rolling around in the salon, banging into the walls, but it would have to wait. The bow crashed hard into another huge wave causing both men to stagger forward. They heard whatever was rolling around in the salon roll quickly towards them in the darkness and stop with a loud thud.

Billy had the throttles at 1,400 rpm, and with the navigation screen back in view on his lap top computer, he noticed that their speed over ground was almost five knots. They were making five knots into the back side of the storm! If they could survive for just one hour, almost one third of the storm would pass them, and surely the wind speed would lessen.

Billy looked at the fuel gauge and knew that it was going to be tight. They had run at cruise speed for about a half hour in the eye of the storm, and in doing so, burned a precious fifty gallons of fuel. *We had to do it,* he thought. *I had to get my bearings and we needed to check the yacht. There's nothing I can do about fuel. Right now we just have to stay alive.*

They pressed on into the storm. During another extreme roll to one side they heard a crash from down below. Marco bounced down the stairs like a pinball and checked out the damage. Clutching the handrail on his way back up the stairs he yelled to Billy, "The other shower door shattered. Other than that all is okay."

Fatigue affected Billy's every move. He hadn't slept in more than twenty-four hours. He had a large egg on his forehead that was still throbbing and bleeding intermittently and the burn on his arm was still oozing. His legs were like rubber bands from all the bouncing around they had been doing for the last ten hours. In addition, he realized he hadn't eaten anything since the morning they left Honduras. His body ached all over, and his vision was hazy.

It was getting harder and harder to keep a diligent watch and keep the yacht on course. The lights emitted from the computer screen and control panel felt like needles in his eyes. Images were blurring into one another. Intermittently, he felt like he was going to throw up, but his stomach contained only bile. He forced things to stay where they were.

Billy stared down at his watch. It took more than five seconds for the dials to become readable to his blood shot eyes. They had been battling the second half of the storm for only forty-five minutes. *Please Lord, help me make it through this.*

The ferocity of the storm changed as they passed through. Occasionally, he could detect slightly less wind, as if the storm was inhaling, giving just enough of a break to fake Billy into thinking they were exiting the hurricane. Then, in an instant, the wind would gust hard. The yacht rocked and shuddered like it was about to burst into a thousand pieces.

They bashed headlong into several huge waves back to back when they heard a loud crash from the galley. Marco got down on his hands and knees and crawled over to take a look at what happened. He still had his head lamp on which helped out tremendously. He could use both hands to move around and the lamp shone in the direction he was looking. After crawling slowly to the galley, Marco looked over to the left, towards the stove, and saw that the oven had been ripped out of its wall mount and had crashed onto the floor. The glass in the oven's front door had smashed.

There was nothing Marco could do with the yacht gyrating so violently. He crawled back to give Billy the news. "It was the oven, amigo."

"Did you kill the circuit breaker?" Billy asked. "Never mind, it's on the same leg as the TV." Billy realized that his mind was beginning to slip. He was beyond exhaustion. *This is how you die,* he thought. *It's just like you read about-the whole cascading thing. One problem happens, then another, then it snowballs out of control, and before you know it, you're waist deep in water.*

They had been fighting the second half of the hurricane for just about an hour and a half when Billy saw a red flash on the alarm panel. Did he see it, or was his mind playing tricks on him? He steadied his eyes on the panel for a few moments. Nothing. He moved his gaze to the black, rain soaked windshield. Out of the corner of his eye, he saw the red flash again. He stared at the alarm panel for a full back and forth roll of the yacht. Sure enough, the engine room high bilge water alarm blinked on again. However, the alarm light illuminated only when the yacht rolled far over to starboard. He knew that the float switch for the bilge alarm was located on the starboard side. It meant that water had accumulated in the engine room and was rolling back and forth with the roll of the yacht. When they rolled hard to starboard, the water pooled up high enough to trigger the float switch.

"Marco, we've got water in the engine room bilge again. Maybe one of the pumps is fouled. Hopefully, there is not another leak. Check it out, but be careful."

"Okay."

Marco had put his boat shoes on after the giant TV had smashed in the salon, spraying broken glass all over the floor. There would be no way to avoid stepping on the shards of glass in the dark. Marco slid his head lamp down around his neck so it wouldn't blow off and took a step outside.

Immediately, he was doused in saltwater and driving rain. He shut the salon door, but hadn't thought of where to put his hands after that. While he tried to round the corner to get to the engine room door, a massive wave struck the side of the yacht. Almost four feet of water swiftly rushed down through the narrow walkway and swept Marco's legs right out from under him. Reaching about frantically he couldn't feel anything but water. As the water began to recede off the yacht, he realized that he was going to be swept overboard. He blindly lunged out with his hands and felt something pass down the length of his arm to the inside of his elbow. What was it? It didn't matter, he pulled his wrist in and locked his elbow, and held on with all his might as the water rushed by, pulling him down.

He had been blown over the side and was hanging on by one arm to the hand rail that ran the length of the yacht. His feet were dangling in the air as the yacht reversed its roll and began to sway back to other side. The yacht righted and then continued to roll to starboard.

Marco swung his other hand up and now had two hands on the rail. He could feel his body press against the hull as the yacht rolled hard over. He kicked his feet up and met the rub rail with one foot. Using the rub rail as a foot step, he pressed down hard with one leg and shimmied over the handrail. He fell to the deck with a painful thud just as the yacht rolled back over to port. Another wall of water crashed down on him, blowing him to the stern with arms and legs flailing and kicking. He crashed head first into the door to the swim platform steps, which sent a jolt of pain through his right shoulder, but it stopped him from going overboard again. The wave was not as large and drained off the yacht quickly.

Marco staggered to his feet and ran towards the engine room door. He grabbed the latch with both hands and spun it counter clock wise as fast as he could. He could feel that the yacht was about to roll to port again. He jumped inside and tried to shut the engine room door behind him, but was only able to get it halfway closed when the next wave struck. With the power of half a dozen semi-tractor trailers, another massive wall of water enveloped the entire port side of the yacht.

The huge wave hit the engine room door, slamming it shut with enormous force and sending Marco flying. Marco tried desperately to hold onto the latch handle with both hands when the wave hit, but it was like trying to hold onto a cannon ball shooting from a cannon. The impact sent him flying off the ladder and crashing into the wall behind him. His head snapped like the recoil of a gun and the back of his head struck the wall hard, knocking him out cold. Unconscious, he ricocheted off the wall, back to the ladder, but his arms and legs were limp, so he fell to the engine room floor, haphazardly bouncing down the seven-foot ladder like a pinball.

Standing at the helm station, Billy could feel that the yacht was rolling over and staying there too long before coming back off the roll. Once again there was too much water in the bilge. Billy knew that Marco had to get the water out soon, or the yacht wouldn't recover from one of these rolls. Marco had been gone for too long. Or had he? Billy's sense of time was off, and his mind was aching. Had Marco been gone for five minutes or fifteen? Billy honestly didn't know. He was having trouble with the simplest things. Off to his right, he continued to see the red light for the engine room bilge high water alarm, but now it was more frequent and staying lit longer. *Damn it, what's going on?*

Billy's concern for Marco grew. *I'll give Marco five more minutes, and if he doesn't come back, then I'll have to go down and see what happened.* He focused on the small clock in the lower right hand of the computer screen. It took almost ten seconds before he could make out the numbers. The yacht was moving around like a roller coaster, his head was pounding, his stomach empty, and his legs about to give way. It was like perpetual vertigo.

An eternity of five minutes elapsed, and there was still no sign of Marco. Billy realized that something must have happened to him. Billy throttled back to 800 rpm, just enough to hold the yacht into the storm, and then he turned the auto pilot on knowing that it wouldn't be able to hold a course in such rough seas, but maybe it would hold for a minute before the course offset alarm sounded. Then the yacht would be at the mercy of the storm. It didn't matter. Billy had to find out if Marco was alive.

Billy bent down and grabbed the spot light with one hand, while holding on to the wheel with the other. He flashed the light down the salon and tried to identify potential locations of both his steps and his hand grips. With seas this rough, there was just no way to simply walk through the salon to the aft deck. It was like trying to walk across a trampoline with a galloping elephant. He turned from the helm station and began to make his first move toward the stern of the yacht. He let go of the steering wheel and took one step forward just as a sixty foot wave crashed down directly on top of him. *Boooom!* It was a wonder the windshield did not implode, never mind the make-shift repair on the port window.

Instantly, Billy was thrown backwards down the steps to the lower deck. The spot light went flying from his hands as he landed on his back. He reached into the air, but there was nothing to grab. Even if he had felt something, he was so weak that he couldn't hold on. Everything continued to spin out of control as he rolled down the stairs backwards, his neck bending sideways as he rolled over his head. He came upright once on his ass as he hit the lower deck. Just then the yacht hit another wave and Billy's head snapped whip-lash backwards into the metal of the laundry machine. Billy exhaled a moan as he slumped over sideways, unconscious.

In the engine room, the yacht continuously filled with water.

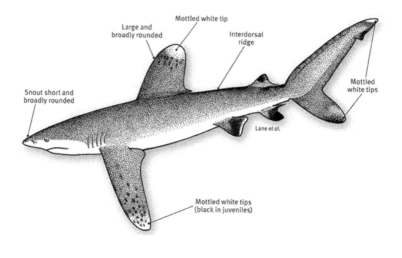

Large and broadly rounded

Mottled white tip

Interdorsal ridge

Mottled white tips

Snout short and broadly rounded

Lane et al.

Mottled white tips (black in juveniles)

CHAPTER 33   OCEANIC WHITE TIP

Miguel Chavez hid in the pocket of air beneath the overturned Honduran coastal police boat. Holding on to the rail near the windshield, he kept his knees tucked into his chest so that his feet and legs could not be seen from above water. The bullets Marco fired into the boat to sink it had barely missed his head as he tried to keep out of sight, but there was only so much room to maneuver. Twice, he clearly saw the perfectly straight line of bubbles left by the deadly bullets as they pierced the hull and zipped underwater. He could hear the low rumble of big diesel engines nearby, but did not dare to look out from beneath the boat. Sunlight pierced through the holes left by the bullets, and Chavez quickly realized the pocket of air was getting smaller as the precious gas whisked out through the holes, and the boat continued to sink. Very soon, he would have to come up for air. Chavez was sure they would just wait and shoot him when he surfaced, but then he heard the sound of the diesel engines growing faint.

Chavez waited until there was no more air left in the small compartment where he hid. Although he had not heard the big diesel engines for some time, he thought that the yacht might be silently drifting nearby. If the Americans were waiting, they could easily shoot him when he surfaced, but he had no choice. He was out of air. Chavez ducked underwater and surfaced sliding one hand up onto the overturned hull. He quickly looked all around and was relieved to see nothing but ocean. The feeling of relief was short lived, however, for he had another problem: staying alive adrift in the middle of the sea.

Wasting no time, he filled his lungs with air and ducked back underwater to retrieve whatever he could to help him live. He grabbed two life jackets, a first aid kit, and a set of flares from one of the compartments below the helm station. Swimming back up to the surface, he threw the items on the overturned hull and went back down to see what else he could salvage. On his second trip to the surface, he became very excited when he noticed that the boat was not sinking, but rather had become neutrally buoyant. He began to tie off several sections of rope so that he could climb up onto the bottom of the overturned boat. He fastened a lifeline in the shape of a cross on the bottom of the hull, running from bow to stern and from port to starboard. Since the small boat had flipped over, the only portion above water was the black painted bottom of the boat usually *below* the waterline. He put on one life jacket and tied the second one to his lifeline along with the flares and first aid kit.

He swam back down to see what else that he could salvage from the flooded compartments of the overturned boat. In the United States, the Coast Guard, and local marine enforcement boats were very well equipped with all kinds of emergency gear funded by the taxpayer. In Honduras, on the other hand, official boats did not contain much, if any, emergency gear. With salt burning his eyes, Chavez managed to find a knife and an old jacket. He swam back up to the surface and used the lifeline to crawl up onto the bottom of the overturned boat. Taking stock of his inventory, he made sure that none of the precious items he had collected would float away by tightly securing all but the knife to the lifeline he had rigged. He gently slid the knife under his belt and could feel the cold steel against his hip.

The adrenaline generated from the boat chase, gun shots, and capsize started to fade, and Chavez began to feel the reality of his situation. In chasing the yacht so far out into the open ocean, Rodriguez had practically written Chavez's death sentence.

Being born near a small harbor port in Honduras, Miguel Chavez had spent a substantial amount of his life on the ocean. As a child, he could always be found playing at the fishing docks. Watching men leave for days or even weeks at a time, and then returning with a boat full of fish, he seized his first opportunity to get on a fishing boat at the age of thirteen and worked it until he was seventeen. During those teenage years at sea, he had witnessed some precarious events and learned a great deal about living on the ocean.

As the first night approached, he donned the still damp jacket he had recovered. Chavez knew from all his time on the ocean that the problem with getting something wet in saltwater was that it never really dried unless the salt was rinsed from it. The ocean soaked garment contained so much salt that it kept pulling moisture from the air to quench the salt's endless thirst. For the same reason, humans couldn't drink saltwater. Ocean water contained roughly four times the salt that human blood contained. If a person ingested saltwater, water would be pulled from the body's organs and tissue to equalize the strong chemical bond between salt and water. If saltwater were continually ingested, eventually, the salt content in the human blood stream would rise to a fatal level.

Chavez wasn't desperate enough to drink from the sea, *yet.* In fact, he focused on staying calm and tried to think ahead. His hands and arms were covered with black from bottom paint of the overturned boat. He could barely see his hands in the pitch black night anyway. He had laid the jacket out earlier in an attempt to dry it, but knew it would only partially dry. In any case, it would only take one large wave for everything to be soaking wet again. Even though he felt exhausted, sleep was impossible. His instinct kept him awake, looking, listening, and thinking about his surroundings. At one point during the early morning hours before any sign of sunrise, he felt a thump on the side of the boat, accompanied by a distinctive *thud.* Trying to placate his fears, he willed the object to be flotsam. However, he had a very strong feeling that the noise was generated by something alive. He awkwardly positioned himself on his hands and knees on the overturned hull, and strained to see into the abyss. The quarter moon's reflection created a solitary line of dim light that ran off toward the horizon. Chavez thought he detected motion on the water, but could not be sure until he saw the unmistakable triangle shape pass through the moon's reflected beam on the surface of the ocean.

His pulse quickened as he tightened his grip on the lifeline. Even in the darkness he could tell it was a very big dorsal fin. He had seen the work of large sharks while commercial fishing in his youth. Chavez had witnessed firsthand a massive bull shark eat a several hundred pound tuna that they had reeled up to the boat, only to be devoured by the bull shark. All that was left on the line was the bloody stump of a head with the tuna's eyes staring wildly open and the jaw reflexively quivering. Chavez hoped that the shark would investigate the overturned boat and if it didn't find any food, it would move on. That was what he hoped, anyway. Suddenly, the shark struck the bow of the boat hard and Chavez was jolted forward, the one direction in which he was not braced against. He couldn't get his hands out in front of him fast enough, so his face smashed into the hull. His nose throbbed as he quickly recovered back to his hands and knees. He carefully brought one hand up to his face and pressed his nose between his thumb and forefinger to see if it was broken. He couldn't tell if he had broken it, but he could feel warm, sticky fluid pouring from his nostrils. "Sangre! Santo Christo! Blood! Oh Christ!"

Like most sharks, the oceanic white tip shark was a competitive, opportunistic predator. It got its name from its exceptionally long pectoral fins, which were white tipped. Its dorsal and tail fins might also be white tipped, or mottled. The oceanic white tip was generally not a threat to beachgoers. Rather, it was a solitary traveler that slowly cruised the open ocean in search of food. It conserved its energy by swimming slowly, but was capable of high speed bursts and extremely aggressive behavior when competing for food. The shark could sense blood at concentrations as low as forty parts per billion, which was the equivalent of one eye drop in 275 gallons. Jacques Cousteau described the oceanic white tip as "The most dangerous of all sharks."[6] A rather daunting reputation, when one considered the ferocity of the great white shark.

All of the World War II veterans who survived the sinking of the *USS Indianapolis* and the *Nova Scotia* would surely agree with Monsieur Cousteau.

Chavez knew that if just one drop of blood mixed into the ocean, it would be like ringing the dinner bell for the shark. Once the shark sensed blood, instincts would be automatically triggered from prehistoric DNA within the shark's brain. These instincts included violent, thrashing outbursts, easily capable of launching Chavez off the slippery hull. He turned over and lay on his back on the overturned boat, tilting his head back in an effort to reduce the blood flow from his nose. He also tried to lower his center of gravity so that the shark couldn't knock him off the bottom of the capsized boat. With his heart pounding in his chest, he wedged himself under the lifeline. He crossed his ankles around the stern section of lifeline and spread both arms out wide from his sides, holding the second section of lifeline as tightly as he could in each hand. Looking up into the dark heavens, he realized he was positioned like Christ on the cross and began to pray.

CHAPTER 34   BLACKOUT

Is this death? Am I dead? What is death? Billy had never really contemplated death before. Did death have a feeling or was it void of all feelings? Logic indicated that death was devoid of life. Life was full of feelings; therefore, death must be void of feelings. If that was the case, than Billy must be alive. Every square inch of his body ached and burned like fire.

Billy blinked several times, but couldn't tell if his eyes were open or shut. He could see no light whatsoever where he lay. Taking a couple of deep, painful breaths, he tried to remember how he wound up here. *Where is here?* Billy thought. As he lay there, he slowly regained his senses and began to process information. He couldn't see, and there was not much to taste or smell, but he could hear the sound of water splashing and he could feel some sort of slow, rocking motion. *Splashing? Water? Rocking? Yacht! Destiny! I'm on the yacht! What the hell happened?* Feeling around, he reached up the nearest wall and felt the cold metal of the washing machine door, which seemed to be somewhat dented, but he couldn't tell in the dark. Crawling on his hands and knees, Billy shuffled to his room, where he kept a flashlight in the drawer next to the bed. Using the Braille method, he located the flashlight and turned it on.

Using one arm to pry himself up from his bed, Billy got to his feet and felt a head rush that made him stagger backwards. He fell against the wall, took a deep breath, and closed his eyes. He leaned his head back to the wall and felt an extremely sharp pain at the back of his skull. Remaining there for a moment, bits and pieces of the past slowly began to replay in his head.

Synapses in his brain fired wildly like the grand finale on the fourth of July. Thoughts were flying by and standing still in the same instant. He had flashes of childhood, running toward an old tire swing in the back yard. The dog he loved so much in his youth. Images of former lovers briefly came into view. Billy's heart began to race when Bridget appeared. She did the little hip shake that he loved and blew him a kiss as she faded into the mist of memory. The image of Bridget urged Billy to try and focus. He loved her dearly and had to get back to her. Her image stirred a bit of *the feeling* in him and he had a flashing thought that she was in danger, or reaching out to him in some way.

Everything moved in slow motion, yet a sense of urgency overwhelmed Billy. Like a drunkard's blackout, partial images of the storm began to invade his mind. Billy started to feel panic, but didn't know why, compounding the chaos. He stepped out of his room and walked toward the steps that led up to the main deck. Flashing his light around, he saw the hand held spotlight off in the corner of the VIP room. Picking it up, Billy thought it would be useless, but it still worked. With the added light he walked upstairs to the main deck and flashed the spotlight around to survey the wheelhouse and salon.

Billy did not see Marco.

When Billy looked up at wood patch on the window, everything started to come back to him: the broken window, the eye of the storm, heading back into it, water in the bilge. *Water in the bilge! Marco!*

Billy dashed to the aft doors, opening them in an instant. The now calm ocean only added to the madness. *There's no wind; the hurricane has passed. How long was I out?* He scurried toward the engine room door and quickly grabbed the handle. The latch was already fully open, the door free to swing. Billy's hart sank. *Oh, God, no! Please no!* He feared that Marco had been ripped over the side by a huge wave while trying to open the engine room door. He ripped the door open and flashed the spotlight down into the engine room.

"Oh, Christ! Marco!" Marco lay sprawled out facedown at the base of the ladder. His arms were spread out, hanging down into the bilge which had filled with water. One arm was wet up to his bicep.

Billy quickly shuffled down the ladder and bent down to Marco. Billy grabbed Marco's shoulder and tried to shake him gently. "Marco, Marco can you hear me?" Marco's body remained eerily motionless. More thoughts flew through Billy's head. *Broken neck? Is he dead?*

Billy found the carotid artery on Marco's neck and took his pulse. *He's alive! Thank God! Pulse is fairly strong. Good, good.* Billy rolled Marco on his side and pulled him up so that Marco was sitting at the base of the ladder with his back propped up, and his legs stretching straight out in front of him. "Marco, Marco can you hear me?"

Marco's lips moved slightly, but no sound came from them. Billy reached down, cupped a handful of saltwater from the bilge and splashed Marco's face. Marco responded sluggishly by pursing his lips and moving his head slightly. He muttered something in Spanish that Billy couldn't understand and slowly lifted his head as his eyes blinked open.

"Amigo! You're alive!"

Marco looked around and blinked, obviously trying to put the events leading to his present situation into place. He began speaking in Spanish and mumbled halfway through a sentence before realizing that he wasn't speaking English. "...and then a huge wave hit the door. That is all I remember."

"I'm just glad you're alive, amigo!"

Billy helped Marco stand up, and both men looked around the engine room. The reality of the situation hit Billy fast. There were almost five feet of water in the bilge. The transmissions were submerged in saltwater. No lights were on. In fact, nothing was on. No engines, no generators, nothing.

Quickly the men realized that they were in a death trap. The yacht was taking on water and there was no way to pump it out. Nothing was working. What the hell had happened? Billy directed the spotlight to the main electrical panel. The bilge pump circuit breakers were on, no, wait! One was off. Billy reset it and waited. Nothing. He looked up and saw that the volt meter for the service batteries was below ten volts. *Shit, we drained the service batteries! Damn! How long was I out?*

"Marco, start pumping with the manual bilge pump! I'm going to see if I can stop the leak from the stuffing box."

"Okay, amigo." Marco made his way over to the manual bilge pump and rotated several ball valves to divert the flow from the electrical pumps to the manual pump. Most large yachts were equipped with a manual pump of some sort, and this particular pump had a lever arm that when rotated, resembled pulling the arm of a slot machine. Marco could feel water flowing with each pull of the arm. It was a slow, laborious process that realistically only moved about a quart per pull. The manual pump couldn't match the flow rate of incoming seawater, but at least it bought them a little time.

Billy ripped off the bilge plates and went to work. He removed several large diameter hose clams from the tool box and grabbed the rag bag. He fished through the rags and found an old, small towel. He ripped it in half and folded it over to about a four inch width. The propeller shaft was completely under water now, so he did most of the work by feel. With his fingertips, he could feel the saltwater flowing in around the stuffing box. He took the towel and wrapped it around the shaft like gauze around an arm, doubling then tripling the layers of the towel. He put two hose clamps in his mouth as he loosened a third one with both hands. He had to loosen it all the way, in order to circle the shaft and towel. Lining it up, he tightened it only slightly to keep the towel in place while he put the other two clamps around the shaft. With the three hose clamps loosely secured around the towel, which was wound tightly against the propeller shaft, Billy slid the whole contraption aft toward the stuffing box. He pushed it hard against the source of the leak and tried to tighten the nearest clamp. However, he couldn't hold pressure on the towel and tighten the hose clamps at the same time, and in the midst of his effort, the screw driver slipped from his hand and sank into the bilge full of water.

"Marco, I need a third hand! Grab another screw driver out of the tool box." Marco handed Billy the screw driver and then climbed down to help. Both men were now waist deep in water, but it didn't matter because they were already soaking wet with sweat. Leaning into the stuffing box, Marco pressed the towel firmly against the stuffing box with both hands.

"Great, right there!" Billy said. With agonizing difficulty, Billy tightened the hose clamp nearest the shaft seal, and worked his way toward Marco by tightening the other two clamps.

When Billy finished, he felt around the towel for signs of flowing water. He could feel something, a small leak perhaps, but the leak had been drastically reduced. "Okay, that's gotta help. Keep manually pumping Marco, and I'll see if we can get some power down here!"

Billy looked about the engine room and quickly summed up the volume of water in the bilge as Marco began to crank the pump again. He knew that it would take at least twenty-four hours to manually pump out the bilge. There had to be another way. At least now, they could tread water and buy some time.

Up at the helm station, it didn't take Billy long to figure out what had happened. Looking at the fuel gauge he saw that they were bone dry. No diesel left whatsoever. He and Marco got knocked out and the yacht ran around in big circles until all the fuel was consumed, and one by one, the main engines and generators died. Once there was nothing to charge the service batteries, it was just a matter of time before all of the DC loads–radar, engine room lights, etc.–drained the batteries. *But they should have had more than four or five hours of life in them,* he thought. Billy recalled that when the generators shut down, the refrigerator and freezers were designed to automatically shift to DC. He dashed into the galley and saw that both the refrigerator and freezer doors were still shut and the locking pin was in place.

When he made his way up to the fly bridge, he saw that both the refrigerator and freezer doors there were wide open, lazily flopping back and forth with the gentle rocking of the yacht.

Billy looked around and noticed barely any wind. In fact, the sea had become relatively calm. He examined the water from *Destiny* to the horizon and continued searching the ocean in a 360 degree pattern, but did not spot a single vessel. On the horizon toward the east, he observed faint light in the distance and had to think for a second if it was sunrise or sunset. Fifteen-foot high swells were lifting the yacht up in the air and then gently setting her down again like a giant horse on a merry go round. More light began to flow from the east, illuminating the vast sea around them.

Where the hell are we?

Billy scurried back down to the wheel house and checked his lap top and the portable GPS that he had rigged up, but both were completely drained of battery power. He fumbled around in the chart drawer and found four new AA batteries for the GPS. It took a few minutes for the GPS to acquire the satellites, but Billy had obtained *Destiny's* coordinates in less than five minutes. He plotted them on the soaking wet paper chart and got his bearings.

Studying the chart, Billy grabbed the dividers and things became clearer. *We were in the eye, here, when we began heading into the storm and we had run for about an hour and a half. That puts us here,* he thought, as he set one point of the dividers on the chart. "Now we're here." He said out loud as he drew a small "X" on the chart. Then he placed the other point of the dividers at their current location. *Destiny* had traveled fifty miles from the last place Billy remembered seeing on the GPS.

I must have been out for four or five hours, he thought. *And I bet we ran out of fuel right after I got knocked out.* Billy realized that nothing he was currently thinking about made a difference to them at the moment; he was wasting time. *What I have to do now,* he thought, *is get the water out of the bilge and then see what we can do about getting some fuel.*

Marco continued manually pumping, which kept up with the volume of saltwater coming in, so they weren't sinking. That was good, but not good enough. Billy knew they were still taking on water. *The service batteries are dead, so I can't use the regular bilge pumps.* "Wait a minute, wait a minute!" Billy said out loud. "I can use the main engine starting batteries!"

Billy had installed a parallel battery switch on *Destiny* years ago. He had installed it in case the main engine batteries were inadvertently drained, resulting in insufficient energy to start the big diesel engines. He had run parallel lines to the service batteries to tap into their energy. If the big engines wouldn't turn over with the energy in the starting batteries, he could press the parallel switch, which would temporarily divert power from the service batteries. Since the service batteries were constantly charged by a separate charger, they were good backup. Billy had never thought they would have to use the system backwards; draw energy from the main engine batteries to run items wired to the service batteries.

Billy descended into the engine room and turned off all other DC loads except the bilge pumps. He told Marco to listen for the pumps to make sure they were running and come up in two minutes to tell Billy the status. Billy climbed back up the ladder and rushed into the salon. He double checked the circuit breaker panel at the helm station to make sure he had turned off all other DC loads, radar, refrigerator, freezer, navigation lights, etc. No sense in using energy unnecessarily. He turned around and prayed that it would work. Then he pressed the parallel battery button with his thumb and waited.

Marco came up two minutes later and said, "One of the breakers tripped, but, em, the other bilge pump is working. I checked the outboard flow and it looks good."

Billy nodded excitedly. "See if you can get the other bilge pump working. Check the intake, there's got to be something in there that is making the breaker trip. We'll cut our pump time in half if we can get that running."

"Okay, amigo." Marco said, heading back to the engine room.

Billy started thinking ahead. *If we get the yacht dry, we can survive for a while. We have food and water. So what if we drift for a couple of days? It can't be any worse than what we just went through! That would give us time to lick our wounds and get some temporary repairs done.*

Billy still didn't know exactly how they would get to the Cayman Islands, but if they could flag down, or radio a boat, maybe they could buy some diesel from a local fisherman. *But, how would a fisherman transport the diesel? It would be better if I gave them an empty drum, and then they could just fill it up in their boat and come back to us.*

Finding an empty fifty-five gallon drum in the States was relatively easy, but in the islands, drums were valuable, and never just thrown away. They made great storage containers on fishing vessels for bait, water, or fuel. Or, drums could be used in homes for storing rainwater collected from tin roofs. Billy had even seen one used as a hot water heater. It had been mounted over a fire pit, and once a week the family would heat the water and have hot showers. Drums were also used as musical instruments. They were cut down to a specific height and the bottom of the drum was hammer-tuned. When the steel drum was played with mallets, it emitted a xylophone sound, integral to Caribbean music.

We need our own empty drum, Billy decided as he continued to hold down the parallel battery button.

Marco returned from the engine room with a three inch long, rusted, old screw. He had pulled it out of the second bilge pump intake. Both pumps were working now and they were getting rid of water at a flow rate of almost thirty gallons per minute each. In ten minutes, they would remove 600 gallons of saltwater from the bilge. Billy patted Marco on the back and said, "Great, amigo! Thanks!" Then Billy grabbed an eraser from the chart drawer and broke it in half. It just fit into the square button of the parallel battery switch. Then he placed the log book on top of the eraser which held down the button.

Billy climbed back down to the engine room and double checked the bilge. The shaft plug he made out of rags was working well to reduce the amount of water coming into the bilge. The flow from the leak was like a faucet barely turned on, maybe a gallon every couple of minutes. The other shaft was only dripping a few drops per second. The bilge would be dry in less than one hour.

If only we had some fuel! But, how could we get it? Maybe there's a delivery service out of the Caymans, like the one they have in Ft. Lauderdale, where a fuel barge ties up alongside and pumps fuel onto the yacht. But the more Billy thought about it, the less likely it seemed there would be anything like that down here in the Caribbean. In fact, he had never seen the fuel barge leave port in Fort Lauderdale. It always delivered right around the downtown area. *There would be no market for a rig like that way down here,* he thought.

It would help if he could use the radar to locate any boats in the vicinity. However, Billy needed to be careful using energy from the main starting batteries. A few hours of bilge pumping was one thing, but hours of radar use was another. The radar consumed a lot of power to transmit and receive radar wave information. More thoughts began to ricochet around Billy's head and he realized that he had a throbbing headache and wasn't thinking straight. He needed some sustenance and rest.

The sun had risen over the horizon and the sky was clearing to the east. Usually after a massive low pressure system like a hurricane passed, there was fairly good weather afterward. This day was no exception. The wind had died to nearly calm and all that rocked the yacht were the remaining swells. The wave period of the swells was in excess of twenty seconds, so they were barely noticeable inside the yacht. Billy had to be looking out to the horizon to see the rise and fall over each swell.

"Okay, amigo, here's the plan." Billy began. "We take an hour and get some food, rest, and maybe a shower so we can think clearly. I don't know about you, but I can barely focus, and I'm completely famished." Both men had forgotten the last time they had eaten anything, and other than the being knocked out cold, neither of them had gotten any sleep in the last forty or fifty hours.

"We're not going to sink and we can last for a few days out here, so I say we get something to eat and..."

D-d-d-da-da-da-ding. D-d-d-da-da-da-ding.

"What in hell is that?" Marco asked.

Billy couldn't believe it. The satellite phone! Of all the things to buzz, ring, or alarm, the last thing he ever imagined was the damn phone. If Billy hadn't had the batteries in parallel, the call never would have gone through because the sat phone ran on DC power and the service batteries were dead. Billy walked over to the helm station and pulled the sat phone from its bracket. He stared at the liquid crystal display on the sat phone in disbelief. It was his boss on the phone. *D-d-d-da-da-da-ding.*

Instantly, thoughts flashed through Billy's aching head. *If I don't answer it, he'll try me on my cell, if he hasn't already. Then he'll want to know why I'm not answering either phone. I always answer my phone. Shit! He'll send someone down to check on the yacht!*

D-d-d-da-da-da-ding.

CHAPTER 35   REVENGE

Chavez tried as hard as he could to stay flush with the overturned police boat. He lay on his back and pressed himself against the bottom of the hull by gripping the lifeline in each hand and bending his arms at the elbows. His ankles burned from being doused in saltwater where the skin had been ripped raw from rubbing against the lifeline. His biceps ached from the relentless effort to hold on, but it was better than being torn apart and eaten alive by a shark. The sea had become much rougher, and he sensed that the weather was going to get worse before it got better. Thankfully, the half sunk boat remained just that, and had not lost much buoyancy. Waves began to crash over the boat, the saltwater stinging his eyes.

　　He could feel the wind speed increasing as it whipped saltwater across his face. While holding on for his life, his fear manifested into anger toward the men responsible for his current situation, and he vowed to seek revenge if he lived through the night. But as the sea began to show its true fury, Miguel Chavez became more and more convinced that he would not see the light of day. He tried to keep his eyes closed, but it was impossible. He needed to see what would happen. The size of the waves increased to the point that if he relaxed his grip on the life line, he would be ripped from the overturned boat by the force of water flowing over the hull. His muscles ached, but he refused to let his grip loosen. After several hours, his hands were cramped closed and he could not feel his fingers, but at least he had secured himself to the boat-or so he thought.

CHAPTER 36   BY THE WAY

"Hello, motor yacht Destiny." Billy said in his best non-terrified, I-didn't-almost-sink-the-yacht, and I-don't-have-pounds-of-cocaine-aboard, sort of voice.

"Hi there, Billy! How's my yacht?" the boss asked in an overly cheery voice.

Billy felt so mentally and physically depleted that he didn't have the creativity to lie. He tried to think fast, but his brain would not respond, so he tried his best not to garble his words on the phone. For a split second, he considered coming clean with his boss and telling him everything. "Well actually boss, not so good," Billy said, as an idea slowly crept into his throbbing head.

"Oh really? What happened?" The boss sounded concerned.

"Last night when Marco and I came back to the yacht after dinner, I noticed that the water line just didn't look right. Even in the darkness, the yacht seemed to be riding too low in the water. I went down in the engine room and we had a lot of water in the bilge." Ideas were starting to come to Billy now.

"Was it saltwater?" The boss asked.

"The first thing I did was taste it, and yes, it was salt. To make matters worse, the primary bilge pump wasn't working."

"What?" His boss asked with concern. "Did it burn out?"

"Well boss, as you know, Murphy's Law works overtime on boats, so actually it took me a while to diagnose the problem." Billy's words began to flow. "We had to pump out the water with the main bilge pump, you know, the one with the long hose, to get it down to where we could get at the primary pump. Turned out there was a piece of a plastic wire tie caught in the impeller. Once we got that running and pumped the water down, I could clearly see the leak coming from the stuffing box."

The boss responded with a frustrated attitude, "Well, the girls are flying down tomorrow night and they want to stay on the yacht."

"That's going to be tough boss. We're on our way to the yacht yard for repairs right now."

"Why didn't you call me?" The boss said, irritation clearly evident in his tone.

"Boss, all this just happened last night. Marco and I took turns on watch throughout the night to make sure the yacht didn't sink. Neither one of us got much sleep. Since we have to get hauled out to fix the stuffing box, I thought we'd knock off a few items on the punch list before our next big trip to the Bahamas. I was going to call you when I had the repairs all lined up. I don't like to call you with problems. I like to call you with solutions."

The boss knew and appreciated that Billy dealt with all the difficult problems that occurred on the yacht and didn't call to whine about them. Billy just got it done correctly and inexpensively.

"Well, the girls can stay on the yacht at the yard, right? I mean, they're only coming down for the weekend."

Oh Christ, Billy thought. "Sure, if they don't mind continuous noise, no air conditioning, a shitty view, and toothless guys clutching power tools checking them out all day while they sun tan."

"All right, all right, they'll get a hotel."

"Do you want me to book it for you?" Billy asked, although he already knew the answer.

"No, no, that's okay. The girls may not know how to operate a washing machine, but they sure as hell know how to make a reservation! Let me know how you make out in the yard."

They exchanged some pleasantries and the obligatory, "how is the family," before the boss remembered that they were on his satellite phone and getting charged by the minute. "Okay, Billy gotta run, good luck with the repairs, and we're looking forward to the Bahamas trip!"

Billy clicked the satellite phone back into its cradle, took a deep breath, and exhaled heavily.

Marco looked at Billy and shook his head in disbelief and said, "Amigo, you are not like most men."

CHAPTER 37   NO MERCY

Hanging onto the overturned police boat during the raging storm had pushed Chavez's body to the limit. He could no longer feel his hands or feet, but miraculously he stayed attached to the overturned boat. The wind howled like a madman, while the seas raged all around, tossing the overturned boat like a toy in the bathtub. Chavez could barely breath, much less open his eyes, but he tried to get a glimpse of what was happening around him. No ambient light existed, as the moon hid behind the thick, dark storm clouds. He felt an odd momentary reprieve from the wind and opened his eyes. Looking up, he saw a massive wave continue to rise before him, and could make out white wisps of sea flying off the top of the seventy foot wave. He cried out in mortal fear.

"Nooooo!" He screamed as the top of the wave started to crest above him. The force of the water alone would probably kill him, smashing his body against the boat's hull. Or he would roll over and over with the boat as the wave crashed through him and drown, unable to get loose from the lifeline. He squirmed wildly trying to get free from the line intended to save his life but would surely seal his fate. He felt like a fish being hauled up to a boat with the end clearly visible and no means of escape. Having produced the final reserves of adrenaline hours ago, his body could no longer respond to fear. Chavez watched in terror as the massive wave succumbed to gravity and descended upon him like the devil himself.

The colossal wave hit Chavez with such force that it smashed his head against the boat's hull and instantly knocked him unconscious. The small boat rolled over three times as the enormous wave crashed over him like a Nazi invasion.

The insurmountable strength of Mother Ocean blew him off the barely floating boat and tore him viciously from the lifeline. Flesh ripped to the bone at both his wrists and ankles. Chavez was now truly at the mercy of the ocean. He lay there unconscious and was whipped about like a rag doll by the raging sea all around him. The twenty-year old life jacket he was wearing barely kept his head above water as blood flowed from his wrists and ankles into the salty abyss.

CHAPTER 38   ADRIFT

The sun continued to rise and Billy performed another 360 degree scan of the ocean, but did not see a single boat. Large swells were still present, but the interval between them was almost two minutes, so unless they were looking out onto the water, the rise and fall of the yacht was unnoticeable.

Billy racked his brain for a way to obtain diesel fuel. According to the GPS coordinates, they were about forty miles from Grand Cayman, but he knew it would not be wise to bring the yacht into Grand Cayman, even if they could do so on their own power. The authorities had a zero tolerance for drugs. There had been numerous cases of the naïve college spring breaker ignorantly smoking a joint on the beach, only to have his high thoroughly destroyed by police taking him to jail. Jail usually lasted several days, and the fines extremely expensive, around $10,000 per joint.

The last time Billy visited Grand Cayman, a friend of his told him about a man trying to get an old sail boat up and running. The sailor hired a cheap day worker, who decided to smoke a joint while washing down the boat. The police were notified and when they arrived all that was left was a roach and a few seeds, but that was enough to impound the boat for more than one year and force the captain into bankruptcy.

It was probably not a good idea to bring 200,000 grams of cocaine into Grand Cayman.

How the hell am I going to get enough diesel to get to Little Cayman? He thought. Billy's physical and mental exhaustion made it difficult to plan and execute anything. He had trouble just moving around the boat.

Billy walked over to the navigation area and noticed that they were drifting at about two knots *toward* Grand Cayman. "Marco can you keep watch for two hours?"

"Yes, amigo."

"Okay, I'm going to lie down and close my eyes. Wake me up in two hours if I'm still asleep. We're drifting toward Grand Cayman, so just keep a look out for other boats and disconnect the parallel battery switch when the bilge pumps dry."

"Okay, amigo. Em, get some sleep and see you in two hours." Billy wasn't sure if he had ever appreciated Marco's companionship and reliability as much as he did right then. He was asleep before his head touched the pillow.

The next thing he knew, Billy felt Marco's gentle shake. *Another boat must be approaching. There's no way two hours have passed.* Billy still ached from head to toe and felt thoroughly exhausted. When he tried to move, it felt like swimming in concrete.

"Amigo, sorry to wake you, but you said to get you after two hours."

Billy blinked. *Christ, two hours!* "Okay, okay, Marco. Will you put some coffee on please? And make it strong."

"Yes, no problem, amigo."

Billy rolled over and tried to resist the overwhelming need to go back to sleep. The urge to close his eyes was unbearable. *This must be what it's like to be a recovering heroin addict resisting enticement,* he thought. Yielding to temptation, he instantly drifted into a dreamlike memory of a childhood friend, who had become a heroin addict in his mid-twenties. Billy had run into Ladd in Lynn, Massachusetts and, while chatting, it became obvious that Ladd had serious problems. Billy remembered how sad he felt walking away from their conversation on the street. A few years later, Ladd was found dead in a bathtub full of water with the needle still in his arm.

Watching some good friends screaming, "Let me out!"

Billy drifted further back in time to when they were teenagers. He could vividly remember riding mountain bikes through town on a hot summer night.

"Psyched for some cold ones!" Ladd said.

"Yeah, me, too. Where do you want to go?"

"Let's ride out to Castle Rock on the Neck. There's good moonlight tonight, and we can look out over the water."

"Great idea!" They hopped on their bikes and started riding the twisted streets of Old Town Marblehead. They rode past Maddie's Sail Loft bar, past the Old Town House, and then toward Lee Street. They encountered some beautiful views of Marblehead Harbor in the moonlight as they made their way toward Glover's Landing. They rode down Chestnut Street and cut through the baseball field at Seaside Park, where Ladd got a little air when he sped over the pitcher's mound on his bike. In no time, they were on the causeway that joined Marblehead neck to the mainland. Ladd wore an unbuttoned long sleeve shirt with his sleeves rolled up; the back of his shirt floating around in the air as they zipped along the causeway. The moon gave off plenty of light to see the boats in the harbor and Billy watched Ladd's shirt wave around in the air like a luffing sail. Ladd looked over and said, "Amigo, amigo..."

Billy opened his eyes and felt even more tired than before. Fortunately, Marco had brought down a large cup of strong coffee. "Thanks, Marco. Sorry about that." Billy took the cup and just the smell was so good, he knew it couldn't be a dream. "Okay, I'm up, amigo. Thank you." With that, Billy took a sip. The instant coffee was cold. Billy gave a frown. "If nothing else, we have to get some fuel so we can run the generators and have some hot coffee." Marco nodded with a half grin. Looking at him, Billy realized that neither of them had laughed or smiled in several days. "We'll get through this, Marco. We will. Now that I've had some rest, I'll look at this fuel situation with a fresh set of eyes.

Even though the coffee was cold, it perked Billy up. He began to search his mind for a way out of their predicament. *We're only forty miles from the Cayman Islands. There has to be a way*, he thought. Billy remembered that they were drifting toward the island at almost two knots last time he checked. *That means in twenty hours or so we can flag down a local fisherman and try to get some fuel. We can't be the only ones who have run out of fuel around here!* He walked up to the wheel house and checked their position. According to his hand held GPS, they were still about forty miles away from Grand Cayman, and drifting at 1.8 knots. Billy transferred their current position coordinates onto the paper chart and drew a line from their last charted position from a little over two hours ago. Immediately, he realized that there must be a current that ran parallel to the island. They had been moving generally toward the Cayman Islands, but on their current course, they would pass the islands about twenty miles to the west. *Damn!* Billy thought. He felt the wind begin to pick up just a little, and knew that even the slightest breeze would turn the huge yacht broadside, and like a square rigged sailing ship, they would travel whichever way the wind blew. *Hell, in ten hours, we could be more than fifty miles away!*

Billy grabbed two protein bars from the storage area under the salon couch cushions and walked out to the aft deck to think. He began eating the second bar before he

realized he had devoured the first one. *Guess I was hungry.*
He walked to the stern of the yacht, took two steps down
toward the swim platform, and sat on the top step. Before
him, the sea stretched out endlessly.

How can we move this big ol' pig with no damn fuel?
The tender has a small tank of about 14 gallons, but that's
gasoline and no good in the diesel engines. Even if we could
use the fourteen gallons, it would barely prime the big
engines! We could launch the tender and try to tow the yacht,
but that's a huge load on the outboard engine. We'd never
make it on the amount of fuel in the tender. I could take the
tender with an empty drum or two, and try to make it to the
Caymans and leave Marco on the yacht. Refuel the tender
with gas and fill the drums with diesel. Why didn't I think of
that before? It's so simple! The hard part will be finding
Marco on the way back. We must still have enough battery
power to lower the tender down using the davit. Billy's mind
began gyrating through the calculations of fuel burn rate of the
tender at top speed, making sure he'd have enough gas to get
to the Caymans. Then he thought about how much time it
would take to find diesel fuel, fill the drums, and get back to
Destiny. He had to account for the distance *Destiny* would
drift while he was gone, and hopefully, the direction of her
drift.

With a rebirth of energy, Billy could feel a feasible
plan coming together. For a moment, he thought of sending
Marco to get the fuel and staying on *Destiny* himself, but
being from Honduras, Marco would have more trouble on
the island if he were stopped by officials for any reason. Billy's
mind was racing now as he thought about all the things he
needed for the voyage in the tender. *I'll need my passport,*
loads of cash, hand held VHF radio, two empty drums,
drinking water, foul weather gear, navigation chart... Billy was

still quantifying the items needed for his voyage when he strutted into the salon to tell Marco the plan.

Marco began removing tie down straps and getting the tender ready to launch from the fly bridge, while Billy planned the voyage in his mind step by step to make sure he didn't forget anything. A forty-mile trip in the tender was something Billy had completed many times, but not in the middle of the Caribbean Sea with his entire existence at stake. He was aware that the round trip would be substantially longer than eighty miles. He felt sure that he could cruise at twenty knots on the way to Grand Cayman. That would take about two hours. Add another two hours to locate fuel and fill the drums. Billy knew diesel fuel weighed about six pounds per gallon, and figured that he couldn't cruise as fast on the return trip, because two drums full of diesel would contain 110 gallons, or 660 additional pounds. So he used a conservative figure of ten knots, and quickly realized that the return trip alone would take about four hours. However, he still had to add the distance that *Destiny* would drift. They were currently drifting over a depth of 2,000 feet of water, so trying to anchor the yacht was not an option. Billy figured it would be at least eight hours before he returned with fuel. At a drift rate of two knots, that would add about sixteen miles, or another hour and a half, to his trip. A shiver ran down his back as he realized he would have to locate *Destiny* in the middle of the Caribbean Sea at night after almost ten hours of her drifting in an unknown direction.

To complicate matters even further, Billy knew the tender had a fuel burn rate of four to five miles per gallon. Just getting to the island was pushing the margin of safety. *Doesn't matter,* he thought, *I've got to do it.*

"Ready to launch the tender," Marco yelled down from the fly bridge.

"Okay, Marco. Toss me the guide lines and let's go."
Marco used the hand held remote control to lower the
inflatable tender from the fly bridge down to sea level. Billy
used the bow and stern lines to keep it from swinging around
and banging into *Destiny*. He secured the tender to the swim
platform.

Together they loaded the two empty fifty-five gallon
drums onto the tender and secured them tightly with rope.
Marco handed Billy his bag of gear for the trip.

"One more thing, Marco," Billy said. "Grab the empty
five-gallon jerry jug in the rudder room. I might need it on the
way back." Marco quickly returned and handed a five-gallon
jerry jug over to him on the tender. Billy was elated when he
felt almost two gallons of gas sloshing within. He stored the
liquid gold securely behind his seat and tied it off with a spare
line so as not to lose it overboard.

"Marco, I wrote out instructions and left them on the
control panel of the wheel house, but let's go over the plan."
Billy went on to instruct Marco on illuminating the yacht after
dark, battery power consumption, and most importantly, the
detailed communication plans that would be necessary later
that night if Billy could not find *Destiny* in the darkness. He
stressed the importance of adhering strictly to the plan.
Deviation from the plan would lead to greater confusion, and
the possibility of Billy not returning. On that somber note,
Billy did his best to smile. "I'll see you later tonight."

Marco watched as the fourteen-foot tender got up on a
plane and sped off. He glanced at his watch and noted the
time. It was 2:10 p.m.

Billy looked back after ten minutes of cruising and
watched as the fly bridge of the yacht bobbed in and out of
view before fading completely under the ocean horizon. A
little over an hour into the trip, Billy focused on keeping the
tender on course when an alarm sounded and a red light

began flashing on the dash board. Billy throttled back and noticed the red light in the shape of an old oil can. *Oh, shit. Low on oil.* He always made sure that an extra quart of oil was stored on the tender and located it in no time. Removing the outboard engine cover, he removed the fill cap to the small oil tank and carefully added the whole quart of oil. *Glad I don't have to do this at night in rough seas,* he thought. Then he drained the jerry jug into the gas tank. Even though he'd preformed the routine procedures dozens of times, Billy was extremely relieved to be back up on a plane and running at twenty knots toward Grand Cayman Island.

His heart skipped a beat when he got his first glimpse of the island, which didn't look like an island at all. In fact, it looked like several sail boat masts far off in the distance, but Billy knew better. Due to the curvature of the earth and the line of sight from the tender, the tallest items would be the first things visible from a distance on the water. Water storage tanks, smoke stacks, power lines, and recently constructed cell phone towers always preceded land when viewed from any distance offshore.

Billy raised the binoculars to his eyes and felt a surge of adrenaline when he focused in on the lighthouse on the south side of the island. *Yes!*

Several years ago, Billy had flown to Grand Cayman and spent two weeks scuba diving and mountain biking all over the island. During his visit, he learned that only a few marinas carried diesel fuel. Now, as he approached the island, he wasn't sure exactly where the fuel docks were located, and he didn't want to waste time searching the island for a marina that sold fuel. He didn't care what the price was, he just wanted to fill up the drums and head back out toward *Destiny* as quickly as possible.

Billy had the island in full view now, and could see the lighthouse about four miles ahead. He altered course toward the west side of the island where he figured the nearest fuel dock was located. He passed Bodden Town, still several miles off to the starboard side and headed for George Town. Fifteen minutes later, Billy pulled the throttle back with the George Town Harbor docks in clear view ahead. The long, industrial looking cruise ship dock looked completely vacant. In fact, as Billy approached the smaller dinghy dock to tie up, he noticed that everything seemed eerily quiet. A huge wave of panic swept over him as he realized that the hurricane that had damn near killed him had also ravaged the island. Most of the local residents were still licking their wounds after the storm. He looked around and noticed the Customs and Immigration building and thought, w*hat if they heard the Mayday call?* He made note to stay far clear of it. It would be a very simple matter to deduce that the small boat with two fifty-five gallon drums strapped to the bow was indeed the tender to a larger yacht. Billy nudged the tender in between two other small boats and tied off the bow line. He ran up the dock with the five-gallon jerry jug in his hand. When he reached the small building containing the dock master's office, the door was locked with no one inside. He walked past the building out onto Church Street, usually bustling with activity, but the whole street appeared deserted. He spotted a gas station and ran across the street, but it too, looked closed.

Billy began to panic and thought about running up the street to find any store open, or somebody to talk to, when just then he heard, "You there, stop!" Billy turned around and saw a very polished uniform heading straight for him. The Customs Officer, a large man well over six-feet tall, walked with confidence and authority as he approached Billy. The officer looked down at Billy and said with a strong island accent, "I'm ef-rayed you be in a great deal of trub-al."

Billy looked around to see where he could run, but spotted another officer about twenty yards away. His heart started to pound while he tried to think of something to say, but no words could come to him. The tremendous amount of stress, lack of proper sleep and food, combined with everything he had dealt over the last few days caught up to him and he felt as if he were going to pass out. Billy began to experience a sense of vertigo coming on and his vision started to blur when the officer said, "You'll have trub-al findin fuel. 'Lectricity out all over de island, cept for de large O'tels with dheir own generatah. Even if de gas stey-tion was open, dhey couldn't pump gas whidout 'lectricity."

Billy shivered with relief, but tried to hide the true reason for his jitters. He gave the officer a lame smile and said, "Oh, well. That's what I thought, but I had to give it a try. Are you sure there's no gas station that might have power, you know, like a generator?"

The officer eased up a bit, smiled and said, "No mon, doubt' it much. All de phones are down, even de cell towah been damaged from de storm. We should have powah tomorrow, or de next dhey." Billy nodded politely and thanked the officer.

He walked back toward the tender out of sight and sat down on the dock. *What the hell am I going to do? I can't even get back to Destiny. Marco is drifting away.* Billy began to shudder uncontrollably as he realized what a failure he had become. Tears streamed down from his eyes, as he buried his head in hands.

Several minutes later, Billy shook off his momentary lapse of reason and looked out at the ocean. His gaze fell down to the tender, then to the boat next to his. Right there in front of his eyes was an eight gallon gasoline tank. He looked around for the customs officers, but they were nowhere to be seen. Then, he hopped into the adjacent boat and discovered that the tank was almost full, but chained to the seat. Working quickly, Billy grabbed the funnel from his tender and filled the jerry jug. Then he poured the jerry jug's contents into the tender's gas tank. He repeated the process until the eight gallon tank was empty. Feeling guilty, he pulled two twenty-dollar bills from his wallet and stuffed them in the cubby hole by the steering wheel.

Billy looked at the empty two drums on the bow. *Okay, I can make it back to* Destiny *now, but I'm here and I've got to find some diesel fuel.* He untied the bow line in a flash as a bolt of enthusiasm struck. Five minutes later, he was running full throttle towards the nearest hotel on Seven Mile Beach. On any other day, he would have been far more courteous, but time was running out. Billy swiftly pulled up the outboard engine just as the tender ran up onto the white sand beach. There were a few hotel guests milling about on the beach who did not give Billy a second look. He quickly jogged up to the front desk and politely asked the attractive receptionist for the operations manager. She smiled revealing a dazzling set of bright white teeth that beautifully contrasted with her dark, island skin and said, "Oh, Sidney is quite busy with repairs after the storm."

"Please," Billy pleaded, "I really must speak with him. It's a matter of life and death." The receptionist's expression changed from the obligatory smile to a look of inquisitive concern, and she picked up a hand held radio and called for the operations manager. Five precious minutes later, the operations manager appeared. Billy walked Sidney away from the front desk, and began to tell the tale of running out of fuel and surviving the hurricane, and explained that he would pay whatever was necessary, but he simply had to get some fuel.

Sidney listened closely and when Billy finished speaking, the operations manager nodded slowly and said, "You are very lucky to be alive my friend. There were several fatalities on the island yesterday during the peak of the storm. I can't imagine being on the ocean when nature's wrath is in such a fury. It's a good thing my boss is off island, because he would not approve of selling you fuel when island folk want it just as badly. Now, where are these drums you are talking about?"

Billy felt an enormous surge of adrenaline as Sidney called for two maintenance men to grab the empty drums from the tender. It took a full hour to fill the drums with diesel fuel and then roll the drums back down the beach to the tender. This time, the beach goers were a little more curious about Billy's activities and watched with interest as the maintenance men rigged up a ramp using two by four wooden beams to roll the drums up and onto the tender. With a substantial effort, the men helped Billy push the tender off the beach. Billy gave each of the men $100, which put a smile on their faces. Sidney had been reasonable with the price of the fuel, and didn't take advantage of Billy's situation. In fact, Billy was prepared to pay whatever amount the operations manager demanded, even $1,000 per drum, or roughly, twenty dollars a gallon. Billy tipped Sidney who refused the tip at first, but after much encouragement from Billy, reluctantly accepted. Billy was overjoyed when Sidney even filled his jerry jug with precious gasoline.

The sun was setting as Billy motored the fully loaded tender away from the beach at slow speed. He wanted to run full throttle back to *Destiny*, but with the extra weight of the drums, he couldn't get the tender up on a plane. He was forced to settle for cruising at twelve knots.

Using the last known location of *Destiny* as his waypoint, Billy used his hand held GPS to plot a course back to where he left the yacht. Time passed excruciatingly slowly as Billy kept a close eye on his heading. He knew that a small cross track error in heading could put him miles away from *Destiny*.

With his current speed, the time required to reach the waypoint was three hours and twenty minutes. From there he figured he'd stop the tender and look carefully for *Destiny* in all directions. If he could not spot the lights of the yacht, he would determine which way he drifted and whether the direction was from the wind or the current or both. Then would come the tricky part. He would run the tender in the direction of the drift, hoping that it was the same direction in which *Destiny* had drifted.

As the lights of Grand Cayman faded in the distance behind him, Billy thought about his predicament. Finding *Destiny* in the dark in the middle of the ocean might be a very big problem. In fact, he very well could run out of gas while desperately searching for the yacht. Billy tried to stop his runaway train of thought every time it started down that path, because there was no use in wasting time thinking about failure and death. He would deal with that situation when, and if, it occurred. But it was similar to a song that was stuck in your head and couldn't get out. Time had slowed to a crawl and with nothing around him but the vast, empty ocean encased in pitch black night, the problem of finding *Destiny* kept jumping to the forefront of his mind.

Billy reached over, grabbed a handful of saltwater and splashed his face. He used his shirt to dry off and took a big, deep breath. As he exhaled, he looked up and noticed the abundance of stars. Very little moonlight enlightened him from above, but far from land in the unpolluted atmosphere, thousands of stars were shining brightly. Billy tried to put his mind someplace else, somewhere pleasant. He felt fortunate that he'd had a full and exciting life with numerous adventures. But even with the vast number of memories to choose from, for the first time in his life, he began thinking seriously about death.

If I were to die right now, tonight, he thought, *would I change anything? I can't, so what does it matter? I guess it's more about having any regrets. Do I have any regrets for things I did or didn't do?*

Well, smuggling 400 pounds of cocaine from Honduras was a pretty stupid thing to do. I really should be thankful for everything I have. Bridget loves me. I'm healthy and have a pretty cool job. Why did I risk all that for some silly green paper? Am I any different than the greedy Wall Street bankers?

Cruising along with nothing but his thoughts, he wished he could turn back time. But the events that had occurred put him far past the point of no return.

If I get out of this alive and don't go to jail, I'm going to live my life to the fullest. I'm going to marry Bridget, raise kids and enjoy every moment and every little detail each and every day. The thought of Bridget stirred his heart. Would she marry him? Lord, he hoped so. How he longed to run his fingers through her soft, silky hair and kiss her. *Why did I get myself into this crazy, fucked up situation? What was I thinking?*

Roughly two hours into the trip, the first splash of saltwater sprayed up from the side of the boat and hit Billy in the face. He had felt the waves getting slightly larger, but didn't want to accept that the seas might be building. There was still about an hour and a half to go to get to the location where he left *Destiny,* and he was hoping that the sea wouldn't get much rougher. He was able to keep up the same speed for another half hour, but as the waves continued to build, he had to throttle back so that the heavy drums full of diesel fuel wouldn't bounce around and damage the small boat. Billy pressed on through the clear night air. High above, the stars glittered white against a veil of darkness, but the moon refused to show itself. Onboard the tiny tender, the only light visible was the faint green glow from the instrument gauges on the dashboard.

Billy had spent tens of thousands of hours on the sea and always felt at home on the water, but as he looked around at the endless pitch black night in all directions, he felt very small and insignificant. Gazing into the abyss, he could not determine where the sea ended and the sky began. Previously, Billy had experienced similar weather conditions on other nights and felt euphoric. However, in the past, he had been an ethical man of principle. Now, as he stared into the darkness, panic and fear began to edge into Billy's mind. He realized that the atmospheric conditions around him were the same as in the past; however, it was he who had changed; same type of night, different Billy. By sacrificing his morality and yielding to greed, he lost the ability to interpret his surroundings with a clear conscious. He feared that his capability to perceive life had been permanently tainted. The canvas on which to paint was no longer white.

Billy looked deep into himself to try and find strength, but it was extremely difficult. He was agnostic, but now he envied the faith and religion that propped people up through desperate times. *It would be offensive and most likely somewhat sacrilegious to pray for help now,* he thought. *Why would the man upstairs assist me in something so selfish and idiotic? Maybe He's trying to teach me a lesson.* Just then the tender hit a wave and one of the drums banged against the floor of the boat, making a dull thud sound. Goose bumps rose all over his body, as the thud triggered the memory of Rodriguez pounding on the engine room door while suffocating. The memory of the dead men, the men *he* had killed, would haunt him for the rest of his life. He gazed at the steering wheel in his hands and flashed back to holding the water tight door latch against the doomed men on the other side. It felt as though Rodriguez was channeling through the ocean and applying torque against his grip of the wheel as he tried to steer. *Keep it together, Billy.*

He started to think about how the human body worked to protect itself. With a severe flesh wound, the body first responded with nerve signals generating pain so that the brain acknowledged the wound. Then the wound was physically tended to and natural healing began. Finally, a scar formed, but even that faded with the passage of time.

When psychological trauma occurred, the human mind did not recover in the same way. Some people cried for days after an emotional wound, while others barely shed a tear. As time went by, the wound never really completely healed. The memory remained forever, and often just a brief sight, the slightest sound, or even a faint smell would lift the latch to the memory vault.

Billy hoped that every time he heard someone knock, he wouldn't flash back to holding the engine room door shut as the men on the other side pounded away while suffocating to death. *I had to do it,* he thought. *They would have killed us. It was us or them.* He knew he was rationalizing murder, but it was all he could do. Another splash from a wave hit his face, and it snapped him back to the substantial task at hand. *I need to bury that memory for the time being and stay focused,* he thought. He looked down at his watch, moving it over to the instrument panel to get enough light to read the time. Billy had instructed Marco to turn the yacht's lights on for ten-minute intervals on the hour and half hour with twenty minutes of blackout in between. That would aid Billy only twenty minutes every hour, but it would save the batteries on board. They had synchronized their watches, but he was running much later than anticipated and had missed the first two hours of signal lights.

After eternity itself had come and gone, Billy finally reached the location where he had left *Destiny* more than twelve hours earlier. It was 2:30 a.m. He drifted for ten excruciatingly long minutes and noted the drift direction and speed from his GPS. Twelve hours at almost two knots of drift meant that *Destiny* was more than twenty miles away. He ran the tender in the direction of the drift for two more hours, then using a serpentine pattern, began running in large "S" shaped turns about a half mile wide. His eyes scanned the horizon with and without the binoculars, while keeping an eye on the GPS.

Billy emptied the jerry jug of gas into the tender's tank at 4:38 a.m. When he turned to stow the jug he saw a white light on the horizon. He strained with the binoculars to see if it was *Destiny*, but just as he started to focus the light went out. Billy's watch read 4:39 a.m. *Could it be that Marco's watch is a little fast, or mine is a little slow, or both?* He thought. *That's too coincidental, it must be Marco.* Billy altered course toward where he had seen the white light and headed straight for it. Sure enough, almost twenty minutes later at 4:57 a.m., Billy saw the light flash on a little higher up off the horizon. He was getting closer! "Yes!" He yelled, as the tension drained away and he felt tremendous relief. At 5:05 a.m., the light went out again. Were the batteries dead aboard *Destiny?* Maybe there was another boat approaching and Marco needed to be stealthy. *Pirates?* Billy hadn't factored in the threat of pirates whatsoever in his equation of madness. *The damn Honduran Coastal Police were pirates enough!* Billy looked through the binoculars and saw the light flicker on, then off again. *Is he signaling me? Am I in trouble?*

Instantly Billy's whole world came crashing down. The light he had seen was a star rising on the horizon. Intermittent clouds were causing the illusion of the light turning on and off. That, combined with the star rising in the air, had completely fooled Billy into thinking that he was getting closer to a yacht that wasn't there. His hopes shattered, he shut off the engine and collapsed on the seat. He felt himself losing control. He started to shake uncontrollably and screech at the top of his lungs. He collapsed onto the deck and flopped about like freshly caught fish, arms flailing about, screaming. Then everything went black.

The piercing brilliance of the morning sun woke Billy. It took several seconds to piece together what had happened. At the peak of his meltdown, Billy's mind had reached critical mass, and he had passed out from stress and exhaustion. He stared at his watch and realized he had collapsed more than an hour ago. Even though he was lost on a fourteen-foot inflatable tender in the middle of the ocean, the rising sun had inspired some hope and helped to ease his nagging worry of never finding *Destiny*. Billy looked down at the gas gauge and knew he only had one or two more hours of search time. Splashing some saltwater in his face, he resolved to give these last two hours everything he had. If that failed and he didn't find Marco, then he would die a horrible death of starvation and dehydration. He forced those thoughts from his mind and scanned the horizon with binoculars.

Before leaving Marco on *Destiny*, the men had agreed to maintain radio silence throughout the night just in case the Honduran mayday call had been heard by officials, and they were now monitoring the VHF radio. However, if Billy hadn't found *Destiny* by morning, then something had gone wrong, and they would need all the help they could get to find each other. The men had worked out a simple code in the event they needed to break radio silence. Naturally, they would change the name of the yacht when broadcasting, and if *Destiny*'s coordinates were to be transmitted, they would add two digits to latitude and subtract two digits from longitude. In doing so, the actual location of *Destiny* would be more than 150 miles to the southwest of the location transmitted through the airways.

Billy grabbed the hand held VHF radio from his bag, closed his eyes, and took a deep breath. He opened his eyes and looked down at the small, black device. His life was literally in his hands. He switched on the radio and stood up on the seat so as to get as high as possible, maximizing the broadcast range.

Come on Marco, please hear me. Billy pressed the transmit button and in his best Caribbean accent said, "Bliss, Bliss, Bliss, this is Loco. Do you read? Over." Thirty seconds turned into one minute and still no reply. "Bliss, Bliss, Bliss, this is Loco. Do you read? Over." Billy cursed himself for being so foolish as to think he could find *Destiny* by dead reckoning in the middle of the night. He felt that he should have used the VHF last night as soon as he returned to their original location. But there was nothing he could do about it now, and time spent blaming himself for being overly cautious was a waste of mental energy that he severely needed.

Billy looked at his hand held GPS and marked his current location. After much deliberation over whether to shut the VHF radio off to save battery power or leave it on, Billy decided to keep the radio on and clipped it onto his upper shirt pocket so he could hear it over the sound of the outboard engine. *Shit, it doesn't matter now. The gas will run out before the VHF's battery does.* Billy accelerated the tender up to twelve knots and travelled five miles in the same direction as the wind. He hoped *Destiny* would be broadside to the wind, drifting in the same direction directly in front of him. However, he also knew that he might be many miles away travelling in a parallel path, but it was the only plan his brain could muster up.

He throttled down and gave the VHF another try, "Bliss, Bliss, Bliss, this is Loco. Do you read? Over?"

Forty-five seconds later the radio crackled with barely decipherable words, "...Co. This... Bl... Em, at eightee...point seven north, and ...nine point...west."

Billy's mind began to race out of control with excitement. "We're within a few miles!" he yelled out loud, "We have to be!" Billy wrote down the partial coordinates on the margin of the navigation chart. He couldn't be sure if *Destiny* was to the east or west of him, but by subtracting two digits of latitude, he knew that she was somewhere on the sixteenth parallel. *I'm so close!*

Billy hit the transmit button on the VHF and said, "Bliss, Bliss, Bliss, broken transmission. Please repeat." After a minute with no reply, Billy repeated the message. No response. "Shit! Shiiiiiiiiit!" Billy wanted to smash something, anything. He raised his fist up in the air ready to smash it down on the seat when he felt overcome by a calming force from outside his own being. *Don't waste precious time and energy on what's not happening. Think about what* is *happening. I heard Marco's voice on the VHF. I know I did. At least I* think *I did. No, I did.*

Billy scanned the horizon with the binoculars in a full 360 degree circle, but could not see *Destiny* anywhere. "Damn! Wait!" Billy said out loud as he grabbed the pen and recited two formulas as he wrote them down on the chart:

"Xmit = $\sqrt{(1.5 \times Af)}$. Where Xmit is the VHF transmit distance in miles, and Af is the antenna height in feet."

"Vis = $1.3 \sqrt{(h)}$. Where Vis is the line of sight distance in miles, and h is height off the water measured in feet."

Adrenaline surged through Billy's veins as he realized what was happening. *I can hear* Destiny, *but I can't see her.* Although he couldn't exactly calculate square roots in his head, Billy was able to approximate the transmitting distance of the VHF radio and the visible distance on the horizon. He began talking out loud to reassure himself, "Okay, so Marco can't hear me, but I can hear him. Yeah, that makes sense. Right? Yes, that's right! Okay, I'm six feet tall, so square root of nine is three, and square root of four is two, so say the root of six is two point five..." Billy went on to calculate that the limit of visibility on the horizon for a person six feet tall was about three miles. "Now, the VHF antenna on *Destiny* is thirty feet high, so 30 times one point five is 45, and the square root of 45 is about..."

In under a minute, Billy had figured out that he could only see a little over three miles in all directions, even with binoculars, but the VHF radio on *Destiny* could transmit more than six and a half miles in all directions. *Of course! That's why I can't see her! Marco's transmission was garbled, so he has to be at the limit of the broadcast radius!*

Billy looked down at the chart and could barely contain his excitement. He double checked his current position on the GPS and plotted his coordinates on the chart. Using his pen as a ruler, he drew a circle with a six-point-five-mile radius around his position on the chart. He knew that *Destiny* had to be located somewhere on the circle he just drew. Knowing Marco's latitude, he studied the circle until he found a longitude position that made sense. "It's GOT to be 81 degrees, 29 minutes west! It has to be!"

Billy punched in the coordinates on the GPS and hit the throttle. The urge to push the throttle to the max was tempting Billy like a South Beach model. The boat slowly crept up to a cruising speed of twelve knots. It would take more than thirty minutes to reach his destination. Glancing down at the fuel gauge, Billy's stomach flipped over. The needle was bouncing on empty. Billy pulled the throttle back to keep the boat at ten knots and figured that he would maintain this speed until he had visual contact with *Destiny*, then he would throttle back even further and conserve fuel. Twenty agonizing minutes later, Billy caught a glimpse of white on the horizon. Having been beaten, bruised, teased and crushed by Mother Nature, Billy didn't trust his eyes at first, but after another minute, there was no mistaking *Destiny* dead ahead! Employing discipline and patience that would make a monk dance, Billy throttled back to idle speed with just two miles to go. The fuel gauge had stopped bouncing altogether, and he knew it was just a matter of time before he ran out of gas.

Billy grabbed the VHF and said, "Bliss, Bliss, I have a visual. See you soon."

"Oh! Thank Christ!" Marco Cried. "Em, good to see you!"

Billy saw Marco on the fly bridge waving his arms frantically, and started to wave back with both arms over his head when the engine sputtered. Without actually waiting for the engine to completely stall, Billy grabbed the emergency paddle and began paddling toward *Destiny.*

It took Billy over an hour to paddle to the yacht. With the dead weight of the drums full of fuel, he barely made any head way with the small paddle. Marco had thrown a life ring with 150 feet of line attached that saved Billy the last few hundred strokes.

"Amigo, I thought you were dead!" Marco said, as he pulled the small tender up to the stern of *Destiny.*

"Oh, Marco! I can't tell you how good it is to see you!" The men embraced like brothers and excitedly discussed Billy's trip and the events leading up to their reunion.

"Let's get this fuel transferred to the main tank and get out of here!" Billy said with excessive enthusiasm.

The men quickly went to work hauling both drums aboard and transferring the fuel into the main tank using two siphoning hoses. "Marco, let's start priming the engines. It's going to take a while for the drums to drain by gravity." They both climbed down into the engine room and Billy surveyed the situation.

Since each generator has its own separate starting battery, and those batteries are not wired into the main engine or house battery systems, there should be plenty of power to start either generator, Billy thought. They could easily wipe out any remaining charge in the main engine batteries trying to start the massive engines, particularly since they had been run dry of fuel. "This fuel won't do us any good if we can't start the engines because the batteries are dead. We'll start one generator and get all the batteries charging while we prime the main engines."

"Em, yes, that makes sense."

"Marco, while I'm priming the generator, will you fill up a five-gallon bucket of diesel and prime all the fuel filters for the main engines? It will take forever to prime them using the tiny priming pump."

"Yes, amigo."

The men worked together in the engine room, Billy priming one of the generators and Marco filling the primary and secondary fuel filters on the main engines. They could hear the fuel from the two drums above them trickling into the main tank as they worked. The diesel meant much more than just fuel for the yacht; it was fuel for their souls. Both men felt lifted. They had survived a hurricane!

After several turns, Billy got the generator started and checked the battery charger. It took several attempts to get the first main engine running, but soon both engines purred quietly.

They had to conserve fuel, so Billy ran the yacht at idle speed all the way to Cayman Brac. They arrived at the small island later that day, just before the fuel dock closed. Although they both needed a good night's sleep, Billy did not want to spend the night on the island. He had Marco get a couple of supplies for the trip back while they were taking on fuel. Two hours later, they were underway, heading back to the United States.

CHAPTER 39   UNITED STATES COAST GUARD

The red and white striped smoke stacks of Florida Power and Light looked like three enormous barber shop poles on the horizon. Never had those smelly, pollution belching, eye sores looked so good to Billy. *Destiny* was only ten miles from Fort Lauderdale and unless the yacht burst into flames in the next half hour, it looked like Billy and Marco were going to make it.

The men took turns at the helm so that each of them could make something to eat. Once in port, they would have many more hours of work before they could get off the yacht, so now was a good time to get some nourishment. Billy hastily ate the last half of a sandwich in two bites and relieved Marco from the helm. With the smoke stacks clearly in sight, they were only three miles out, nine minutes at twenty knots.

Being one of the busiest ports in Florida, Billy had to negotiate a high volume of bottle neck traffic while approaching the Port Everglades channel entrance into Fort Lauderdale. Several large container ships were anchored just north of the red and white "PE" buoy, awaiting US Customs clearance to enter the port. As they approached the channel entrance, they passed a huge cruise ship loaded with passengers heading out of the channel, bound for Nassau, Bahamas.

Outside on deck, Marco organized the lines and fenders, in preparation for tying up. Billy picked up the channel marker on the radar, but had already spotted it by eye. He had just lined up for a straight shot down the channel when the VHF radio crackled to life.

"Motor vessel Destiny, motor vessel Destiny, this is the United States Coast Guard."

Billy's hart sank. He grabbed the mike and responded, "This is Destiny on channel one-six. Go ahead Coast Guard."

"This is the United States Coast Guard. Reduce your speed to idle and prepare to be boarded!"

As Billy slowed the yacht down, a profound feeling of dread overwhelmed him and he broke into a cold sweat. The guilt generated from orchestrating a drug deal, and ultimately becoming a murderer, coursed through his veins to the point where his sweat felt like slime. Prison flashed into his mind. What if he could never see Bridget again? He looked around. *Where the hell are these guys? I don't see them anywhere.*

As *Destiny* slowed down, Marco walked in through the salon and told Billy that a Coast Guard boat was heading straight for them. Billy replied, "They called us on the radio, but I don't see them." Billy took a few steps back and peered around the wood patched window on the port side and saw the Coast Guard boat approaching fast from 100 yards away.

"Stay cool Marco, stay cool. If these guys smell that you're nervous, they'll tear the yacht apart. Let me do all the talking."

"Okay," was all Marco said.

The Coast Guard pulled up in typical military fashion with two men standing on either side of a bow-mounted machine gun. The gunner stood at the ready with his hands firmly on the handle bar-type trigger, just waiting for the opportunity to kill something. "Christ," Billy mumbled under his breath as the Coast Guard fenders bounced off *Destiny*'s port side.

A short man stepped forward and said in a raised voice with an overabundance of attitude, "Captain, I am Petty Officer Third Class Johnson. My men and I have stopped you for a routine safety inspection. Do you have any firearms onboard?"

Billy looked down at the little man. *He is just the kind of little prick to cause us major problems.* "No, no, we have no guns."

The two men shook hands out of formality. Billy noticed that Johnson shook with too firm a grip. Petty Officer Johnson scrutinized the yacht up and down, looking at every detail as he hopped up onto the gunwale.

"My name is Bill Forbes. Would you like something to drink, a water or soda?"

Johnson shook his head quickly as if the mere thought of hospitality were an insult. "Captain Forbes, how many men are onboard your vessel?"

"It's just me and my mate."

"Advise your mate to relocate his presence to the aft deck area while we conduct our inspection." *'Relocate his presence.' Christ, this guy must own every episode of COPS on DVD,* Billy thought.

Billy stuck his head into the salon and told Marco to wait on the aft deck until the inspection was over. Marco came out and tried to give his best, "Hello," and smile.

Johnson picked up on the Spanish accent and said, "What is your name?"

"Marco Villanueva," he replied.

"Are you a U.S. Citizen?"

"No, I have work permit."

"I need to see your immigration papers," Johnson said in a demeaning tone.

"I go and get them now," Marco said.

Billy glimpsed around the Coast Guard boat, trying to sum up the rest of the guys. He had known a few "Coasties" over the years, and most of them were pretty decent guys. The other Coast Guard men on the adjacent boat were talking amongst themselves and occasionally chortling, probably at Johnson's expense. Billy guessed there were assholes in every profession.

Marco walked back out onto the aft deck with a file full of papers and handed it to Johnson. Marco had every work permit for the past seven years and all of his papers arranged chronologically. He really only needed the current issue, but the thickness of the folder added merit to his legality. Johnson snapped the file out of Marco's hand without saying a word, opened it up, and started reviewing the papers in earnest. A moment later, he looked up at Marco and said, "You are from Honduras?"

"Yes," Marco replied.

Johnson closed the file and set it on the aft deck table. He reached for the remote radio mike on his shoulder and pressed the transmit button with his thumb, "Captain, we have the boat. You'd better get out here and bring the dog." And with that, Johnson reached down and unsnapped the leather strap on his side arm.

CHAPTER 40   LOCAL SAVIORS

Miguel Chavez blinked several times as his eyes slowly began to focus. He did not recognize his surroundings and had no idea where he was. He was staring up at old, faded paint with intermittent rust stains weeping through. His body ached from head to toe, and he could not lift any portion of his body. However, he seemed to be moving in a swaying motion. A sense of panic started to come over him when he tried to remember how he got to wherever the hell he was. He tried to lift his head to get a better view, but the physical effort was too much. His eyes rolled back into his head, and he passed out with a soft moan.

  The reflective tape on the life jacket he was wearing had caught the keen eye of a fisherman from Nicaragua in the early morning sunshine after the hurricane had passed twelve hours earlier. The fishermen thought Chavez was dead when they hauled him aboard. Chavez was unconscious. His skin color was as pale as a dead person, the wounds on his ankles and wrists looked fatal, and they could not find a pulse. It was only when they carried him into the V-berth of the fishing boat, out of the distraction of wind and noise from the engine, that one man was able to feel very soft breathing coming from Chavez. The breathing was so faint that to be sure Chavez was still alive, they mixed up some soap and water and splashed a very light mist onto Chavez's mouth. When the soap bubbles slowly grew in size, they knew he was exhaling. The men worked quickly to try and save his life.

CHAPTER 41   PROVIDENCE

Billy felt himself break into another cold, slimy sweat, but damned if he was going to let a little shit like Johnson take him down after all he'd been though. *Stay cool, Billy, stay cool.*

Marco looked over at Billy, and Billy shrugged his shoulders and tried to compose the most innocent face he could muster up. However, it felt to Billy as if he were on stage in front of a thousand people, with every move being examined. Just then, the Captain stepped through the door of the Coast Guard vessel and walked out onto the aft deck. In his fifties with salt and pepper hair, he was a ruggedly built man with broad shoulders and thick forearms, wearing a crisp, freshly pressed dark blue uniform. Another officer walked out behind him trailing a German shepherd on a choke chain leash.

"Captain Billy Forbes?" The Captain of the Coast Guard vessel asked as he looked up to take the step onto *Destiny.*

Billy knew the man, but from where? Had he boarded him before? No, that wasn't it. Billy searched his mind, trying to remember how he knew the Coast Guard Captain and hoped it didn't show on his face. In an instant, it all came to him, and he said, "Chuck O'Brien! How are you?" The two men shook hands heartily, much to the chagrin of Petty Officer Johnson.

Johnson interrupted the moment, pointed to Marco and said, "Captain, this man is from Honduras and this yacht fits the description. I must insist we do a thorough search with the dog."

"Settle down, Johnson. Billy and I went to school together."

About five years earlier, Billy had taken a two-week training class on Caterpillar diesel engines. The class went over the principles of diesel combustion and the operation and maintenance of the engines in fine detail. The guy sitting next to him in class had been Charles O'Brien. They talked during breaks and had lunch together almost every day with several other class mates. At the end of the two weeks, the teacher took them all out for a celebration at the Southport Raw Bar, where some of the guys showed their true colors. Billy remembered eating several dozen raw oysters with Chuck over a few beers, watching some of the other guys, and laughing at their drunken antics. Beers flowed all afternoon, and the teacher ended up taking car keys from four or five of the boys. Billy hadn't seen O'Brien since then.

"Yeah, that was a good class, I learned a lot," Billy said smiling, trying to take the spot light off of his nervousness. "But I gotta ask, Chuck, what's going on?" He pointed down at Johnson's gun holster. "Johnson here was just getting ready to shoot me in the head with his sidearm."

Captain O'Brien looked down and saw that the strap to Johnson's sidearm was unbuckled. He gave Johnson a scornful stare. "Well, we're doing safety checks on all vessels your size, but there's a little more to it. Why don't you and I go inside and..."

"But!" Johnson interrupted, "But, Captain, I must insist!"

"Damn it Johnson! You interrupt me one more time, and I'm going to recommend you for hazardous waste cleanup duty!"

Billy heard a few muffled chortles from the men on the Coast Guard boat, and noticed that Johnson's face resembled that of a scolded puppy dog, as he looked down at the deck. O'Brien nodded toward the salon door, which Billy opened and gestured for Chuck to enter. Billy slid the door shut behind them and offered O'Brien a seat. O'Brien sat on the couch with his elbows on his knees like a football player on the sidelines bench. He was a built like a football player, but not that tall, more like a fire hydrant.

"You got to excuse the kid," O'Brien said. "Johnson flunked out of the Navy and his old man, who's a friend of mine, is riding him pretty hard."

"Oh, that makes sense," Billy said nodding.

"Yeah, he can be a real pain in the ass sometimes, and I think the kid shits regulation feces, but he's not all bad. Just a little too gung-ho right now."

Billy noticed that while O'Brien was casually relaying the information on Johnson, he was looking around, taking everything in with watchful eyes. *Dumb like a fox,* Billy thought. *You're not out of this yet.*

"So, anyway, Johnson's old man calls me up and tells me about a report they had from a Navy warship 200 miles south of Cuba. Turns out, the warship recorded a VHF 'mayday' call from what was alleged to be the Honduran Coastal Police. The mayday call was kind of a garbled account of a patrol boat that had come under attack. The caller was being shot at. At first, the Navy thought it was a hoax. But S.O.P. requires diligent follow up on all reports of that nature, so they made a few calls to Honduran officials. It turns out that a Honduran patrol boat with four men aboard is several days overdue."

"Huh?" Billy replied.

O'Brien looked up directly into Billy's eyes. "Did you kill anybody from the Honduran Coast Guard?"

"Jesus, Chuck!" Billy said, throwing his head back, mocking a smile and spreading his arms out. "We don't even have any guns onboard! The owner has kids, hates guns! You wouldn't believe what we've been through in the last few days!"

"Sorry, Billy, but I had to ask." Looking around O'Brien said, "Yeah, you look pretty well torn up." He nodded towards the shattered TV. "What happened?"

"We were down in Jamaica when I first heard about the hurricane. Of course, I watched its development and direction closely. In fact, it looked like it was going to miss us completely, so we were hunkered down and waiting it out when I get a knock on the hull. It's the dock master of the new docks down there in Montego Bay, you know, by the Four Seasons Hotel. He told me that if the hurricane came through here, we had to evacuate the marina. I told him, 'No way' and that he should have told us about the mandatory evacuation several days ago. We were already under a hurricane watch, and the storm was only forty-eight hours away. At the time, the predicted path was going to miss Montego Bay, so I kept asking him why we had to move. I even went so far as to tell him that it was illegal in the U.S. to force boats to evacuate a marina when a hurricane was approaching, just to save some potential real estate damage. The dock master was very firm and pointed out the incredibly small print on the back of the dockage agreement, where it clearly stated that any vessel could be forced to evacuate the marina at any time at the dock master's discretion. He was yelling and screaming at me, and told me that if I did stay, we would damage their brand new docks, and the owners of the marina would sue me for triple damages under Jamaican law."

Billy took a breath and continued, "Well, all my life I swore I'd never try to outrun a hurricane, but with the speed and direction the storm was moving, I thought we could make it around Cuba, and then tuck into some hurricane hole in Key West, so I tried to get ahead and outrun the storm to the west."

"What happened?" O'Brien asked.

"Well, we were doing pretty well, and got some decent distance between us and the leading edge of the storm when it accelerated and made that hard turn to the south."

O'Brien nodded in agreement and added, "Yeah, that high pressure system that came in from the northwest bumped it right out of our path."

"Right, well I'm sure you all were very happy, but I was shitting Twinkies sideways!" Billy said with a grin.

That caused O'Brien to chuckle out loud and lean back in his seat.

Billy continued, "Had that high pressure been a day earlier, it would have really knocked the storm down a notch, but as it was, it kicked it in the ass and it nearly doubled its speed. So now, all of a sudden, the hurricane is moving right at us at twenty-four knots! Hell, we only cruise at twenty! As the storm gained on us, it shook us up pretty good. Rocked us so much in fact, that we stirred up the tanks and fouled the fuel filters with sediment, even though I had just changed them in Montego Bay."

As Billy was explaining the fuel filters clogging, he walked over to the helm station and pulled the ship's maintenance log from the array of nautical books on the shelf above the electrical panel. He walked over to O'Brien and showed him the entry. "We only had twelve hours on the filters, and we both know they should be good for at least 100 hours of run time."

O'Brien glanced at the entry in the log book. "So did the engines stall out, or did you try to change the filters underway?"

"The engines started coughing at higher speeds when we were burning a lot of fuel, so I had to slow down. I was hoping we could change the filters underway, but we were rolling all over the place. Marco got one new one in on the port side, but it got too dangerous to be in the engine room, so I slowed down and hoped for the best. It was maddening because we could see the storm gaining on us on the radar, but we couldn't out run it!" Billy had a strange sense of déjà vu about time and wanting to move, but not being able to. He had a flash thought of Rodriguez pounding on the engine room door. *Stay cool, Billy.*

O'Brien nodded slowly, then asked, "Is that what happened to your arm?"

"Oh this?" Billy said as he looked down at the bandage on his bicep. "Yeah, turbo charger got me good on a fierce wave. That was when I decided that there was no way we could change the filters underway."

Out on the aft deck, Johnson continued to walk around the yacht, examining every detail and making Marco very nervous. It would be difficult for Marco to explain the damage caused by bullets. As Johnson walked back from the bow, he stopped and looked at the chipped fiberglass area where a bullet had just missed Marco's head. "What happened here?" Johnson asked pointing up at the damage.

"Emm. My English, it is no good. Captain, please," Marco said, and pointed to the salon.

Johnson could see that the Honduran mate was nervous and enjoyed making the immigrant feel uncomfortable, so he took a step closer and watched as a drip of sweat rolled off Marco's chin and hit the deck.

Johnson had been a small kid and was the runt of the litter in his family. Growing up he had constantly tried to please his overbearing and dominant father. However, no matter how hard Johnson tried, he continually let his father down by failing at the things his father shoved down his throat. When he flunked out of the Navy, he felt very tempted to just take off and say the hell with everything, including his family, but he couldn't elude the mental stronghold that his father had over him. When his father asked him why he had failed the Navy, Johnson was forced to answer, "No excuse, Sir!"

All of the rejection, disappointment, and failure that Johnson had experienced throughout his life eventually forced him to create an external shell that he used to deflect any criticism from anyone with the exception of his father. The shell took the form of acting like a complete asshole to everyone he met and exert his limited power to the full extent possible, whenever he could. Oblivious to his own demeanor, Johnson actually wondered why the other guys on the Coast Guard boat didn't like him.

Marco had experienced many men like Johnson in Honduras, although in Honduras, they were far worse. They were criminals with badges like Rodriguez, killers with immunity, and they knew it. They could smash a rifle butt into your head, take all your money, and you had no recourse. If you did try to report the officer, you might wind up dead, or at least severely beaten. Marco tried to tame his nerves and appear calm, but knowing that he stood near a very large quantity of cocaine was causing an emotional overload of panic. Marco feared that he might crack at any second. If the Coast Guard found the cocaine, not only would he would spend a very long time in jail, he would be deported, and never be allowed to enter the United States again.

In the salon, Billy tried his best not to show guilt. He was eternally grateful for the air conditioning, because he was sweating up a storm as it was. The Coast Guard boat remained tied up alongside of *Destiny*, and both vessels had drifted beam to the wind. Since they were located in the approach channel to one of the busiest seaports on the East Coast, numerous vessels were cruising by. A sport fish boat producing a large wake zipped by, and the waves unexpectedly knocked *Destiny* and the Coast Guard boat together.

Outside, Johnson grabbed the binoculars and was squawking away on the VHF radio at the sport fish boat, threatening this and that in the name of the almighty Coast Guard.

Inside, the sideways jolt caused by the sport fish wake jarred a coconut loose from under the salon couch. The coconut rolled over and hit O'Brien's foot. He picked it up and handed it to Billy. Billy looked at the coconut and was truly puzzled. *How the hell did a coconut get in here? We didn't have any onboard in the galley.* "Huh," was all Billy could muster up, when all of a sudden it clicked.

"Of course!" Billy said excitedly. "This must have been what took out the window! Damn! At first I thought it was just the force of the water, but a coconut makes much more sense." O'Brien stood up and gave Billy a curious look.

"See, look here." Billy walked forward pointing to the window that had blown out on the port side. "We were cruising along and *Bam!* But, we never knew what blew out the window. It had to be that coconut!"

O'Brien looked at the coconut and turned it over in his hands. He nodded and said, "Yup, that would do it. And see here, this must have been where it hit." O'Brien pointed to an area on the coconut that had been flattened from the impact. "Okay, Billy, show me your immigration papers from Jamaica and we'll get out of your hair. Looks like you have enough work to do without us holding you up."

Billy turned around to the bookcase, where he kept the log book and other official paperwork, and did his best not to physically tremble as thoughts of prison flashed into his mind.

Several days earlier, after Billy had waved goodbye to Bridget at the airport, he flew to Jamaica where he bribed an immigration officer for ship's documents. Hopefully, it was worth it.

Billy reached up with a shaky hand, grabbed the file, and handed the paperwork to O'Brien. Sweat beaded up on Billy's forehead, and he could hear his heart beating loudly as O'Brien looked at the dates of arrival and departure and checked the stamps for authenticity.

"Okay, Billy," O'Brien said, as he handed the yacht's official papers back. "All looks good here. Where you headed for repairs?"

A new surge of adrenaline filled Billy's veins like a damn bursting from a flood, but he tried to act as nonchalant as he could. "Ah, gee. We're probably going to lick our wounds for a couple days, make an inventory of needed repairs, and get some estimates. Somewhere up the New River I guess." Billy slid the salon door open to the aft deck and both men stepped outside. Billy immediately noticed that Marco did not look good. He leaned over to O'Brien and whispered, "I think poor Marco is ready to piss his pants."

O'Brien quickly looked at Marco and chuckled. He then corralled his men and boarded the Coast Guard boat. Before they untied, O'Brien yelled over, "Hey Billy, if you hear anything about what we talked about through the coconut telegraph, I'd appreciate a heads up."

"No problem, Chuck," Billy replied, as he held up the coconut in his hand. "I've got a direct line on that palm tree!" Both men smiled as the deckhands untied the lines and the United States Coast Guard vessel eased away.

Billy could not believe they had just been boarded by the United States Coast Guard. Had it been any other commanding officer, Billy and Marco would be cruising into port in handcuffs.

They made their way into the Port Everglades channel and joined in with the regular boat traffic as *Destiny* turned north onto the Intracoastal Waterway.

CHAPTER 42   NEW RIVER

Billy wanted to call Bridget as soon as they entered Port Everglades. He couldn't wait to hear her soft voice, and tell her how much he loved her. However, he forced himself to make arrangements with the yacht yard first, and then call her. He missed her terribly, but knew they would need some time to catch up. It had been her idea not to speak by phone during her exam week. She had said that, in order to pass her exams, she really needed to focus, and talking to him would be too great of a distraction-they always talked for hours.

Billy called her on his cell and smiled from ear to ear when she answered her phone by saying, "That was the longest week of my life!" They chatted away for the entire hour and a half cruise up the New River and would have kept talking, but Billy had to hang up when the yacht was getting hauled out of the water.

Once *Destiny* was securely jacked up on the asphalt lot, Billy allowed himself to relax a little and enjoy the fact that he had not been caught, *yet.* He knew that selling the quantity of coke he had onboard was not going to be quick-he had 200,000 grams. Nor would it be easy, but he had made it this far and felt sure that the worst had to be over. He left the coke hidden on the yacht. After all, the hiding place had eluded Rodriguez and his men. Men who *knew* drugs were hidden on board and still couldn't find them. As long as the boat was in the yacht yard, Billy felt it was safe. Now, he had just ten days to find buyers.

When he stopped and thought about it, Billy couldn't believe that he had made it back to the United States without getting killed or caught. *I've come this far and I'm not going to make a mistake now. As much as I want to, I can't just quit working on the yacht and walk away. The boss would be furious with the damage to the yacht, and he would seriously investigate. Now is no time for rash actions, I just need to stay calm, get the repairs done and do the trip to the Bahamas. While we're over there, I'll mention something to the boss about the possibility of another job, so he won't be surprised when I leave.*

Now that the yacht was out of the water, Billy went to work on the leaking shaft seal while Marco worked topsides repairing the bullet holes. Billy had the shaft seal partially disassembled when Bridget called back on his cell phone. Once again, the sound of her voice raised his spirits. She said cheerily, "Hey Babe, I've got some good news!"

"Oh yeah," Billy replied, "Don't keep me waiting!"

"Well, now that I've finished all my exams, I switched shifts around so that I can take ten days off and do the Bahamas trip with you!"

"Really? That's great!" Billy could hear the excitement his own voice.

"Yeah, I'm really ready to work as a chef and put some of this nutrition knowledge to work!"

The thought of Bridget coming aboard for the upcoming trip made Billy feel euphoric. Granted the owner and family would be onboard most of the time, but having Bridget with him would make the voyage so much nicer. If she liked the islands, he could talk to her about the catamaran he wanted to buy and starting a charter business together. Billy just had one little problem to take care of before the trip: he had to unload more than 400 pounds of cocaine.

The repairs to the yacht took a full eight days to complete. Even a trained eye could not locate the repaired gelcoat area where the bullet had almost ended Marco's life. As the trip with the boss rapidly approached, Billy continually worried about getting rid of the product. Finding large quantity buyers proved to be far more difficult than he had anticipated. He didn't want to increase the risk of getting caught by moving his special cargo to an apartment or storage unit. He just wanted to unload it as quickly as he could.

The night before they were scheduled to re-launch *Destiny*, Marco's son, Ernesto, met Billy and Marco at the Quarterdeck Restaurant in Fort Lauderdale. Ernesto was dressed in a tee shirt, shorts, and flip flops. He fit in like a leaf on a tree at the local bar. They sat outside and let the ambient noise drown out their conversation. Once the waitress set a round of beers down and walked away, Ernesto leaned forward over the table and quietly said, "I've found a buyer."

Billy could barely contain his excitement. "Really? How much are they willing to pay?"

Ernesto shuffled in his seat and gave Billy a look of exasperation. "That's the problem. They only want to pay two million."

"What!" Billy checked himself and lowered his voice, as he did the math in his head. He leaned forward, "But that's only ten thousand a key. It's worth at least fifteen!"

Marco's son nodded in agreement and said, "I agree with you, but they were firm on the price. You'll move all of it at once, and your return is not that bad."

Ernesto had made two valid points. Billy sat back in his chair and took a long sip from his beer. Several moments later, he leaned forward and said, "When can they have the money?"

"Give me a sample to bring back to the buyers in Miami tonight, and I'll find out." After that, they finished dinner quickly with little conversation.

Once the waitress had cleared their plates, Billy asked, "Marco, are you okay with the return on your money? We'll both make roughly ten times what we invested. You put up twenty-five thousand, so you'll get a quarter of a million."

Marco smiled quickly and said, "Amigo, that kind of money goes a very long way in Honduras. I am an old man and just want to retire."

"Okay, then," Billy said and turned to Ernesto, "Tell them that we'll agree to that price, but it has to be done within the next two days."

All three men left the restaurant and went back to the yacht.

Billy had used an inflatable bladder in *Destiny's* water tank and filled it with the coke from the fifty-five gallon drum in Honduras using a small shop vac. That way they still had a decent supply of fresh water during their return voyage from Honduras, and any inspection from officials would require removing the access plate to the water tank, which was located mid ship, beneath the floor of the VIP guest room. The hidden location had frustrated Juan Rodriguez to such an extent that it ultimately led to his death. Billy's main concern now was that the bladder had not punctured during the washing machine effect of the hurricane.

Billy and Marco had lowered the volume in the water tank on their way back to Florida with daily activities, and it was an easy matter to drain the remaining few gallons. Billy removed the flooring from the VIP guest room and unbolted the stainless steel access plate to the water tank in order to get at the flexible bladder tank. He felt an enormous wave of relief when he observed that the bladder was still intact and had not ruptured. He filled a small glass vial with the fine, white powder.

Billy pulled Ernesto aside and handed him the vial. Making sure Marco was out of earshot, he said, "No fucking around with this. This sample goes straight to the buyers!"

Ernesto nodded, slipped it into his pocket and said, "I'll call you as soon as I have any news."

Marco woke Billy up at 1:30 a.m. later that night. "Amigo, wake up!"

"Christ Marco, what's wrong?"

"Em, they will do the em, deal. They can meet us in two days!" There was no way Billy could fall back asleep after that.

Early the next morning, Billy and Marco decided to pay Ernesto $20,000 for being a full liaison with the buyers, provided that the deal was executed with no snags; that is, no one got killed or arrested. Billy insisted that the transfer of cash and product had to be done in broad daylight in the yacht yard. At first, the buyers refused. Billy thought they were just thugs, pretending to have money, who would try to kill them for the product during the exchange. But Marco's son talked them into doing the deal at the yacht yard. They still had to remove the product from the bladder tank. Billy knew they would lose some residual coke inside the shop vac, and in the long hose that ran up to the aft deck where a new fifty-five gallon drum was located, but what the hell, it would only amount to a few grams. To the average person walking by at the yacht yard, it just looked like someone cleaning oily water out of the bilge. Billy didn't have a means to weigh the product, so he had to guess by the volume in the drum. The process went smoothly, and he filled the drum until the bladder tank was empty.

Per Billy's instructions, Ernesto had told the buyers to arrive at the yard in a hazmat truck, and that the drum aboard *Destiny* would be marked as waste oil. Billy was surprised when two men showed up in worn jumpsuits, complete with sewn on patches of a local hazardous waste removal company. The buyers looked so authentic in their disguise that Billy began to worry that they were undercover police or DEA agents. Who else could come up with two million dollars cash overnight?

Billy had the davit ready to lower the drum onto the flatbed truck from the aft deck. He pulled one of the men inside the salon and said, "We get the money before we lower the drum onto the truck." The man looked around the salon, gave Billy a long look, nodded and walked out onto the aft deck. Billy's heart was pounding. *This is it,* he thought. *Either I'm going to make a hell of a lot of money, or I'm going to jail for a very long time.*

The man returned to the yacht carrying a cloth tool bag and set it at Billy's feet without saying a word. Billy opened the bag and saw more money than he had ever seen in his life. The bag contained all $100 bills vacuum sealed in clear plastic, complete with light blue paper tags indicating $10,000 increments. There were ten bundles of bills, about the size of a brick, presumably $200,000 each. Billy grabbed one and sliced it open with his knife. He removed a highlighter from his pocket and tested a bill at random to see if it was counterfeit. He felt a surge of relief when the color of the highlighter did not change. It would take him several days to test all the bills that way, so he had a simple test to verify the authenticity of the remaining bundles.

Billy knew that U.S. currency is printed with ink that contains iron particles, so it is attracted to a magnet. He removed the plastic casing from all ten bundles of cash and placed a high power magnet that was the shape of a business card on top of one of the neatly stacked bundles. Then he rotated the bundle, if the magnet fell off, some or all of the currency was counterfeit. He repeated the process ten times and the magnet stayed attached to all ten bundles.

Billy was now a wealthy man.

CHAPTER 43   THIRD WORLD JUSTICE

Three weeks after being rescued at sea, Miguel Chavez sat recuperating in his hospital bed. When he had first regained consciousness nineteen days earlier, Chavez felt extremely thankful to be alive. However, as he slowly recovered during his near month-long stint in bed, he had much time to think, and his thoughts morphed from thanks into anger. With each passing day, Chavez thought about the Americans who had tried to kill him, and then left him stranded at sea alone to die. Rage coursed through his veins, and he vowed to seek vengeance for his cousin's death.

Francisco Lopez walked into the hospital accompanied by two body guards. All three men were dressed in dark suits as they walked briskly past the reception desk and made their way uninterrupted through the hospital. Chavez's thoughts of revenge were momentarily interrupted when the three strangers walked into his room. Chavez looked up from his bed and studied his visitors curiously.

The man dressed in a finely tailored suit walked over and sat down in a chair next to the hospital bed and motioned for his associates to leave the room. Lopez leaned in closer and asked Chavez, "¿Se siente mejor? Are you feeling better?"

Miguel Chavez had never met the leader of the largest illegal cocaine trafficking organization in Honduras, so with a confused look he asked in Spanish, "Who are you?"

Lopez smiled. He was rarely asked that question. "My name is Francisco Lopez. Juan Rodriguez reports to me, or at least he used to."

"Oh!" Chavez quickly sat up in his bed. Chavez knew the name, but had never seen a photo of Lopez, much less met him. Nervously he continued, "I'm... I'm well; I'm getting better. I can almost walk now, but I have to use crutches. I have partial paralysis in my left hand, but the doctors say it might come back."

Lopez leaned back in his chair and nodded. "I see; well I hope it all comes back. Can you write?" Lopez seemed to be truly interested in Chavez's medical condition, but what he really wanted to know was if Chavez could still use a handgun.

"Yes, I'm right handed, so I can manage. In fact, I'm supposed to get discharged today."

"I know. I had them keep you here a few extra days, because I could not visit until today." Chavez now understood that it had been Lopez who arranged for a private room in the crowded hospital. Lopez said softly, "Please, tell me what happened."

Miguel Chavez told the story of boarding the yacht and thoroughly searching it, but not finding anything onboard or in the drums. He explained how he had fled when Rodriguez and the others were trapped in the engine room and killed. He could only recall bits and pieces of being adrift on the small boat, but he told Lopez everything he remembered.

When Chavez finished telling his story, Lopez nodded thoughtfully, paused for several seconds, and said, "I want you to go to America and kill the men responsible for this. You must seek vengeance for your cousin's death, and I must have revenge for losing my men. You will be paid well, and I will arrange for everything you need once you get there. When do you think you'll be able to make the trip?"

Miguel could not believe what he was hearing. Every day since he regained consciousness he had been scheming to kill the men who had tried to kill him and then left him to die. Now he would be paid to do it. "I'll leave as soon as I can walk."

CHAPTER 44   BAHAMAS

Billy and Bridget were having a blissful time working together aboard *Destiny*. Bridget kept saying to Billy, "I can't believe I'm getting paid to do this! What a fun job!" Her words were music to Billy's ears.

Several days earlier, Billy's boss and family had flown into Nassau, and now *Destiny* was cruising south through the Exuma Islands section of the Bahamian Island chain, stopping at marinas and anchoring out on the shallow waters of the Bahama Bank.

Billy maneuvered *Destiny* up to the Staniel Cay Yacht Club dock after being at anchor for two nights. All onboard were ready to walk on terra firma and eat off the yacht for a change.

As Billy finished securing the yacht he asked the boss, "Would you like to take the tender over to Hog Island?

His boss looked at him curiously and asked, "Hog Island? What's that?"

Later that evening, the boss took his family, Bridget and Billy to dinner at the yacht club restaurant. After preparing all the meals and cleaning up after everyone onboard for two nights at anchor, Billy knew that Bridget would welcome being waited on. Prior to being seated, Billy tipped a waitress that he'd known for years to help him play a little joke on Mrs. Boss. While they were being served by his special waitress, Billy brought up the legend of the infamous killer swimming pigs. "Now, I've never seen them," Billy began, "But I've been told that there are several very large pigs that haunt a nearby island. The pigs are huge and white like ghosts and they stalk anyone who has eaten their kind."

Mr. Boss turned his head, looked at Billy and gave him a stealth wink, but Mrs. Boss said, "Oh come on Billy, really? Pigs on an island? And killer pigs at that!"

The waitress set a dinner plate down in front of Mrs. Boss and said in a thick Bahamian accent, "Dehm words is true. I never seen dehm ghostly white pigs e-dah, bot many here swear dhey seen dhem."

The boss's three children were in their teens and couldn't be bothered with island folklore regarding farm animals, so they returned to their cell phones and promptly forgot the conversation.

The next day, Bridget packed a large cooler with a delicious three course lunch for the family to enjoy out on a beautiful, deserted Caribbean beach. Billy used the paper chart to show his boss some of the uninhabited islands that would be great for a picnic lunch. Billy's boss smiled, and patted Billy on the back before yelling down to his wife, "Honey, I'm going to take the tender with Billy and find us a nice beach on a deserted island. Billy will come back and pick you and the kids up in a half hour or so." Billy and his boss departed on the tender, complete with the big cooler and a camcorder discreetly packed in a beach bag. Billy dropped his boss off on a deserted white sand beach several miles away and hurried back to *Destiny.*

To Billy's complete surprise, everyone was ready to go when he returned to the yacht. The three kids and Mrs. Boss climbed aboard the tender, and Billy sped off back toward the beach. Billy slowed the tender down as they approached the deserted island where he had dropped off his boss. The island was fairly small, but contained a long, bright white sand beach that extended thirty yards from the water's edge and turned into island thicket and palm trees. One of the kids looked back and forth, pointed to the white cooler sitting on the beach and asked, "Where's dad?"

"I dropped him off a little while ago. He said he was going to explore a little bit and would meet us back here soon."

When Billy had maneuvered the tender about twenty yards from shore, a bright white, 400-pound pig bashed through the thicket at the top of the beach and came bounding down the sand, heading straight for the tender.

Mrs. Boss pointed in horror and screamed, "Ahhhhhhh!" Just then the outboard motor died. "Billy do something!" She cried.

While the tender drifted helplessly toward the beach, two other large white pigs appeared from the thick island bush and quickly made their way down the sandy beach. The largest pig paced about the water's edge and everyone onboard could see his massive nostrils flexing as he moved his head back and forth, examining the tender and its inhabitants.

With a surprisingly quick, agile leap, the 400-pound pig jumped into the ocean and started swimming rapidly toward the tender.

"Ahhh! Oh my God! Billy! He's coming right for us! Get us out of here!"

"The motor won't start! I don't know what's wrong!" Billy fiddled with the ignition switch and turned the motor over, but it refused to start. "I can't get it started!" The massive pig was gaining on the tender quickly and the other two pigs had also jumped in and were now swimming quickly toward the tender.

One of the kids yelled, "Mom! It's getting really close!"

Billy removed his Leatherman from its sheath and flicked open the blade. "Don't worry, I'll save us! They won't get us without makin' some bacon!" The massive pig swam with surprising speed and grunted and snorted as it approached the side of the tender, its five-inch wide pink snout discharging saltwater spray with each loud snort.

All passengers were glued to the far side of the tender when the pig reached the boat. Mrs. Boss was bordering on hysterics. "Oh my God, he'll sink us!" The children were all huddled together and one of them looked like she was about to cry.

The pig raised his head over the pontoon of the tender and snorted loudly.

Mrs. Boss screamed, "Ahhh! No, it's the killer pigs!"

Billy quickly moved over and sat down next to the huge pig and patted his massive head. "This is Jumbo," he said, as he grabbed some carrots from his pocket and began to feed the enormous pig.

CHAPTER 45   OBSESSED

Miguel Chavez limped slowly as he walked through the hospital front doors, and took a taxi back to his small apartment. Lopez had arranged for him to remain at the hospital until he was able to walk. He was scheduled to fly to the U.S. the following day and had been ordered to pack his suitcase light, as if he were a tourist. Lopez had also arranged transportation to the airport where a ticket would be waiting for Chavez on JetBlue nonstop to Miami. Lopez also assured him that a man named Carlos would be waiting for him at the Miami airport when he arrived. Carlos would be his contact in the U.S., and would get Chavez whatever he needed: information, weapons, a place to stay, and anything else Chavez requested.

　　Miguel Chavez touched down in Miami right on schedule and Carlos introduced himself right after Miguel cleared customs. Carlos had the dark brown skin of a Central American native, with several days worth of growth on his beard and sunken eyes. They left the airport in a nondescript Ford Taurus and headed east toward Miami. The men did not speak very much during the car ride. Miguel noticed how the surroundings changed as they made their way to the city. Carlos headed south on Biscayne Boulevard, and they stopped at a restaurant in little Honduras to get some dinner.

As they walked in, Miguel was pleasantly surprised that the atmosphere of the restaurant reminded him of his home country. He could hear everyone speaking Spanish, the food looked and smelled familiar, and he even noticed telenovelas in the background on TV.

They sat at a table, ordered drinks, and Carlos said, "Podemos hablar libremente aquí. ¿Qué necesitas de mí? We can talk freely here. What do you need from me?"

Miguel responded in Spanish, "I'll need a gun, but first I need to find out where the boat is docked."

Carlos nodded. "This is America, so getting a gun is no problem, but what kind do you want?"

Miguel had not really considered what type of gun he should use for the job, so he thought for a moment and said, "It will need to be small, so I can conceal it, but it needs to be powerful as well."

"I see. How many targets do you have?"

"Two, but they may not be at the same place at the same time."

"I know just the gun. What the Americans call a 'thirty-eight special.' It's a Smith and Wesson thirty-eight caliber handgun, very reliable with a six-round cartridge that will give you two rounds per target, plus two reserve shots. The barrel is not that long, so accuracy is tricky, but it will be easier to hide. You'll need to be fairly close when you fire."

Their food came and Miguel asked, "How will we find out where the yacht is docked?"

"I have a contact at the customs office. All yachts are required to clear customs within twenty-four hours after they arrive in U.S. waters. The data base shows that the yacht *Destiny* cleared into Fort Lauderdale from Jamaica a little over three weeks ago, but that's not all. The customs officers also have access to Homeland Security databases, so my contact pulled all information on yachts named *Destiny* in Fort Lauderdale."

Carlos slid a printout across the table to Miguel, who picked it up and studied it silently. Carlos continued, "Every time a bridge opens for a yacht, the yacht's name is filed in that database."

From the printout, Miguel learned that *Destiny* had traveled up the New River, where several bridges had opened for her. "It looks like they are docked up the New River somewhere."

Carlos nodded, "Yes, but scroll down a little. They went back down the river about two weeks ago. There are several large yacht yards on the New River, so they probably went up for repairs and then came back down river. That means they should be docked somewhere in Fort Lauderdale."

CHAPTER 46   TRUE LOVE

The ten-day trip cruising the Bahamas had gone exceptionally well. The meals Bridget prepared underway were spectacularly displayed, delicious but not sinful, and she had done it all with a great attitude.

On the last day of the trip, the boss took Billy aside and said, "Bridget did a great job, so tip her accordingly. You both made the trip very special for us, and I really appreciate it, so why don't you two stay an extra night or two here at Atlantis on me." Then the boss slipped five 100 dollar bills to Billy as he shook his hand and said, "That was the best trip we've ever had!"

The boss and family were scheduled to fly out of Nassau on their private Falcon 50 jet. Billy accompanied them to the airport to help load the mass of luggage onto the sleek aircraft. The boss finally waved goodbye from the steps of his plane late in the afternoon, and Billy rushed back to join Bridget on the yacht, but first, he made the taxi stop at the diamond district in downtown Nassau.

Once back onboard, Billy popped a bottle of Cristal champagne, and the two of them sat on the aft deck of *Destiny*, looking out at the Atlantis Marina while remembering highlights of the trip.

Bridget said, "You and the boss get along very well."

Billy smiled and said jokingly, "Yeah well, I bite my lip a lot of the time."

"No seriously," she continued, "Not too many people would dare to play a practical joke on their boss's wife. When you came back from Hog Island, and told me the story, I couldn't believe it!" They both laughed out loud about the encounter with the "killer" pigs. Bridget shook her head laughing and asked, "How did you get the engine to stall? Did you disconnect the gas hose?"

"Actually, there is a kill switch with a lanyard on the tender for when you're running by yourself. You connect the lanyard to, say, your belt loop, and if you fall overboard the kill switch is pulled from the ignition, and shuts the motor off. That way you're not left stuck in the water with the tender flying away at full speed. I had the lanyard in between my big toe and I just pulled it out at the right moment. The engine won't restart unless the kill switch is replaced. It worked perfectly!"

Then Billy asked, "Did you enjoy the trip?"

Bridget smiled and said, "Oh, I'm surprised you have to ask! I had a great time, but honestly, I don't think I would have been able to do it without you. You made it very easy and non-stressful. It really didn't feel like work."

Billy smiled, "The boss was very pleased with your work and told me to tip you well. I'm also taking you out to dinner tonight at a wonderful restaurant, so you don't have to cook, and we can have a nice night out together." Billy raised his glass and said, "To a great trip with the woman I love."

Bridget clinked her glass to his and added, "And many more with the man I love."

Billy made a reservation at a magnificent five-star restaurant inside the Atlantis complex, and made sure their table abutted the floor to ceiling glass wall of the world renowned aquarium. As they were being seated, an enormous manta ray swam by their table. Bridget had never seen one underwater before, and her eyes went wide. "Wow!" She said, staring awestruck. The hostess smiled knowingly, having heard the "oohs" and "ahhs" many times before. Although Billy had seen the Atlantis aquarium several times, he always enjoyed viewing the vast array of species. In addition to being the world's largest open air marine habitat, the enormous, yet tasteful aquarium hosted some very rare species, like the saw tooth shark.

Billy looked at the menu, nodded toward the thick glass of the aquarium and said, "I feel a little guilty eating their brethren, but I'd love some lobster tonight!" Bridget smiled and studied the menu. They had an exquisite meal with a bottle of wine and talked about the trip and future plans. Billy mentioned that the boss had offered to treat them to another night at Atlantis, but both Billy and Bridget wanted to get back to the States, so they decided to leave the next morning on the yacht.

They departed Atlantis casually at seven thirty a.m. Once they departed Nassau Harbour, Billy ran the yacht from the fly bridge. He had the navigation system set on auto pilot, so it was really a matter of making sure they didn't hit any floating debris. The sun was shining brightly, and the ocean was flat calm when they passed Chub Cay and Northwest Passage Light two and a half hours later. They made the transition from thousands of feet of water to the shallow Bahama Bank, where the water became absolutely still. The water on the bank appeared so clear it seemed as if they were going to run aground, but there was actually ten feet of water below them. Billy had his arm around Bridget as they cruised across the magnificent, bright blue-turquoise waters. Both Billy and Bridget felt terrific, from both a job well done, and their wondrous surroundings. The crystal clear water of the Bahama Bank created a sense of enchantment, accented by flying fish that would take flight as the yacht approached, and magically glide through the air for several seconds before splashing back into the sea. Billy looked around in a full 360 degree circle and did not see another boat. He leaned over, kissed Bridget and said, "As absolutely perfect as this is, I have to do an engine room check."

Bridget smiled as he removed his arm from around her shoulders. "Aye, aye, Captain!" She said, as she gave him an exaggerated salute.

Bridget scooted forward on the seat to look for anything in the water. She had just been thinking how perfect the moment felt; cruising across beautiful Caribbean water with the man she loved in a multimillion dollar yacht. She knew in her heart that Billy was the one. She loved that he respected her and really *listened* to her opinions. He didn't *tell* her how things were in life. She smiled as she thought of their wondrous sex and the things Billy did with his tongue. She would never get tired of *that!* She gazed out at the ocean daydreaming about their future together, when suddenly the rpm of the engines slowed down and the yacht came off a plane, and slowed to a stop. Both engines died.

Bridget snapped to attention and looked at the throttles, but they had not moved. She felt an immediate surge of concern for Billy and quickly scurried down to the main deck to see what happened. She ripped opened the salon doors. Soft music, Bob Marley's *Turn Your Lights down Low,* was playing. She stepped inside and looked around, but did not see Billy. Instead, she noticed a bottle of Cristal Champagne on ice in an opulent silver bucket set on a white linen napkin on the coffee table. Billy walked out from behind the wheelhouse smiling and all of her concern swiftly faded. He looked handsome wearing a navy blue blazer, tie and khaki dress slacks, which was rather comical because he was barefoot. She did not have time to figure out what was happening before Billy wrapped his arms around her and began passionately kissing her. He pulled her in tight with his strong arms, rubbing them up and down her back. He kissed his way down her cheek then slowly made his way down her neck, then her cleavage and stopped at her belly button. He was on one knee now and he looked up at her and said, "The sea has become part of my life, and so have you, Bridget Ann Smith. And as eternal is the sea, so is my love for you." He removed a small black velvet box from the right pocket of his blazer. He opened it, gazed deep into her eyes and whispered softly, "Will you marry me?"

The moment hit Bridget like a thunderbolt. "Oh, Billy!" Tears of joy streamed down her face as she nodded, but couldn't speak. Simultaneously laughing and crying, she choked out, "Yes! Oh God, Yes!" He stood up and they embraced in a passionate kiss. He picked her up and carried her up to the fly bridge and set her down on the sun pad. Their clothes flew off in less than three seconds, and Billy was inside her in three-point-five. They made passionate love on the fly bridge beneath the hot, Caribbean sun. Billy climbed on top first, but then Bridget rolled over, pinned down Billy's wrists and straddled him. Gradually, her pace increased and soon she was riding Billy as hard and fast as she could until neither could hold back any longer and they both climaxed together. Afterward, they lay naked in blissful silence, savoring the moment as they drifted on the Bahama Bank, etching every detail into long term memory.

"I'm so happy," Billy said quietly, as he lay on his back looking up into the heavens.

Bridget had her head propped up in her left hand as she rubbed her right hand over his chest. "I love you so much, Billy."

He rolled over and kissed her. "Would you want to run a charter business together? We'll get a catamaran sail boat and live on it while doing charters in the Caribbean."

"That sounds like a wonderful plan, and I'd love to run a charter boat with you. We'll work out the details later, but right now, I want you deep inside me." She moved her hand from his chest down in between his legs, and it didn't take Billy long to respond.

After their second love session, Billy set the anchor naked as the day he was born. The water was only fifteen feet deep, so the process went quickly. He made sure the anchor was set fast, and the yacht was secure before he popped the bottle of Cristal champagne. They brought the champagne bucket to the aft deck and set it down on the swim platform where they could reach it from the water. They both dove into the crystal clear, warm water naked and embraced at the surface. They swam over and poured champagne into crystal glasses and toasted to each other. Both Billy and Bridget felt euphoric and spent the afternoon in total bliss anchored on the astonishing turquoise waters of the Bahama Bank, swimming, drinking champagne, and feeding each other shrimp the size of lobster tails.

Later that night, Billy lay in bed with his arm around Bridget as she slept. He could hear her softly breathing while he thought through the next few months. *I'll pay cash and buy a new catamaran sail boat in South Africa, then I'll sail it back to the Bahamas where I can start a legitimate charter business. We'll pick and choose only the best guests for charters that we want to work. Over time, I'll use the Bahamian banks to deposit the remaining cash. I won't deposit too much cash at once. That will surely alert American authorities. Instead, I'll use safe deposit boxes to store hard cash, then, over the next few years, make cash deposits into my account. That way, the accounting will mimic that of a legitimate charter business.*

If we get tired of living on the boat in four or five years, we could sell the business and move back on land. Even though the catamaran will depreciate, it would still be worth several hundred thousand dollars, and that, combined with the money in the Bahamian bank, will secure our future.

Billy had no worries and could barely control himself; he was so happy. He smiled, rolled over, and kissed Bridget on her back before closing his eyes. With Bridget by his side, they would sail around the islands doing the occasional charter and live life to the fullest. It was perfect.

CHAPTER 47   *DESTINY* CLEAR

It didn't take long for Carlos to find out where *Destiny*'s slip was located. In fact, he did it by phone in less than an hour. He called the marinas in Fort Lauderdale one by one and pretended to be a diesel mechanic who had worked on *Destiny* and left expensive tools in the engine room. The eighth marina he called was the City Dock Marina, and the dock master informed him that *Destiny* had left for the Bahamas two weeks ago and was actually due back yesterday.

The dock master said, "They've paid for the slip for the whole season, so I have to keep it open for them, but the captain is really good about telling me when he's definitely not going to be here so I can rent it out. He told me they'd be back yesterday, so I'm expecting them any time now."

Carlos smiled on the other end of the phone and replied, "Thank you. You've been very helpful."

Chavez and Carlos drove down to the City Dock Marina to perform field reconnaissance of the layout and walk through how Chavez was going to carry out his assassination. As soon as they drove into the parking area, both men immediately noticed the small, satellite police station located adjacent to the city docks. They parked and shut off the motor, but did not get out of the car. Chavez spoke in Spanish, "There's no way I can do it here. Of all the fucking docks, they have to choose the one with a police station right next to it!"

"You're right, you can't do it here," Carlos responded, "but you have the element of surprise. From what you've told me, they think you're dead, and they've never seen me. So, for now, we wait. My contact at Customs will tell us when the yacht returns to Florida. Then, I'll follow them and let you know where they are. You'll have to be flexible and catch them somewhere off the yacht when they least expect it."

Destiny rested peacefully at anchor with variable winds less than five knots on the shallow Bahama Bank. The sun broke the horizon a few minutes before six a.m., but Billy and Bridget were blissfully asleep. The only sounds were the gentle lapping of water against the hull and the occasional sea bird. Billy's internal clock woke him up naturally a little after six. He rolled over, surprised to see Bridget awake and smiling at him.

"Good morning," she said, her hair falling naturally about her face.

A huge grin formed on Billy's face as he said, "This is one of the best... no wait... this *is* the best morning of my life." She cuddled up next to him with her head on his chest and his arm around her. They lay in total peace, and Billy overflowed with joy. *If she's feeling half of what I'm feeling, then she's still got to be really happy.*

She ran her fingers over his chest and said, "I've never felt this way before. I'm so head over heels in love with you that I'm actually a little scared. Please promise me that if things get tough, we'll always try to work it out. I'm emotionally opening up all the way with you and in doing so, setting myself up for real pain if anything were to happen. But at the same I am experiencing new feelings of joy that I didn't know were possible."

Billy rolled over and looked deep into her eyes. "Babe, I feel the same. We're connected in a way that I've never felt with anyone before, and I'm totally in love with you. I promise to always try to work things out, and I don't mind completely opening up with you because I believe in us, and it's worth it the risk." Then he smiled and said, "Now, since we're only eighty miles from Florida—only four hours at cruise—we can enjoy our morning at a nice leisurely pace." He leaned in and kissed her soft lips. He held her lower lip in between his lips and gently massaged it until she beckoned him with her tongue. Billy took his time, savoring every detail as he kissed his way down her neck and slowly made his way to her nipples. All of their inhibitions were long gone. Both Billy and Bridget gave way to the wondrous euphoria of passion as they pleased each other.

Billy hauled the anchor at nine-thirty. *Destiny* climbed up to her cruising speed of twenty knots less than five minutes later. The weather had been incredibly cooperative. The forecast for the often nasty and unpredictable Gulf Stream called for waves two feet or less. *Destiny* cruised along effortlessly in a westerly direction on the Bahama Bank, toward Hen and Chicken shoal. The water remained crystal clear, and the view from the fly bridge was limited only by the curvature of the earth. All of the weather and sea conditions combined had created a truly beautiful Caribbean day. As he sped across the sea with his arm around Bridget, Billy didn't have a care in the world.

When they approached the Gulf Stream, Billy could not believe how calm it the ocean appeared. He had never seen the water surrounding the Gulf Stream so peaceful. "Enjoy this, Babe. It's rare to see the Gulf Stream this calm."

Bridget had only crossed it once before, when it was relatively flat, so she had not seen the havoc that a strong north wind created. She leaned her head over onto his shoulder. "I must be good luck."

Billy kissed the top of her head. "That you are!"

Three hours later, Billy called the city docks on the VHF radio and the dock master said he'd meet them at their slip to give them a hand tying up. Billy turned the bow into the current generated by the outgoing tide and backed the eighty-five foot yacht into the slip with ease. The dock master grabbed one of the shore power cables from Billy. "Hey Billy, a diesel mechanic called me earlier and said he left some tools on the boat. He said he'll come by grab them."

"Really? Huh. I didn't see any in the engine room, but I did have some work done when I was up river. I'm sure he'll track me down." Billy handed the dock master a twenty-dollar tip and shook hands.

"Thanks Capt'. Let me know if you need anything."

Billy could hear Bridget talking excitedly to her mother about the engagement on the cell phone and smiled as he undressed for the shower. She surprised him by jumping in with him several minutes later. They enjoyed a nice, long shower, changed, then headed off the yacht to clear U.S. Customs.

One hour later, Carlos received a text message on his cell phone that read simply, "Destiny Clear."

On the way back from the Customs Office, Billy and Bridget stopped at the Southport Raw Bar and ordered a pitcher of beer and several dozen oysters. The oysters were served on a bed of crushed ice with spicy cocktail sauce and sliced lemon on the side. As Billy slid the third oyster into his mouth, he grinned and said, "You know what they say about oysters, right?"

"Well if it's true, I'm going to need crutches to walk tomorrow," she replied laughing.

She took a sip from the icy cold beer mug with her right hand and put her left hand on Billy's thigh. She set the mug down with an "Ah," and said, "Sometimes the simplest things in life are the most profound."

Billy's eyes popped open. "I can't believe you just said that! My father used to say that. I have a vivid memory of fishing with him as a boy, watching a beautiful sunset, and he said those exact words! I remember, because I didn't know what 'profound' meant and he explained it to me." He raised his glass and they clinked their beer mugs together. "To profound simplicity!"

Bridget said, "Let's take tomorrow off and just chill out."

Billy nodded as he swallowed another oyster. "Sounds great, what do you have in mind?"

"Well, I've never been to South Beach, but I've heard a lot about it, and saw some pretty cool pictures on line. There's a place on the beach where you can lay out on a big bed that has a cloth enclosure, so there's privacy, but it's right on the beach, next to the water."

"Yeah, I know where you're talking about. I saw those beach beds while riding my mountain bike along the beach last time we docked at the South Beach Marina. That sounds very cool and a great way to spend the day. We'll just swim, lie out, and let someone wait on us for a change."

The next morning they packed up a couple of beach bags and walked down the dock toward the parking lot. Neither one of them noticed a swarthy man in a baseball hat and mirrored sunglasses sitting in a chair, fishing on shore near the dock. Billy put the bags in the backseat, and they drove out of the parking lot.

Carlos left the beach chair and fishing rod where they were. He jumped into a car and followed Billy. He had Billy's car in sight and was three cars behind him at the first traffic light. Carlos used a Wal-Mart disposable cell phone to call Chavez. "Están en el coche en movimiento. Te permite conocer la ubicación tan pronto como pueda. They're in the car on the move. I'll let you know the location as soon as I can." He hung up without waiting for a response.

Carlos followed the car west, away from Fort Lauderdale Beach on SE 17th Street, toward the highway. He had to run a red light to follow them south onto U.S. 1. He kept several cars in between them, so as not to alert Billy that he was being followed. Billy took Griffin Road, and Carlos guessed correctly that they were headed south on I-95 toward Miami. Twenty minutes later, Billy merged onto the off ramp for I-395 and Carlos knew where they were headed.

He picked up the cell phone and called Chavez. "They are going to South Beach. Leave now, it won't take you long to get there. I'll follow them and tell you exactly where they are when you arrive."

Undercover DEA Special Agent Mitch Stevens leaned back against his chair at the outdoor café and took a sip of coffee. He pretended to look at the menu, but was actually surveilling his section of South Beach along Ocean Drive. There had been a sharp increase in gang violence directly related to drug distribution around Miami, and Special Agent Stevens was performing field reconnaissance to identify street dealers who would hopefully lead him to the big time drug movers. He was no novice to the violence generated by the illegal drug trade. In the last year, Stevens had been shot at several times. In the process, he had defensively shot and killed two people.

Stevens blended into the South Beach scene the way a scorpion fish blends into a coral reef. He was wearing flip flops, khaki shorts and a white collared shirt with an embroidered yacht broker's logo on the chest. To look at him, he was just one of the two million employees in the yachting industry in South Florida.

"Miami is so built up!" Bridget said, as they drove east through the high rise buildings of downtown Miami and headed toward MacArthur Causeway.

"Yeah, I don't know if I could live here," Billy replied. They opened the windows and sun roof and let the eighty degree air blow against them. They passed two enormous cruise ships off to the right, as they sped along the causeway toward South Beach. They parked and walked up Collins Avenue, then cut over toward Ocean Drive.

The ocean temperature had reached the high seventies and the light breeze off the water gave a little cool relief as they stepped onto the sand. They found a spot without too many people about ten yards from the water's edge. Bridget pulled off her tee shirt and shorts and said, "I'm definitely going for a swim!" Billy admired how the white string bikini accented the dark, golden brown tan that she had perfected in the Bahamas. She was wearing a thin, silver belly chain that Billy had never seen before. Bridget noticed him staring at her and said, "What?"

"I'm the luckiest man in the world. And by the way, never, *ever* take that belly chain off."

"Oh?" Then she put her hands on her waist and did the little hip shake that had become her trademark. It was just one of the many little things that Billy loved. She gave him a mischievous grin and said, "You like?"

He gazed at her, fully aware of just how cute, fun, sexy and smart she was, and fell in love all over again. "Oh, me like-ee very much!" He pulled off his tee shirt and chased her down the beach into the water. They both dove into the warm water and embraced when they came up for air. She wrapped her legs around his waist and interlaced her fingers around his neck. Billy reached down and grabbed her ass with both hands and pulled her in close. They held their embrace in silence as they gently swayed in the warm, chest deep water. She looked deep into his eyes and said, "I get to be with you the rest of my life." The words touched Billy's heart so deeply that he shivered, and felt his eyes well up with tears. She saw his reaction, and blinked back her own tears.

One hundred yards away Carlos paid three dollars to a street vendor for twelve ounces of water. He walked away, sat down on the beach wall and drained the bottled water in one long gulp. Then he quietly spoke into his phone, "Están en la playa. Los tengo a la vista. ¿Dónde estás? They are on the beach. I have them in sight. Where are you?"

Billy and Bridget walked up to their spot on the beach and lay down on large beach towels. The hot sun felt good on their wet bodies. Billy rolled over, and Bridget rubbed suntan lotion onto his back. "Oh, that feels great!" Billy gushed. She rubbed his back long after the suntan lotion was applied, and soon, Billy drifted off to sleep. He woke up a little later and felt his stomach rumbling. "Are you getting hungry, Babe?" He asked.

"Sure, let's go grab a bite in the shade." They shook off the towels and packed up their beach bags.

Billy pointed to the area where the beach beds were located. "Let's swing by and see what the deal is with those." They walked over and inspected the beds. They were quite large, king sized beds that were suspended by four ropes, one on each corner, allowing the bed to swing. The mattresses where made up with fine, white linen and there was a lily-orchid flower bouquet placed in between the two large pillows. The four ropes extended up vertically to a large wooden frame shaped like a cube. Each side of the cube had cloth drapes that were tied back. When the drapes were pulled closed, the only open surface of the cube faced the sky, allowing sunlight in from above, yet total privacy. The wooden frame was composed of solid, dark teak. Billy was impressed by the robust design and beauty of the wood. "These are nice," he said.

Bridget displayed her wonderfully mischievous grin. "I definitely think we should get one of these after lunch."

Billy smiled back, "Absolutely!"

They showered off the saltwater before heading across Ocean Drive to find a place to have lunch. They walked past several overly-chic restaurants all flaunting glittering décor that did not appeal to either Bridget or Billy. They decided upon a small, older café that had been there for many years, and seemed to care more about the food than the furnishings. They waited a few minutes for an outside table and were seated in the shade on the sidewalk next to Ocean Drive.

Carlos followed Billy and Bridget to the restaurant and watched them from across the street until they were seated. Then he hurried to the parking garage where Chavez was waiting.

Chavez had been pacing the stuffy Miami apartment earlier that morning waiting for his cell to ring. He was anxious and nervous. He had killed before, but in remote settings far from the public eye, and in Honduras, not America.

Carlos climbed into the passenger's seat and explained exactly where Billy and Bridget were sitting. Then he gave Chavez his mirrored sunglasses and baseball hat. "You can walk right up to them if you approach from the north side. Keep your head down and he won't notice you."

Bridget studied the menu. "Everything looks good. What are you in the mood for?"

"You," Billy replied.

She winked. "Save room for dessert, Billy-boy, I rented that beach bed for the whole afternoon!"

"Well then, we really better fuel up! Let's start with some cold beers!" They ordered two Coronas and salads with fish; Billy ordered rare tuna and Bridget, wild Salmon. Their beers came, and they sat back in the shade, people watching.

"This is way more entertaining than TV," Billy said. Dozens of people from all over the world were walking by. It was a fascinating display of humanity. Men and women of all different shapes and sizes sauntered about; the obvious cruise ship couple, complete with name tags attached to their Hawaiian print shirts; scantily clad, artificially inflated young women trolling the strip for wealthy men; a rather out of place looking cowboy dressed in jeans, a black shirt and a large cowboy hat; women holding hands with women; men holding hands with men; a muscle bound couple in spandex pants and matching tee shirts tightly displaying a gym logo; and numerous young women wearing bikinis that defied the laws of gravity.

"Check out this dude!" Billy said with a chuckle. A man in a fluorescent green bathing suit came walking up the sidewalk, toward their table behind Bridget. The "suit" was shaped like a "V" and had two shoulder straps that came together at the crotch, barely covering what was down there. Behind, it ran like a G string up the back to the shoulders. Billy bit his cheeks to keep from laughing. Bridget took a sip from her Corona just as the man approached. She saw his side profile and then his back as he passed by. Beer came out her nose as she lunged forward laughing. Embarrassed, she grabbed her napkin and tried to compose herself.

"Would you like me to get Borat's autograph for you?" Billy said.

Bridget shook her head, and put her hand up, still laughing and coughing. "Stop it! Seriously, my nose is killing me!" Billy laughed heartily at both Bridget's condition and the Borat wannabe.

"A hairy man's ass in a G string is not the visual I wanted with my salad," Bridget said when their food came.

"Okay, here you go. This is better," Billy said nodding. A young, attractive couple walked by, smiling as they held hands.

"I bet they're engaged," Bridget said.

"How can you tell?"

"They remind me of us."

They continued people watching as they ate, and it morphed into a kind of game where they labeled someone walking up the sidewalk with a word and then watched each other's reaction as the person walked by. A man in suit and tie approached, and Billy said, "Business."

Bridget smiled and offered, "Saline," when a woman with huge, fake boobs walked by in a skin tight top.

A man dressed in flamboyant colored drag, with far too much make-up came by. "Confused," diagnosed Billy.

Bridget finished her salad and set down her fork. She looked up nodding in the direction behind Billy and said, "Scary." He turned around to see the person she was talking about. Ten yards away, the man in the baseball hat looked up for a second, and Billy looked into mirrored sunglass. A cold feeling of trepidation hit him like a freight train. Something was seriously wrong. *The feeling*.

Billy was not the only one with his eyes on the man in a black, untucked, long sleeve tee shirt, jeans and sneakers as he limped down Ocean Drive. Special Agent Stevens had positioned himself in the café so that he had a 180-degree view of Ocean Drive and the beach across the street. Stevens had watched Billy and Bridget sit down three tables away, but immediately summed them up as a young couple having some fun on South Beach.

Stevens instantly picked out the man in mirrored sunglasses as a person of interest. For one thing, the man appeared anxious and was sweating profusely. Stevens also noticed that the man's right hand was stuffed in his jeans under his baggy tee shirt, which made it look like he was playing with himself, but Stevens knew otherwise. As the man limped towards him, Stevens wondered if he were about to be to the target of an assassination. Revenge for people he killed or an initiation killing for a new gang member? It didn't matter. Stevens did a rapid peripheral scan for other potential perpetrators, but didn't see any. He removed the hand gun from the holster at the small of his back and stealthily slid it under the table. He clicked off the safety and then gently slid his index finger onto the trigger as the man in mirrored sunglasses limped toward him.

Billy took a full second to process who was behind the mirrored sunglasses. In that second, Chavez took two more steps forward and pulled the 38 special from his waist.

As soon as Agent Stevens spotted the black metal of the 38 special, he jumped up with his gun raised in both hands. "Freeze!" he yelled at the top of his lungs. The rapid burst of action from the table next to Chavez happened so quickly that Billy did not have time to react. Shocked by the unexpected commotion, Chavez reflexively looked to his right, while raising his weapon. In that instant, Agent Stevens fired his gun, hitting Chavez with a body mass shot in the center chest, throwing him backward. Billy watched in horror as Chavez convulsed and reflexively pulled the trigger as he fell backwards. The bullet just grazed Billy's shoulder and kept going, but the shock sent him flying off his chair. Billy hit the ground accompanied by the sound of shattering glass and scattering flatware.

The sounds of hysterical screams and breaking dishes were abruptly overcome by Stevens yelling at the top of his lungs, "Nobody Move!" Agent Stevens was standing now, with his gun trained on Chavez's head. Chavez was sprawled out on the concrete sidewalk with blood pooling beneath his chest. Stevens did a quick scan of the area as he slowly walked over and kicked the gun away from the right hand of the motionless body.

Billy jumped up and rushed over to Bridget. She was face down on the table. "Babe? BABE!" He pulled her back and saw a pool of blood on her tee shirt and a gruesome hole in her chest. "NOOOOOOOOOOOOO!"

CHAPTER 48   DEFINITION OF WEALTH

Billy felt paralyzed during the wake and funeral. The reception was held at Bridget's parent's house outside of New York City. Billy made small talk and listed to strangers tell him what a shame it was and how sorry they were. However, Billy really wanted all the people to leave, but simultaneously, didn't want to be alone. If he was by himself, he just couldn't handle the solitude and might kill himself. As it was, he didn't care if his heart stopped beating because that would spare him the pain he felt with every breath. Bridget was everything he loved. His future was shattered, and he did not have the mental fortitude to contemplate moving on.

One by one, the guests made their departure and eventually Billy was left alone with Bridget's father. Mr. Smith sat across from Billy in the kitchen and looked directly into his eyes. Neither man said anything for several minutes. Billy could feel Mr. Smith's pain from across the table. Billy desperately wished he could turn back time. The bullet meant to end his life had missed Billy and killed the woman he loved. He would trade places in a second. Guilt rose from Billy's soul and coursed through his veins. He physically trembled as he tried to look at Mr. Smith. However, Billy just couldn't keep eye contact with Bridget's father and lowered his gaze down to the floor. The shooting flashed into Billy's mind. The image of Bridget's once beautiful chest now bloody and torn apart, combined with the piercing stare from her father pushed Billy over the edge. He brought his hands up to his face and broke down crying. Mr. Smith stood up and walked out of the room without saying a word.

Billy sat in the kitchen and stared at the leftover food for hours. Only the clock hanging on the wall broke the silence with a menacing, *tick-tock, tick-tock*. Later, he drove to his boss's house in East Hampton. Billy's boss was away and had offered to let him use it. When Billy pulled into his boss' mansion he couldn't remember driving there. Billy sat alone in the opulent living room. He looked around at the exquisite furnishings and couldn't care less about them. He inhaled deeply and shuddered as he exhaled a painful breath. Now, there was nothing to break the silence but his thoughts.

He was exhausted, but he couldn't sleep, so he started drinking. He opened the bottle of rum at eleven, and it was gone by one o'clock in the morning. At two thirty, Billy woke up on the couch, went to the bathroom, and staggered into his bedroom. The room was spinning, and he thought he was going to be sick, but he shut his eyes and struggled through it.

All of a sudden he had a clear vision of his deceased father, who talked to him as if he were in the room. "It hurts me to see you so upset, son. I know you loved her very much. Finding true love can be a difficult challenge, but you did, and now she's gone. I'm not here to make you feel guilty; you have the rest of your life to do that, but how could you rationalize the crime you committed by comparing it to investment bankers running the government? Come on son, big money has always run government in this country and all the others. You know that. Governments are far from perfect, but if you really had to choose a country to live in, which one would it be?

"Son, we all know wealthy people who are unhappy. You're rich now, but that money will haunt you for the rest of your life. You have time and money, but you also have a lot on your conscience, and that can be a very dangerous combination. Be careful son, I'm worried about you. If you're truly happy, it doesn't matter how much money you have. The painful lesson you've learned is that love is worth much more than money."

NAUTICAL GLOSSARY

Aft: Towards the rear, or stern of the vessel.

Beam: width of the vessel.

Bow: front of the vessel.

Chef/stew: A combination of two employment positions on a yacht, chef and steward/stewardess.

Davit: Small crane/lift mechanism used to haul/launch tender and lift large loads aboard.

Dead Reckoning: Navigation method using course, speed, and time to determine current location. Can be subject to combined errors such as drift and current.

Ditch Bag: A duffel bag, usually water proof, which contains important items in the event of abandoning ship. Typical items include, but are not limited to, copies of passports, pocket knife, sunscreen, dried food, water, and survival gear required if set adrift on a life raft.

Fly Bridge: The open deck area of a yacht, usually above the main deck, equipped with a second set of navigational devices.

Fore: Towards the front, or bow of the vessel.

Gaff: A large, sharp hook attached to a long handle used for hauling big fish aboard.

Gelcoat: An epoxy-type coating used as the finish, or outer shell, of a fiberglass vessel.

Gunwale (pronounced, *gunn'l*): The top edge of the sides of a boat or yacht.

Head: Bathroom.

Helm station: Throttle control, navigation and steering area.

Hull: Watertight portion of a vessel below the main deck.

Knot (rope): Used to secure a rope; an object made by tying a line or rope.

Knot (speed): 1.15 statute miles per hour, as in: "The boat is cruising at ten knots."

Lanyard: A cord or rope used to secure an item.

Leeward side: Downwind side.

Luffing (sailing): The point at which the direction of the sail is so far from optimal trim that airflow causes the sail to flap, or "luff."

Midship: The area in the middle of the vessel.

Mile Marker: A numeric numbering system used on the Intracoastal Waterway (ICW) to denote statute miles along the route. The Atlantic ICW begins at Mile Marker "0" in Norfolk, Virginia and ends with Mile Marker "1243" in Key West, Florida. The mile markers are listed in five-mile increments on most navigational charts that display the ICW.

Nautical Mile: 1.15 statute (land) miles.

No Wake Zone: A water body area where low vessel speed and minimum wake are required by law.

On the hard: A nautical slang term used to describe a yacht hauled out of the water, dry docked, or in storage.

Port: left side of the vessel.

Starboard: right side of the vessel.

Stern: rear of the vessel.

Stuffing box: The water tight area surrounding the propeller shaft where the shaft penetrates the hull.

Tender: A small boat, sometimes referred to as a 'dinghy,' used to go to and from a larger boat or yacht. It can be towed behind or carried on a larger boat or yacht.

The Bends: A severe medical condition caused by nitrogen bubbles forming in the blood stream. Often caused by too rapid ascent while scuba diving. The condition is extremely painful and sometimes fatal.

V-berth: A "V" shaped sleeping or storage area located in the bow, below deck.

Windward side: Upwind side.

Yaw: To rapidly deviate from a straight course.

A NOTE FROM THE AUTHOR

Many people have asked me about the storyline of this book. Since I may be running for political office someday, my short answer is: "No, I didn't do it." However, within the aforementioned sentence, the context and definition of the word, "it" were not fully elaborated upon. Therefore, previous sentence notwithstanding, I hereby substantiate that I have operated many large yachts as a captain while cruising all over the world. As far as nefarious drug smuggling activities are concerned, the reader shall be reminded that this is a work of fiction; however, there are real characters and scenes contained herein.

See? I would make a good politician...

The following is a brief, true history of one of the largest drug traffickers in history.

CRIME AND PUNISHMENT

Juan Ramon Matta-Ballesteros, aka Ramon Matta, is most noted for his role in the Iran-Contra affair in the mid 1980's, where he controlled the airline that provided the Nicaraguan contras with weapons financed by the United States. However, every time his Honduran DC-9 flew into New Orleans to pick up an arms shipment for the rebels, Matta unloaded *tons* of cocaine onto U.S. soil. As such, DEA officials estimated that Matta was responsible for importing more than half the cocaine into the U.S. in the mid-eighties.[7]

Matta was arrested in Columbia in 1986, but managed to bribe his way out of jail for two million dollars and returned to Honduras.[8]

In 1988, U.S. Marshalls seized him from his home in Tegucigalpa, Honduras, and flew him to the United States where he was convicted for the kidnapping and murder of undercover DEA agent, Enrique Camarena.

Following his abduction in Tegucigalpa, thousands of Hondurans rioted in the streets. When the dust settled, six people had been killed and the annex to the U.S. Embassy was burned to the ground. The U.S. DEA resident agent in Tegucigalpa "...rapidly came to the accurate conclusion that the entire Honduran government was deeply involved in the drug trade."[9]

The United States Penitentiary, Administrative Maximum Facility (ADX Florence), in Fremont County, Colorado, is known as the "Alcatraz of the Rockies."[10] ADX Florence contains a vast combination of motion detectors including lasers and subterranean pressure pads. Heat sensitive night vision cameras, attack dogs and multiple razor wire fences virtually eliminate any means of escape.

ADX Florence houses many of the world's most dangerous criminals. Most notable are the numerous Al-Qaeda operatives responsible for both the 1993 and 2001 World Trade Center attacks, including Ramzi Yousef and Zacarias Moussaoui. The movie, *Breach,* was based on a resident of ADX Florence named Robert Hanssen, who sold top secret information to the Russians for twenty-two years. Hanssen is spending twenty-three hours per day in solitary confinement for the rest of his life. Other infamous inmates include: Theodore Kaczynski, aka The Unabomber; Chicago organized crime bosses; and international drug lords.

During the design of the prison, sensory deprivation was high on the list of priorities. The tiny four-inch by four-foot long cell windows were installed far from reach, and only allow a view of the sky, thereby providing the inmate with no information about his location within the complex. A former warden has referred to the prison as, "a cleaner version of hell."[11]

Ramon Matta is currently serving twelve life sentences at ADX Florence.

REFERENCES

1. Steve Kroft, "Prosecuting Wall Street," *60 Minutes*, CBS, December, 2011.
2. *Encarta Dictionary*, English (North America) via Microsoft Word *Research*.
3. "The True Cost of the Bank Bailout," PBS, September, 2010, http://www.pbs.org/wnet/need-to-know/economy/the-true-cost-of-the-bank-bailout/3309/.
4. "AP IMPACT: After 40 years, $1 Trillion, US War on Drugs has failed to meet any of its goals" http://www.foxnews.com/world/2010/05/13/ap-impact-years-trillion-war-drugs-failed-meet-goals/.
5. http://insightcrime.org/personalities/el-salvador-criminal-personalities/chepe-diablo-texis-cartel/item/1544-honduras-murder-rate-set-to-soar-to-86-per-100000
6. Cousteau, Jacques-Yves & Cousteau, Philippe, *The Shark: Splendid Savage of the Sea*. Doubleday & Company, Inc., 1970.
7. http://en.wikipedia.org/wiki/Juan_Matta-Ballesteros
8. Jerry Melden, "The CIA's Ghosts of Tegucigalpa," July 2009, http://www.scoop.co.nz/stories/HL0907/S00240.htm
9. Alexander Cockburn and Jeffrey St. Clair, *Whiteout: The CIA, Drugs and the Press,* Verso, 1998, ISBN 1-85984-258-5, p283.
10. http://en.wikipedia.org/wiki/ADX_Florence
11. http://en.wikipedia.org/wiki/ADX_Florence"Supermax: A Clean Version Of Hell", CBS News, October 14, 2007 http://www.cbsnews.com/stories/2007/10/11/60minutes/main3357727.shtml. Retrieved 2009-05-31

PHOTO/IMAGE CREDITS

Chapter 1, Hurricane map image by Jeff Ford

Chapter 5, Fifty-five gallon drum image by Jeff Ford

Chapter 6, Yacht *Destiny* image by Jeff Ford

Chapter 14, Atlantic Intracoastal Waterway sign photo by Jeff Ford

Chapter 16, Image modified from Google Images;
http://1.bp.blogspot.com/_9atQ7zpfZ0w/TMh1Ap4n_eI/AAAAAAAAH2
I/mO2l3HwR9gc/s320/PA270208.JPG

Chapter 20, Photo provided by the Jekyll Island Club Hotel, courtesy of David Fisher

Chapter 22, Satellite rocket launch photo by Jeff Ford

Chapter 32, Hurricane Tanya/*Destiny* image by Jeff Ford

Chapter 33, Oceanic White Tip Shark image by Lane et. Al, modified from: http://www.daff.qld.gov.au/fisheries/species-identification/shark-identification-guide/photo-guide-to-sharks/sharks,-part-1/oceanic-whitetip-shark

Crime and Punishment, Modified from Google Images;
http://www.google.com/imgres?sa=X&rlz=1T4ADFA_enUS436US518&bi
w=1440&bih=729&tbm=isch&tbnid=ySlWtjTvgykpWM:&imgrefurl=http://
/www.armyofgod.com/EricRudolphSuperMaxPrisonIssues.html&docid=sy
0cToqAkHu0mM&imgurl=http://www.armyofgod.com/EricRudophPicSu
perMax1.jpg&w=150&h=250&ei=qBANUsnhAaflyAGL-
4GgCQ&zoom=1&iact=rc&dur=109&page=1&tbnh=140&tbnw=85&start=
0&ndsp=36&ved=1t:429,r:7,s:0,i:102&tx=63&ty=68

About The Author, photo by Heather E. Bradley

ABOUT THE AUTHOR

After receiving an engineering degree from the University of Maine, Jeff Ford worked in Boston as an environmental engineer, and became a published engineering author. He then became CEO of The Water Company, Inc., and a partner of Cheryl Fudge Designs. An accomplished musician, Jeff has played percussion on six different albums with multiple artists. He is also a licensed U.S. Coast Guard Captain and PADI certified SCUBA Divemaster.

Working on multimillion dollar private yachts, Captain Jeff Ford has cruised the waters from Maine to Brazil, and spent a substantial amount of time in the Bahamas and Caribbean. For the past 20 years, he has divided his time between New England in the summer and the Caribbean in winter.

www.locoford.com

The following is an excerpt from Captain Billy Forbes next adventure entitled,

Imminent Hazard

Billy came to with a throbbing head. His head was actually making a throbbing sound, *Beep, Beep, Beep. Wait,* he thought, *is that an alarm of some sort?* He blinked his pasty eyes and tried to sit up, but the motion made him feel as if he was going to be sick. It took several seconds before he figured out where he was. Somehow, he had passed out on the floor of the salon with one leg haphazardly draped up on the couch at the knee. *Beep-Beep-Beep!*

"Okay, alright, Jesus!" he said to no one. As he stood up, he felt a giant *whoosh* and staggered before stopping his fall with the galley counter.

His concern grew exponentially to fear when he gazed out the salon window and saw nothing but ocean. The last thing he remembered, his catamaran was tied to the dock. *What the...?*

Billy ran over to the navigation station. The radar alarm continued emitting a loud, monotone beep. On the screen, a large box made up of red asterisks outlined the flashing word: "COLLISION!"

Billy's heart sank as he looked up into every captain's nightmare. Dead ahead, coming straight at him was the massive black steel wall of a container ship slicing through the water at twenty-eight knots. The container ship appeared so close that he couldn't see the deck of the ship, just weeping rust flowing down the side of the enormous steel hull that looked like a screaming bearded madman fast approaching to swallow him whole.

CPSIA information can be obtained
at www.ICGtesting.com
Printed in the USA
FFHW021119220119
50259140-55249FF

9 780989 859103